The Sleeping
And The Dead

Ann Cleeves lives in West Yorkshire with her husband
and their two daughters. As a member of the 'Murder
Squad', she works with other Northern writers to pro-
mote crime fiction.

She is also the author of the Inspector Ramsay
series. More recently she has turned to writing psychological suspense novels, of which *The Crow Trap*
was the first, followed by *The Sleeping And The Dead*.
Her latest novel, *Burial of Ghosts*, will be available in
Macmillan hardback in early 2003.

By the same author

A Bird in the Hand
Come Death and High Water
Murder in Paradise
A Prey to Murder
A Lesson in Dying
Murder in my Backyard
A Day in the Death of Dorothea Cassidy
Another Man's Poison
Killjoy
The Man on the Shore
Sea Fever
The Healers
High Island Blues
The Baby-Snatcher
The Crow Trap

Ann Cleeves

The Sleeping And The Dead

PAN BOOKS

First published 2001 by Macmillan

This edition published 2002 by Pan Books
an imprint of Pan Macmillan, a division of Macmillan Publishers Limited
Pan Macmillan, 20 New Wharf Road, London N1 9RR
Basingstoke and Oxford
Associated companies throughout the world
www.panmacmillan.com

ISBN 978-0-330-45507-7

3 5 7 9 8 6 4 2

A CIP catalogue record for this book is available from
the British Library.

Printed and bound in the UK by
CPI Group (UK) Ltd, Croydon, CR0 4YY

Visit **www.panmacmillan.com** to read more about all our books and to buy
them. You will also find features, author interviews and news of any author
events, and you can sign up for e-newsletters so that you're always first to hear
about our new releases.

Prologue

She had the lake to herself. She wasn't given to fancies, but on a morning like this she knew the water was what she was born for. The water, then her and the canoe. Like they were one creature, one of the strange animals out of the myths they'd had to read when they were at school. But she wasn't half horse. She was half boat.

The spray deck was fastened so tightly round her waist that every movement she made with her upper body was reflected in the canoe, and if she capsized her legs would stay quite dry. Not that there was any chance of that today. The sun was already burning off the last of the mist and the lake was flat. There were mirror images of mountains all the way up the valley. The blades of her paddle sliced sharply through the water, pushing her back towards the shore.

The water level must have dropped again because the row of staithes, which had only recently appeared running out from the beach, seemed more prominent. She turned the canoe towards them, partly out of curiosity, partly to put off the moment of her return to the school. The figure floated just under the surface, moving gently. From a distance she'd thought it a piece of polythene. She tilted the paddle so one blade was submerged and pushed against the pressure of the water to stop the canoe. Still interested. Not scared. Waiting for the silt to clear. Then she found she was shaking and held on to the wooden post with her free hand to steady herself. It was as if she'd stumbled into a bad horror movie. The corpse swaying below her was white, like a wax, witchcraft effigy.

PART ONE

Chapter One

Peter Porteous walked to work. It was still a novelty. He liked it all, the overgrown hedges, birdsong, cow muck not dog muck on the road. Having made the decision to walk, he walked every day. Whatever the weather. Even in this heat. He was a man of routine. On the edge of the town he went into the newsagent's by the bridge to buy the *Independent*. He checked the time on the church clock. In the office he would drink a mug of decaffeinated coffee and begin to sift through the overnight reports before meeting his team at the ten o'clock briefing. And at the briefing he knew there would be nothing to cause anxiety. Cranford was a small town. The team covered a huge geographical area, but there was seldom the sense of being swamped by uncontrollable events which he had experienced in his previous post. That was why he had transferred to Cranford and that was why he would enjoy it. He knew colleagues who functioned better under pressure but he hated panic and chaos. Stress scared him. He had designed his working life to avoid it.

He was waiting for the kettle to boil for his coffee when the telephone rang.

'Porteous.' He continued to make neat, pithy notes in the margin of the report on his desk.

'We've got a body, sir.'

He took a breath. 'Where?'

'In the lake. Only visible now because the water's so low. It was found by an instructor at the Adventure Centre.'

'Natural causes then?'

'Unlikely, sir.'

'Why?'

'It was tied to an anchor. Weighed down.'

'So.' The kettle clicked off. Still holding the phone he poured water on to coffee granules. 'Murder.'

There was a brief silence. Perhaps the sergeant was expecting a rush of orders. Instructions and queries fired one after another. None came. Instead Porteous asked calmly, 'Any identification?'

'Can't even tell the sex. It looks as if it's been there some time.'

'No rush then. They haven't done anything daft like trying to lift it from the water?'

'I'm not sure.'

'Tell them to leave everything as it is. Are you clear? Exactly. I want the pathologist there. I seem to remember that water has a preservative effect. Once the corpse is lifted from the lake it'll start to decompose very quickly. Make sure they understand.'

'Right, sir.'

'Get hold of Eddie Stout. Tell him I'll meet him there. And Sergeant?'

'Yes, sir.'

'I'll need a car.'

Before leaving his office Peter Porteous drank his coffee and finished reading the report on his desk.

The town had its back turned to the lake, was separated from it by a small hill and a forestry plantation. There were no views. Many of the older residents could remember the valley before it was flooded to create a vast reservoir and still disapproved. They had quite enough water. In the hills it never stopped raining. Let the city dwellers fend for themselves.

The road to the lake was signposted Cranwell Village and showed a No Through Road symbol. Beneath it was a brown tourist sign which said Cranford Water Adventure Centre. Cranwell Village was a scattering of houses on either side of the single-track road. There was a church and a pub and a country-house hotel where, the month before, Porteous had briefly attended a colleague's engagement party. Then there was a bend in the road and a sudden, startling expanse of water, this morning dazzling in the sunlight. The lake had a circumference of thirty miles. The valley twisted, so although Porteous could see across the water to the opposite bank, each end of the reservoir was invisible. The lane ended in a car park, with a grassed area to one side and a couple of picnic tables. There was a noticeboard with a map showing a series of walks and nature trails. A gravel track followed the lake a little further north to the Adventure Centre, a wooden building of Scandinavian design, surrounded by trees. Porteous parked by the noticeboard and studied it before walking up the track.

Detective Sergeant Stout had arrived before him.

His car was parked in one of the residents' marked spaces next to the building. He wore, as he always did, a suit and a tie, and looked out of place in the clearing, surrounded by trees, with pine needles underfoot. An officious garden gnome. Next to him stood a fit, middle-aged man in shorts, a black T-shirt with the Adventure Centre logo on the front in scarlet, and the rubber sandals used by climbers. Porteous always treated Stout carefully. The older man had been expected to get the promotion which had brought Porteous to the team. He was well liked but too close to retirement now to move further.

'Thank you for getting here so quickly, Eddie.' As soon as the words were spoken he thought they sounded sychophantic, insincere. Stout only nodded. 'Perhaps you could introduce us.'

Stout nodded again. He was a small, squat man with the knack of speaking without appearing to move his mouth. He would have made a brilliant ventriloquist, though Porteous had never passed on the compliment. 'This is Daniel Duncan. He's director of the Adventure Centre. One of his instructors found the body.'

Porteous held out his hand. Duncan took it reluctantly.

'Perhaps I could talk to him,' Porteous said.

'Her,' Duncan said. 'Helen Blake. She's a bit upset.'

'We should give her a few minutes then. Is there anything we can see from the shore?'

From where they were standing the view of the lake was obscured by trees. Duncan led them along a path to the back of the building, to a dinghy park, where there were half a dozen Mirror dinghies and a rack of canoes. A concrete slipway sloped gently into the water. He walked very quickly, bouncing away from them on the balls of his feet, as if he hoped the matter could be dealt with immediately.

'This is the last thing we need,' he said crossly. 'We've only been going three years and this is the first season we've shown any profit.'

'But the building must have been here longer than that.' It looked weathered. Lichen was growing on the roof.

'It's nearly ten years old. It used to be run by the council but in the last round of cuts they had to sell it off. I took it over then.'

'What was here before that?'

Duncan shrugged. 'I wouldn't know.'

'It was a caravan site,' Stout volunteered. 'A sort of holiday centre. I think the people who owned it went bust. The wooden building wasn't here then, though, and the trees have grown a lot. There was the reception and a bar nearer the lane. Brick and concrete. An ugly place. I remember it being demolished.'

Porteous leaned against the stone wall which separated the dinghy park from the shore. There was the smell of baked mud. A slight breeze moved the water but seemed not to reach him.

'Where did Ms Blake find the body?'

Duncan pointed to a rotting wooden staithe which jutted out from the water about thirty yards from the wall.

'This is the driest summer since the reservoir was built. The water's never been so low. Those posts haven't been exposed since I've been here. Not until a couple of weeks ago. I think they formed part of a jetty or a pier when the lake was first flooded. The body's near that far post.'

'So it was probably weighted and thrown from the jetty? Before it collapsed?'

Duncan shrugged again as if he wanted to disassociate himself from the enquiry.

Porteous gave up on him and turned to Stout. 'I don't suppose you remember when the jetty fell into disuse. That might help us date the body.'

'I don't think it fell down. I think the council knocked it down when the Adventure Centre was built. They didn't want the kids drowning themselves.'

Porteous pursed his lips in a soundless whistle. 'So we're talking a ten-year-old body. At least. When was the reservoir completed?'

'1968. The year Bet and I moved here.'

'So, a twenty-odd-year window of opportunity, if we accept the body's been in for ten years. It'll be a nightmare just sorting through the missing-person records.' He didn't talk as if it would be a nightmare. His voice was suddenly more cheerful. 'I don't suppose anyone obvious comes to mind? As a candidate for the victim.' He'd learned already that Eddie was famous for his memory and his local knowledge. According to the desk sergeant he went to bed reading the 'Hatches, Matches and Dispatches' column of the local paper.

'Give us a break, sir. We've no age or sex. I'm not a miracle worker.'

'That's not what I was told.'

Duncan had wandered away from them and was pulling one of the dinghies on to a trolley. Porteous joined him but didn't offer to help.

'How deep is the water there?'

'The bank's steep at this point so usually it's very deep. The post must have snapped off sometime because the jetty would have been higher than that. It's silty there too. This year? You'd probably be able to walk out in thigh waders.'

'Thanks. We'll see how the forensic team want to play it.'

He found it hard to imagine Carver, the pathologist, in thigh waders. He was a dapper man given to flamboyant ties and waistcoats. His hair was a deep oily black, which could only have come out of a bottle. Even in the Teletubby paper suit he put on to enter a crime scene he gave the impression of neatness and vanity.

'Will you wait here for Mr Carver, Eddie? I'll see if Ms Blake's up to a few questions. Mr Duncan, if you wouldn't mind . . .'

Duncan seemed at first not to have heard. He finished coiling a piece of rope, straightened, then reluctantly set off towards the Centre. Porteous followed.

'Where do you get your customers from?'

'That's hardly relevant to your enquiries, is it? If the body's as old as you think.' He stopped in his track so suddenly that Porteous almost walked into him. 'Sorry, that was rude. Everything I own is sunk into this place. I'm worried. In the summer holidays most of our clients are kids whose parents think it would be good for them to do more than sit in front of the computer screen all day. At the moment the whole place has been taken over by one school party. We're starting to attract more adult groups too – companies looking for a quick fix in corporate bonding.' He opened double doors into a wood-panelled lobby with a couple of chairs, a payphone and a drinks machine.

'Helen's through there, in the common-room. I'll be in the office if you need me.'

Helen Blake was a large-boned redhead in her early twenties. Her face was still drained of colour, so the scattering of freckles on her nose and cheekbones looked livid and raw. She was alone.

'What have you done with all the students?' He hoped the joky tone would reassure her but she looked up, startled, and some of the coffee she was holding spilled on to her jeans.

'They've got pony-trekking this morning.'

'Would you normally be with them?'

'No. I only do water sports.' She gave a laugh which rattled at the back of her throat. 'I did try riding once. I got a blister on my bum and the beast bit me.'

'How long have you been working here?' He wanted her more relaxed before he started on the difficult questions.

'This is my first season. I did sports science at university. Canoeing's my passion. I compete. I'm hoping for an Olympic trial.' She set the coffee mug on a low table. Her hand had stopped shaking.

'Do you like it here?'

'Yeah it's OK. Dan Duncan could do with being a bit more laid back, but as he always says, he's got a lot resting on this place.'

'Did you have a group with you on the water this morning?'

'No, thank God. I practise on my own before breakfast every day. One of the perks of the job.'

'Could you take me through exactly what happened?'

'I was on my way in.' The words came in breathless pants. 'I never take the students close to the old jetty. It would be tempting fate. They'd get stuck or hit one of the underwater planks and capsize. I suppose I was curious. There seems to be less water in the lake every day and I wanted to see what else might emerge. I didn't expect a body. It seemed to be floating not far from the surface. Very white. Hardly human. Not human at all.' She shivered and pulled her knees up to her chest and wrapped her arms around them.

'Could you see the anchor?'

'Not then. It was covered in silt. I put my blade in to steady the canoe and the movement of the water cleared it long enough for me to see the shape. I came in then. I couldn't look any more. Dan called the police. Two men rowed out in one of our dinghies. Perhaps they didn't believe me. Perhaps they thought I was imagining it. I wish I had been.'

'They had to check,' he said gently.

'What will happen now?'

'We're waiting for the forensic team.'

'I won't have to see it again, will I?'

'Of course not.'

'What I can't bear,' she said, 'is the thought of him out there all this time and none of us realizing. It's as if nobody missed him. As if nobody cared.'

If it was a he, Porteous thought. As she spoke he saw beyond her, through a long window, to the scene outside. Carver's Range Rover was pulling into the drive. The pathologist parked it neatly beside the Centre's minibus and climbed out. From the back seat

13

he pulled out a pair of rubber waders. They were spotless and shiny, as black as his hair. Porteous hid a small grin behind his hand.

'What time will the children be back?' He didn't want an audience of sniggering, pointing teenagers.

'Not until late this afternoon. They've taken a picnic.' She followed his gaze. 'You'll be busy. Don't worry about me. I'm OK.'

Later he, Stout and Carver sat in the Range Rover to compare notes. Carver had with him a silver thermos flask of coffee which he passed around, wiping the cup each time with a paper handkerchief, like a priest at communion.

'Really,' he said in the prissy voice which made some of Porteous's colleagues want to thump him. 'It's most interesting. I've read about it of course, but this is the first time I've seen it.'

'Seen what?' Porteous had come across Carver when he was working in the city and was prepared to be patient with him. The man was a good pathologist and he could usually be persuaded to commit himself. Porteous would put up with a lot for that.

'Adipocere. That's what it's called. It's caused by saponification. Literally the making of soap. The effect of water on the body fat. One of the first pathologists to describe it said it's as if the corpse is encased in mutton suet. Remarkably apt as I'm sure you'll agree. Sometimes the adipocere preserves the internal organs. I won't be able to tell you that, of course, until the post-mortem. I'll do that as soon as I can. This afternoon if it can be arranged. I wouldn't be surprised

14

if some of my colleagues didn't want to be present.' He took a fastidious sip of his coffee. 'Really, I can hardly wait.'

Chapter Two

Porteous lived in a barn as big as a church, which had been converted into three flats. He had the top floor to himself. Exposed rafters stretched to a sloping roof. There were two long windows, a view over farmland. Occasionally, if the light was right, he could see the glint of the lake in the distance, like a child's imagined glimpse of the sea. One wall was exposed stone, the others plastered and whitewashed. On these he hung the paintings he collected. He always went to the fine-art students' finals exhibition at the university in the city. Usually he saw something he liked.

It was early evening. Porteous didn't believe in unnecessary overtime. It messed up his budgets, and tasks which could normally be fitted into the working day expanded, became more complicated, to fit the time allowed. Tonight, despite the body in the lake, he sent his team home at the usual time. There was nothing they could do until they had identification. Besides, he wanted them calm and reasonable in the morning. He hated the frantic, febrile atmosphere which sometimes enveloped a murder case. Rational judgement was lost. It was as if there was something heroic about the obsession with one victim, one per-petrator, about the lack of sleep, the passion stoked by alcohol. He had, however, brought work home with him. He had carried six large box files up the open stairs. They contained the flimsy copies of missing-person reports between 1968 and 1985. The last five of the years which were of interest to him, 1986–1990, had been computerized, and he would check those in the morning.

He had attended Carver's post-mortem. As the pathologist had suggested, there was quite an audience. The little man had played up to them, preening himself, throwing out scientific jokes and puns which meant little to Porteous but raised a titter amongst his colleagues.

Porteous had taken notes in impeccable shorthand, following Carver's commentary exactly. The pathologist had performed like a music-hall magician, and there was likely to be as much information in the suggestion, the conjecture, the surprise discovery as in the completed official report. Porteous set his notes on the painted table which stood under one of the windows and went to the tiny kitchen to make a pot of tea. He liked Earl Grey, weak with a slice of lemon. He poured a dribble, was satisfied that it was ready and filled the cup. Then he returned to his notes and translated them in his head.

Carver had confirmed that the body had been in the water for at least ten years. The victim was a young male, aged between sixteen and twenty-five. He was five feet ten inches tall and, despite the adipocere, which usually occurred only when the victim had considerable body fat, he was of slender build. Carver had been excited by that fact, had thought it might warrant a note in a scientific journal. Enough of the organs, protected by the hard white layer of adipocere, remained for Carver to give a cause of death. The young man had been stabbed. By a knife with a short but unusually wide blade. A dagger of some sort. He had been stabbed in the back. A sharp upward movement into the heart. Either the perpetrator had known what he was doing or he had been very lucky. At this Carver had looked at his friends and grinned.

'Very exotic, gentlemen, very theatrical, as I'm sure you'll agree, for our small town in the hills.'

The body had been tied to the anchor by a piece of nylon rope, which had been looped around the waist. The young man had been clothed, though most of the garments had rotted and only tatters remained. The scraps had been retained and the forensic team was examining them. He had been wearing boots made of a soft leather or suede. Around his wrist was a plaited leather bracelet, which looked home-made. Perhaps from a bootlace.

At this Porteous stopped for a moment and took a sip of tea. He had been a child in the seventies. His only brother had been ten years older, and Porteous pictured him preparing to go out for the night. He saw him quite clearly, standing in front of the mirror in his parents' room, the only long mirror in the house. He was wearing wide trousers, desert boots, a fringed suede jacket. Around his neck was a leather thong threaded with wooden beads. The victim's bracelet suggested to Porteous the fashion of the seventies. The end of flower power. Not punk or the new romantics. He made a note and continued.

There had been some dental work. Carver announced this as if they should be grateful to him.

Which Porteous certainly was. After all this time it held the best chance of positive identification. There had not been extensive work on the teeth – one extraction and two small fillings – but a record of the mouth, perhaps even an X-ray would have been taken. There was no guarantee that the dentist was still in business or that the records had been kept but at least it provided an avenue of investigation. Porteous thought it would give his team something to do the following day. He liked to keep them busy.

He leant back in his chair and emptied the pot into his wide blue cup – part of the tea service which had been a present to himself when he moved into the barn. He stretched with satisfaction. This was why he had joined the police. Not to save the world. Not to race around the countryside in fast cars or strut the city streets in a uniform. But to bring order, to solve problems, to understand.

He set the post-mortem notes to one side and pulled the first box file towards him, savouring a moment of anticipation before opening it. This was what he loved, this precise and meticulous sorting of facts. He had never understood why his colleagues thought such work tedious.

Each report was a minor human tragedy, baldly told, given a dignity because the facts were unembellished. He sorted them first into gender and age, rejecting the menopausal women with depression, the elderly wanderers from care homes, the occasional heart-breaking ten-year-old who had gone to a friend's house to play and never returned. Still he was left with a mountain of paper. The majority of missing-person reports was for young males. They'd left home after problems at school, a row with parents, or in search of a more exciting life. He knew that many would have returned or got in touch. The relatives, simply relieved that the panic was over, would never have thought to inform the police.

He became engrossed in the task and couldn't let it go. He had planned just to sort through the paperwork but began phoning the contact numbers for relatives. Inevitably some had moved or died, but Cranford was the sort of town where people knew one another. Other phone numbers were given, alternative names suggested. The people wanted to talk. Porteous listened patiently to tales of lads who'd been scallies as youngsters but who'd gone on to do well for themselves, who'd taken university degrees, settled down, had families. The worst calls were when boys were still missing and no contact had ever been made. Porteous heard the flurry of hope in elderly voices.

'Does this mean there's some news?'

'No, no,' he said gently. 'Just checking old files.'

Some had heard about the discovery of the body in the lake on local radio and put two and two together.

'But that can't be our Alan,' one said. 'He could swim like a fish.'

He stopped when the light faded and it was too dark to read the scrawled names and numbers on the copy paper. He had reached 1980. If nothing came of the names he had set to one side he would check the files for 1980–1990, but he thought he had gone far enough. He had a picture of the victim in his head. A boy who was a teenager in the early seventies just after the lake had been flooded; who wore desert boots and a leather bootlace bracelet; who had been stabbed in the back.

He stood up and pressed the light switch. The room was lit by spots fixed to the ceiling beams. They shone through the rafters, throwing shadows on to the stripped wooden floor. He was hungry. He loved to cook; the process of peeling and chopping relaxed him. But today he wanted something quick and simple. He filled a stainless-steel pan with water for spaghetti and sweated garlic and red chilli in olive oil then covered the lot with freshly sliced Parmesan. He ate as if he hadn't seen food for days, shovelling it in with a spoon and a fork. He was sitting at the table where he'd been working and he looked out through the uncovered window at the lights which were all that remained of the roads and the farmhouses. Later he poured himself a glass of wine.

He liked to go to bed early but tonight found it impossible to let the investigation go. He thought he was as bad as the macho colleagues who bragged of their nights without sleep in pursuit of their prey. Still with his glass in his hand he read through his shortlist of candidates again, hoping to pick up on some minute detail which would point him to the man he was looking for.

He judged them, just as a betting man would pick a horse from a racing paper, using a mixture of fact, experience and superstition. There were three. After those he had picked a dozen or so more to follow up if nothing came of the first group. He set the three sheets before him in alphabetical order and read them again.

The first was Alan Brownscombe, the boy who

could swim like a fish. His parents still lived in Cranford. They came originally from the West Country and had planned on moving back there when they retired, but even after retirement they had stayed where they were – 'otherwise how would Alan know where to find us?'

Porteous had spoken to the mother. She had worked as a dinner lady in Cranwell Village First School. The father had worked for British Gas and taken a redundancy package when the company was privatized. Mrs Brownscombe could remember exactly what happened when Alan disappeared. She had the story pat, word for word, like a favourite bedtime tale repeated over and over to a child. He was the eldest of three, a bright boy, and he'd gone to Leeds University to read electrical engineering. He'd never been away from home before. Perhaps he was homesick. Perhaps the course was more demanding than he'd expected. At any rate when she managed to get through to him on the phone she sensed he was unhappy. It was Easter when he went missing. He was nineteen. It was 1978, a bit outside Porteous's preferred time-scale but not by much. Alan had come home for the holidays and managed to get a job on the caravan site by the lake, cleaning the vans before the start of the season, doing small repairs. One day he set off for work and never arrived. He didn't take anything with him other than the packet of cheese-and-pickle sandwiches she'd made up for his lunch. So far as they knew he had no money. He didn't return to university and they never saw him again.

'You say he was unhappy,' Porteous had said. The woman's West Country accent was preserved intact. If they could tell her what happened to her son, even if he were dead, she'd feel she could move home. He'd wanted to help her. 'Could he have been clinically depressed?'

'I don't know,' she'd said. 'It wasn't something you thought of then. Not with a nineteen-year-old lad. And he was home with us. We'd not have sent him back if he didn't want to go, whatever sort of noises his father was making.'

The height and the build fitted the body in the lake. She gave Porteous the name of Alan's dentist without asking why he wanted to know.

Michael Grey was reported missing only after his foster parents had died and the executors of their wills had tried to trace him. They'd left him the small house where they'd been living. He'd have been twenty-two at the time, but when a firm of solicitors tried to track him down they discovered that no one had seen him since he was eighteen. That would have been in 1972. It was a peculiar case but Porteous tried not to read too much into it. Social Services seemed not to feel too much responsibility for kids in care once they were sixteen. They drifted in a twilight world of hard-to-let flats, hostels and mates' floors. And if the next of kin had been named as one of the executors presumably there wouldn't have been much incentive to trace the boy. Perhaps they would have received the profit from the house in his absence. The description was vague. Porteous had the feeling that the person reporting Michael as missing had never seen him. Nothing ruled him out from being the dead boy in the lake, but there was nothing to suggest it. There was nothing as useful as a photograph.

Carl Jackson had lived twenty miles from Cranford with his parents, who farmed sheep on the other side of the lake. He beamed gappily from a school snap attached to the file. He was sixteen and had learning difficulties and was described by the constable who'd taken the first missing-person report as 'mentally retarded'. Because of his vulnerable status there'd been a big search for him, involving not only the police and mountain-rescue team but also members of the public. He attended Cranford Adult Training Centre and was collected every morning from the end of the farm track by a bus which picked up all the trainees from rural areas. His parents were elderly, considered by the staff at the centre as overprotective. Usually one of them waited with him for the bus and was there to meet him in the evening. In an attempt to encourage Carl's independence it was suggested that he could make the half-mile walk down the track alone. What could go wrong? The track led only to the farmhouse. It would be impossible for him to get lost. But one day, the third that this experiment in independent living was tried, he failed to arrive home. His parents waited less than half an hour before going out to look for him. Two hours later they alerted the police. It was as if he had disappeared into thin air.

Porteous had phoned the contact number without much hope of success. The Jacksons had been in their fifties when Carl had disappeared in 1969. He was answered by a machine. 'You're through to Balk Farm Computing. No one is available to take your call . . .' The farmhouse had been sold to yuppies, the land dispersed. It was happening to hill farms all over the north of England. It had happened to the farm where he was living.

He looked again at the photo. Carl was dressed in a check shirt, corduroy trousers and a hand-knitted V-neck pullover. Old man's clothes. It was hard to imagine him wearing a hippy leather bracelet.

The long case clock in the corner chimed the half-hour. Half-past midnight. Porteous rinsed out his glass, stoppered the bottle and put it in the fridge. In bed he took ten minutes to go through the breathing exercise which usually helped him to relax, but he slept fitfully, haunted by the grainy photographs of Carl Jackson and Alan Brownscombe, by the fat white body in the mortuary and by Carver's grin.

Chapter Three

They sat in Porteous's office, which was so small that their knees almost touched, making an effort to get on.

Eddie Stout had seen Porteous cart off the boxes of files the night before and wondered what was going on. Was the man some sort of control freak? That wasn't his job. Didn't he trust the rest of the team? But Eddie was a Christian, a lay minister on the Methodist circuit, out every Sunday preaching to a handful of old ladies in the windswept chapels in the hills, so he had to forgive Porteous for being promoted over him and he had to make allowances. It was a strain for him, Porteous could see that. The silence between them was awkward.

Porteous liked Stout. Perhaps it would have been easier if the man had been less hospitable and generous. Why was Stout trying so hard? When Porteous had first arrived Stout had invited him to dinner at his home – an overture of friendship which had been impossible for Porteous to refuse. It had been an unexpectedly pleasant evening but Porteous felt he had disappointed Stout because he had given too little of himself away. He had taken flowers and chocolates as gifts instead of wine. Methodists didn't drink, did they?

But it seemed that nowadays they did, and after several glasses of home-brewed beer Stout had become mellow, almost Dickensian, sitting in a fat armchair, puffing his pipe, surrounded by evidence of his family. Porteous had drunk little and maintained his guard.

Stout's wife, Bet, was plump and motherly. There were two grown-up children, settled down with babies of their own, and photographs of them were on the mantelpiece and the window-sills. Then there was Ruthie, the baby, ten years younger than the others, a wild adolescent with cropped hair, who had eaten with them, entertaining them with stories about school. Afterwards she had disappeared off to a party with her boyfriend, but not without giving her father a big hug first.

'You've no family?' Bet had asked, as if it were a loss in his life, something to be pitied, to be compensated for with comforting casseroles and sticky puddings.

He had shaken his head. 'Never married.'

He had seen them looking at each other and had read their thoughts. At first they had considered that he might be one of them – a Christian. Perhaps of the happy clappy born-again variety, saving himself for the right girl. That might have explained his reluctance to go to the pub after work, to join in the swearing, the banter about women. But he hadn't used the right phrases, as recognizable as a Masonic handshake. He hadn't made himself known.

So then they had wondered if he might be gay. That too was something he was used to. It was a way for colleagues to explain his apparent celibacy, his love of art and theatre. He had heard the sniggers and the jokes, though he never responded to them. Eddie and Bet hadn't sniggered – they were too kind and too tolerant for that. But they had felt cheated because he hadn't been more open with them and they were curious. Later he was sure they would ask Ruthie what she thought. Porteous wondered what the answer would be.

Now, in his office, so close to Eddie that he could smell the tobacco, he had a sudden urge to explain. It would have been like talking to a priest or a shrink: 'Ten years ago I had a nervous breakdown. Stress. Now I avoid it. You know, prevention better than cure. And I take the medication. I like my life ordered, predictable. That's why I live alone. So I can control what goes on. It runs in the family, actually, psychiatric disorder. My dad was a nutter. He jumped off a bridge in front of the Birmingham Intercity. It's like diabetes. Genetic.'

But it wasn't like diabetes. Diabetes would have been no big deal; his promotion wouldn't have been a cause for self-congratulation on the part of his superiors. 'This shows that we take equal opportunities seriously, Peter. You're a trailblazer. But we suggest that you don't make a song and dance about it. You need authority, the confidence, you know, of your troops. Your past illness is no business of anyone else, is it?'

He was aware suddenly of Stout watching him, waiting for him to speak. God, he thought, it won't take him long to work out that I'm a headcase if I sit here with my mouth open, staring into space. He pulled the three files out of his briefcase, lay them on the desk.

'Do you remember any of these, Eddie?'

Stout read them quickly, flicking his eyes occasionally back to his boss's face.

'Carl Jackson. I remember that one. I was up on the hill with everyone else searching, even when I'd come off shift. It was March but the weather was foul. Low mist. Rain. I thought I'd been mad to move away from the coast.'

'Could it be our chap in the lake?'

'I don't know why I didn't think of it before.' He seemed angry with himself.

'So it could be him?'

'Carl was murdered, if that's what you mean. There's no way he just wandered away from the track and got lost.'

'But it doesn't say anything here about a murder investigation.'

'There wasn't one. Everyone was content to put it down as an accident. According to the press, if anyone was to blame it was the social worker who suggested that he should be allowed to walk home on his own. But I talked to her in the day centre and I was impressed. She said Carl was deaf. No one had picked up how profound that disability was, and she thought he was more capable than his parents allowed him to be. In the few months since she'd known him he'd begun to read quite fluently. She thought he might catch up enough to move on to the technical college, perhaps hold down a real job. But his parents were horrified by those plans. They wanted nothing to do with them.'

'Hard, I suppose, to stop being protective after all those years.'

'There was more to it than that. They were a

strange family.' It was Stout's turn to stare into space, to drag back the memories, image by image.

'You think one of the parents was responsible for his death?'

'Not directly. The wife, Sarah, had a younger brother. I can't believe I can't remember the name. He caused me enough sleepless nights at the time. He didn't live at the farm but he'd never married and he spent a lot of time there. He was assistant manager in a hardware shop in town. It's been closed for years but it was a big place then, dealt in agricultural supplies and machinery too. In his spare time he got involved in community work.' He turned his head so he wasn't looking directly at Porteous. 'Quite a saint if you listened to Sarah. He was a scout leader in Cranford for years and ran the youth club in our church until I persuaded the committee it wasn't such a good idea.'

'Child abuse?'

'Nothing proved. Never charged.' Stout paused. 'It was before all the child-safety legislation, don't forget. Before Childline. Some people even treated it as a bit of a joke. If a pervy old man liked to touch young lads' behinds when they were horsing around, so what? At least it kept the kids off the streets. And no one else wanted the responsibility of organizing the group.'

'What put you on to him?'

'Rumours. Some of the things the kids said. The fact that he was such a loner. He never liked working with other adults. If he had an assistant it was an older lad who'd gone through the group. I had just enough to persuade my church to drop him. Tactfully of course, with a letter of thanks and a ten-quid book token. But not enough to take it further.'

'Until Carl Jackson disappeared.'

'Even then it wasn't a central line of investigation. I was a young DC. New to the district. No connections. I passed on the rumours and some enquiries were made but it seemed that the bloke had an alibi for the time Carl disappeared.' Porteous waited for Stout to continue but he was frowning, preoccupied. 'I've just remembered his name. It was Reeves. Alec Reeves.'

'You don't think much of the alibi?'

'It was half-day closing at the shop so his boss couldn't vouch for him. Reeves claimed he was at home taking one of his lads through his paces for the Queen's Scout badge.'

'And the boy bore it out?'

'Too scared or too involved not to. So far as I know no other checks were made on where they both were that afternoon.'

'Would you be able to dig out the name of the witness?'

'Aye. I made sure I kept all my notes on that one. I knew it would come back to haunt me.'

'Do you know what happened to Carl's parents? I tried to phone the farm last night. The number's the same but it seems to be some sort of office now. Computers.'

'Alf, the father, died. We didn't think he was involved in any way with Carl's disappearance. He was a grafter but not the sharpest tool in the box. Last time I heard, Sarah was in one of those old folks' council bungalows near the river. I presume she's still alive. She's one of those women you imagine would go on for ever. She'll be a good age now.'

'And Reeves?'

'Funnily enough he left the town soon after the investigation was wrapped up.' His voice, which was heavy with sarcasm, turned to a quiet desperation. 'To work as a care assistant in a children's home. I should have told someone. Said something. But he hadn't been charged and he had a lot of powerful friends. I really didn't think anyone would take any notice.'

'Do you remember where he went?'

'I don't think I ever knew. Look, I can't tell you if that body in the lake was Carl's, but if it was, I can tell you who killed him and I'm glad I'll be there to see him go down.'

'There's nothing we can do until we've checked the dental records. That's happening this morning.'

'I'd like to talk to Sarah. Now. While we've got an element of surprise.'

Porteous had never seen Eddie Stout like this. He was usually the one in the team to caution detachment: 'We don't get paid to act as judges,' he'd say. 'That's for God and the chaps with the hairy wigs.'

'She'll surely have heard about the body in the lake.'

'But no details. Not that we're calling it murder.'

Porteous wanted to say no. If he didn't feel he owed Eddie, he'd have refused immediately.

Eddie sensed the hesitation. 'If it is Carl it would give us a head start. Let me see what she's got to say for herself. You're right. Of course she'll have heard about the body in the lake. She might give something away. And I want to find out what happened to Alec Reeves. If he's still working with children I want to know about it. Things are different these days.'

God, thought Porteous, suddenly feeling very tired, I haven't been that passionate about anything in years.

He sensed that Stout wouldn't let it go and couldn't face a confrontation. He shrugged.

'Why not?' he said. 'But I'm coming with you.'

Stout drove. There was no air-conditioning in the car and even with the windows down Porteous felt sticky, slightly light-headed in the heat. The bungalows were grouped around a square of grass which was brown through lack of water. Two old men in white hats stood chatting and broke off their conversation when Stout knocked on the door.

Porteous had worked out that Sarah Jackson must be at least eighty, but she opened the door to them herself, and she recognized Stout immediately.

'Oh, it's you.' She had an underbite and a way of thrusting her jaw forwards to emphasize it. She was skinny and short and the mannerism gave her the air of an aggressive child. A cotton floral dress added to the impression. 'You might as well come in.'

She led them into a small room packed with shabby furniture which must have come from the farm.

'I heard you sold up after Alf died,' Stout said.

'I could hardly work the place on my own.'

'Good timing, just before the bottom fell out of hill farming. You were lucky.'

She glared at him. 'You make your own luck in this world.'

Porteous had the impression that this was a continuation of the sparring which had gone on twenty years before. He sat on a fireside chair that had been covered in pink stretch nylon, and watched.

'I hear there's a computer business in the old house now,' Stout said. He was still standing, looking out of the window.

'Is that what it was about?' She hardly seemed interested. 'I suppose there would be plenty of space.'

'You don't miss the place?' Stout persisted.

'It was never the same after Carl went.'

'No,' Porteous interrupted. He could feel Stout's anger across the room. 'It can't have been.'

She sniffed, slightly mollified, and perched on the edge of an overstuffed chesterfield.

'What do you want?'

'You'll have heard we found a body in Cranford Water?'

'That's nothing to do with me.'

'Why are you so certain it's not Carl in the lake?'

'Because he just wandered off. It was the sort of thing he did. I told the social workers he couldn't take in what you said to him. And it wasn't because he couldn't hear. Even with his deaf aid he had his head in the clouds. And he couldn't have walked that far without anyone seeing him. Where did you find the body? Near the Adventure Centre. That's the opposite side of the lake from the farm. A twenty-mile walk. At least. You lot were out searching before he could have made it. And, before you ask, he couldn't swim. Or row a boat.'

She spoke with confidence. It was a well-rehearsed speech.

'Someone could always have driven him in a car,' Stout said softly.

'Which someone are we talking about now?'

'Alec had a car, didn't he? A Morris 1100. Navy blue. It was his pride and joy as I remember.'

'I wondered how long it would be before you got round to Alec.' She was contemptuous, turning her back on Stout and directing the rest of the conversation at Porteous. 'My little brother was hounded out of the town by your man, just when I needed his support the most. It was rumours at first. Gossip. Snide, like a lassie. Don't trust Alec Reeves with your children. Then he went to his boss and accused Alec of taking our Carl. As if he would. He was good to the boy, more patient than me or Alf could ever be. He took him for treats, things we never had the time or the money to give him. The pictures on Saturday afternoons, picnics in the hills . . .'

She wiped the corner of her eye with an embroidered handkerchief. Porteous, who was looking closely, could see no tears.

'Please don't distress yourself,' he said. 'We thought you'd rather we came ourselves to tell you what was happening. My people are checking the dental records now – we know that Carl saw a dentist while he was at the day centre. The records are still available. You shouldn't have long to wait. We'll have a positive identification by this afternoon.'

Sarah Jackson was so angry that she seemed not to care. 'That's all very well,' she cried. 'But you shouldn't have brought that man here. It wasn't tactful. It wasn't right.'

She stood up as if she expected them to leave but Porteous stayed where he was.

'What happened to Alec when he left Cranford, Mrs Jackson?'

'He did well for himself. Better than if he'd stayed here.'

'Oh?'

'He got a job in a home for kiddies. They sent him

away to college.' She was as proud as if she'd been talking about her own son.

'Is he still there?'

'He retired. I thought he might come home then. We'd been so close, him and me. Our parents died when he was still at school. I brought him up. But he couldn't face it after what happened before. All those lies. He bought a bungalow in the Pennines not far from the school. I visit when I can. I'll go again when it's not so hot.'

'Whereabouts in the Pennines?'

'What's it to you? I'll not have him harassed.' She walked towards the door and threw it open. 'I'm an old woman. I need my peace. I've nothing more to say to you.'

They walked out into the glare of the sunshine. 'I'll be in touch this afternoon,' Porteous said, 'when we've heard back from the dentist.' But she had already shut the door on them.

They were in the station, walking up the stairs towards Porteous's office, when they heard footsteps running up behind them. It was Claire Wright, a young DC, flushed, excited, out of breath so she could hardly speak.

'We've got a match.' She bent double, gasping.

'You look as if you've just won the Great North Run.' Porteous forced himself to stay calm, to keep his voice light.

'Who?' demanded Stout. When she did not reply immediately he added, almost in a whisper, 'Is it Carl Jackson?'

By then she had caught her breath. 'Nah, nothing like. It's the lad called Michael Grey.'

36

'Ah.' Porteous continued up the stairs, unlocked his door and flicked the kettle on. He waited for Stout to follow.

Chapter Four

Stout stood in the doorway of Porteous's office.

'You don't seem surprised.'

'Not too surprised, no,' Porteous said. 'You were right about Sarah Jackson. She does know what happened to her son. But when we talked about the body in the lake she wasn't bothered, hardly interested. She knew it wasn't him.'

He made a mug of tea for Eddie, strong, as he knew he liked it, and waved it at him to invite him in. 'We'll have to save Carl for another day.' The words sounded unbelievably trite. 'I'm sorry, Eddie, I mean it. Now we have to concentrate on Michael Grey, find out everything there is to know about him.'

Porteous could tell the man's mind and heart weren't really in it. He was still thinking about the deaf boy everyone had labelled as dumb. When this investigation was over he'd give Eddie his head for a few weeks, let him dig around for a bit. Even if nothing came of it he deserved that much.

Soon it became clear they would find out very little about Michael Grey. Not immediately at least. At first Porteous had thought it would be easy. A piece of piss, he said to himself, though not to Eddie who disapproved of such language. Michael Grey had been fostered to a couple called Brice. Fostering meant Social Services and that meant records as long as your arm – reports for the court, case conferences, personal records kept to cover the back of whichever poor social worker had been in charge of him. There would be details of the natural family at least and of any contact between them and the boy. Michael hadn't been adopted, so he would still have been officially in care when he disappeared. Some attempt would have been made to trace him.

He sent Eddie to talk to the solicitor who'd triggered the first missing-person report after the foster parents' death. 'Find out who benefited from the will in the absence of the boy. Did anyone? Is the cash still being held in trust for him? What happens to it now?'

Stout slunk away like a sulky teenager. As soon as he had gone Porteous made an appointment with the senior social worker on duty at the town hall. The man was prepared to see him at once. The town hall was in the same street and of the same design as the police station – redbrick Victorian Gothic – though it had a depressing concrete and glass extension at the back, where the Social Services department was housed. A small middle-aged man named Jones met Porteous at reception and led him upstairs. They left behind them the screams of an elderly woman, demanding to see her social worker, and the increasingly irate reply of the receptionist who said she would have to wait.

They sat in a cubby-hole looking out on a busy open-plan office where one of the phones always seemed to be ringing. Jones was tidy, with a few wisps of hair combed over a balding pate. He was apologetic. 'After you phoned I checked our records. I like to think we're efficient in that department. But we've no details of a couple called Brice being registered as foster parents. Nothing at all. No application form, no record of training.'

'Would you still have the file after all this time?'

'Oh yes. We go back thirty years. Longer. Child protection, you see. It's important to know who's been looking after our children.'

'Could the Brices have been working for someone else? A charity, perhaps? Another authority?'

'That's what I thought!' He seemed impressed that Porteous had been thinking along the same lines. 'But I've phoned around and I can't find anyone else in the field who's heard of them. I'm not saying it's impossible that they were registered with another agency, but – if it doesn't sound too big-headed – my contacts are second to none. I'd certainly say it's unlikely.'

'You'll have a record, though, of Michael Grey?'

'No.' The man closed his mouth firmly, allowing no question. He sat back in his chair and clasped his hands round his small paunch. He seemed to be delighted by the mystery, and by Porteous's discomfort.

'But I gave you his date of birth. We found it in the dental records.' Porteous could tell he was sounding desperate. That'll teach me, he thought. A piece of piss.

'It doesn't help, I'm afraid. I've phoned the court. They keep their own records. No care or supervision order was placed on anyone called Michael Grey in the seventies anywhere in the county.' He paused, savouring the moment. 'Social Services were never involved with him either.'

'But they must have been.'

'Not necessarily.' Jones leaned forward, but didn't elaborate.

'I don't understand.'

'How old was he?' The tone was patronizing. An infant teacher talking to a particularly thick six-year-old. Just what I deserve, Porteous thought.

'When we think he went missing? Eighteen.'

'There you are then.' Jones leaned back in the chair once more and smirked. 'Over sixteen and we wouldn't get involved. He could have been younger than that when he started living with the foster parents, if it was an informal arrangement.'

'Perhaps you would explain.' Porteous had never minded eating humble pie. It was surprising how people liked you to grovel. The social worker was loving it.

'Let's take a hypothetical situation. Something we come across all the time. Say there's a single mum with a teenage lad. He starts to run a bit wild. Perhaps it's nothing that would get him in trouble with the police, but he's staying out late, skipping school. She begins to feel she's losing control. Now, it could be that the boy has a good relationship with her parents and they offer to have him to live with them for a while. To take the heat off her until things calm down. That would be fostering of a sort, wouldn't it? Nothing official. No need for Social Services to be involved even if the lad were under sixteen. In fact that's usually the last thing a family under stress wants. A nosy cow from the Welfare knocking on the door.'

Porteous smiled.

'So you're saying these Brices were probably relatives?'

'They might have been. Or friends. They might even have been doing it for money. All I can tell you is I don't think they were official.'

'Where do you suggest I go from here?'

'Have you got the name of the school?'

'Cranford Grammar.' That too had been in the dental records.

'Try there then. If it was an informal fostering they'd still have wanted the names of the natural parent. It's possible that he moved away from home after he started the school. Most problems of that sort start in adolescence. You might even find a couple of teachers who remember him. My kids go there and some of the staff must be close to retirement.'

He led Porteous down the concrete stairs. In the waiting-room the old lady had begun to sob.

Cranford Grammar had since become Cranford High, and when Porteous phoned the school from his office he was told that it was the last day of the summer term. The secretary sounded on the verge of hysteria. In the background he heard the high-pitched yelps of children, an impatient teacher calling for mislaid reports, a yell for silence.

'It really isn't a good time.'

Then he explained that he was running a murder inquiry and suddenly her attitude changed. Porteous had noticed it before. It wasn't a desire to be a good citizen and help the police. Murder had the same effect as the mention of celebrity, of a pop idol or football star. She was excited. Later she would boast to her friends that she had been involved.

He told her again what he wanted.

'I can only think of one member of staff who would have been around then,' she said. 'Mr Westcott. He's head of history. I know he has a free period first thing after lunch but that's probably not the best time to talk to him.'

'Why not?' he asked politely.

'Oh well. I suppose it'll be all right. I'll tell him you're calling. And I'll check our records. If you come to the office first I'll have everything ready for you.'

The electric bell sounding the end of lunch was ringing as he got out of his car. By the time he got to the school office the children were contained in their classrooms. No pretence was being made to teach them. He heard whoops of laughter, the blare of rock music. The secretary moved away from her computer screen when she saw him and held towards him a manila envelope. He could tell from the weight that there were only a couple of sheets of paper inside.

'It's not much I'm afraid. After all this time . . .'

He knew that she would have done all she could to help. There was no point in pushing for more. He followed her directions to the staff-room. Jack Westcott was plump and round and when Porteous pushed open the door to the cluttered room, he was asleep. Despite the heat he wore a tweed jacket with a loud check and there were beads of sweat on his forehead. Porteous leaned over him to tap him on the shoulder and smelled whisky fumes. That explained the secretary's feeling that the first period after lunch might not be a good time to speak to him. Jack Westcott had been celebrating the end of term in the pub. He opened rheumy eyes and with an unembarrassed jolt he sat up.

'You must be the policeman chappie.'

Porteous admitted that he was.

'Help yourself to coffee.' He nodded unsteadily towards a filter machine in the corner. 'I have mine black. Two sugars if the bastards have left any.'

He pressed on the arms of his chair as if to hoist himself out of it, but the effort was too much for him. The three remaining teachers in the room picked up their bags and wandered out. Porteous carried back the polystyrene cups of coffee and sat beside him.

'I'm here about a boy called Michael Grey. Your secretary said you might remember him. We think he could have been a bit of a troublemaker.'

'No, no no.' The words were thundered so loud that Porteous was startled. Jack Westcott set the cup on the table and shook his head as if to clear an alcoholic fug. 'He was a good chap, Michael. One of the best.'

'So you do remember him?' Porteous felt a wonderful relief. He had begun to think that Michael Grey didn't exist at all, that he was some figment of Carver's imagination.

'Of course I do. I remember all the kids. Hundreds of them. That's what teaching's all about. Not attainment targets. Not literacy hours. Not . . !' He looked about him, saw that the bulk of his audience had disappeared and lapsed in to silence.

'Tell me about him.'

'I didn't teach the boy. History wasn't one of his

subjects. Shame. He'd have been an asset to the sixth-form group. Articulate, you know.'

'So you didn't know him well?' Porteous felt the image of Michael Grey fade from his grasp. A ghostly apparition disappearing through a wall before it has even taken shape.

'I didn't say that. He was in my tutor group for nearly two years so I probably knew him better than his subject teachers.' Westcott sat back in his chair like an elderly Billy Bunter and shut his eyes. He continued to speak, unaware of Porteous taking notes. 'Michael joined us at the beginning of the lower sixth, a year older than most of them. I can't remember where he came from. Some private place, I think. I know there was a problem getting the paperwork from them. It hadn't even arrived by the time he left. I was never told why he resat the lower sixth and I didn't ask. Not my business. Some illness perhaps or emotional problem. It happens at that age. They're very intense. That's why they're such a joy to teach. I'm an old man, can't get up to much now. So I live through them. Voraciously but second hand. Much the safest way . . .'

He paused for a moment. Porteous worried that he might have fallen asleep again, but the words continued in a low-pitched growl.

'He was an exceptional boy. There was something about him. Charm, I suppose you'd call it. He had a way of winning people over.'

'Did he talk about his home life?'

'He was living with the Brices.' He lapsed again into silence. Porteous resisted the temptation to prompt him. 'Good people, the Brices. I didn't really know them myself. Met them occasionally. Parents' dos. The school play. But that's what everyone said. Of course they were religious.' He snorted, as if religion was to be disapproved of, then began to snore. He was more drunk than Porteous had first realized.

'Did he have friends?'

'What? Oh, bucketsful. I could give you a list. There was a girlfriend. What was her name? Shy little thing.'

'Did he talk about his family? I mean his real family.'

'No, but parents are an embarrassment at that age, whatever they're like. It doesn't mean anything. None of the kids talk about them.'

'Is there anything else you can tell me about him?'

'He was an actor. Brilliant. I remember his Macbeth. The best production the school ever did.' He lurched suddenly to his feet and began to quote hammily: 'Is this a dagger which I see before me?'

He flung out one arm and collapsed back into the chair. Then he fell into a deep sleep and Porteous found it impossible to rouse him.

Because it was the end of term the students must have been released early; as Porteous got to his car it was surrounded by a tide of screaming and dishevelled children. He was grateful to reach the peace of the police station. It was only when Porteous was back in his office that he opened the envelope given to him by the secretary.

There was one sheet of paper and a faded photograph. The paper was a reference, handwritten by Jack Westcott, for use in the universities selection process. It described Michael Grey in the same glowing terms he had used to Porteous. The boy's predicted A-level grades were good. It seemed that he would have had no difficulty in securing a university place. The photograph was in fact a cutting from the local paper and included a review of the production of *Macbeth*. A grainy figure stood centre stage. He was dressed in a costume obviously put together by the home-economics department. In his hand he brandished a wide-bladed knife.

Chapter Five

Porteous felt suddenly restless. He re-read Westcott's reference for Michael and set it aside. Sometimes it happened. He'd happily sit for days going over a mechanical task, then all at once feel that he was caged. He needed to pace up and down, to be somewhere, anywhere different. He'd discussed the problem with his doctor, who'd agreed that it could be a side-effect of the medication he was taking. But didn't everyone feel like that once in a while? Didn't everyone feel the need to break free?

He wandered down the stairs to the car park and was hovering there, trying to think of a legitimate journey he could make, when Eddie Stout returned from his meeting with the solicitor who'd handled the Brices' affairs.

'Any joy?' He thought he sounded businesslike. Not like someone trying to dream up an excuse not to go inside.

'I don't know. More complications.'

'We'll talk about it over a cup of tea, shall we?' Porteous said. 'Not here. Not the canteen. Let's go somewhere else.' To his own ears he sounded hysterical, but Stout seemed not to notice, even to be pleased by the suggestion.

'There's quite a nice place along by our church . . .'

The walk calmed Porteous, made him slightly less jumpy. He felt his pulse slow. The café was attached to the church and was obviously run by its members. It was called the Mustard Seed. Besides tea and cakes it sold religious books and sentimental greetings cards. Again Porteous wondered if Stout saw him as a subject ripe for conversion. The building was new, airy, but as they went in Porteous had a fleeting smell of damp books and old ladies' perfume.

Perhaps Stout sensed his discomfort. He said defensively, 'It's run by volunteers. All the profit goes to our charities. I like to support it. Anyway it's a quiet place to talk.'

They were fussed over by two grey-haired grandmothers. There were frilly tablecloths and silk flowers, but the women made him Earl Grey to his exact specification and the shortbread was excellent. The church had been built as part of a new housing development, along with shops and a community centre. They looked out on to a street. A funeral service was taking place in the church next door. One of the undertaker's men was standing by the hearse, smoking a cigarette. The women were interested in what was happening and kept coming out into the room to peer through the window. At a nod from Stout they retreated behind their counter and soon became engrossed in their memories of the dead man. Porteous resisted an impulse to fidget. He wanted to arrange the sugar cubes into towers, to straighten the birthday cards on a nearby stand.

'I've finally met someone who knew Michael Grey,' he said. 'The social worker wasn't much use. He decided the fostering arrangement with the Brices must have been informal, set up between them and the parents. He'd have no record of that. But he put me in touch with the school. There's a teacher called Jack Westcott, head of history. He remembered Michael quite well.'

'I'd take what Westcott said with a pinch of salt,' Stout said tartly. 'He'll have been in the Percy Arms all lunchtime.'

'Is that a regular event? I thought it was just because it was the last day of term.'

'Regular enough. He's retiring now, so the school hasn't made an issue of it. He never taught Ruth but I kept an eye on what was going on.'

I bet they love you at the school, Porteous thought. He said, 'There's written confirmation, anyway. A reference from Westcott to help Michael get a place at university.'

Stout didn't reply.

'I'm surprised you didn't know the Brices,' Porteous went on. Thinking, You know everything about every other bugger in the place.

'For some reason we never bumped into each other. I've been asking around though. Stephen Brice was an ordained priest with the Church of England. He worked in Africa before coming back to be rector here. After he retired he still did a lot of writing and teaching. People I've spoken to can't remember the lad, but they say it would be just like the Brices to take someone in. They liked young people. Set up a youth group. Run, coincidentally, by Alec Reeves.'

'Was it now?'

'Unfortunately he'd already left the area before

Michael went to live with them.' Stout shrugged. 'Like
you said, I'll have to let that go.'

'What did you get out of the solicitor?'

'Everything he had to give. The Brices died just
over a year after Michael disappeared. There was a car
crash on the A1. Stephen died immediately. Sylvia was
taken to hospital but passed away a couple of days
later in intensive care. The wills were drawn up by the
couple without the help of a solicitor. He said that if
he'd been involved he would have worded things a bit
differently, but the intention of the couple was quite
clear and he has no doubt the wills are legal docu-
ments. They were found with the rest of the Brices'
papers after their deaths. He was one of the executors
and determined to carry out their wishes as best he
could.'

Stout pulled a notebook from his pocket. 'Each of
the wills was identical. The estate was to be left first
to the other partner. In the event of the survivor dying
it should go to "our foster son, our gift from God,
known as Michael Grey, so he can lead an independent
life". That was it, quoted word for word.'

'No legacies to charity or to the church?'

'No. According to the solicitor, they gave regularly
in covenants while they were alive, but there was
nothing in the will.'

'Doesn't that seem odd to you?'

'I don't think so. It wasn't a huge estate. Only a
small terraced house and a couple of thousand in
savings. Perhaps they wanted to give as much as possible to Michael.'

'Their gift from God.' Porteous tried to keep the
sneer from his voice. 'They obviously thought he was

still alive at the time of their deaths or they'd have changed the wills. And they must have believed the solicitor could trace him without too much difficulty. Didn't they think it odd when Michael didn't get in touch for months?'

'The solicitor said he'd never had any other clients like them. They were unworldly, as trusting as children. They didn't worry about things they couldn't change.'

That's what I try to do, Porteous thought. But I never manage it. 'What do you make of the "known as" in the phrase "known as Michael Grey"?'

'I supposed it meant the Brices considered him their son, even though he used a name different from theirs.'

'Not that Michael Grey was an assumed name?'

Stout looked up sharply from his tea. 'That would complicate matters.'

'Wouldn't it just.' But, thought Porteous, if that's the way it is I can't change it, so there's no point worrying.

They sat for a moment in silence. The coffin was carried from the church and replaced in the hearse, which drove slowly away. The congregation had spilled out on to the street and elderly men in shiny black suits stood chatting in the sunshine. One of the ladies behind the counter plucked up courage to call over to them. 'Can we get you anything else, Mr Stout?'

'Some more tea, Mavis, would be lovely.'

Still there were no other customers. After the tea had been presented Porteous said, 'What steps did the solicitor take to trace Michael Grey?'

'Much the same as we've done today. He contacted the school. He thought it most likely that Michael had gone on to further education and that the school would have the name of the college or university even if it couldn't give him his home address. At that time he thought it would be quite straightforward to find him.'

'But it wasn't.'

'Apparently Michael left quite suddenly without taking A levels.'

'The Brices must have thought they knew where he was or surely they would have got in touch with us.'

'I don't know. Unless they talked to a friend about it, we'll never find out. The solicitor did report him as a missing person when he couldn't get an address from the school. His main objective was to prove that he'd done everything possible to find Michael. Apparently that's a legal requirement. He advertised for information in the local Cranford paper, the *Newcastle Chronicle* and the London *Evening Standard*. It's standard procedure.'

'No response?'

'Not even from cranks.'

'What did the solicitor do then?'

'He didn't feel there was anything else he could do. He'd fulfilled all his legal obligations.'

'What happened to the money?'

'It went to Sylvia Brice's next of kin. Because she survived her husband by a couple of days *her* relative was the beneficiary, not his. It was actually a nephew, a commodity broker in the city. He hardly needed the cash. According to the solicitor all the family have done well for themselves. Perhaps that's why the Brices decided to leave the estate to Michael.'

'I'm glad they never knew,' Porteous said, 'that he couldn't be traced.'

'There is one complication.'

'Only one?'

'The solicitor's very keen for us to fix a date of death.'

'Aren't we all!'

Stout ignored the sarcasm and ploughed on. 'You see, if Michael's death predated the Brices' then the arrangement by which the nephew inherited was fair and legal. But suppose Michael was still alive when the Brices had the car crash. Suppose he'd just gone to earth somewhere and he was killed and dumped in the lake later. Then that would affect the inheritance.'

'In what way?'

'The cash should have gone to *his* next of kin, not the Brices.'

Porteous found that he could concentrate again on the detail. The dreadful restlessness seemed to have left him. 'I don't think that's likely, do you? He wasn't the sort of lad I imagined at first. I don't see him disappearing for months, moving from one squat to another, spending time inside. He was bright. He had a lot to lose. I think he was killed soon after he was missed at school.'

Outside, the congregation had dispersed. The grandmothers were banging pots in the kitchen to show they wanted to lock up.

Stout stood up. 'What now?'

'Back to the station to organize a press conference. It's time we went public. The school gave me a photo, a cutting from the local rag, but it could be anyone. Let's see if the paper still has the original. I know it happened nearly thirty years ago, but people round here have good memories. There'll be friends still living in the town. And enemies. Come on, Eddie. Let's make you a star.'

In fact Porteous took the press conference early the following evening. There was all the media interest he could have wished for. The body had been discovered because of the drought and the drought was a big story, so the national press was there. He had wanted to hold the conference in the high-school hall. The only certainty he had in the case was that Michael Grey had been a pupil at Cranford Grammar. He thought it might jog a few memories. But the head teacher wasn't keen. He seemed to think that even after all those years murder would be bad for the school's image. He used as an excuse the fact that the hall had already been hired out for an event in the evening. Nothing Porteous said could make him change his mind.

Instead they used the community centre next to Stout's church. It still smelled of the lunch that had been provided for the pensioners' club which had met earlier in the day – steamed fish and cabbage. Porteous sat on the stage behind a trestle table hidden by a white cloth. His answers to the press emphasized his ignorance. He didn't have an exact date of death. He hadn't traced the boy's relatives. That was why he needed their help. All he had was a body that looked like a lump of lard – this he phrased more delicately – and an old photo of a white-haired boy with a knife.

There was one moment of excitement. In the second row sat a big woman who worked for the town's free paper. When the photo was passed round Porteous could have sworn that she recognized the face. But when he looked for her later she had rushed away.

PART TWO

Chapter Six

It was hot again. The local news was all about the weather. A magistrate had been prosecuted for using a sprinkler at midnight. Tankers were driving the region's water south. The lake at Cranford was so low that flooded buildings were starting to emerge from the sludge and a body, trapped under a pier for years, had been found by a canoeist.

Hannah switched off the radio and parked her car. There was a new officer on the gate so she had to show her pass. The photograph was two years old and she saw him look at it then back at her, squinting, unsure at first that it was the same person. He pushed it back under the glass screen and Hannah stared at it too. It didn't look like her. The woman in the photograph was younger. She was smiling. Not relaxed exactly – Hannah had never been that – there was a tension around the mouth. But content, complacent even. It was taken while she was still part of a family. Before Rosie hated her. Before Jonathan left with a twenty-five-year-old PE teacher, to set up home all over again.

She had to wait for a moment in the gate room for two officers to come in through the outer door. The inner door wouldn't open until the outer was locked. Then she stood back to let them go ahead to collect their keys. She was in no hurry, early as usual. Punctuality had been a curse since childhood. She threw her tag into the chute and waited for the new man to find her keys. Ahead of her the officers were talking very loudly. She recognized them but they were too engrossed in conversation to acknowledge her. She gathered there'd been some trouble on the wing the night before. Nothing serious. She thought it had probably been caused by the heat. Those huts must be insufferable in this weather. The men walked off before she could hear any more, the heels of their highly polished shoes reflecting the sunlight. They were still talking. Every other word, she knew, would be a blasphemy.

Hannah followed them from the gatehouse and thought that generally, in the prison, the officers were less polite than the inmates. *They* were usually courteous, grovelling even, like the child in a class who is always bullied. Especially if they wanted something – to use the library on an unscheduled day, for example, or to be let off a fine for a lost or damaged book. 'Please, miss, it's not my fault. Honest,miss.'

Of course, they weren't all like that. Neither were the officers all boors. Today she was feeling particularly jaundiced, because the photograph had reminded her of a time of certainty, and because she'd had a row with Rosie last night. Rosie. Named by her parents Rosalind, she'd changed her name with her personality in adolescence. She was Hannah's only child. The night before, Rosie had come in drunk again with a gang of friends. It was midnight. Hannah's room was over the kitchen and she'd heard the freezer door open and the banging of a cooker shelf, and she knew that when she got up in the morning there'd be plates everywhere and half-eaten pizza ground into the carpet. And probably a body snoring on the sofa in the dining-room and two more in the spare bed. So she'd gone down and made a fuss. Rosie had stared at her in apparent horror and amazement, actually enjoying every minute of the drama.

'Get a life, Mum,' she'd said. 'Make some friends and get a life.'

Then she'd stormed off to spend the night in someone else's spare room.

Jonathan had never minded the late nights, the loud music, strange kids in the house. At first Hannah had been surprised by his tolerance. Then she'd been jealous of his ability to get on with Rosie's friends.

'We've all been young,' he'd say. 'Even you, Hannah.'

He'd take them to the pub at the end of the street, buying them drinks even before they were eighteen, talking music, reminiscing about bands he'd seen and festivals he'd attended. That side of his life had been new to Hannah. Perhaps he hadn't wanted to admit to a vaguely hippy past until the sixties became fashionable again. Perhaps he'd made it all up to impress the stunning sixth-form women who sat around the beaten copper tables in the Grey Horse, downing their pints of Stella as if they were glasses of lemonade. Perhaps, stirred by their admiration, that was when he recognized there were other possibilities in his life and he turned his attention to the lycra-clad Eve.

Not Eve the temptress, he had said earnestly when he explained that he was leaving. She was shy. She hadn't wanted it to happen. She'd be the last person ever to want to break up a family. They'd both fought it.

When Hannah failed to respond he had gone on more petulantly, 'At least we waited until Rosie finished her A levels before making it public.' As if that had deserved a prize. As if it hadn't been more about embarrassment, because Jonathan and Eve both taught in Rosie's school. As deputy head, Jonathan was Eve's boss.

Before leaving the gatehouse Hannah clipped the keys on to her belt and tucked them into the leather pouch which was designed to keep them hidden from view. The pouch was hardly an attractive garment but she always wore it. It was a rule and she'd never had any problems with rules. Perhaps that was why she'd settled without too much difficulty into the routine of the prison. There was a comforting hierarchy: governors of different grades, prisoners with different privileges, a system and a structure. Rosie's life seemed to have no order and that was why Hannah was alarmed for her. She had personal knowledge of how unsettling disorder could be.

The prison was category C, medium security, taking men who had been dispersed from local jails and lifers nearing the end of their sentences. It had once been an RAF base. There was still an enormous hangar which housed the workshops. The lads slept in billets where once conscripts spat on boots and folded blankets. Hannah had slipped into the way of calling them lads, though some of them were older than her. That showed, she thought, that she had become institutionalized into prison life.

The library was in a hut of its own, attached at the

back by a brick corridor to the education department. The site of the prison was vast. Now, at the beginning of July, it was a pleasant if sticky walk from the gate. There were flowers everywhere. Huge circular beds had been planted in formation as in a municipal park. The grass was closely cropped. The prison regularly won prizes for its gardens. In the winter it was a different matter. Then she came to work dressed for an expedition to the Arctic. The wind blew straight from Scandinavia. Horizontal rain and sleet seemed to last for days. Men who'd grown up in cities further south spoke of their sentence as if they'd been sent to a Siberian work camp. They called it the Gulag. The nearest railway was twenty miles away.

Hannah's orderly, Marty, was waiting outside for her, leaning against the door where the week before she had stuck a poster saying: NO SHORTS PLEASE. Since the beginning of the heatwave the men had started to dress as if for the beach. The exposed flesh and muscular thighs had seemed inappropriate for a library and, with the Governor's authority, she'd put a stop to it. As Hannah approached she realized the phone was ringing inside. Marty must have heard it, but he hadn't called or waved to hurry her along. By the time she'd unlocked the door it had stopped. Automatically she wondered if it had been her daughter. Anxiety about Rosie stayed with her constantly, eating away at her. She knew it was a silly habit, like checking the gas was switched off before leaving the house and always being early, but she couldn't help it. Knowing the history of the habit didn't help at all.

'You can't be on her back all the time,' Jonathan would say. 'Relax. What's wrong with you? Hormones, I suppose.' And if Rosie was there too they would snigger together. After all, what was more amusing than a middle-aged, menopausal woman scared to death that her reckless daughter would get into trouble? Because Rosie was reckless in an overreachingly confident way that left Hannah breathless.

Of course, she hadn't come in that morning before Hannah left for work and Hannah didn't know which friend she'd imposed on for a bed for the night. When she'd heard the phone it had occurred to her briefly that Rosie had called to apologize, but she dismissed the thought as ridiculous. Some chance. She picked up her bag, let Marty through ahead of her and locked the door behind them.

Marty was new to the job, different from any other orderlies she'd been given. It was a cushy number and the other men she'd worked with were eager to please, desperate to make themselves indispensable so she wouldn't find it easy to sack them before the end of their stint. They were only allowed six months in the job. It was a security concern. Supervisors and prisoners shouldn't have the chance to get too close. Marty was self-contained, efficient. He didn't tell her about his family or try to impress by talking about the books he'd read. He didn't say anything much unless it was about the library. Hannah thought he was probably in his thirties but he had one of those pale-skinned, freckled faces which always look boyish. She watched him lift a pile of newspapers on to a table and begin to sort them.

'Why don't you put the kettle on, Marty?'

He looked up, surprised, then nodded. Usually they had a cup of tea just before opening for the first session and today business didn't start until the period of lunchtime association at eleven thirty. But it wouldn't have occurred to him to comment.

For the first time she wondered what crime he had committed. Her friends – because she did have friends, despite Rosie's jibe – always asked about that.

'But what are they in for, Hannah?' they'd say with the disapproving curiosity of a *Telegraph* reader sneaking a look at the *Sun*. 'Who do you have to mix with in there? Rapists? Muggers of little old ladies?'

They were surprised when Hannah said she didn't know. She was never sure that they quite believed her. It was etiquette, this lack of interest. She wouldn't have enquired of the borrowers in the community library where she'd previously worked if they'd ever been prosecuted for speeding or tax evasion. Besides, it was irrelevant. It didn't matter. The prison was separate from the outside world. So long as the men fitted into the system and caused no bother, nobody much cared what had happened to bring them there. Except perhaps Arthur, her colleague. It seemed to matter to him very much.

Looking at Marty filling the kettle at the small sink in her office, she thought suddenly: it must have been an offence of violence. It was a revelation and she wondered why she hadn't realized it before. He was angry. Continually angry. He controlled it well and kept it hidden but now that it was obvious to Hannah she thought it explained a lot about him. That was why he kept himself to himself. It was the only way he could keep his anger in check.

She phoned home. There was no reply. Of course. Rosie would still be in a bed in a strange house, sleeping off the excesses of the night before. Not that she'd wake with a hangover. The young never seemed to have hangovers. Then, with the same sense of startling revelation she'd had when looking at Marty, it occurred to her that Rosie might not be on her own in bed. They never discussed her relationships with men. If ever Hannah broached the subject, talking elliptically perhaps about safe sex, she'd roll her eyes towards the ceiling and say, 'Oh Mum. Please!'

Hannah thought there was a boy. Joseph. He phoned and when Rosie was out she took messages. If she was in they talked for hours and she'd hear Rosie laughing. But when he came to the house it was always as part of a crowd and often he had his arm round another girl. If Rosie was hurt by that she didn't show it. Hannah hoped Rosie did have a love. She wanted something magic and gut-wrenching for her daughter. Don't wait, she wanted to tell her. Do it now. Soon you'll have responsibilities. You'll be too old. Trust me. I know what I'm talking about.

While Marty squatted by the tray on the floor, squeezing tea bags in the tasteful National Trust mugs she'd brought from home, Hannah started opening her mail. There wasn't much. A memo from her boss in the Central Library about budgets. An agenda for the prison librarians' summer school. A plain white envelope with a handwritten address which she recognized immediately. Something similar came every year. Before she could open it the phone rang again. It was Rosie, bristling with righteous indignation.

'Well,' she said, 'I hope you're ready to apologize.'

It caught Hannah on the hop. She didn't know whether to snap back a sarcastic answer or make an attempt to be conciliatory. She knew why that was. She was afraid Rosie would up sticks and move in with Jonathan and Eve if she upset her too much. Rosie had never mentioned it, hadn't used it as a threat, but Hannah was always aware of the possibility. In the end she wasn't given a chance to respond.

'Look,' Rosie said. 'I'm sorry. It must be a difficult time at the minute.'

Hannah could have fainted with shock. 'And for you. Waiting for your results . . .'

'Oh, sod the A levels.' She paused. 'I'm working this afternoon but I'll be home by six. You can take me to the Grey Horse. Buy me a pint.'

Hannah bit back a lecture. She was always telling Rosie she drank too much. 'OK,' she said. 'Why not? That would be great.'

When she replaced the phone Marty was standing looking at her, a mug in each hand.

'Trouble?' he asked, in an offhand sort of way to show that he wasn't prying.

'No. Not really. You know what kids are like.'

'I know what I was like when I was a kid.'

'Trouble?'

'All the time.' They smiled. He went back to sorting newspapers.

Dave the prison officer attached to the library came in, jangling his keys, demanding tea. Hannah opened her letter. Inside there was a printed invitation and a handwritten note. She read the note first. The hand-writing was scrawled but familiar. She recognized it from way back. It had been dashed off in a hurry and there was a stain which could have been coffee on the back.

Hannah
Hope this reaches you in time.
You can always stay with me.
Do try and make it this year.

She didn't need to look at the signature. It was from Sally. At school Sally had been her best friend. She hadn't seen her for years but they kept in touch, spoke occasionally, sent Christmas cards. The card was an invitation to a school reunion. Cranford Grammar. Sally tried the same tactic every time something similar was arranged. Recently the invitations were always sent to the prison. Perhaps she thought it was Jonathan who prevented Hannah's attending.

Hannah threw the card on to the desk where she sat to stamp the books, then picked it up again to look at the date of the party. It was only a couple of days away, one of her late shifts. She thought it was typical of Sally to allow her so little time to come to a decision and arrange her affairs. For the first time she was tempted to go to the reunion, to see Sally and her other friends again. It was only pride which had kept her away. She propped the card between her mug and a box of library cards.

Hannah was never sure how the argument started. Perhaps she'd done something to provoke it, but she didn't think so. Rosie's phone call had made her more mellow. Later she remembered the conversation she'd heard on her way in about a disturbance on the wing. Apparently there'd been rumours of an early lock-up because of a Prison Officers' Association meeting and the whole place was still tense. There'd been no sense of that though when she'd let the men in.

In the first group there was a lad she didn't recognize as one of her regulars. He was young, squat, muscular. A tattoo of a snake twisted from his wrist to his shoulder. His hair was cropped so short that pink skin showed through the stubble. He mooched around the shelves for a bit, but Hannah didn't have the impression that he was looking seriously for anything. She noticed that Marty was keeping an eye on him too. She wondered if he was new, though he hadn't been at the last reception talk she'd given.

She came out from behind the desk. Dave was in her office with the door shut. She'd heard that he was moonlighting in one of the clubs in town. Certainly he liked to catch up on his sleep in the mornings. She approached the lad with the tattoo, thinking she could be making up a ticket while he was choosing. 'Can I help you with anything?'

He turned to face her squarely. He was slightly shorter than she was.

'Not doing you any harm, am I?'

'Of course not. I'll leave you to it.' She was thinking she'd had enough of oversensitive adolescents. Perhaps something of the weariness showed in her face, but she wasn't aware of it.

Suddenly he banged his hand on the edge of a metal shelf then lifted it towards her, a gesture of warning. She could see the red mark from the shelf on his palm.

'Don't look at me like that.'

'I'm sorry. Like what?' Out of the corner of her eye

Hannah saw Marty standing behind the man, his knees slightly bent, watching. She willed him to keep out of it.

'Like I was a piece of shite. Like I was something on the bottom of your shoe.'

'I think you'd better leave,' she said, much as she'd said to the drunken kids lounging around her kitchen the night before. 'Come back when you know how to behave properly in a library.'

'Don't worry I'm going.' He pushed out and sent one of the shelves flying. On the top was a plant – one of her attempts to cheer up the room. The pot shattered. The books were covered in dry compost. 'Do you think I want to stay here and look at an ugly cow like you?' He spoke quietly, with intense contempt, looked around the room and swaggered out.

It was the sort of incident that happened every day in the prison. There was no physical violence against her. No threat of it even. She'd handled worse in her time there. Much worse. But Hannah went to pieces. She started to shake and then to cry.

Dave the library officer emerged from her office, yawning, wanting to know what the noise was about. He was embarrassed, desperate to play the incident down so he'd not get into trouble. Hannah got rid of the other prisoners then sent him away.

Marty pulled the shelf upright and replaced the books, shaking out the compost, checking the spines so they were in order. Then he put on the kettle and made more tea.

'You need a break,' he said. 'A holiday.'

'I don't know.'

'We have to stay in this place. You can escape whenever you like.'

'Perhaps.' She sipped the tea. He'd used powdered milk and the liquid was very hot. It burnt her mouth. 'My husband left me three weeks ago. I'm not sure where I'd go on my own.'

She thought she shouldn't have spoken to a prisoner like that. They'd been taught not to give personal details away.

'What about a trip to the hills? You could look up your old friends.'

She was shocked. He must have read the card when he collected her mug. She wasn't surprised that he'd read the invitation but that he'd commented on it. It wasn't like him.

'Sorry,' he said, blushing slightly as if he'd read her thoughts. 'None of my business.'

'No.' The temptation returned to run away. 'No. It's an idea.'

Arthur Lee was sitting in his office in the education block. His door was open. He saw Hannah walking down the corridor and waved her in.

'Aren't you busy?' She had walked that way hoping to talk to him, but had to pretend she didn't want to intrude.

'Nah, it's good to see a friendly face.'

Arthur was a Home Office imposition on the education department and they'd never liked him. He was too clever and reported straight to the Governor. A psychologist by training, he ran courses in anger management, victim awareness and special sessions for sex offenders. That was another reason for his unpopularity. Since Jonathan had left, Hannah had taken to dropping in on him more often, using him, she sometimes thought, as a personal therapist. He was in his early fifties, the age her father had been when he died. She'd have liked a father like Arthur, plump, comfortable, understanding. He'd been born in Liverpool and had never lost the accent. John Peel, she thought, without the beard.

'I hear you've had a bit of bother.'

She should have known it would be impossible to keep the incident in the library quiet. She shrugged, explained what had happened. 'Some lad kicking off. Marty thinks I should take a break.'

'Marty?'

'My orderly. Fox. D Wing. You haven't had him on one of your courses?'

She was thinking anger management. Arthur shook his head. Perhaps he wouldn't have told her anyway.

'Sounds like good advice.'

'There's a school reunion. In Cranford. Up in the hills where I grew up. But I'm not sure . . .'

'I'll come with you if you like.'

Hannah was surprised. She knew he was on his own but they'd never met outside the prison. She hadn't thought of him at all as the sort of person she'd take to a party and needed time to get used to the idea.

'It's too far to come back the same night. I thought I'd stay with my pal Sally. Make a weekend of it.'

'That's fine then.' His tone was easy but she felt she'd been unkind. She didn't want to offend him.

'I'm taking my daughter out for a drink tonight. Why don't you join us later?'

'Yeah,' he said. He seemed pleased but he never gave much away.

Hannah wondered what Rosie would make of him. At least, she thought, it would prove to Rosie that she did have a life outside the family. She did have friends of her own.

On her way home Hannah called in to her boss at the Central Library and told her she wanted to take a week's holiday. It was short notice but something had come up. Marge, her boss, was so sympathetic that Hannah knew she'd heard about Jonathan and Eve. 'Have as long as you like, pet.'

They lived in a small town. By now it would be common knowledge.

Chapter Seven

Her mother always made her feel so sodding guilty. Rosie replaced the receiver, glad the conversation was over. The house was quiet. Mel was still asleep and Mrs and Mr Gillespie had left hours before to go to work. Mel was Rosie's best mate and had been since coming to the school three years before. She had spiky red hair and green eyes and she played the bass guitar. Rosie was starving but she could hardly pour herself a bowl of cornflakes in someone else's house. Besides, she needed to go home to change or she'd be late for work. Mel, whose parents were seriously rich and seriously generous, hadn't felt the need for employment between A levels and college. Rosie didn't mind working. It was a distraction.

Outside it was hot already, though here on the coast there was usually a breeze. Just as well because she had on what she'd been wearing in the club the night before – a lacy black dress and tarty sandals. The shoes were OK for dancing but they knackered her ankles if she tried to walk any distance. She took them off to go barefoot and as she stepped in and out of the shadow thrown by the trees she felt the changes of temperature on the soles of her feet.

The houses round here were big Edwardian semis

set back from the road. In one of these houses Joe lived. She took care not to turn her head as she sauntered past.

Her home was more ordinary. A tidy semi on a tidy estate. Her parents had bought it from new when she was five. It would have been her mother's choice. They must have realized by then that there'd be no other children. This boring three-bedroomed box would be big enough.

Inside she switched off the alarm and went straight to the kitchen. She put on the kettle, stuck a couple of pieces of bread in the toaster, took orange juice from the fridge and drank it straight from the carton. Inside her head she heard her mother telling her off about that. How pathetic could you get? She was eighteen, an adult, and there was her mother, nagging away at her, a worm inside her head: 'For goodness' sake, Rosalind, can't you get a glass?'

In her bedroom, when she switched on the light the bulb fizzled and died so she had to open the curtains. She saw the place in daylight for the first time in months. There was an unpleasant, musty smell, which she'd tried for too long to ignore. She pushed a window open. In the garden next door a neighbour was pegging baby clothes on to the line. Rosie waved to her. Before the job in the pub she used to babysit quite often. The woman waved back. Rosie saw pity on her face, imagined her gossiping to the rest of the street. 'Poor kid. Her dad's left. And they seemed such a happy family.' When the woman bent to lift more laundry from the basket Rosie stuck up two fingers at her back. She turned over the pile of clothes on her floor like a peasant turning hay with a fork. For the pub she had to wear a uniform – black trousers, white shirt, stupid little green apron and green bow-tie. The tie and the apron were still in the bag from her last shift. There was a white shirt in the pile but the collar and the cuffs were filthy and there were spatters of red wine down the chest. Her father had left clothes when he'd decamped the month before and her mother had been too civilized to throw them out. She'd moved them instead into the spare-room wardrobe. As if he might return one day as a lodger. There, on a hanger, was a single white shirt.

There was no sign of the trousers and the hassle was starting to bug her. Her mother had recently dreamed up a rule about Rosie doing her own washing and since then things had been chaotic on the clothes front. She'll not have stuck to it, Rosie thought. It'll be like all the other threats and ultimatums. She'll not have been able to stand the thought of her daughter going out in mucky pants. And sure enough her trousers were washed and dry with a load of towels in the tumble in the utility room. In the spirit of concili-ation which had led her to phone her mother she folded the towels and loaded the washing machine with part of the muck heap from the bedroom floor. She rolled the trousers into a tight ball and shook them out. She never understood why anyone bothered with ironing.

She looked at her watch. She could have done with a shower but there was no time, so she cleaned off last night's slap, put on more and she was ready. She only realized how dirty her feet were when she pushed them into her flat work shoes. No one would see. The pub was a big, white place close to the sea front. It was called the Promenade, known as the Prom. She'd got the job because she had the nerve to ask. Like all her friends she'd been drinking there since she was sixteen and she'd thought working in the place would be a dream. In fact when it was full of kids in the evenings, being behind the bar was a bit of a drag, not the buzz she'd expected. She had to watch her mates drinking, having a good time and usually she was too busy to exchange more than a couple of words. Sometimes she saw more than she wanted to, heard more too. It was as if the uniform made you invisible.

The first inkling she'd got about her father had been in the pub. Two lads, who she'd known fine well were in Year 11 and shouldn't have been in the place anyway, were playing darts. She'd been emptying ashtrays. It was a Friday night, somebody's birthday. The Prom was packed. They'd had to yell.

'They say he's going to get the sack.'

'You don't get the sack for screwing someone you work with.'

'You do if you screw them on the staff-room floor. My dad's a governor. He should know.'

'You can't blame him though, can you? I mean, have you seen her on the trampoline?'

'But what does she see in him?' The boy put his fingers in his mouth and pretended to throw up.

She'd almost gone up to them to find out who they were talking about, curious, eager to share the gossip. Then they'd seen her and something about the look that had passed between them had warned her, made her pretend not to have heard. Episodes, which had meant nothing to her at the time, slid into sharp focus. Miss Petrie volunteering to do the choreography for the play her father was directing. Miss Petrie on the school trip to Stratford, though what interest could a brainless PE teacher have in Shakespeare? Every time she thought of the two of them together she lost control of her body. Her breath came too fast and she almost fainted.

She didn't mind the pub during the day. There was a different kind of customer then. Grown-ups. Old men sitting for ages reading a paper, office workers wanting lunch, tourists.

When she got there Frank was outside watering the hanging baskets. He looked at his watch and grinned. She always turned up with only a second to spare. Frank was the manager, fat and forty, divorced. He'd been the one to give her the job. She'd chatted him up when he'd had a few drinks and allowed them a lock-in, then she'd turned up next morning for an interview he couldn't remember having arranged. She thought he'd given her a job out of embarrassment. It was only after learning about her dad and Miss Petrie (she couldn't bring herself to call her Eve) that she wondered if he might fancy her. He'd never tried anything on but she always made sure to keep her distance.

It was only twelve o'clock and the pub was nearly empty. Two old ladies with wispy hair and floaty dresses sat by the window in the dust-speckled sunlight, sipping brandy and lemonade. When Rosie went over to collect their empty glasses they continued to sit, engrossed in conversation, making no move to leave or to order more drinks. They were lost in memory. They had come to the coast when they were girls on charabanc trips from town. Back behind the bar, Rosie heard them giggle suddenly over a shared memory. It was a slightly awkward giggle. A boy was involved. Rosie thought, Is that how Mel and I will be when we're old? We'll sit in the Prom getting pissed on brandy and reminiscence, laughing about Joe. If Mel lives long enough to get old, that is.

Then, almost as if the thought had conjured him out of thin air, there Joe was, standing at the door, skinny as one of the pipecleaner men her granda used to make. She had to make an effort to compose herself, to breathe slowly and regularly. Joe saw her and smiled, showing a mouth of gappy teeth. He looked crumpled, as if he'd slept in his clothes – baggy cotton trousers and a T-shirt so tight that she could see the frame of his ribs. What could anyone in their right mind see in him? He had bigger feet than anyone else in the world. Black hair tied back in a loose ponytail. He loped to the bar.

'Mel said you'd be working.'

'You've seen Mel this morning?' She was surprised. She thought Mel would be dead to the world.

'Spoken to her on the phone.'

'Everything OK?'

He frowned without answering. She poured him a pint. Mel was usually the subject of their conversations. She demanded their attention. She had an eating disorder – anorexia, Rosie thought. Rosie didn't know the details, didn't like to ask. She suspected Joe knew more than she did.

Joe fidgeted in his pocket for money. 'Has she said anything to you?'

'What about?'

'She's really stressed out about something.'

'Isn't she always?' Rosie regretted that immediately. It sounded petty. But what was Mel about? She was bright and gorgeous and her parents doted on her. And so did Joe. So why all the shit?

Joe took the pint, stared into it. 'Have you started doing food yet? Any chance of a burger?'

Although he was so thin, there was nothing wrong with Joe's attitude to food. She shouted his order through to the kitchen. Frank came in with the watering can still in his hand, letting it drip on the carpet. He nodded to Joe, winked at Rosie. She knew she was blushing but Joe seemed too preoccupied to notice.

'We're going away,' he said. 'Mel and me.'

'I thought you were skint.' Joe worked all night shifts at the big supermarket on the ring road, but he never had any money. He spent it on drink, junk food, music, stupid presents for them all. His parents were both doctors and could have bailed him out but they said he had to learn to budget before going to university. They took university for granted; Rosie wasn't so sure. Joe hadn't done much work before the exams. He'd been too busy obsessing over Mel.

Joe shrugged. 'Mel says she needs to get away. It's like she's really spooked by something. She won't let go. But she won't talk about it either. Haven't you noticed?'

No, Rosie thought. I've had my own problems lately. If you hadn't realized.

Joe was continuing. 'Her mum and dad say they'll pay. We're only going for a week. They think she could do with a holiday. It would do her good. A friend of theirs has a villa in Portugal.'

'Very nice.' This time Rosie managed to keep her

voice noncommittal. She was thinking, It's not Mel who wants to go away. It's their idea. They've just had enough of her illness. They're fed up with seeing her like that. They want the problem to disappear for a while.

They'd sent Mel away before and Rosie couldn't blame them.

'I'm not sure I can handle it,' Joe was saying. 'It's the responsibility. What if something happens while we're away?' He paused. 'They want her to think about going into hospital but she's dead against it. They want me to persuade her.'

'She doesn't seem too bad to me,' Rosie said. 'No worse than usual.'

A punter came up to the bar. A salesman, she thought. Suit and a briefcase. He was sweating. It was very hot out now. From where she stood she could see the glare on the water as far as the horizon. Families walked past in shorts and skimpy tops and they seemed to turn pink as she watched them. Making the most of the summer. She expected the man to order a meal and a bottle of lager, but instead he barked, 'Scotch. A large one.' His voice was desperate. She watched him take it to a table in the shade, knew he'd be back in five minutes for another.

Joe slid back along the bar so he was facing her again.

'You don't have to go,' she said reasonably. 'Explain how you feel.'

'I can't let her down.'

They teased him sometimes because he'd been a choirboy as a kid. He said he'd been dragged along to church by his parents but she thought some of it had rubbed off. He had too many principles.

'When do you leave?'

'A couple of days.'

'Mel didn't say anything to me.' Rosie convinced herself that was why she was so angry. She felt herself close to tears. They were supposed to be best friends.

'She wanted to keep it a secret. I don't know why.'

Because she likes secrets, Rosie thought. She likes keeping things to herself. She's a hoarder. Perhaps that's what the stuff with food is about.

'What was all that with your mum last night?' he asked with a complete change of tone. He pulled a prim, schoolmistress face. This was the Joe the others knew, the gossip and the clown.

Rosie was cross. Hannah was an easy target. 'She's had a bad time. All the talk. You know what it must be like, finding out that your husband's a rat after twenty years. And she has it rough at work. It's not a bunch of laughs in the prison.'

'No,' he said quickly, seeing that he had offended her. 'It won't be. I didn't mean . . .'

The businessman came back to the bar. He held out his glass to her. She saw that his hand was shaking.

'Your mum's all right,' Joe said. 'We were being stupid.'

Rosie served the customer and let it go.

His burger came. He ate it quickly, holding it in his hand and tearing away at it as if he were ravenous. He stood still when he'd finished and she thought he was going to say something else about Mel. Perhaps he wanted to enlist Rosie's support in finding out what lay behind the paranoia. But he just nodded.

'See you in a week then. If I don't catch up with you before we go.'

And he was gone.

That evening at a different pub, Rosie's local, it was still warm enough to sit outside. She'd eaten the veggie lasagne her mother had cooked for dinner, had a shower and changed into a sleeveless frock. The beer garden was at the back, away from the road, though there was still a far-off hum of traffic. A row of conifers separated the pub from playing fields. There were tubs on the terrace and shrubs under the trees, a faint exotic smell of flowers and pine.

'Melanie and Joseph are going away,' Rosie said, using the full names as if it were a formal announcement. As in 'I, Melanie, take you, Joseph'. That wouldn't surprise her either. Joe was besotted enough to do it and he'd always been into crazy gestures. Melanie's parents would be delighted. Melanie would have a full-time minder and they could go back to the real business of making money.

'Isn't Melanie's name Gillespie?' her mother asked.

Rosie hardly heard. She was imagining Mel's dress, the church, the flowers. Her as chief bridesmaid. 'Yeah,' she said. 'Melanie Gillespie.'

'And her dad's the businessman?'

'That's right.'

When she'd first asked Melanie what her father did she'd said he ran a chip shop. Computer chips, it turned out. He'd set up a huge plant on the site of a derelict factory, was a major local hero because of all the jobs it provided.

'He was on the television again tonight,' Hannah said.

Mel's dad was always on the television.

'They're going to the Algarve,' Rosie said. 'Mel and Joe.'

'Will you be at a bit of a loose end then?'

'I have got other friends!'

For a while she had been watching a small, plump man hovering just out of her mother's line of vision. She thought he had been listening in, waiting for them to finish their conversation. Now he was approaching and Hannah stood up to greet him. Rosie thought, She planned this all along. She knew I'd not come if she warned me.

'This is Arthur,' Hannah said.

Rosie could tell her mother was nervous and decided to be gracious. 'Hi.'

'Arthur works with me at the prison. He's a psychologist.'

Rosie nodded. What could you say?

'Rosie was just telling me that two of her friends are going on holiday.' Hannah shot her the look Rosie remembered from Sunday-afternoon tea at her grandma and granda's house. A pleading look which said, Please behave, please don't show me up.

Rosie said nothing. Arthur smiled. It would be easy, Rosie thought, to be taken in by that smile.

Hannah continued, 'I was just going to tell her about my trip.'

'What trip?'

'There's a school reunion. I thought I should go . . .'

'Great. Can I come?' It was a malicious offer. She didn't want her mother to go off with this little round man with the beguiling smile. She wanted to pay Hannah back for treating her like a six-year-old.

'Do you really want to?'

Hannah looked so pathetically grateful that Rosie couldn't say she didn't mean it. Anyway, what was wrong with running away for a couple of days?

'Why not?'

Arthur smiled again as if this was what he'd been planning all along and he went to the bar for drinks.

Chapter Eight

Although Hannah had avoided Sally since she'd left the town to go to university, she had kept in touch with her friend's news. Sally had gone up in the world since they'd first become mates in Cranford. At school she'd lived with her parents on a small council estate, a couple of streets which ran down the hill to the west of the town. Her father had been a barber. Her mother had worked in the chemist's in the high street. There'd been a younger sister, a pretty child called Joanne. Hannah's dad had worked in the only bank in the town and they'd owned their own home, but the families' lives had been very similar. There'd been an emphasis on good manners and tidiness. Of course, after Hannah's father had died things were never the same again. Then she'd loved spending time with Sal's family. Everything in their little house had seemed safe and respectable.

Sally didn't go to university. She'd had no academic ambition though she'd been bright enough. Instead she'd got a job as office junior on the local paper. She was still there in a more glorified form, writing features and running the women's page. She'd sent Hannah a cutting when she first got the post as features editor. There had been a photograph at the top of the page and she'd put on a lot of weight. Hannah thought she made the job sound grander than it was. The paper had turned into one of those free weeklies which are seventy per cent adverts. She did write back to congratulate Sally about the promotion. She hadn't wanted to appear mean spirited.

When she was nineteen Sally married Chris, a lad they'd knocked about with. A baby arrived soon after. Chris worked for a printer and on summer evenings ran a disco in the caravan site near the lake. There was one more baby then Hannah heard that they'd separated. Much later she saw a piece in a Newcastle paper saying Chris had been sentenced to twelve months' imprisonment for selling drugs. She wondered if he would turn up at the prison, but if he had she'd never met him. Not so far as she knew. Would she have recognized him after all this time?

When Sally wrote to say that she was getting married for a second time to a local businessman, Hannah had imagined a shopkeeper or someone running a small unit on the business park near the river. A barber even, like her dad. But it turned out that Sally's new husband was an hotelier. Hannah might have gone to the wedding – in fact had been building herself up to it – but in the end she was never invited. Sally said it was a very small affair because she and Roger were busy preparing for the holiday season. The hotel was close to the lake and attracted tourists.

On the drive to Cranford Rosie fell asleep before they'd left their estate and didn't wake until they'd nearly arrived. She sat with her head tipped back, snoring slightly through an open mouth. Hannah didn't mind. It was a reminder of what she'd looked like as a small child.

She had only been back to Cranford once, for her mother's funeral, and that was in her third year of university. Because she was so far away – she had been at university in Exeter – the funeral had been organized by Hannah's aunt. Hannah had stayed with her for one night then returned to the West Country, glad of the excuse of exams.

Jonathan couldn't understand her refusal to return to the place of her birth. In the beginning at least, he had been interested in going. 'For Christ's sake, H, it's only fifty miles away. We could be there and back in an afternoon. Show me the scenes of your wild youth.' He'd thought he was being funny. Hannah had made no attempt to explain her reluctance.

They came upon the town almost before she realized, and then she saw with a start that it had hardly changed at all. It felt as she remembered it: stately, quiet, seductive; a place which was hard to leave, very different from Millhaven, the town on the coast which was now her home. That was rakish and full of people passing through – students, hotel workers, yuppies using it as a staging post. And affluent businessmen like Richard Gillespie who lived there to show they had a certain style and personality. Though no doubt he would be moving on too.

The hotel was in a village called Cranwell, very close to the lake. She must have passed through it on her way to the caravan site but she had no recollection. It was pretty enough. There was one main street with stone cottages, a small first school backing on to open fields, a large church. The hotel was down a track next to the church and was called The Old Rectory. It was a big, grey Victorian house with steep gables, an immaculate garden and a view of the graveyard. Hannah had been imagining something seedy, with draughty corridors and stained baths, and was pleasantly surprised. It had an air of class and of money. Rosie had stirred as they pulled on to the drive and now stretched, yawned and scrabbled under the seat for her shoes. Hannah wished she didn't look quite so grubby or dishevelled. She wanted Sally to admire her daughter.

There were other cars in a courtyard at the side of the house. All of them were newer and larger than Hannah's Polo – Jonathan of course had taken the Rover when he left. Rosie got out of the car and Hannah saw that the seam of her skirt had split at the back. She began to feel nervous, as if they had no right to be there. There was complete silence, of the sort that you find in small Spanish towns at siesta time. It was even hotter here than on the coast and Hannah was reminded of the dense, bright heat of a Mediterranean afternoon. Although the house was close to the main village street there was no sound of traffic or conversation. They walked through an arch and round the house to the main entrance. The front lawn was set for croquet. Two mallets lay with balls on the grass. Beyond a green wire-mesh fence was a tennis court, freshly marked. No one was about.

Rosie whistled and said, 'Not bad.' She pulled the hair back from her face, twisted it and fastened it with a comb. She looked immediately tidier. 'I can't see a pool,' she said regretfully. 'Still, in a normal summer, when would you use it? Really, it's not bad at all.'

The front door was open and led to a large wood-panelled hall with a stone fireplace. There was no reception desk, no bell to ring to attract attention. They stood for a moment. It seemed very dark after the glare outside, and wonderfully cool. Three doors led into the hall but all were shut.

'Well,' Rosie demanded. 'Are we going to stand here like lemons?' There were times when Hannah wondered that she had created such an assertive young woman. Rosie raised her voice. 'Hello,' she shouted. 'Anybody home?'

'Ssh . . .' Hannah felt awkward, as if she'd wandered into a private home and sworn at the hosts. She would have stood there all day.

Rosie began to shuffle impatiently. There was a woodblock floor. She'd learned tap dancing as a child and began to tap her heels and toes to some rhythm in her head. It was an irritating habit and came upon her whenever there was space to move. She'd never been able to stand still. In the distance a door opened and shut and they heard footsteps. Rosie continued to hop and shimmy and click her fingers. Hannah motioned at her to stop. The middle door into the hall opened and a man appeared. Beyond him she saw a corridor, a sunny window. She didn't at first take him to be Sally's husband. He was older than she would have expected, at least fifty-five, but it was more than that. He wasn't the sort of man she thought Sally would be married to. He wore an open-necked shirt, brown trousers with a neatly pressed crease and, despite the heat, a cardigan with pockets. His hair was thin and grey, too long at the back. Perhaps after Chris Sally had had enough of wild men. Rosie slid to a halt.

The man blinked in a way which Hannah found oddly familiar, smiled a thin, long smile and held out his hand.

'You must be Sally's friends.' His voice was light, clipped, a little spinsterish, and again she felt she should recognize it. 'Not a good day for a drive, I'm afraid. Poor you. This weather doesn't show any sign of breaking. I suppose we shouldn't complain. By the time you've had a chance to freshen up Sally will be home. She was sorry not to be here when you arrived, but today's a busy one for the paper. She's looking forward to the reunion.'

He picked up Hannah's holdall and directed them towards a curving staircase. Rosie went first and he stared as she walked ahead of him at the long brown legs appearing through the slit in her skirt. Hannah wanted to hit him, but knew Rosie would probably take the attention for granted. Across the graveyard the church clock struck five. The noise seemed to shock him out of a trance and he turned to Hannah, muttering something about the age of the tower. Their room was at the back of the house. It was large and high ceilinged with a full-length window looking over a rose garden and across more lawn. Beyond that, dazzling in the sunlight, was the lake.

Roger seemed to have regained his composure. He gave them an arch little smile as if he were enjoying some private joke and left them alone.

'Hey,' Rosie said. 'This is a bit of all right.'

Hannah dragged her attention from the lake and looked at the room. Solid Victorian furniture was lightened by pale yellow bedspreads and curtains. Rosie dropped the sophisticated pose she put on for her friends and became a child again. She bounced on the bed and danced around the room opening drawers and doors. 'No mini-bar but two sorts of biscuits on the tea tray and very nice smellies for the bath. And Sky.' She began to strip for the shower with a sort of mock striptease, not caring that the curtains were still open. Remembering Roger, Hannah closed them.

They had made themselves tea and were watching the early-evening news when Sally came in. Hannah thought she *had* put on weight, especially on the hips and the bust, but that she'd have known her anywhere. She was stylishly dressed in a thrown together, ramshackle way, in a cream linen skirt which came down to her ankles and a long cream top, crumpled at the back where she'd been sitting. There wasn't any awkwardness. She pulled Hannah towards her so she bounced against the pneumatic bosoms. Then she sat on the bed and started talking.

'God, what a gorgeous daughter. You're so lucky, H. I only had boys and they were monsters. They left home long ago, thank the Lord, and they only appear when they want something. Roger puts up with it, the sweetie. God knows why.' She paused. 'You know, it's so good to see you. I'd given up thinking I'd ever get you here.' She grinned wickedly. 'You didn't recognize Roger, did you? He didn't think you did.'

Hannah was embarrassed. She dredged back in her memory for the circumstances when she'd heard the pedantic voice. She had a fleeting image of school, of sitting with a crowd of others on the edge of the stage in the hall, then it was gone.

She mumbled, 'Something about him was familiar,' knowing how pathetic she sounded.

'Probably best forgotten,' Sally said. 'That's what I thought until I met him again. I came to do a feature on him when he bought this place. You won't believe it but he swept me off my feet. Perhaps this will jog your memory.' She stood up, put her hands behind her back and in a surprisingly accurate imitation of her husband's voice said, 'If that homework's not handed in tomorrow, Miss Marshall, I'll be down on you like a ton of bricks.'

It was the final phrase that released the memory. It was the threat for every occasion. Hannah started to giggle, quickly put her hand over her mouth to cover it.

'You married Spooky Spence?' It was impossible to keep the astonishment from her voice. She wanted to ask Sally how on earth she came to do anything so ridiculous.

'Exactly,' Sally said, enjoying Hannah's surprise. 'Spooky Spence.'

He had taught them Latin for O level. At the time Hannah had thought of him as middle-aged, verging on the elderly, but he could hardly have been more than thirty. Now that she had fixed him in her memory she thought his appearance had hardly changed over the years. She remembered those lessons as restful occasions. A quiet sunny classroom. Mr Spence's voice a drone in the background as they plodded through Virgil and Caesar's *Civil Wars*. And he had been involved in the school play. That was what the flash of memory had been about.

'But you couldn't stand him,' Hannah said.

Sally had never liked drama and had hated the Latin lessons. She'd never got to grips with the grammar. Spence had been quietly but menacingly sarcastic.

She grinned. 'He couldn't stand me either. He hated teaching. I mean, he didn't mind fiddling round with the theatre club but standing in front of a class all day was a nightmare. Food's always been his real passion. You wouldn't recognize him in the kitchen. When his mum died she left him a house and a bit of money. It gave him enough to set up this place. It's been an exciting project for us both.'

Rosie had been watching the conversation with interest. Perhaps she was wondering what it would be like to get involved with a teacher much older than her. A bit close to home.

'Why did you call him spooky?' It wasn't a tactful contribution, but again Sally didn't take offence.

'It was his way of appearing beside you without warning. Apparently out of thin air. When you least needed it. Like when you'd just lit a fag behind the changing rooms. Or you were planning to mitch off early before his lesson.' She grinned again at Rosie. 'Not that your mother ever did anything like that. Hannah Meek was the biggest swat in the school.'

Hannah didn't say that she remembered things rather differently. They'd called Roger spooky because of the way he looked at them. At the hems of their skirts which were still very short at the time, at the shirts bursting at the buttons over newly formed chests. There were stories that he'd been caught staring through the gym window at third-form gymnasts, at the girls in their knickers and airtex vests doing straddle jumps on the box and cartwheels on the beam.

*

Sally didn't go with them to the school for the reunion. She said she'd meet them there. She had to nip back to town. It was work. The editor was away and there was a press conference she needed to cover. Again Hannah felt she was making her work sound grander than it was.

Still, she was pleased to go in on her own, with only Rosie to keep her company. Sally would have rushed round introducing her to everyone, and she wanted a moment of anonymity. She wanted to stand just inside the door and look for Michael. She had dreamt that he would be there. If she was honest with herself, that was what the trip had been all about from the start. Michael was what had kept her away from the town for all those years and now it was Michael who had brought her back. When Roger dropped them off at the school – it seemed that he was too busy to attend the party – the futility of the venture hit her. She was embarrassed that she had allowed her fantasy to develop this far.

Michael Grey had come to the school when Hannah was in the lower sixth. He was a year older than the rest of them but for some reason had been placed in their year. She remembered having been given a number of reasons for that – he had been living abroad, had been ill, there had been a family problem. Still she didn't know which, if any, of them had been true. Certainly he hadn't been asked to retake the year because he was thick. He was quick and conscientious and the teachers loved him. He was doing art, English and biology, but art was his thing. He noticed the way things and people looked. She remembered the big, battered portfolio he used to cart around, the way he always had a smear of paint on his face.

So she collected her name badge, stood just inside the door and looked around. He wasn't in the room. She saw that immediately. Even after nearly thirty years she would have recognized him. She didn't think that was self-delusion. She would have stood there longer, but Rosie gave her a shove in the back.

'Go on then,' she said. 'Do the business.'

It turned out to be easier than Hannah had expected. Sally still hadn't arrived but Hannah was greeted by people who knew her, who were pleasant enough to say that she'd hardly changed. The name badges were in sufficiently large print to allow the possibility that this was a kind fiction, that they remembered the face only after reading her name, but soon she felt less nervous.

This hall was newly built when she was at school. Previously the dining hall had been used for everything. For the first time the students had somewhere for assembly and drama that didn't smell of school dinners. She recalled her first speech day there. Some sixth-form boys always ran a book on the length of the headmaster's lecture. Parents were invited and when Hannah won a prize for English her mother had turned up. Her husband had just died and people were still talking about it so it was a brave thing for her to do, but she was the only woman to be wearing a hat and Hannah wished that she'd stayed away.

The new hall was where school plays were performed. In Hannah's final year, Michael was Macbeth. He looked like a Viking warrior with his long white hair and papier-mâché armour. Jenny Graves was Lady

Macbeth. People said she was very good, but Hannah had been prompting and too busy following every line to notice individual performances. What she did remember was the knife, because she'd helped with props too. She didn't know where Mr Westcott had found it, but it was seriously sharp. One of the first years was messing around and cut herself. Hannah thought that nowadays, when everyone was so conscious of health and safety, it wouldn't be allowed.

Once she'd persuaded herself that of course it would have been impossible for Michael to be there, Hannah even started to enjoy herself. At first the music was far too loud for sensible conversation but someone persuaded the disc jockey to turn it down. She could catch up on news of people who had once been close friends. No one mentioned her father. She supposed, even in a town as small as this, that had been forgotten long ago.

She was talking to Paul Lord when Sally arrived. Hannah saw her from the corner of her eye, but continued the conversation. In school Paul had been something of a figure of fun – a spotty scientist, too conventional for his age, more conventional even than her. He had become rather handsome. Certainly he was married. He mentioned a wife and child. It seemed he had his own business and was doing rather well.

'What happened to that blond lad you used to knock around with?' he said suddenly. 'Did he go away to art school in the end, or did he settle for university?'

Hannah said calmly that she had no idea. Then Sally interrupted them quite rudely, taking Hannah's arm and dragging her away. Something had excited her. She could hardly contain herself. But she kept her face serious.

'There's something you have to know.'

'What is it?'

She turned everything into a drama. Hannah was expecting a piece of local gossip. Someone had run away with someone else's wife. She should know not to mention it in front of the people involved.

'The body in the lake,' Sally said.

Hannah must have looked at her stupidly. It wasn't at all what she was expecting.

'You had heard that they'd found a body in the lake?'

Hannah remembered a snatch of a radio report. 'Yes. It came to light because the water level's so low.'

'That was what the press conference was about. The police have got a positive ID at last. Dental records or something. It's too horrible to think about.' She shivered theatrically. 'It's Michael Grey. He'd been down there for nearly thirty years.'

She was whispering. Perhaps she wanted to add to the theatre of the occasion. Perhaps she didn't want to spoil the party. Hannah felt the room spin around her.

'Pull yourself together,' Sally said sharply. 'You'll have to speak to the police. We all will, but you're most likely to have something useful to say.' She looked at Hannah, waiting for a sensible response before adding impatiently, 'Michael Grey was murdered.'

Hannah remained silent. She could hardly say that the news had come as something of a relief.

Chapter Nine

So far, Rosie thought, she'd been very good, very much the mummy's girl, putting on a clean frock, tying back her hair in a French plait, saying what a brilliant time she'd been having.

The school was pretty much what she'd expected, comprehensive now, but still to Rosie's eyes, rather grand. Her high school on the coast was a seventies glass and concrete slum. The window frames had warped and the roof leaked. This was a stone building, approached by a drive through trees. There was a couple of new blocks, a scattering of mobile class-rooms, but still it was hard to imagine kids dealing dope in the toilets or sniffing glue behind the bike sheds. More Mallory Towers than Grange Hill. Rosie wasn't sure about being there. 'Look,' she had said. 'I'd just be in the way.' Hannah had given her a look so geeky that Rosie could have strangled her but not deserted her.

They had been early of course. Her mother was always early. It drove Rosie crazy. There had been people in the hall, but they were still setting out food and glasses. Rosie had taken her mother's arm. She was shaking.

'Why don't you give me a guided tour of the place before we go in?'

They had walked together round the outside of the building, peering in through windows. Hannah had pointed out the domestic-science block, the room where Roger had taught Latin, the sixth-form common-room. Rosie had listened. She had felt supportive and grown up. She had even wondered if she should bring up the subject of Eve and Jonathan – they had never really discussed it – but she hadn't wanted to spoil things and had left Hannah to her memories.

When they returned the party had begun. The hall doubled as a theatre and it was blacked out by heavy curtains and lit by coloured spots. Outside the sun was still shining. On the stage sat a DJ playing seventies music. The lines on his face were so deep that they seemed chiselled. It was hard to tell whether his head was bald or shaved. But he still seemed younger than the people standing awkwardly in the hall, juggling paper plates and plastic glasses. He put on a David Bowie. 'Life on Mars'. It had always been one of Rosie's favourites and she was itching to dance. If Joe had been there she'd have dragged him on to the floor to get things moving.

There'd been a bit of a queue at the door, where a fat woman stood behind a table doling out laminated name badges. She was short sighted and had to squint like a mole over the table to find the one she was looking for. Hannah had found her own. Hannah Meek. How bloody appropriate, Rosie had thought. The fat woman had stared at them, as if the name or her mother's face should trigger a memory, but the effort had seemed too much for her because she just shook her head, smiled vaguely and let them walk on into the hall.

At first everything was as tedious and civilized as Rosie had expected it to be. She was introduced to old friends of her mother's. She smiled a lot, was polite and dutiful. When she laughed she felt as if she were making too much noise. The people she met seemed frozen in middle age. It was impossible to imagine them being yelled at by a teacher in this hall, or sitting at small tables to take exams. They talked about their children, the iniquities of student fees and student loans, their homes and their foreign holidays. All the time the rhythm of the music nipped at her ankles and made her want to sway away from them back into the middle of the floor.

This is *your* music, she wanted to say. Doesn't it take you back to how you were?

And sometimes she saw a woman or a man with dreamy eyes, who would look at her with a start, as if they were staring at themselves or a girl they fancied. But it didn't last, and when someone did start the dancing it was a peculiar shuffle as if they all had arthritic knees or a broom handle strapped to their spines.

Then she looked up at the stage and saw the DJ, who must have been at least as old as her mother and the others in the room, but who didn't seem it. He seemed to be laughing at them too. She moved through the dancers and hoisted herself on to the stage so her legs dangled over the edge. He didn't look at her.

'A bit young for this, aren't you?'

'I came with my mum.'

'Who was she, then?' Now he did turn to eye her up. 'I might know her.'

'Did you come to this school too?' For some reason

it seemed unlikely. He looked too different from the smartly dressed men and women. She thought he must be a refugee from the city.

'No, not bright enough. I was at the secondary modern. But I used to hang around with some of them.'

'Hannah Meek,' she said. 'That was what my mother was called then.'

'Yes,' he said. 'I can see.'

'Can you?' She had seen the occasional photo of her mother as a young woman and saw no resemblance. Her mother was so reined in. Her features were small and sharp.

'She was skinnier of course.'

She felt her face colour. Most people were skinnier than her. Hannah said she was over sensitive. 'Carry on like that and you'll end up like Melanie Gillespie.' As if she wouldn't have adored to be the same weight as Mel.

'But you're bonnier,' the DJ said after some consideration. Rosie could have kissed him.

'Can you recognize her?' she said, falling into the joky, flirty voice she used with the older punters at the Prom. She didn't have to shout. Someone had moaned about the music being too loud and he'd turned it down. He scanned the room but so briefly that she thought he wasn't really bothered.

'Can't see much at all in this light,' he said.

There was a bit of a scuffle at the door as Sally came in. She pushed her way through the blackout curtain and was silhouetted briefly against the light outside. The woman behind the table knew her and tried to offer her a badge but Sally ignored her. The DJ was watching the scene too, with the same detached amusement as when he'd been looking at the dancing.

'That's Sally Spence,' Rosie said, wanting his attention again. 'She's my mum's best mate. We're staying at her hotel tonight.'

'Oh, I know Sal very well. When you see her say Chris sends his love.'

The track he was playing came to an end. He murmured a few words into the microphone. No one seemed to be listening. Hannah was deep in conversation with a tall man, dressed in black. He had more style than the rest of them and Rosie might have fancied him if he'd been twenty years younger. Suddenly Sally broke in on the couple. She said a few words to Hannah then steered her away from him. From her position on the stage Rosie watched. Caught in a livid green spotlight, with Roxy Music in the background, she saw her mother's face crumple. The normally sharp features fell in on themselves. Sally led her out of the room and Rosie followed. At the door she stopped and looked up at the stage. Chris, the DJ, gave her a little wave and a knowing grin.

Outside it was still light, and at The Old Rectory four guests sat on the flagged terrace having drinks before a late dinner. Sally had driven them back from the reunion immediately. Rosie thought it was a fuss about nothing. Sally playing the drama queen. An old body dragged out of the lake. What could that have to do with her mother?

Roger insisted that they shouldn't decide anything until after dinner and Sally had deferred to him.

Hannah seemed to think she had no right to express an opinion. Rosie thought Roger had been transformed. That afternoon he'd been a crabby and grey old Latin teacher. Now, talking to his guests, dressed in a brocade waistcoat and floppy bow-tie, he was in his element. When they arrived he was taking a tray of drinks to a couple in the lounge and he sat beside them for a moment to chat. He flattered the woman without annoying her husband, camping it up a little to make himself harmless. Rosie, who was no mean actor herself, appreciated the show. She knew the effort which went into a performance.

Over dinner Sally and her mother talked in a series of elliptical comments which made little sense to her. At one point Sally said to Roger, 'But you must remember Michael Grey, even if you didn't teach him. Everyone knew Michael.'

Roger stared into his wine. 'Of course I remember him,' he said in a sad, solemn voice. Then he made an excuse to go into the kitchen and when he returned he was his old self, solicitous and funny.

At the end of the meal they were the only people left in the dining-room. The main lights were switched off. Their table was lit by a wall lamp with an engraved glass shade, which could have covered a gas lamp. The room had been designed to look like a Victorian parlour, with glossy-leafed pot plants, red plush, heavy furniture and silver. For Rosie it took on a nightmare quality. She prided herself on being able to hold her drink, but Roger had filled her glass every time it was empty and by the end of the meal her head was swimming. She listened to snatches of the women's conversation, and the image of the white corpse from the lake caught her attention immediately and stayed with her.

It was partly to shake off this feeling of melodrama, partly because she was so drunk that when the thought came into her head she couldn't stop it coming out, that she interrupted their conversation.

'Oh, by the way, Chris sends his love.'

'Chris?' Her mother seemed puzzled.

'The DJ.'

Hannah looked at Sally. 'That was Chris?'

'Didn't you recognize him?' Sally seemed pleased. 'He hasn't worn very well, has he?' Then she seemed to think Rosie deserved an explanation. 'Chris,' she said, 'is my unmissed ex-husband.'

Soon after, Rosie left them to it. Roger winked and wrapped a half-drunk bottle of wine in a napkin for her to take with her. Hannah would have objected if she'd noticed but she was too preoccupied to see what was going on.

In her room Rosie drew the curtains. The window was open and she heard young voices, smelled the grilling flesh of a barbecue. By the edge of the lake someone was having a party. She switched on the television and flicked through the channels, but nothing held her interest for long.

She poured wine into a beaker from the bathroom and wished she were outside. Leaving the set on, but with the sound turned right down, she dialled the Prom on her mobile. Frank answered.

'Hi,' she said. 'It's me.'

He recognized her voice. She wondered idly if he'd

know all his part-time staff by voice. 'Good God, girl,' he said. 'Can't you keep away from the place? I thought it was your night off.'

'Sad, isn't it?' She thought it really was sad.

'You're pissed,' he said. It was a statement of fact.

'Shit, Frank, you sound like my mum. Is anyone in?'

'Can't you hear them?' He must have held the receiver over the bar. The roar was deafening.

'Not *anyone*. Anyone I know.'

'Nah. They were in earlier. The whole crowd.'

'Except Mel and Joe.' She thought they'd be in Portugal by now, sitting by the pool under the orange trees.

'I've got some news about them.' He was like an old woman about gossip. He paused, tormenting her, knowing she'd be gagging for the information.

'What?'

'They're still here.'

'Why?'

'Mel refused to go, didn't she.'

'What do you mean?'

'She refused to go on holiday. They called in here on their way to the airport. Bags all packed. It was supposed to be just to say goodbye. Then all of a sudden she threw a wobbly. She said her parents wanted to get rid of her. The holiday was a trick to get her out of the country. They never intended to let her back.'

She kept her voice flat. 'Was Joe OK?'

'He didn't say much, but what was there to say? His girlfriend had practically accused him of kidnap. That girl needs help.'

She switched off her phone and dialled Joe's house.
The answerphone clicked in straight away. She left a
message for Joe saying she'd call him the next day.
She thought then that she should phone Mel and check
that she was all right but knew that should wait until
she was sober. She'd only lose her temper. She seemed
to lie awake for hours but she didn't hear her mother
come in.

Chapter Ten

Sally was very eager that Hannah should go to the police station as soon as they returned from the school reunion.

'It'll be all over the papers tomorrow. They've got a picture. Someone will tell that detective you were Michael Grey's girlfriend. Better he hear it from you. Of course, I'll come with you if you like.'

Of course, Hannah thought. That was what Sally wanted. She was a journalist, even if not a very grand one. She saw a story she could sell.

'Let the poor woman eat,' Roger said.

Hannah was grateful. Perhaps it was the shock but she was ravenous.

In the end two detectives came out to the hotel. It was Sally's suggestion. She said the national press was already sniffing around in the town. On second thoughts this would be more discreet. And, thought Hannah, it would give Sally more control. Hannah didn't mind. She felt very tired. She didn't think she could face going out.

It was after ten when the detectives arrived, just dark, still very warm. Rosie didn't seem to have grasped the significance of the body in the lake. She went, a little unsteadily, to their room. The staff were clearing up in the dining-room and there were still guests in the lounge, so Sally let them use her private sitting-room. Roger brought in a tray of coffee. There was a bowl of roses on the table. Later Hannah would remember their fragrance, the scent of filter coffee and another smell which she realized was pipe tobacco. Although the older detective made no attempt to smoke on that occasion, it seemed that he was an addict and his pipe was always in his pocket. It must have been hard for him to sit there for so long without it.

She couldn't decide at first which was the senior officer. The older man was shorter, slight and dark, with an accent which suggested he came from the coast, from one of those villages where the pits used to be. He had the look of a collier about him. He wore a grey suit. The trousers were too big for him and held up by a thin belt. His shoes were as black and shiny as a prison officer's boots. The younger man was tall, prematurely balding. If she'd met him on a social occasion, Hannah would have guessed that he taught humanities at a college for further education. He could even have been a librarian. He wore odd socks and scuffed suede boots. The older one was called Stout, the younger Porteous. They must have given their ranks when they introduced themselves but Hannah had been in too much of a daze to take in the information.

They were very polite, but something about their manner put Hannah on her guard. She drank a cup of Roger's good, strong coffee and tried to clear her head. She had heard the prisoners talking and knew that the police weren't always to be trusted. What they wanted now was to clear up their case as quickly as possible.

There wouldn't be two detectives here, at this time of night, if they didn't think there was something in her story for them. For the first time she wondered what Sally had told them. There had been a muttered conversation at the door before she'd shown them in. She had been surprised when Sally had left them alone together without any fuss. But perhaps she was standing at the door now with a glass to her ear. Or perhaps there was a tape recorder hidden under one of the cushions on the sofa.

'I don't know what Sally has told you . . .' she said. She wanted to take the initiative, to appear purposeful, to let them know she couldn't be browbeaten.

Porteous, the younger, answered. He seemed diffident, almost apologetic. The voice was educated, but somewhere behind the polish there was a Midland whine.

'She said that you and Mr Grey were close at the time of his death.'

Stout interrupted briskly. 'We think it's possible, Mrs Morton, that you were the last person to see him alive. That, at least, is the information we've been given.'

Hannah stared at them. Trust Sally to stir things up. Trust her to turn this into the plot line of a soap opera. Hannah thought her judgement had been right all along. She should never have been persuaded to come back.

'I know it's a long time,' Porteous said. 'But if you could just take your mind back . . .'

'How did he die?' Hannah demanded. 'You must have done a post-mortem if you know he was murdered. You pulled him out days ago.'

They seemed shocked and the words sounded callous even in her own head, but Hannah needed to get the facts straight, neatly catalogued like books on a shelf. Stout looked at Porteous who nodded imperceptibly. She realized then that Porteous must be the superior and was glad to have another fact sorted.

'He was stabbed,' Stout said, 'with a sharp, wide-bladed knife.'

Hannah had an image of Jenny Graves at a school play rehearsal. It must have been a dress rehearsal because she was in costume. Her dress had been hired from the local amateur-dramatic society and was scarlet, laced at the front, daringly low cut. She had fake blood all over her hand. Mr Westcott had been so pleased with her performance that he had clapped. Hannah realized that the detectives were staring at her, waiting for her to speak.

'Have you told Michael's family?' she asked, not putting off answering but fishing again for information. She was still curious about Michael's family.

Again Stout and Porteous looked at each other. Again, it seemed Stout was given permission to answer.

'Ah,' he said. 'Well, we seem to have come up with a bit of a problem there. We're having some difficulty tracing them. He seems to have been a real mystery your young man, a real mystery. That was one of the reasons why we were so keen to talk to you.'

They looked at Hannah expectantly. At last she felt obliged to tell them at least something of what she knew.

'When we were at school together Michael Grey lived with foster parents. His mother had died and his father had worked abroad a lot. Or was ill. I'm not sure.' It had seemed to Hannah even in the beginning that Michael had made himself up as he went along. He changed his story to suit his audience. She had caught him out a few times and at first it had seemed to disconcert him. Later, when he realized how she felt about him, he had only grinned.

'What did the father do?' Stout asked. 'Work, I mean. The boy must have said.'

'I got the impression that he was employed by the Government. Some high-powered diplomat or civil servant. Something that took him away a lot.'

'He must have come back sometimes to see his son.'

'No. Never. Not that I remember. I never met him.'

'Didn't that strike you as odd?'

Hannah didn't answer. Michael's strangeness had been part of his attraction.

'What about the foster parents?' Porteous asked. His voice was gentle. Hannah thought he had set out to win her round. 'You must be able to tell us about them.'

She knew he would have got that much at least from the school records, but decided to play the game.

'Their names were Brice. Stephen and Sylvia. An elderly couple, more like grandparents than parents. They'd never had children of their own. Stephen was a retired vicar. They were devoted to each other, kind to everyone, into good causes. They lived in one of those terraced houses near the school.' She looked up at him sharply. 'You must know all this.'

'Part of it. I haven't been able to speak to anyone who knew them.'

'I didn't really know them,' she said quickly. 'I only met them once or twice.'

They had come to the performance of *Macbeth*. From her position as prompt, Hannah had seen them sitting proudly in the front row. At the end they had stood up and cheered, more like elderly eccentrics on the last night of the Proms than the audience of a school play. She could imagine them dressed up and waving a Union Jack. They had seemed to her then very old and even now, looking back from middle-age, she thought they must have been in their late sixties or seventies. They both had silver hair. Sylvia wore hers long, pinned back with a tortoiseshell comb. Their house was the quietest Hannah had ever been in. There was no television or radio. She remembered a ginger cat which purred and a clock which chimed the quarter-hour. She presumed this was not the sort of information which would be of interest to Porteous or Stout.

'They never reported him missing,' Stout said in a slightly aggrieved way, as if he took the Brices' failure to make a fuss personally. 'Nobody started looking for him until they died. Then the solicitor tried but couldn't trace him.'

Hannah wondered what had happened to the small, tidy house. It seemed unfeeling to ask. She had gone there first for tea. Michael had asked her. Although the Brices hadn't been expecting her they were thrilled to see her. 'We're always telling Michael he should invite his friends in.'

His attitude to them was delightful. He was thoughtful and playful. He called them Sylvie and Steve. But as they sat in front of the fire in the tiny drawing-room, eating seed cake and crumpets, the thread of the conversation had led Hannah to think that they knew little more about his past than she did. It seemed that Stephen had been invited to a theological college in Idaho to give a lecture on the Psalms. They had been discussing flight plans, when Sylvia asked suddenly, 'Have you ever been abroad, Michael? I can't remember your saying.'

It was as if they had depended on what he told them for their knowledge of him. Hannah struggled to explain that to the detectives. 'I don't think they were relatives. They probably didn't think there was anything sinister in his disappearance. They'd be sorry he hadn't kept in touch, but they wouldn't see it as their affair to meddle.'

'What was he doing with them then?' Stout demanded. 'You wouldn't just invite a strange teenager into your house.'

'I think they were the sort of people who might.' She paused. 'They called him their gift from God.'

She'd always thought it was a strange thing to say. Michael had spoken of it in a slightly shamefaced way. 'Look, Steve, that's a big thing to live up to, you know?' But the detectives remained impassive and unsurprised. She continued talking, trying to give an explanation they would accept as reasonable. 'He arrived with them out of the blue, then disappeared in the same way. Perhaps that's why they never reported him missing. They felt they had no claim on him.'

'The Lord giveth and the Lord taketh away,' Stout said. 'That's all very well, but they must have met up with him somewhere. He wouldn't just have knocked on the door.'

'Perhaps it was arranged through a charity,' Porteous suggested. He looked at Hannah hopefully. 'Was anything like that mentioned, Mrs Morton? Can you remember the name of any organization which might have put Michael in touch with the Brices?'

She shook her head. 'He wouldn't have told me,' she said. 'He liked being a mystery.'

'All the same he must have said something. When you asked about his family, his previous school, he must have given some scrap of information.'

Despite her resistance, memories were already clicking into her brain, jerky images like an old home movie.

'He told me a lot of things,' she said. 'Not all of them were true.'

'But . . ?' Porteous prompted.

'But I really think his mother died when he was little. He was quite specific about that. She died of leukaemia and he could remember the funeral. Nobody had explained to him properly what was going on. He couldn't understand where his mother was. When a black car turned up at the house, he thought it was to take him to see her.' Hannah stopped, then continued hesitantly, 'It was early spring. There were crocuses on the lawn. I don't know if that's any help.' She thought: Unless that was one of his fictions too.

Porteous said, 'At present everything is helpful.'

'There is something else.' She paused. She didn't want to make a fool of herself and she had a sense too that she was betraying Michael. But it was a matter of self-preservation. She had to give the detectives something to get them off her back. 'He resat the lower sixth. He was a year older than the rest of us.' Again she saw she was telling the men something they already knew and wondered what other secrets they were keeping to themselves. 'He made up a tale about his having been ill, but it was quite similar to his story of his mother's illness. I was taken in by it at the time. Why wouldn't I be? But now I work as a prison librarian and it's occurred to me that there might be another explanation for his missing year. I wondered if he might have been in trouble. Youth custody. Borstal, I suppose it would have been then. That would be something he wouldn't want to admit to the Brices or to me. That wouldn't fit into the Michael Grey myth.'

She realized she sounded bitter and to hide her confusion poured herself another cup of coffee, though by now it was cold. Porteous jotted a few lines in his notebook but gave no other indication of what he thought of the theory.

'Was he the sort of lad who might have been away?' Stout asked.

'What do you mean?'

'You work in the nick, Mrs Morton. There aren't many well-read, nicely spoken blokes in there.'

'More than you'd realize.' She thought of Marty, whose consideration had led to her being there.

'But you know what I mean,' Stout persisted. 'Most of the men will have been brought up with some degree of physical and emotional deprivation.'

It seemed an odd thing for a policeman to say. She took his point more seriously.

'Michael was a brilliant actor. And he was quick and bright. He could be whatever anyone wanted him to be. Do I think he was brought up in the west end of Newcastle or on a council estate in Wallsend? Probably not, but I wouldn't be astonished if that turned out to be the case.'

'Where *was* he brought up then?'

'West Yorkshire. At least that's where he said he went to school.' Hannah waited for another question: And before that? But it never came. Besides, she had told them the truth. On Michael's first day a girl from the upper sixth had asked which school he'd come from and he'd answered, without pausing a moment, giving her a smile: 'A place in West Yorkshire. You won't have heard of it.'

When Hannah told Porteous that, he wrote it down and said seriously to Stout, 'It seems a strange thing to make up, that, off the cuff. Check out approved schools, borstals and detention centres for that period in Yorkshire. Or perhaps that's where his family lived. We might find his mother's records.'

I don't think you will, Hannah thought, and wondered why she didn't speak the words out loud. Porteous turned to her with his diffident smile, which wasn't very different from one of the expressions in Michael's repertoire. 'Is there anything else you remember from that first meeting, Mrs Morton?'

She didn't answer. She thought she'd given him enough.

'You don't know how much this is helping us. We're very fortunate to have found a reliable witness at this early stage. What about his voice? Could you believe that he came from Yorkshire?'

'It depended to whom he was talking.'

'Sorry?'

'It was a habit. I explained he was an actor but I don't think this was self-conscious. He didn't realize he was changing his voice to suit the occasion. But he was. When he was speaking to us he spoke as we did. With the Brices it was old-fashioned English. We had a biology teacher from Edinburgh. She thought he came from there too because when he spoke to her he had something of the accent. It wasn't imitation or that he was trying to impress. He was a sort of verbal chameleon.'

Hannah sipped cold coffee. She thought she had nothing left to tell them. Surely now they would let her go. But Porteous shifted uncomfortably in his very comfortable chair.

'Tell us about you relationship with Mr Grey,' he said gently. He was more like a counsellor than a police officer. 'In some detail if you wouldn't mind, Mrs Morton. If you could cast your mind back.'

'We were friends,' Hannah said.

'More than friends surely.'

'Not at first.'

The men waited for her to say more.

'What are these questions about?' She'd had enough. 'You know who he is. Sally told me you found the dental records. There must be more efficient ways of finding what you want than listening to my ramblings.'

Porteous gave another little apologetic smile. 'Unfortunately not. Apart from your ramblings we've very little. We know that the body in the lake was that of a young man known as Michael Grey. One day he had toothache and Mrs Brice took him to her dentist. We're lucky that the practice kept records, but it hasn't provided us with a conclusive identification. It hasn't helped us to trace the victim's family. Because no birth certificate was issued to Michael Grey on the date he gave as his date of birth. There are no medical records or child-benefit records for him. There is no record of his having existed before he started school with you.'

They looked at her. It had been a long time since anyone had given her their full attention. She found it flattering. No doubt it was a technique they often used. She was taken in by it. She dragged her memory back almost thirty years.

Chapter Eleven

Her father died the summer Michael arrived. He committed suicide. He rigged up a hose-pipe from the exhaust of their Austin and the fumes killed him. Hannah didn't find him. He had timed it so her mother would do that when she went into the garage to fetch potatoes to peel for their supper. Mr Meek had an allotment. He kept the potatoes in the garage in wooden trays in the dark to stop them sprouting.

Looking back, Hannah thought her father and mother had never got on. He was nervy, quick to snap. Any noise or disruption to his routine threw him. She thought perhaps she'd inherited her own intolerance of change from him. He was a chain smoker. Every evening he came home from work, threw down his briefcase and would sit for an hour, sucking on cigarette after cigarette, going through the imagined slights of the day. He felt he was much undervalued at the bank. No one appreciated the work he put in. The only time he was anything like content was in the allotment. Perhaps the physical activity helped him to relax. Perhaps in the mindless routine of digging and weeding he could forget his troubles.

Hannah's mother didn't like the idea of the allotment. She pretended it didn't exist. She had been pretty as a girl and could have had her pick of the lads in the town, the ones who came back after the war. She had chosen Edward Meek over the plumbers and bricklayers because he worked in the bank. He wouldn't have to get his hands dirty. It put her on a par with other professional wives. Perhaps she imagined dinner parties and coffee mornings, but in fact she was awkward in company and if the invitations had ever come they soon dried up. When Hannah was a child Audrey Meek seemed to have no friends at all. She confided in her daughter, shared her loneliness and her disappointment with her. She had spent her life being disappointed.

At first Hannah thought that this disappointment had been reason enough for her father's suicide. She supposed he felt responsible for her mother's unhappiness; he had never been able to live up to her expectations. Then Hannah learned it was much worse than that. By the time of his death he'd progressed to the post of assistant manager, and he'd been stealing. Perhaps he hoped to buy his wife's approval with little luxuries for the house, but Hannah thought it was more that he felt the bank owed him what he took. It was his way of fighting back. Of course, he wasn't very good at covering his tracks and he knew he would be caught. He couldn't face it. But Hannah and her mother *had* to face it. They had to face the questions from the bank and the police, the prying neighbours, the dreadful sympathy. And Hannah had to come to terms with the fact that her father hadn't loved her enough to stay alive. He had put her through this embarrassment to save himself the ordeal of it.

Then it was September and time to go back to

school. Hannah was dreading it. Her father's face had been plastered all over the local paper. Even if the teachers were too sensitive to mention the suicide she'd be aware of their curiosity, and some of the kids, at least, would be merciless. Hannah wasn't popular. She was known as a swat. Rock music was important then. Status was conferred by knowledge of obscure groups and Hannah couldn't join in those discussions. There wasn't even a record player in her house and anyway she wasn't really interested. Over the holidays she'd avoided most of the people from school. She'd seen Sally a couple of times, but only in her home. She'd kept away from the pub and the parties.

On the first day of term Michael Grey turned up. There weren't many new kids at the school and he was immediately the centre of attention. For Hannah his appearance was a relief. It took the heat off her. While the rest of them were gathered around him at registration she slid into the room, dumped her stuff in her locker and slipped away to her first class. There was such a crowd around him that she didn't even see his face. At the mid-morning break she wanted to hide again, but Sally dragged her to the common-room.

'Look,' Sally said. 'You'll have to face them sometime. Better now when they've got the beautiful Michael to distract them.'

He always was Michael. Never Mike or Mick.

The sixth-form common-room was a mobile classroom. It was square, flat roofed, freezing in the winter, but that September was hot, an Indian summer. Sixth formers didn't have to wear uniform and they'd all chosen their clothes on that first day with care. It was a season of peasant fashion. The boys wore wide trousers and cheesecloth shirts. The girls, even Hannah, were in smocks and long flowery skirts. Michael stood with his back to the window so the light was behind him. That could have been deliberate. He had what Mr Westcott called a theatrical eye. He wore a pair of denim jeans which looked new, a black T-shirt, and desert boots with black leather laces. His hair was blond, almost white. He had a suntan. Foreign travel was unusual those days and it was hard to get a tan in her northern town, so that made him stand out too. There was something about him that made the others listen. It wasn't just the novelty.

Sally nudged Hannah in the ribs. 'What do you think?'

'I think he's cocky,' Hannah said. 'He's good looking but he knows it.'

He can't have heard what she said. There was music playing and everyone talked at once. But he looked over the heads of the others towards her as if he knew what she was thinking. He gave a self-deprecating little shrug. I know, he seemed to be saying. This is all bullshit. But it's a game and I've got to go along with it.

Later Hannah saw her first meeting with Michael as a turning point. After that she was seen differently within the school. She could face them all without embarrassment. It was possible that her memory played tricks – that there were unpleasant comments about her father, days when she wanted to stay at home. It was possible that her re-creation of her friendship with Michael was as great a fiction as the story he told about himself. But his arrival did make a difference. Some incidents remained clear and vivid. These, she was convinced, were true.

There was the day he first invited her to the Brices, for example. Hannah remembered that as soon as she started talking to the detectives. Michael was placed in the same English group as her, and on the day of his arrival he chose the seat next to her, at one of the old-fashioned desks with the lift-up lids that you never see now. Despite her disdain, her sense that he was too cocky by half, there was a rush of excitement when she turned and saw him there. Through habit they kept the same seats all term. They were reading *Middlemarch*. The rest of the group hated it. They found it tedious and Hannah suspected that most of them didn't make it to the end. She loved it and so did Michael. There'd been this guy in the old place who'd been passionate about it, he said. Who'd done it as part of his Ph.D. and passed on his enthusiasm. Hannah presumed then that the 'guy' was a teacher, the 'old place' a school. Later she was to presume nothing. Michael said he had some notes at home. Perhaps she'd like to borrow them to help with an essay they'd been set? If she wasn't in a hurry she could go back with him, have a cup of tea. The old folks would be thrilled to bits.

Recreating the scene in her head, Hannah thought it had been the beginning of December. She could remember the cold. He must have been in the town for three months but still she had no idea that his family was different from anyone else's. They hadn't talked about it. She hadn't told him about the drama with her father, though it was possible that the others had been whispering behind her back. At that age families weren't as important as friends.

'Old folks?' she said. It seemed an odd way to talk about parents.

'Sylvie and Steve. You'll see.'

'You call your mum and dad by their first names?'

'No. They're not my parents. My mother's dead. My father . . .' He seemed thrown for a moment. 'Well, I don't get to see much of him.'

They walked slowly up the school drive to the house. It was almost dark by the time they arrived at the house, one of a small row, flat faced. As the light went the temperature plummeted. They stood for a moment on the pavement, looking in. There was a street lamp and they could see their breath as a white mist. The lights were on inside but the curtains had not been drawn. There was a fire in the grate and an elderly man sat on a leather armchair, with a cat on his knee, reading.

'That's Steve,' Michael said with enormous affection. He took out a Yale key and let himself in.

Inside there was a smell of fruit and spice. A small kitchen led straight from the hall and she'd seen Sylvie, red faced, turning a cake on to a wire tray. She looked slightly flustered. Her hair had come loose from her comb. Michael put his arm around her.

'This is Hannah,' he said. 'She's a George Eliot fan too. I've brought her home for tea. You don't mind?'

'Of course we don't mind.' She smiled at Hannah. 'We haven't met any of his friends before. I think he's ashamed of us.'

'How could I be?' he said.

Hannah didn't know what to make of the relationship between Michael and the Brices. Usually she was jealous of other people's home lives. Her own was so bleak. Her mother struggled on to keep the house as she wanted it. They hadn't been forced to sell, though at one time that had been a possibility. There was even less money than there had been before and Audrey hated the forced economies. She pretended not to mind the gossip and in fact seldom went out to hear it. Television had become her consolation. Hannah was grateful because it provided a safe topic of conversation. Without it they would have had little to say to each other. Later she thought that her mother had been depressed and had been brave to keep things as normal as she did. Then she longed to be a part of a different sort of family. That's why she spent so much time with Sally. Her dream family would have been quite like Sally's, but the parents would have been younger, interested perhaps in different things. There would be a brother as well as a sister and they would have shared meals together discussing ideas about books and plays. There would have been noise and laughter. At the time she didn't consider Michael's situation as ideal. It was too different from her dream. Everything was so quiet. There was discussion but it was calm and measured.

There was one room which served as living- and dining-room. They sat at a round mahogany table and drank tea from translucent china cups, ate crumpets which Michael squatted by the fire to toast, and the cake Sylvie had baked. They talked about Stephen's lecture on the Psalms. At one point Michael reached out and touched Sylvie's hand.

'Why don't you go too?' he said. 'You know you'd enjoy it and I'll be perfectly fine here on my own.'

'I'm sure you would be.' Her voice was serene. 'But Stephen and I have had a lifetime together and I'll have your company for such a short while. I'd prefer to stay and make the most of it.'

Then she asked him the question about his having been abroad.

Hannah had always been an observer. Even in her youth she could usually work out what was going on between people. But the situation in the Brices' home confused her. She couldn't make out at all where Michael fitted in.

After tea the Brices refused the offer of help with the washing-up and Michael took Hannah to his bedroom to find her his notes. She was tidier than most of her friends but his room was almost Spartan in its lack of clutter. She wondered if he had planned to invite her back and had cleared it specially, but she went there on subsequent occasions and it was always the same. It reminded her of a cell.

'Are they your grandparents?' she asked.

'No, we're no relation. They're just friends.'

'Friends of your father's?'

'Yes,' he said, seeming grateful for an explanation that worked. 'That's right.'

It was a small room but there was a big desk under the window, of the kind that you'd have found in offices everywhere. It had three drawers on each side of the knee-hole. It wasn't well made. The varnish was scratched and the top was chipped. Michael seemed flustered when he couldn't find the notes where he'd expected them to be, with others in the top drawer.

'Sorry, I thought I'd brought everything with me. But obviously not.'

'Couldn't they be somewhere else?' Hannah yanked open a bottom drawer which was wider than the others. When it came to school work she was competitive. She wanted the notes, a chance to shine in the essay. She hadn't come along just for the chance to know Michael better. She had expected to find more files in the drawer, neatly labelled, but it was empty apart from a shoebox, the sort she had collected when she was young for use in *Blue Peter* projects. He must have had the box for a long time. It was too small to hold shoes of the size he wore then.

Michael slammed the drawer shut with a ferocity which almost trapped her hand.

'There's nothing in there. I told you, I must have left them behind.'

'Sorry.' She looked at him, expecting an explanation. He said nothing.

The incident seemed to have thrown him. Hannah thought he was angry about the invasion of his privacy and apologized more profusely. It was something she could understand. He hardly seemed to hear what she was saying and when she said that her mother would be expecting her he seemed relieved to see her go. When Hannah saw him at school the next day he greeted her as if nothing had happened.

For several weeks she was haunted by the mystery of the small, blue shoebox. She imagined it contained answers to her questions about Michael.

Just before Christmas she was invited back to the Brices for mince pies and mulled wine. She made an excuse to go upstairs, slipped into Michael's room and opened the drawer. She hated herself for doing it. Her hands were sweating as she tried to turn the knob. She had kept the door open so she would hear if anyone was coming. But it was an anticlimax. The drawer was empty. When she returned to the others Michael looked at her as he had on his first morning in the common-room, as if he knew exactly what she'd been up to.

Chapter Twelve

Throughout the interview both Porteous and Stout went on about Michael having been Hannah's special friend, as if they had been lovers from the start. But they were never lovers, not in the sense the detectives meant, and they didn't even start going out with each other until after the lower-sixth exams. She tried to explain that to them. The detectives listened but she wasn't sure they understood.

The town itself had nothing to attract young people. The cinema had shut and the pubs were gloomy and unfriendly. In the summer at least, they were drawn to the lake. A couple of years before, the valley had been flooded to provide water for northern industrial towns and the biggest man-made lake in Europe was created. It was news at the time. Although it was surrounded by forestry plantations and was miles from everywhere, the novelty of the development and the scale and spectacle of it attracted tourists. An enterprising farmer opened a caravan site, then built a bar and a club, so it was more like a small holiday camp. It hardly provided a sophisticated night life but it was livelier than anything else the town had to offer and it drew the kids like a magnet.

The Saturday after the end-of-year exams they

gathered on the shore in the afternoon and collected dead wood to build a bonfire. Hannah had expected Michael to be there but he didn't turn up. You could never guarantee his presence on these occasions, and he never offered explanations. They ate chocolate and crisps as a makeshift picnic and later moved on to the caravan park, to the bar where Sally's boyfriend was DJ. It was only supposed to serve residents but no one asked questions when they all piled in. It was June, early in the season. No doubt the owners were glad of their money. The bar was a horrible place, furnished like a transport café with Formica tables and plastic chairs. Along one wall a row of one-armed bandits clacked and flashed. Hannah and her friends didn't mind. There were no awkward questions about under-age drinking, and they took it over and made it theirs. When they arrived there were two residents, an overweight Brummie and his wife, leaning against the bar. Soon they shrank away and the Cranford Grammar brigade had it all to themselves.

Hannah still found events like that evening daunting, but she began to enjoy herself. She thought she'd done well in the exams, better than she'd expected. And she'd arranged to spend the night with Sally, so for once she didn't have to worry about her mother. Since Edward's death, Audrey had become increasingly anxious, in an obsessive, unhealthy way. It seemed that anxiety was the only way she could express her concern or her love. When Hannah went out Audrey always waited up. She would be pacing up and down the dining-room, her face knotted with tension, although Hannah was always back before the agreed time. Later she was to understand something of what her mother had gone through – she could never sleep until Rosie was in – but then it had seemed an unnecessary intrusion.

The evening of the party it was a relief to know there would be no prying questions to answer and she felt she could let herself go. She started drinking her usual halves of cider but later Sally's boyfriend, Chris, bought all the girls vodka. He was always throwing his money about, trying to impress. They made him play the music very loud and they started to dance. At closing time, as she stumbled and giggled with the others down the sandy path to the shore, Hannah thought this must be what it was like to be drunk. She had led a very sheltered life.

The bonfire was already lit. They could see the flames from the path, reflected in the water beyond. Sparks from the burning wood shattered in the sky like fireworks. Michael had lit it and he was there, alone, tending it, throwing on more wood as soon as the flames subsided. While the others ran down the bank to join him, pretending to be angry because he'd started the fire without them, Hannah stood and watched him. He was absorbed in his watch over the flames and seemed not to notice the approaching crowd. Even when the others crowded round him, yelling and cheering, he didn't look away.

Of course, she fancied him like crazy. In the beginning she *had* thought him cocky, still did if it came to that, but that was part of the fascination. And perhaps he'd seen her resistance as a challenge, because he'd made an effort to win her over. No one else had bothered to do that. She wasn't seen as much of a catch – skinny with no figure to speak of, black oily hair and the hint even then of dark down on her upper lip. He said she looked Mediterranean. Perhaps he had heard about her father and felt sorry for her, though if his friendship was prompted by pity he hid it well. She could usually pick up a reaction like that. It turned her spiky and moody. Perhaps their unusual homes in this conventional town of happy families gave them something in common. She thought he was happy in her company and for a while that was enough.

After Hannah's first visit to his home the relationship continued to revolve around the books they were reading, the essays they had to prepare. When school finished for the day they went to the library together. Not to the school library where the few recommended books of criticism were fought over but to the dark building in the town centre, a Victorian heap, with enormous polished tables and rows of reference books smelling of damp. Hannah never wanted to go home immediately to face her mother. The Brices placed no restrictions on Michael's movements. That always surprised Hannah. She would have expected such elderly people to share her mother's anxieties. He would have stayed with her all evening if she'd wanted. As a friend, of course. Not a lover. But she had her pride and sent him home at five o'clock in time for the tea Sylvie would have prepared. She knew that the pretty girls with the short skirts who lusted after him never felt jealous of the time they spent together. They didn't consider Hannah as any sort of competition.

By the night of the bonfire he'd been at the school for nearly a year, but he'd never had a proper girlfriend. Some of them saw it as a challenge. He tantalized them with the possibility, snogging them at parties, but nothing came of it. He was indiscriminate in his physical contact in a way which was unusual at the time. He liked to put his arm round people, boys and girls. He often hugged Sylvie, making her blush with pleasure. He had never touched Hannah though, not even a hand on the shoulder, not even brushing against her by mistake. She longed for it.

She didn't make straight for Michael when she reached the shore. The booze had made her up for the games other people played. Let him come to her if he wanted to. That night there was a huge orange moon which lit the scene, so she would be able to see Michael even if he moved away from the fire.

She latched on to a tall lad from the upper sixth, who was a figure of fun, because his picture was once in the paper when he got a Queen's Scout award. Someone had torn it out and stuck it on the noticeboard at school. He had stood in the photo in the ridiculous uniform, blushing in a way which made his acne stand out. Since then he'd got rid of the acne, but the reputation of being what they now called a geek had stuck with him. He did science and maths, and was considered brilliant at both, which didn't help. He came along to parties like this, but always ended up on his own.

'Isn't this brilliant, Paul? I mean this enormous sky. The landscape seems so huge, doesn't it, tonight. It seems foreign. Like we're in a country with wider spaces.'

She leaned against him, knowing as she did it that it wasn't fair. It was the sort of trick that had been played on her. Tentatively he slid his arm around her shoulder. She felt his breath on her neck. On the other

side of the fire Michael was watching. She saw him get
up. He walked over the pebbles towards the caravan
site and the road into town. Hannah waited for a
second, then pulled away from Paul Lord and ran after
him. She caught up with him by the jetty where the
water-sport freaks launched their dinghies and canoes.
She took him by the elbow and swung him round to
face her, exhilarated by the first touch and her daring.
She felt muscle and bone under the denim shirt.

'Where are you going?'

'Home.' He paused. 'To Steve and Sylvie's.' As if the
two were not the same thing.

'Where *is* home, Michael, really?' She hadn't had
the nerve to ask him about his personal life before.
After the incident in his bedroom, she'd been scared
of frightening him off. 'What is going on here?'

He shrugged and walked off like a sulky child, not
bothering to turn on the charm. She realized he
resented the attention she'd given to the other boy,
even though it was Paul Lord, who was a figure of fun,
almost a charity case. He wanted her to himself. She
was flattered but felt a sense of injustice. It was all
right for him to flirt and kiss and touch, but she had
to be there for him whenever he wanted the company.
On other occasions she would have been apologetic,
grateful that he needed her. Tonight, because of the
vodka, she had more confidence.

'Suit yourself,' she shouted and started back towards
the party.

'No.' He called after her and she heard something
like panic in his voice. She hesitated, determined not
to give in too easily, then continued walking. The
tactics paid off because he scrambled over the pebbles

towards her. He put his arms around her and clung on to her as if she were the most important person in the world. Triumphant, she stroked his white hair and told him everything would be alright.

'Shall we go for a walk?' He took her agreement for granted. He knew she wouldn't let him go again. He took her hand and led her along the edge of the lake. Sheep-cropped grass fell away into sand so it was almost like being on a beach at the seaside. But there were no waves. The water was glassily still. If the others saw them she presumed they'd think she was just another of his party conquests.

'Poor Hannah,' they'd say. 'She's been hanging round him for months and now he's taking pity on her.'

At that point the road skirted the edge of the lake. There was the flash of headlights. For a moment she thought it might be the police, that there'd been a complaint about the fire, or even something more serious. She wondered sometimes what Sally was getting into. There'd already been rumours about Chris and drugs. But it was a blue 1100. It stopped and the driver got out, leaving the engine running. He was a small middle-aged man, rather nondescript. Hannah thought it must be a parent, come to collect errant offspring. He peered over towards the fire trying to make out individuals, trying, it seemed, to pluck up the courage to go over. He couldn't see Michael and Hannah. They were in the shadow. But they could see him quite clearly, caught in the headlights. She turned to Michael to make a comment about the man, to ask him to guess which of their friends he belonged too, but saw at once he already recognized him.

'Who is it?' she whispered.

'I'm not sure.'

'But you do know him?'

'Perhaps.'

The man gave up his search, got into the car and backed it erratically up the lane.

Michael put his arm around Hannah and they walked on.

'Why don't you ever talk to me?' she said.

'I do.'

'Not about the important stuff.' Or the not so important. Like a bloke in a Morris 1100 looking for his kids. 'Is it just that you like the mystery?'

'No. You don't understand.'

'Whatever it is I won't be shocked. You must have heard about my dad. So you know about my shady past.'

'That was him. Not you.'

'What do you think I'll do? Shop you? Dump you?'

He didn't answer at once. 'I'm frightened,' he said. 'Not just for me. For you.' She thought that was the old Michael again. The attention seeker. The boy who made up stories in his head and almost believed them himself. She didn't care.

He pulled her beside him on the grass. She thought he was kissing her to stop the awkward questions. By the fire someone had started playing the guitar. There was a smell of pine and wood smoke. She lay on her back and looked at the orange moon.

All that came back when she was talking to the detectives, but of course they weren't interested in the detail, only in the clues which might lead to information about their victim's past. The party by the lake had taken place a year before Michael's disappearance. What happened then could have no relevance to his death.

Chapter Thirteen

So they became a couple. Michael Grey and Hannah Meek. She always liked the way their names scanned. Now, listening to Porteous and Stout talking about the mystery of their victim's birth, she thought it would be a shame if that turned out not to be his name, if the rhythm were lost. Though now of course she was Hannah Morton and she had more important things to worry about, like convincing these policemen that she knew nothing at all about Michael's murder and that she had no reason for wanting him dead.

If their friends thought about it, they must have assumed that Michael and Hannah were lovers. Porteous and Stout, of course, had made the same assumption. After all, they went out with each other for nearly a year. Their intimacy was for everyone to see. They walked round the school hand in hand, despite a rule banning physical contact. It only got them into trouble once. They were walking across the yard towards the common-room for morning break. Michael had his arm around Hannah's waist and they were laughing at a joke, some piece of nonsense. There was a shout and they turned to see Mr Spence bearing down on them. Spooky Spence. Now husband of Sally.

'Mr Grey, Miss Meek. A little decorum, if you please.'

They looked puzzled. Like the ban on smoking in the common-room, the rule was never enforced. Spence must have taken their bewilderment, their failure to comply immediately with his instruction, as impertinence, a personal insult. Suddenly he lost his temper. He stood in the middle of the playground, gathering a small crowd of giggling onlookers, and he ranted about the younger generation in general and Hannah and Michael in particular, about their lack of morals, their failure to comport themselves with decency and modesty. As he yelled flecks of spit came out of his mouth. It took them a moment to realize what had provoked his anger. At last they got the message and pulled apart. Spence regained a shaky control and walked away. They didn't mention the incident to their friends. They were embarrassed by it. It wasn't the way adults were supposed to behave.

They never went to bed together. Spence and the gang they hung around with would have found it hard to accept, but they never even discussed it. Hannah thought that was because Michael was living with the Brices and felt he should conform to their standards. An exaggerated idea of good manners. She wouldn't have known how to raise the subject. Later she wished she had, that she'd lost her virginity to him and not to a plump mathematician after a drunken freshers' ball in her first week at university. Sally was certainly sleeping with her disc jockey. At weekends she told her parents she was staying at Hannah's house, but she'd spend the evening with Chris and the bed in the Meeks' spare room was never used. Her parents never checked up on her. Perhaps they didn't want to know what she was up to. Hannah was worried about her, concerned she'd get caught up in his shady deals. It wasn't only the drugs. There was an air of aggression about him.

'Are you sure you know what you're doing?' she asked once.

Sally had told her not to be stupid. She wanted Chris and he wanted her. That was all that mattered. Sally also wanted the things Chris could provide. He had two jobs, more cash than the rest of them could dream of. She liked the presents, the fact that she never had to buy her own drinks. On the evenings when Sally was supposed to be at the Meeks, she would go with him to work, to the disco at whichever village hall or hotel had hired him, or more often to the caravan site which was his regular gig and seemed to have become her second home. Then she would go with him to the scruffy flat he was renting over the betting shop in a back street behind the police station. She once took Hannah there when Chris was away for the weekend. He'd given her a key to feed his cat – an angry black tom. Inside the flat was surprisingly ordinary. There was the same utility dining suite as Hannah's mum had in their house, and a floral carpet. One of the bedrooms was locked and Sally didn't have a key to that. She said it was where Chris kept his sound system, but Hannah wondered what else was inside. Sally agonized about going on the pill as if it were a decision Hannah must be making too. 'Doesn't it make you put on weight? Chris would hate me fat. It's all right for you. You could do with a few extra pounds.'

Hannah was noncommittal and Sally was too wrapped up in her own affairs to notice. Michael and Hannah didn't spend all their time together. They were ambitious. It was the A-level year and they wanted to do well. Hannah for herself; Michael, she thought, for the Brices. Hannah went through the process of applying to university, filling out UCCA forms, going for interviews. Michael, however, refused to make any plans. None, at least, that he would talk about. It was as if he wanted to shroud his future as well as his past in mystery. He said he'd take a year out, travel perhaps. Hannah wondered if he had more specific ideas. He worked for his exams with a purpose which suggested he had a project in mind. He spoke once of a crusade. He had a responsibility, he said. There was something he had to put right. When she asked what exactly this mission was, in a teasing voice, because she refused to let him take himself too seriously, he clammed up. She didn't push it. Talking to the detectives she thought it was incredible that she should have taken any of his stories at face value. Why didn't she ask where his father was, why they never saw each other? Because she was perfectly content. She knew she would never be so happy again. She was determined to do nothing to spoil it.

The school play was planned for the end of the Easter term. When Michael went for the auditions, just after Christmas, she thought he was mad.

'You *are* joking. Our last full term before the exams. You'll never manage it all.'

'Sod the A levels,' he said, much as Rosie would do, then gave her a grin to show he didn't mean it. Perhaps managing it all was the challenge. Perhaps it was part of his game plan.

Hannah went with him to the audition, not to try for a part, but to offer her support. She thought he might be given a small role. When she saw that Spooky Spence was one of the auditioning panel, she thought he'd be lucky to get that. It never occurred to her that he would go for Macbeth. She perched on a window-sill at the back of the hall and waited for his turn. The teachers sat in judgement on a row of chairs at the front: Spooky Spence, Miss Davies who taught English and drama, and Mr Westcott, still slightly tipsy from his lunchtime in the pub. The actors stood on a block to read, but when it was Michael's turn he didn't stand. He sat with his legs crossed, quite relaxed, and when he spoke, despite the language, it was as if he were speaking just to her. She knew at once that he would be chosen to play the lead.

Hannah saw Jenny Graves audition that day too. She was in the lower sixth, a year younger than them, tall and willowy, rather nervy. Hannah thought it was typecasting. The panel had gone for the look. She wasn't sure she would have chosen Jenny over some of the others. She realized that Michael and Jenny would have lots of rehearsals together. It didn't bother her at the time, but nearer to the performance she thought she could afford to get involved and she volunteered to help with props and to prompt. She never admitted to herself that she wanted to keep an eye on him.

One Saturday, at about the time of the *Macbeth* auditions, Michael and Hannah took a trip to the coast. Occasionally they wanted to get away from home and homework and explore the surrounding district. Hannah liked to have Michael to herself. On this day they went to Millhaven, the seaside town where Hannah would end up living. Where Rosie would be born. Where her husband would fall in love with a PE teacher called Eve. They caught a bus into Newcastle, then another to the coast. It was the longest trip they had made and she wasn't sure how they came to decide on it. On the bus Michael said he liked seaside towns in winter.

When they arrived, however, she could tell that he had been there before. It was a freezing day. Flurries of snow blew in from the sea, gathered like piles of confetti against the lampposts and wrought-iron benches. They walked shoulder to shoulder, hands deep in coat pockets, heads bowed against the wind. But not in an aimless way. Michael knew where he was going, where he wanted to be. He found his way immediately to the sea front, knew which way to turn for the funfair, closed and deserted for the winter. He stood there for a moment, looking in over the pad-locked gate at the entrance to the ghost train and the helter skelter, at the still and tarnished horses under their gaudy awning. Hannah guessed he had been taken there as a child, though it didn't seem to hold any happy memories for him.

'A penny for them,' she said lightly.

'Sorry?' He turned to her, still preoccupied.

'What are you thinking about?' She had to yell above the wind and felt a bit ridiculous. They weren't ideal conditions for a deep and meaningful discussion.

'My mother,' he said. 'Actually.'

She sensed that he was ready to talk, took his arm and pulled him into a pub.

Talking to the detectives, she was aware on a number of occasions of coincidences, links between her life as an eighteen-year-old and her life as a mother. Often she caught herself thinking, What would Rosie have done if that had happened to her? Certainly she would have been more assertive. She wouldn't have waited for almost a year, content with a kiss and a fairly chaste grope. She would have wanted to know what was going on. The pub was the most obvious coincidence. When Rosie first started work in the Promenade, Hannah thought the name was familiar. She called in occasionally to collect her daughter from a late shift but the place stirred no memories. By the time Rosie worked there the Prom had become one big room with long windows painted white. One evening, when she wasn't quite ready for her lift home, Hannah looked at the old photographs on the walls. They hadn't been bought as a job lot by the brewery; they showed the place as it had been before it had been taken over. With a start she realized it was the pub where she and Michael had sat on that winter's day. Then, the Promenade had two small bars separated by a gloomy corridor. The walls were half panelled in wood covered in a sticky yellow varnish, wrinkled like custard skin. They had sat all lunchtime in the corner of the snug, with their half-pints in front of them, and nobody disturbed them.

That was the time he told her about his mother's funeral, the story Hannah passed on to the detectives, without giving them the context, without telling them where she sat to hear it. He talked in short phrases, not trying to call attention to himself this time, but trying to get it right. He described the big car whose purpose he could only guess at. The stern people in black clothes. The crocuses on the lawn.

But the funeral hadn't taken place in Yorkshire. Hannah was sure of that. It had taken place in the windswept town on the coast. Why hadn't she passed on *that* particular gem of information to Porteous and Stout? She had her reasons. Because they had irritated her with their insinuating questions. Because Michael wouldn't have wanted them to know.

In the pub it was cold, so cold that she found it hard at first to concentrate on what Michael was saying. At one point she put her hand on the radiator and pulled it away because it was freezing, almost literally, so she felt her skin might stick to the pipe. They sat, huddled in jackets with the hoods still pulled up, Michael talking in spluttering fits.

'I don't remember much of the time she was ill. A visit to the hospital with my father. He was holding flowers – orange lilies, I think – and when we got to the bed he pushed them into my hand. The smell. In hospital and at home. Disinfectant, I suppose. Her face. I think I remember her face, but I've struggled too much to hold that in my mind and I'm not sure how accurate it is. You lose something, don't you, if you try too hard?'

'You must have photographs,' Hannah said. Even after just a couple of years her memory of her father seemed to come from family snaps. There was one of him, taken at Christmas, with a paper hat on his head and a forced smile on his face, which she'd have been glad to forget.

But Michael shook his head. 'I don't know where they all went.'

'Doesn't your father have them?' He shook his head again. He was so upset that she didn't feel she could push it. Later she knew that to be a mistake.

'Did she take you to the fair?'

'I think she must have done. It's one of the pictures I have in my head. We went down the helter skelter together. I sat between her legs. She wore tan nylons. I remember the mat we sat on. I was wearing shorts and it was prickly like coconut fibre. The sun was shining.' He paused. 'I chose the wrong day, didn't I, to re-create the atmosphere?'

'We can come back in the summer.'

'She was buried here,' he said suddenly. 'In the cemetery by the lighthouse.'

'Shall we go to look for the grave?'

He shivered. 'No,' he said. 'I've had enough now. Let's go home.'

He placed an emphasis on the last word as if he'd come to a decision. Home was the Brices' house. It wasn't this place.

Chapter Fourteen

Rosie stood behind the bar of the Prom with her back to the punters and took a moment to catch her breath. It had been a crazy evening. Friday nights were always busy, but this had been wild. On Friday night the locals came out and trippers and people from the city. They dressed up and paraded along the sea front from one pub to another, ending up after closing in the clubs. On Friday nights every pub along the sea front had a bouncer outside. The clubs were heaving. Scantily dressed waiters and waitresses pranced between the tables with trays held high above the customers. The Prom wasn't really part of this circuit, but some people who did the Friday-night gig as a bit of a joke started off there, because the beer was cheaper, and to show that they weren't really taking it seriously.

Early on, a visiting rugby team had arrived and taken up residence in front of the widescreen television.

'Isn't rugby a winter thing?' Rosie had asked vaguely.

They had explained it was a special tournament but she had already lost interest. She had never seen so many similar-looking men before. They were like clones, she thought. They wore matching sweatshirts with a sponsor's logo on the back. All had square jaws and squat, square bodies. All drank the same brand of lager. As the evening wore on they grew more raucous. They bought two pints each to save queuing at the bar. They whistled and shouted at the female images on the television, but when Rosie went to clear the tables they seemed not to see her.

Tonight was even busier than usual because they were one person down. Lindsay, their most experienced barmaid, had called in sick. Frank was grumbling. Rosie, preparing to dive back into the fray to collect glasses, heard him muttering to himself. She grinned. It'll be his age, she thought. Poor old thing. He can't stand the pace.

Just before closing time the crowd suddenly thinned. The rugby team stumbled away to look for a curry or a late-night bar. The holiday makers returned to their B&Bs. In the distance she heard the wail of a police siren. Then Joe came in. Mel wasn't with him.

Rosie hadn't seen him since she'd come back from The Old Rectory with her mother. He hadn't returned her calls and she'd almost given him up. She'd tried to talk to Mel but hadn't got through to her either. Mrs Gillespie always answered the phone – even during the day, which was a sign that something was wrong. Mrs Gillespie was usually as much of a workaholic as her husband, certainly worked the same sort of hours. At first when Rosie phoned, Mel's mum had been evasive – Mel wasn't available and she wasn't sure when she'd be back. Later she'd come clean.

'Look, I'm sorry, Rosie. She's really not very well.'

'I could come round.'

'Not just at present. Maybe when she's a bit better.'

So when Joe turned up at the Prom on his own that night, Rosie wasn't surprised. She pulled him a pint.

'On me,' she said, because she knew he'd have no money, even if he hadn't been on holiday.

He sat on one of the high stools by the bar.

'How's Mel?' she asked, though if she was honest by now she really didn't care. He cared though, which is why she asked.

He shrugged. 'Her mother says she doesn't want to see me.' He looked over the glass. 'I don't know what to make of that woman. When Mel first introduced us I thought she was OK. Smart. Funny. Mel always made out she was some kind of monster but I didn't get it. Now I don't know . . . I've spent the last few days at home waiting for Mel to phone. I'm not even sure if her mother passed on the messages. I had to get out. I need some air. Or space. Whatever . .'

'Why wouldn't she go to Portugal with you?'

'I don't know. She was excited at first. We were all set to go. It must have been something I did.' He went on in a rush. 'I do everything wrong. I always say the wrong thing. Perhaps it would be better if we finished. What do you think?'

Yes, she cried silently. But he didn't want an answer. Not that one at least.

'She's so delicate.' He spoke slowly, struggling for the words, looking to Rosie to help him. 'So fragile. And I'm clumsy. Perhaps she'd be better off without me.'

Then, for the first time in such stark terms, Rosie saw what she was up against. She understood the competition. She was a size fourteen. Healthy. As strong as an ox. She laughed too loudly and could drink Joe under the table. He didn't want that. He was a romantic. Mel was frail and needed looking after. Consumption would have been better, but now that was no longer feasible, anorexia came a close second.

'Well?' he demanded.

She shook her head. What was the point of speaking?

He drank the beer without thanking her. To be fair that wasn't like him and she couldn't use it as an excuse to be mean. She felt like howling but she couldn't freeze him out. No point throwing a wobbly like Mel. Really she'd always known the score.

'My mum's a suspect in a murder inquiry.'

She thought that would grab his attention. It might not have the romantic appeal of anorexia but she thought it deserved some sympathy, some interest. It should take his mind for a moment off Mel's skinny body, her huge and haunting eyes. And he did look up, suitably curious.

She told him about the corpse in the lake. 'He was the love of Hannah's life.' Keeping her voice cynical, though she had been moved by the tale of first love, at least the bits of it which Hannah had told during the drive home.

Frank was getting rid of the last of the drinkers. As she talked to Joe she was washing glasses, holding them over the machine, then standing them on the draining board to dry.

A taxi stopped outside for three of the other barmaids. Frank asked, 'Do you want to go in that?'

'I'll walk home with you,' Joe said, so she shook her head.

She undid her tie and her apron, rolled them into a ball and stuffed them in her bag. Frank waited at the door for the women who were catching the taxi. The driver was getting impatient and hit the horn. They scurried out swearing and laughing. He watched for a moment until the car drove off then he shut the door and switched off the main lights. Even with the door shut they could hear the noise outside. The street was full of people moving from one club to another.

'Fancy a nightcap, you two?' Frank had never suggested anything like that before. Rosie was glad Joe was there. She thought her boss must be lonely. Word in the pub was that his ex-wife was getting funny about access and he was missing the kids. Rosie didn't particularly want a drink. It wasn't that her mum would kick up if she were late. She was always late on a Friday. Sometimes it took over an hour to clear up. Sometimes she went on to a club with her mates. But she was knackered. And she wasn't too proud to want a bit of time with Joe to herself. Joe seemed to take the invitation as an honour though and brightened up.

'Yeah. Great.'

Frank didn't ask what they wanted. He stood by the optic and poured three whiskies. He'd taken off his jacket and as he stood with his hand above his head they could see the flab spill out over his trousers. When he turned round with their drinks he was sweating slightly. He set one of the whiskies in front of Joe.

'Did that bloke ever catch up with your lass?'

'Which bloke?'

'There was a bloke in here a couple of nights back asking after your Melanie.'

Frank kept his voice casual but Rosie could tell he

was desperate to know what had been going on. That was probably why he'd invited them to stay. She thought it was really sad, this need he had to know all their business.

'What sort of bloke?'

'Middle-aged, respectable. A mate of her dad's maybe. I didn't like to say where she lived. He didn't seem that bothered so I expect he had some other way of catching up with her.'

'Perhaps she's into older men.' Rosie had meant it as a joke, but when she saw Joe's face she wished she'd kept quiet.

'Didn't he leave his name?' Joe said.

'No,' Frank had drunk his whisky and was getting another. 'I asked but he seemed in a rush. He didn't even stop for a drink.'

Out on the street Joe took her arm as he often did and steered her through the crowd on the pavement. A middle-aged woman in a see-through leopard-print shirt was throwing up in the gutter. A teenage girl was sobbing on her friend's shoulder. Joe held Rosie's hand and pulled her at a run across the road and on to the sea front. She had learned to take no notice of these gestures of affection but she still enjoyed them.

'Where are we going?'

'The scenic route.' He paused. 'You don't mind going the long way?'

'No.'

There was enough light from the street to see the white line of foam fall on to the beach. They walked in silence. She was thinking of her mother, of the body in the lake. If Joe disappeared into thin air, Rosie thought she'd make some effort to find him. She'd hassle his family, contact the rest of his friends. If they couldn't help she'd go to the police. Yet from what she could gather her mother had done none of these things. Michael Grey had disappeared and she had accepted it without a fuss. That was a very Hannah-like way to behave, but even so it just didn't make sense. She hadn't even been to see the couple Michael had been living with. She hadn't gone to the police. She'd sat her exams as if nothing had happened and then she'd left the area without trying to trace him to say goodbye. And she'd never gone back.

Rosie stopped. Without the noise of their footsteps they could hear the tide dragging back the shingle.

'That stuff I told you about my mother being a suspect in a murder inquiry. It was a joke, right?'

'Of course it was a joke.' He sounded amused. That was all she was to him. One big joke.

'It's just she's had enough to put up with. Everyone talking about my dad . . .'

'I know.' He squeezed her hand.

Of course her mother hadn't killed anyone. She was the least violent person in the world. When Jonathan walked out on her, she hadn't even raised her voice in anger. But it was odd all the same. Her mother couldn't have told the full story. Something had happened.

They had come to the lighthouse, which had been converted years before into an art gallery. It still had a whitewashed wall around it. There was no need for the light now. The rocks in the bay were marked by navigation buoys on the water. Looking back towards the town, they saw the flashing neon which marked the entrance to the funfair, the strings of street lamps, the inevitable blinking blue light of a police car.

From the lighthouse a footpath led inland, skirting the cemetery and arriving at last at the housing estate where Rosie lived. The free drink and the walk seemed to have cheered Joe up. He didn't mention Mel again, or the stranger who had been looking for her. As they sauntered past the cemetery he started making howling, ghostly noises. There were houses banking on to the footpath and Rosie had to tell him to shut up.

Outside her house Joe lingered. If she'd invited him in for coffee, he'd have accepted like a shot. She could tell he was too wired up to go home. But Rosie couldn't bear any more confidences. Not tonight. She might end up confiding in him. A small wind had got up. Down the street a Coke can rattled against the kerb and startled them. The trees threw strange shadows.

'You'd better go,' she said. Then she imagined him turning up at the Gillespie house, making a scene. 'You're not going to try to see Mel?'

'God no.'

He kissed her on the cheek as if she were a favourite aunt. She gave him a quick hug. Then he loped off. Inside her mother was still up, watching a late film on Channel Four, half dozing.

'Sorry I'm late.' Since the drama after the school reunion Rosie had been sporadically worried about her mother. She wasn't getting much support. When Rosie had told her father about the police investigation he'd had difficulty in stopping himself laughing. 'Hannah! Mixed up with the police. God, she'll hate it.'

Yet if the murder had happened recently, everyone would have considered it horrifying. Rosie could tell that the past had become very real to her mother. She seemed to have become lost in it. Hannah said nothing, but Rosie could tell that in the long silences she was reliving it. Now, half asleep in front of the television, she was probably dreaming it too. To bring her back to the present Rosie offered her a piece of information. Usually she never told her mother anything about herself unless she could help it.

'Joe walked me home.'

Hannah stirred at this but wasn't, Rosie thought, sufficiently distracted. Not as distracted as she normally would have been. Usually she took an unhealthy interest in Rosie's relationships with men.

'The police phoned,' she said. 'They want to come here to talk to me. More questions. After work on Monday.'

'I'm sorry. It must be shitty.'

Hannah was usually prudish about language and Rosie expected her to object to the word. Instead she repeated it. 'Shitty. Yes, it is, rather.'

'It can't be important if it can wait until Monday.'

'I suppose not.'

At the top of the stairs there was a landing window which looked over the street. She stopped and looked out, not expecting to see anyone because Joe walked very quickly and would have been long gone. But someone was there, half hidden by a windblown sycamore on the pavement opposite. Her mother called downstairs to ask if the front door was locked. Rosie turned away to answer her. When she looked again, the figure had gone.

Chapter Fifteen

That Monday the weather broke and Hannah went back to work. She woke too early, unrested, to bright sunlight, but by the time she went out to the car the sky was hidden by thin cloud like smoke. She ran back to the house to fetch an umbrella just in case. The prison was five miles to the north. She drove along the coast road towards mountains of cloud. The first rain started just as the barrier lifted to let her into the staff car park. The drought which had brought Michael's body to the surface of Cranford Water was over.

Apart from the weather it was just like any other morning. She queued at the gatehouse with the officers. Some spoke, others didn't. No one realized she'd been away. After she'd collected her keys she bumped into Arthur, who was sheltering from the downpour, blocking the doorway so the officers had to squeeze past. She thought he'd enjoy being an irritation.

'I thought it might blow over. It was fine when I left home. I'm not really prepared.' Grinning at himself, liking looking such a mess.

He was wearing a short-sleeved shirt, jeans and open sandals. Everything was dripping. His dress was another excuse for the education department's disapproval. The principal thought it set the wrong tone. Hannah had heard comments from the inmates too. They didn't know what to make of him. The officers were openly hostile. Despite his lack of hair there were muttered comments in the mess about ageing hippies.

She opened her umbrella and they ran together towards the education block. The rain was a deluge which had already formed a lake over the hard-packed ground. Inside, she walked with him as far as his room.

'Did you have a good break?'

She paused. 'It's a long story.'

'I'm not doing anything for an hour. I can make you a coffee.'

'My orderly will be waiting. Perhaps I could meet you at lunchtime.' She thought she sounded like a teenager suggesting a date, regretted the words as soon as they were spoken.

'Sure,' he said easily. He unlocked his door and went inside, his sandals squelching on the tiled floor.

Marty was waiting outside, his face pressed to the glass door to see if anyone was in the room. There was no porch and by the time Hannah had opened the door he was soaked. He was wearing a thin, prison-issue shirt which clung to him.

'Oh God.' She pulled the hand towel from her cupboard-sized cloakroom and threw it to him. 'I'm so sorry. I went in the other way and I was talking.'

He rubbed his hair and looked like a five-year-old just out of the bath.

'I'll make some tea,' she said, realizing she was staring. 'Warm you up.'

'It's OK, really.' He folded up the towel and handed

it to her, pulled his sodden sleeves away from his wrists.

'Everything been all right?'

'I'm glad you're back. The guy they sent didn't know the ropes. And he didn't want to be told.'

'No bother then?'

He shook his head.

'The lad that kicked off before I went on leave wasn't in?'

'Don't worry. He'll not be back.'

'You've not done anything stupid?' She was thinking threats if not actual violence.

'Nah. Too much to lose. He's out soon. Doing his pre-release course now. He's lucky you didn't say anything and that Dave's a good sleeper.'

Hannah made the tea, handed a mug to Marty.

'I could get used to this,' he said.

'Don't tell anyone. You don't want to spoil my reputation.' Which was, she knew, as a tough bitch, a bad-tempered cow who was OK at sorting out books, would move heaven and earth to track down a requested title, but who wouldn't listen to excuses about lost or damaged copies, would have you up on report for a bit of chewing-gum stuck to a page.

He smiled. The rain hammered on the flat roof, streamed down the windows so it was impossible to see outside. The perimeter wall had vanished. They could have been in a rain-soaked library anywhere.

'Do you mind if I ask what you're in for?' she asked. Suddenly she felt she had the right to know. Perhaps it was that being the subject of a police investigation gave her some fellow feeling. It made her position in the prison more ambiguous.

'Don't you know?'

'I suppose it was in your file. If I ever did know I've forgotten. Look, it doesn't matter. It's none of my business.'

'Manslaughter.'

She thought that was all he was going to say. She didn't blame him for not wanting to go into any detail. She shouldn't have asked. He'd been kind to her and she'd been rude. But he continued.

'It was a fight in a pub. Stupid. I was pissed and I can hardly remember now what started it off. The court accepted it was self-defence. To be honest I think I was bloody lucky. I had a good brief.' He drank the tea. Hannah didn't know what to say. 'The lad I killed had a wife and a baby. Sometimes I think, well he shouldn't have been in the pub then should he? Getting tanked up and gobby, spoiling for a fight. He had responsibilities. He should have been at home. But that's bollocks, isn't it? I can't blame him. You can't blame the victim.'

Hannah thought of Michael Grey. 'No, I suppose not.'

'Listen to me,' he said. 'I sound as if I've been on one of those courses. Victim awareness.'

'And have you?'

'Not here. But I've been through it all. I can talk the jargon standing on my head.'

'Where then?'

He didn't answer directly. 'I've done supervision, care, probation, community service. Spent more time in prison than I've been out. Long enough to know the right thing to say when you're after parole.'

But he'd meant it, she thought. That thing about not blaming the victim. He'd meant that.

'Have you got a release date?'

He shook his head. 'First board comes up next month.'

'Then what?'

'Then I'm going to stay out of trouble. Of course.' He gave a twisted grin. 'That's what all the cons say, isn't it? I bet you've heard it before. "I'm serious, miss. You won't see me in here again." Then a couple of months later, there they are at your reception talk.'

'And you?' she asked. 'Will you be back?'

'No. Not this time.'

'What's different this time?'

'I've grown up, I suppose. About time.'

'And?'

He smiled. 'You're in the wrong business. You should be a cop. You've got a better interview technique than most of them. *And* there's a girl.' He corrected himself. 'A woman. She's an actress. Younger than me but not that much. Dunno what she sees in me. Crazy.' He shook his head in wonder. 'She said she'd wait. This time. No second chances. We got together when I was on bail. My solicitor wangled me a hostel place. She was running a literacy course. A volunteer.'

'Does she visit?'

'Yeah. Regular as clockwork. With a list of books I should be reading.'

'So. A happy ending.'

'For me, yeah. One last chance. Up to me not to blow it. Not so lucky for the guy in the pub.'

Or for Michael Grey, she thought.

'You said you'd been in trouble when you were a kid . . .'

'Oh yes.' Now he'd started talking about himself it seemed he couldn't stop. 'We were the classic dysfunctional family.' She could hear the quotation marks in the self-mockery. 'My dad beat up my mum. My mum left him and took me with her. She couldn't cope so I was in and out of care. Where I met real little thugs. I was brighter than them so I didn't get caught so often. But often enough to go right through the system. I never did drugs but I drank too much, even when I was a kid. It clouds your judgement. If I hadn't been a boozer I'd probably have been a brilliant criminal. But I needed the drink.'

'Did you ever do youth custody in West Yorkshire?' This is ridiculous, she thought. A waste of time. Leave it to the police. But she held her breath while she waited for an answer.

'Why?'

'I'm just after some information.' She wasn't quite daft enough to trust him with the truth. He might keep it to himself, but if it got round the prison that she was involved in a murder inquiry her position would be impossible. 'A long shot. Something came up at the school reunion. Someone we're trying to trace. There's a place at Holmedale isn't there?'

'Yeah. I was there for a few months. It was all right. There was a farm. Pigs. Some of the instructors were OK.'

'When would that have been?'

'Early seventies.' He was older than he looked. 'I'd have been fourteen.'

'The timing would be about right. Like I say, it's a

long shot but do you remember a lad called Michael Grey? Very blond hair. He'd be a few years older than you.'

He paused and she thought for a minute he'd remembered the name from the news reports. But he must have sorted the daily papers without reading them. Certainly he hadn't seemed to have made the connection.

He shook his head. 'It's a long time ago. And I knocked around with so many lads over the years.'

'He might have been using a different name. You'd have noticed him. Posh voice, well educated, bright.'

He used almost the same phrase Stout had done. 'You didn't get many like that in borstal. Nice boys in trouble got probation or were sent off to see a shrink. I think I'd have remembered a lad like that.'

She could tell there was no point pushing it. 'Thanks anyway.'

There was a jangling of keys. Dave the prison officer came in, snug in his uniform waterproof. He raised an eyebrow at them drinking tea and the papers not sorted. Hannah could tell he would have liked a cup himself but was too idle to make it. He took off the coat, shook the water all over the floor and went into the office for his kip.

When Hannah went to find Arthur at lunchtime he was still running a class. He'd got them to pull the tables together and they sat round as if they were at a board meeting. The prisoner who'd pushed over the library shelf was standing at the front, writing on a flip chart with a fat felt-tip pen. This must be the pre-release course. Hannah knew it was feeble but she didn't want to meet him again so she waited in Arthur's office until they all streamed out. There was a list of the men attending the course on his desk, with their dates of birth and release dates. By a process of elimination she identified her troublemaker as Hunter. The next day he'd be gone.

Despite the rain Arthur took her out of the prison for lunch. It was her choice. The food in the officers' mess was cheap but she hated the noise in there, the banter, the unspoken implication that anyone not in uniform was an outsider. They went to a pub in the nearest village. Often that was full of prison staff too, but today it was empty. They sat in the bay window but low cloud hid the view. Arthur went to the bar for drinks and to order food. As soon as he returned he said, 'I'm sitting comfortably. Let's hear the story.'

She didn't know where to start. She would have liked to go back to the beginning, to her first meeting with Michael and the bonfire on the beach. She would have liked Arthur's opinion. He was an expert. But the friendship hadn't developed to the stage of discussing ex-lovers. And besides, they only had three quarters of an hour for lunch.

'Did you meet up with your friends?'

'Yes, and I'll go back. It's broken the ice.'

'But something happened?'

'Yes.' She sounded abrupt and ungrateful – Rosie on a bad day. She'd found it easier to talk to Marty. Arthur was a professional. The reassuring voice, the laid-back manner, these were techniques he'd perfected. He listened to people's confidences for a living. She felt resentful. She didn't want to be one of his clients. Anyway, wouldn't he resent her spilling out all her fears in his lunch break? It was like asking a mechanic to check your brakes in his dinner hour. Still, she couldn't stop now and she stumbled on. 'Did you hear on the news that a body was found in the lake?'

'Exposed after the drought. Yes.'

'I knew him. When I was at school he was my boyfriend.'

There was a minute of silence. It was obviously the last thing he'd been expecting. 'I'm so sorry.' The response seemed genuine. But so, she supposed, would his Monday-to-Friday compassion with the inmates.

'The police think he was murdered.'

'Can they tell after all this time?'

'There's evidence of a knife wound. Apparently.'

'You went to the hills to escape all the crime and punishment thing here, then you ended up with that.'

'I know.' She forced out a laugh. 'As Rosie says, it's shitty.'

'How is Rosie? Is she giving you grief?'

'No. She's being a sweetie.'

There was a slightly awkward pause. 'She seems a nice kid. Protective.'

'She is. Usually. I'm sorry she was so prickly when you met the other night.'

He shrugged. 'Understandable, isn't it?'

A middle-aged waitress approached with the food. She had flat feet and they could hear her as soon as she left the bar. Arthur waited for her to put down the plates and retreat.

'Just because it happened thirty years ago doesn't mean you won't go through the normal stages of bereavement. You're bound to feel anger, guilt, all the usual junk.'

Of course he was right. Hannah supposed she

should be grateful. No one else had given her the right to mourn. But it wasn't what she wanted to hear. It wasn't any of his business. She didn't need a psychologist.

'It was all a long time ago,' she said briskly.

'But you'll have memories. Intense at that age.'

'No danger of forgetting,' she said. 'The police are coming tonight to interview me.'

'Whatever for?'

She was about to make a flippant remark. Something like – Perhaps they think I killed him. But that was too close to the truth. That was what really frightened her. She didn't want to tempt fate by saying it, even as a joke.

'After all this time they can't find out much about him. They haven't even traced his family. They think I can help.'

'Ah.' That satisfied him. He hesitated. 'Would you like me to be there with you? Not to interfere. Just for support.'

It was tempting. If she hadn't dismissed his earlier kindness she would probably have accepted. But she'd decided the body in the lake was none of his business. She couldn't have it both ways.

'No,' she said. 'Really. It's just a few questions.'

She looked at her watch. It was time to go back inside.

Chapter Sixteen

When Hannah got in from work Rosie was in the kitchen and there was a smell of cooking. A wooden spoon hung over the edge of the bench and dripped tomato sauce on to the floor. Pans were piled on the draining board. Hannah moved the spoon. 'This is a surprise.' A nice surprise. Since the end of exams, Rosie had seldom been there to share a meal with her.

'I'm supposed to be at work at seven but if you want me to stay while the police are here I can phone in sick.'

'Don't be silly. You can't do that.'

Usually they ate in the kitchen but Rosie had laid the table in the dining-room with the white linen cloth Hannah saved for Christmas and special events. It was a monster to iron but she didn't suggest changing it. Rosie proudly carried dishes from the kitchen – a tomato and aubergine casserole with a yoghurt topping, a green salad. She'd bought a bottle of wine.

'You should cook more often,' Hannah said.

Rosie smiled.

Afterwards there was the usual scrabble for uniform and she ran off to work. Hannah watched her through the window. Rosie wore a thin hooded jacket which hardly kept out the rain and every so often she looked at her watch and put on a spurt of speed. She ran like a toddler, legs flailing out from the knees. Then she disappeared round a corner and the house seemed very quiet. Hannah was finishing the washing-up when the doorbell rang. There was wine left in her glass and she drank it guiltily before going to the door. Porteous and Stout stood outside. They wore almost identical waterproof jackets. The sight of them – one tall and lanky, one short and squat – reminded her of a music-hall double act.

'Come in.' She had made sure the living-room was tidy before starting on the dishes. The gloom outside had made it seem almost dark and she turned on a table lamp.

'On your own?' asked Stout. He took off his jacket and waited for Hannah to take it.

'There's only my daughter and I. She's at work.' Usually she hated that explanation, but tonight it made her rather proud.

She offered them tea and was surprised when they accepted. She thought it wasn't a good sign. They expected to be here for a long time. On the way to the kitchen she hung the coats in the cupboard under the stairs. Stout's smelled of tobacco and reminded her of the night in The Old Rectory when she'd learned that Michael had been stabbed.

When she returned from the kitchen with a tray the men were perched side by side on the sofa. They sat with their cups and saucers on their knees, looking all prim. Hannah thought they could have been a committee of volunteers, perhaps organizing a charity jumble sale. She had sat on many such committees. It would have been more appropriate for them to interview her in the prison. That was the natural home for what Arthur had called the 'crime and punishment thing'.

'I'm afraid we're no further forward,' Stout said. 'We checked out your idea that Michael might have been in trouble when he was young. I know you thought he might have done time in Yorkshire. But no joy. There is a youth-custody institution near Leeds . . .'

'Holmedale,' she said.

'Holmedale, yes. It was a borstal in those days. But no one called Michael Grey was there in the years in question.'

'I thought you said he must have changed his name.'

'We've tracked down a couple of staff. There's an officer who's since retired and a senior probation officer who was a young welfare officer there at the time. No one recognizes the lad you describe.'

'It was a long time ago and they'd have worked with a lot of boys.' She wondered what made her push it. Marty hadn't known Michael either. Why was she so sure he'd been inside?

'Not many posh ones,' Stout said. 'Not many who go on to take A levels.'

'We've been looking at boarding schools in York-shire too.' Porteous gave a polite little smile as if to say – You see, we did listen to you, we did take your ideas seriously. 'Just in case Michael was telling the truth when he said he'd gone to school there. We started with boarding schools. If his father were a diplomat as you thought, that would be his most likely education. Don't you agree? We've been asking for a list of boys with the same date of birth as Michael gave to the dentist. We've tracked down every individual. They're all accounted for. No one's gone missing. Of course, it's an incomplete picture. Places close, records are destroyed. The team is working through the state schools now.'

'I see.' She didn't know what to say. Did he want a pat on the back for his thoroughness?

'We haven't found the mother's grave yet,' Stout said. 'But that's hardly surprising when we don't have a name, a date or a place.'

That would have been the time to tell them about the cemetery by the lighthouse. It would be possible to explain it away as a stray memory which had returned. But the tone of Stout's voice frightened her. He made it clear he hadn't believed her, that the story of the funeral was a fantasy she'd made up for her own ends. How would he accept she'd forgotten a detail of such significance, something which might finally pin an identity on Michael Grey? The moment passed without her speaking.

'So we thought we'd look at things in a different way,' Porteous said. 'From the other end, as it were. Not looking into Michael's origins but into where he was going. Or where you thought he was going. Because you didn't report him missing either, Mrs Morton, and that does seem rather odd. You had been his girlfriend for a year. We've been speaking to your friends, to teachers at the school, and everyone says you were very close.' He gave a sympathetic smile. 'Deeply, madly in love, someone said. I don't think you'd simply accept his disappearance. So he must have given you an explanation. Perhaps he told you the same story as he'd told the Brices.'

Hannah wondered which friends had been talking to him. The prose style sounded like Sally's.

'No,' she said. 'No story.'

'Oh but there was.' He sounded apologetic, as if he didn't like to contradict her. 'At least there was a story for the Brices. Unless they made it up.'

'They wouldn't have done that.'

'So it was a story they believed, even if it wasn't told to them by Michael himself. Let me explain. You were all sitting A levels. Michael's first exam was art. We know because we've spoken to the school. It hasn't been easy but we've chased up some of his subject teachers. The art teacher is retired but still living in the area. Michael didn't turn up for the exam. He was one of the few pupils in the class predicted to get a top grade. It was a subject he enjoyed, so it wasn't a case of last-minute nerves. The teacher was frantic – perhaps Michael had made a mistake about dates. He phoned the number on the school record and got through to Stephen Brice, who was perfectly calm, who seemed bewildered by all the fuss. "Didn't Michael tell you?" he said to the art teacher. "He's gone back to his father."

'If there was any other information given during the conversation the teacher can't remember it. He assumed it was a case of family illness or bereavement. It must have been something serious, he said, because Michael had been working hard for the exam and was determined to do well.'

Oh yes, thought Hannah, remembering lunchtimes in the art room, watching Michael, smudged with paint, working on his display. He was certainly determined.

Porteous set his teacup carefully on the coffee table. 'You never heard that story?'

She shook her head. 'I didn't see anyone much at that time. I went in for the exams and straight home. As soon as the A levels were finished I left the area. I'd found a summer job in a hotel in Devon. I didn't even come back for the results. They were posted on to me.'

'You must have noticed that Michael wasn't around?'

'Yes. I realized he'd gone. Back to his family, I thought. Dramatically. The way that he'd come.'

'But you didn't go to see the Brices, to ask what had happened, to get a forwarding address?' Porteous was faintly incredulous.

'No.' She hesitated, unsure how much to say. 'It was a bit embarrassing. We'd stopped going out with each other actually. I suppose I didn't want them to think I was chasing him. Pride, you know.'

'A row, was there?' Stout asked. 'Lovers' tiff?'

He said it casually enough, but then they both looked at her in a way that made her realize the answer was important to them. She sensed the danger just in time. Sally hadn't just told them how much in love she'd been.

Hannah matched her voice to his. Kept it light. Implying, You know what dizzy things teenage girls are. 'I suppose so, but I'm blessed if I can remember what it was all about. Not wanting to face the details, even after all this time.'

'Serious though, at that age.'

'Not as serious as passing the exams. That was our priority at the time. That was probably why we fell out.'

'You were jealous of the time he spent studying?'

'I think it was more likely the other way round.'

They looked at her. They were still sitting side by side on the sofa. It was leather. One of Jonathan's affectations. It didn't go in the room at all. Hannah thought of Michael's audition for *Macbeth* – Jack Westcott and Spooky Spence sitting in judgement on the red plastic chairs at the front of the hall. Porteous and Stout were sitting in judgement too. They thought she was lying but they were trying to decide if it was because Michael had dumped her and she didn't want to admit it, or because she had killed him. It was impossible to tell if they'd reached a conclusion.

'Why don't you take us through the last couple of days of his life?' Porteous said.

'Is that possible? Do you know when he died? Exactly?'

'Perhaps not,' he admitted. 'But we know when he disappeared. If we can believe the Brices.'

She was starting to panic. Incoherent thoughts pitched one after another into her brain. She forced out a reasonable voice. 'It's a long time ago. I'm not sure how much I'll remember.'

'We can help you.' Porteous leaned forwards so his elbows were on his knees. He clasped his hands. More like a priest than a cop. Or a counsellor. Not very different in tone from Arthur. 'There was a school play. *Macbeth*. I've seen an old programme. Mr Westcott has kept them all over the years. There was a photograph of Michael – we'll call him Michael for now, shall we? It's different from the one which was in the paper. It's rather faded and grainy, but it gives an impression. He was a striking boy.' He stopped, miming a man who's had a sudden thought. 'I don't suppose you kept a photograph, did you?'

She shook her head. She'd always regretted not having one.

'No? Pity. Still . . !' He seemed lost in a thought of his own, then ditched all the make-believe vagueness. 'The final performance of *Macbeth* was on the Friday night. You were prompting and looking after the props?'

She nodded, remembered like a slow-motion replay the Brices rising in their seats to cheer.

'Did you talk to him that evening? In the interval perhaps, or afterwards?'

'I'm not sure. Probably.'

'So you were still going out with him on the Friday then. So far as you're aware. The disagreement between you must have happened on the Saturday or the Sunday.'

'The Saturday,' she said. She felt she was being boxed in, tricked. She should have claimed not to remember. How could she be expected to have perfect recall of that sort of detail after so many years? But she did remember. She had played the scene over and over in her head ever since.

'You're absolutely certain about that?'

She nodded. She wished suddenly that Arthur were there. So much for pride. They wouldn't push so hard if another person were present. They'd be more circumspect. She wondered if she should refuse to answer their questions, demand to have a solicitor there. But she'd never been much good at demanding. Besides, then they'd assume that she was guilty, that she had something to hide.

Porteous straightened his back and looked satisfied as if it were just as he had supposed. He was taking the lead in the questions. Stout had taken out a soft, thick pencil and was making notes on a shorthand pad. As Porteous had waited for her answer Hannah had heard the lead move over the paper.

'We'll come back to Saturday later,' Porteous continued. 'If you could cast your mind back to the Friday.' He paused, gave her a look of reluctant admiration. 'You do have a most remarkable memory, Mrs Morton. It was the same during our previous conversation. So tell us what happened in the interval. Did all the actors remain backstage?'

'Yes.' An easy question. 'Mr Spence, the producer, was strict about that. There was to be no running around the hall. The PTA organized refreshments for the audience and took juice and biscuits for the actors and crew.'

'But *you* were prompting, I understand, from the front of the audience. It wasn't a traditional stage with wings.'

'That's right.' Good God, she thought. He's a magician. How can he know all this?

He closed his eyes as if he were picturing the scene. 'Did you go backstage in the interval or stay where you were?'

'I stayed in my seat. Mr and Mrs Brice came to speak to me.' That had been a relief. Her mother had been in the audience too, a gesture of support which she should have welcomed. Hannah wouldn't have known what to say to her and the Brices kept her away. Hannah had seen Audrey from the corner of her eye, circling at a distance.

'Did they mention that Michael might be leaving the area?'

'Definitely not. They talked about the play.'

'Of course. So either they didn't know about his plans at that stage – if indeed there were any plans – or Michael had asked them to keep a secret. Otherwise they would have discussed his leaving with you.'

'Yes, I'm sure they would.'

'What did you do after the performance?'

'We walked into town together and bought fish and chips.' Again to avoid her mother. So she wouldn't have to talk to Audrey on the way home. She saw he was astonished that she had remembered a detail like that and added, 'At least I think that's what we did. It could have been another time.'

'What about the props?' he asked. 'Did you clear them up that night?'

She thought, He knows about the knife. Felt the last of her control slipping. Held it together.

'Some of them. While I was waiting for the others to change and take off their make up. A team of us came in on the Saturday afternoon to do the rest.'

'What did you do with all the stuff?'

'Packed it into boxes. I don't know what happened to it then.'

'Did any of the cast keep anything? A souvenir perhaps. Something to remind them of the play?'

She shook her head. She couldn't trust herself to speak.

'Was Michael there that afternoon?'

'No,' she said sharply. 'He was the star. Too grand to muck about with props and costumes.'

Porteous smiled. 'Well that takes us nicely to Saturday evening.'

'There was a party,' she said. 'For the cast and the crew and a few of the teachers who were involved in the production.'

'Mr Spence?'

'I'm not sure. Yes, perhaps he was there.'

'Mr Westcott?'

'I don't think so. It was mostly the younger staff. I believe there was someone from the art department . . .'

'Don't worry. We can check the names if we need to.'

'We weren't allowed the party in school. Not the sort of party at least that we would have wanted. We hired a room on the caravan park. The DJ ran the disco for nothing.' She paused. 'Chris Johnson. He's still around in the town. He's got a record. You probably know him.' She was going to add that he'd been married to Sally but decided that would be petty. They'd find out anyway if they asked around. She watched Stout scribble furiously on his notepad.

'And you and Michael had a row?'

'Not a row.' She'd had enough. She could hear her voice raise a pitch. 'We just decided it would be best if we didn't see each other until after the exams.'

She expected him to probe with more questions but he nodded understandingly.

'Did you see Michael on the Sunday?'

'No. I had an exam the next day. I didn't go out at all. I was working.' It wasn't a lie.

'And on the Monday the Brices told the art teacher that Michael had gone back to his father . . .'

He sat for a moment as if he was musing the significance of the detail for the first time, but it was all show. He must have gone over that information dozens of times before visiting her. He stood up suddenly, seeming to take Stout by surprise. Hannah fetched their coats and showed them to the door. Stout was still stuffing his notebook and pencil into his pocket as he left. It had stopped raining so Stout was able to light his pipe on the way to the car, curling his hand around the match to nurture the flame.

Chapter Seventeen

Frank sent Rosie home early. Perhaps that's what she'd been hoping for when she told him about the police and her mum. He was a good boss. It had been quiet in the pub anyway and she knew she'd been ratty. Raging PMT. Sometimes it got her so she wanted to roar with frustration. Like a huge lioness. She'd made a real effort with her mum earlier so she'd taken it out on Frank and the others at work. No wonder he'd wanted shot of her.

When she got in Hannah was sitting in the living-room. She must have heard the door, but she didn't get up or turn around. There wasn't the usual inquisition about what had happened to Rosie at work. No television. The only light came from a small table lamp. Hannah was sitting in shadow. She'd opened another bottle of wine and nearly finished it. She hadn't got drunk even on the night Jonathan had walked out, but tonight she was ratted. Rosie sat on the arm of the chair and put her arm around her. She took the glass from her hand.

'You'd better let me have that. You're not used to it and you've got work in the morning.'

'I was used to it once. When I was your age.'

Is that how I'll get? Rosie thought. Pissed after a couple of glasses of wine.

'I take it the police came,' she said. 'Was it dreadful?'

'They were all right. Polite. Just doing their job.' Hannah turned to her and Rosie saw lines on her face she'd never noticed before: on her neck and framing the bottom of her jaw. 'But they think I killed him,' Hannah said in the same flat voice. 'They think we had a row and he dumped me and I stabbed him.'

The next day Hannah must have got up in time to go to work but Rosie didn't hear her. She never woke up much before lunchtime unless she was on an eleven o'clock shift. Today she had a day off. She hadn't made any plans.

She was jerked awake by the phone, which didn't stop, even after the seven rings when the answerphone usually clicked in. Her mother must have forgotten to switch on the machine before leaving for work. Rosie got out of bed, saw it was only nine thirty, swore and took the call in Hannah's bedroom. The bed was made, the few clothes left out were neatly folded on the chair. Even with a hangover her mother couldn't bear to leave the house without tidying. Talk about anal.

'Rosie? That *is* Rosie Morton?' The caller had waited so long that he seemed surprised to get a response. She didn't recognize the voice. It was a middle-aged male. Somewhere in the background a woman was talking very quickly.

'This is Richard Gillespie.' She was still fuddled with sleep and didn't answer so he added with a trace of impatience, 'Mel's father.'

'Oh yes. Hi!' She'd never met Mel's father. She'd seen him on the telly, but whenever she was at the house he was working. 'How's Mel?'

There was a pause. 'We've a bit of a problem here. I wonder if you'd mind coming round.'

'Is Mel OK?' Rosie wondered if it was Mel's voice she could hear in the background. If so, she was almost hysterical.

'I don't really care to discuss it on the telephone. Look, if you like I'll come and pick you up.'

'I can walk thanks.'

'As soon as possible then.'

He hung up. She wished she'd put up more of a fight. She thought she knew what it was about. He wanted her to persuade Mel to go into hospital. Mel hated hospital, always had. She'd hinted darkly about past experiences. Rosie imagined scenes from *One Flew Over the Cuckoo's Nest* and wasn't going to force her into something she didn't want. Then she thought there must be something seriously wrong with Mel to keep Richard Gillespie away from his microchip empire. She dialled Joe's number. He might know what was going on. The line was engaged. Was Mr Gillespie enlisting him to do his dirty work too?

Outside, the rain had cleared the air. The sun was shining again but the day didn't feel so humid or sticky. She paused in front of Joe's house, considered calling in to find out if he had any news of Mel. But there was a car in the drive. Joe's mum only worked part-time. Once she'd seen Rosie very drunk and ever since Rosie had sensed the disapproval. She couldn't face it today. Besides, Richard Gillespie had made it clear he expected her immediately and even over the phone she'd found him intimidating.

She loved Mel's house. It was three storeys, set back from a quiet road. An old brick herring-bone wall separated it from its neighbours. At the back there were apple trees and blackcurrant bushes. There was nothing flash or showy about it. The Gillespies had money but didn't feel the need to flaunt it. Even the Volvo parked in the drive was a couple of years old. She thought that showed real style. Jonathan insisted on a new car every year.

Despite all that, Rosie wasn't sure she'd want Richard and Eleanor Gillespie as parents. Perhaps it was because style mattered to them too much. Image at least. Eleanor had made a career out of it. She was head of marketing for the big brewery which owned the Prom. According to Mel she'd been responsible for the huge posters which had recently appeared all over the city, featuring an elephant and a beer bottle and a slogan about gigantic thirst.

Image mattered to Richard too. Rosie had seen him on television talking about his family. The picture he presented was of a close and supportive group. 'Really, I couldn't cope without them.'

How did a nervy anorexic fit in with that? Mel said he had ambitions to go into politics. 'Power. That's what really turns him on.' It must have bugged him that he couldn't turn her into the daughter he wanted.

Richard opened the door to her. She recognized him from the newspaper articles and television reports. He looked younger than Eleanor, hardly old enough to be Mel's dad. She wondered if he dyed his hair.

'Hello. You must be Rosie.' A firm handshake and a smile. Charm on tap. A habit.

He showed her through to the kitchen. It looked over the garden and she thought, as she always did, that you could fit the whole of her house inside it. The style here was farmhouse chic. There was an Aga, a rack of stainless-steel pans hanging from the ceiling, a huge dresser with shelves of glass jars full of beans and pulses. Rosie had never seen either of the parents cook but she imagined them having dinner parties here at the weekends. Of course, the guests would sit at the scrubbed pine kitchen table. Richard would probably do the cooking – Thai perhaps or Mexican. She could imagine him in an apron. Melanie wouldn't be invited. She couldn't be trusted around food.

Mel's mother was sitting in a wicker chair by the Aga. She was wearing leggings and a big sweatshirt – aerobics-class clothes. Rosie knew she belonged to a gym but had never seen her dressed casually before. Without the suit and the make-up she looked like a different woman. She sat with her feet on the edge of the chair, her knees near her chin, her arms clasped around her legs in a sort of foetal coma.

'Where's Mel?' Rosie demanded, thinking from Eleanor's desolation that an ambulance had already come to cart her away.

Eleanor came to life, shifted position, put her feet on the floor. The wicker creaked. 'She didn't come home last night.'

'I thought she might be at your house,' Richard said. 'But obviously not.'

'Have you tried Joe's?' Rosie wasn't quite sure why they were so worried. Not after one night. They weren't usually like Hannah, who panicked if Rosie was half an hour late.

'She's not with him either. But I've asked him to come round. Between us we should be able to work out where she is.'

Rosie sat on one of the reclaimed pine chairs. 'Is there any chance of a coffee? I came straight out.' Usually she wouldn't have had the cheek to ask, but they needed her help, didn't they?

'Of course.' Richard filled the filter machine.

'Where did she go when she left you last night?' Eleanor demanded.

'I didn't see Mel last night. I haven't seen her for days. You said she was too ill.'

'Last night she insisted on going out. She said she was going to the Promenade. It was only down the road, so we thought . . .' her voice tailed off. 'Anyway, we couldn't stop her.'

That explained some of their anxiety. Mel had left in a strop after a fight. They'd be feeling guilty too.

'What time did she leave home?'

'Late,' Richard said. 'She told us she'd just go in for last orders. She knew you'd be working. We thought she'd be all right with you.'

Christ, Rosie thought. As if it's my fault.

He went on. 'It was probably about quarter-past ten. We went to bed soon after, assumed she'd go back to your house or Joe's and let herself in late. It was only this morning when Eleanor got back from the gym that she realized Mel's bed hadn't been slept in.' And had an attack of anxiety and guilt and summoned Richard back from work.

'I'd already left the pub at ten,' Rosie said. 'Frank let me go early.'

'Were any of her other friends in the pub?'

Rosie thought, shook her head. Monday was usually quiet; people spent all their money at the weekend. 'Have you spoken to Frank?'

'Frank?'

'The manager. To check that she arrived there.'

'Not yet. We didn't want to make a lot of fuss until we were sure it was justified.'

'Do you want me to phone him? He needn't know she's missing.'

'Yes,' Richard said. 'That'd be helpful.' Another flash of the smile.

Rosie would have preferred not to have an audience, but they obviously expected her to use the phone in the kitchen. She looked at her watch. Ten o'clock. Frank should be up by now. He answered quickly. 'The Promenade. Frank speaking. How may I help you?' Very brisk and efficient. He must have been expecting a call from his boss at headquarters.

'Hi. It's me. Rosie.'

'Hey, lass. I hope you're in a better mood than you were last night.'

'Did Mel come in after I left?'

'Aye but only to poke her head round the door to ask where you were. I'd have bought her a drink if she'd hung around. She looked like she could do with one.'

'Do you know where she went after?'

'No idea, pet.'

Rosie replaced the receiver. 'Sorry,' she said. Both

Gillespies were staring at her. 'She *was* there but only for a couple of minutes.'

Eleanor gave a little whimper. Rosie felt sorry for her though she'd never much taken to her before. She'd been friendly enough, but in a desperate way. She tried too hard to be one of the girls.

There was a knock on the door. Richard touched Eleanor's hand, extinguishing the hope before it was lit. 'That'll be Joe.'

Joe looked shattered. He was still wearing his uniform from the supermarket. It had been one of his nights for work. Any other time Rosie would have teased him about the shiny grey trousers, the blazer with the company logo on the breast pocket.

Now she just said, 'You must have had time to change.' His night shift finished at seven thirty.

'It's been a nightmare. I borrowed my mum's car. It broke down on the bypass on my way home. It took the AA an hour and a half to get there and then they couldn't fix it. By the time they'd got it to the garage . . .' He stopped, shrugged, turned to the Gillespies. 'Anyway, I got your message.'

Richard seemed to have forgotten about the coffee. Rosie tipped some into a mug, waved the jug towards the others.

'Yeah,' Joe said. 'Thanks.' She poured one for him and replaced the jug on the hotplate.

'Mel's gone missing,' Rosie said. 'She came to see me at the Prom but I wasn't there. She didn't come to your house? It would have been between ten thirty and eleven.' She felt the need to take charge. Even Richard seemed to have given in to lethargy. He was staring out of the window.

'It was one of my regular work nights,' Joe said. 'She might have forgotten and gone to the house but no one would have been there. Mum and Dad were at the theatre and Grace spent the night with a mate.' Grace was his thirteen-year-old sister.

They sat round the table looking at each other. Eleanor had moved away from the Aga to join them. Richard was at the head. He dragged his attention away from the garden. The chairman of the board, Rosie thought, trying to hold his team together.

'She has other friends,' he said. 'She'll have wanted to teach us a lesson. That's what this is all about. It would be best if the kids phoned around.' He looked at Rosie and Joe. 'You know the names and the numbers and they'd be more likely to tell you the truth.'

They started with a pretence of enthusiasm, but soon it was obvious to them both that Mel wasn't with any of the usual gang. Eleanor would have had them phoning all day. It was Joe, hollow-eyed and fraught, who said, 'Look, I think you should go to the police.'

Eleanor and Richard shot a look at each other which Rosie couldn't interpret.

'This evening,' Richard said. 'I promise. If she's not back this evening . . .'

Soon after, they left – Rosie to town to check on some places Mel might be and Joe to sleep. They were standing, talking together on the corner of the street before going their separate ways, when the Volvo pulled out of the drive and accelerated away. Richard Gillespie off to do some other deal. Rosie imagined Eleanor Gillespie curled up again in the wicker chair waiting for the phone to ring or the door to open.

Chapter Eighteen

Hannah's father had been cremated. Her mother had wanted the whole business over quickly, without any fuss. Hannah remembered the undertaker coming to the house to discuss arrangements. He was young, with impeccable clothes and a nervous cough. Perhaps Edward had been his first suicide.

'No fuss,' Audrey said immediately, before he had a chance to sit down. 'No show.'

'Nothing in the papers then?'

'Certainly not.'

'Flowers?'

'No!' She spoke very fiercely and he asked no more questions.

Hannah and her mother stood alone in the crematorium and watched the flimsy coffin slide behind the curtains. Afterwards they went home for tea and Battenberg, a cake Edward had always particularly disliked.

Michael's mother, however, had been buried. There had been mourners dressed in smart clothes, a black limousine which had taken Michael from wherever he had been living as a child to a church and then to the cemetery by the lighthouse. Had he mentioned a church? Hannah thought he had. The crocuses on the lawn, a church filled with weeping people, then another ride in the car to the cemetery.

Hannah had felt lousy all day. The encounter with the detectives had left her with a thick head and a jumpiness verging on paranoia. She was frightened that they'd turn up at any time to ask more of their questions. In the prison Marty saw at once that she wasn't well and had the kettle on before she asked him. She was tempted to seek out Arthur at lunchtime but something stopped her. More pride. She didn't want to admit to a hangover at her age. She didn't want him analysing her problems, coming to conclusions about her weakness and loneliness. She'd always been a person to give support, never to need it.

When Hannah got home, the house was empty. There was a cryptic note on the table from Rosie saying something urgent had come up and she'd be back by eleven. Hannah'd had nothing to eat all day but she couldn't face supper. She couldn't settle. So she went for a walk to the cemetery to look for Michael's mother.

Michael hadn't started school when his mother died. She was sure of that. It was the way he'd spoken of the wrench of her going into hospital. She must always have been around before. So, Hannah thought, when his mother died Michael would have been five at the oldest, three at the youngest. His memories had a clarity and sophistication which would have been unlikely in a toddler. The death would have occurred between forty to forty-two years previously. Even then it would have been unusual for a woman to die so young. Perhaps on the headstone there would be mention of a child. At the very least, Hannah thought, she should be able to provide Porteous and Stout with a short list of possible names. Information for the team to check, to get them off her back.

She walked along the sea front towards the lighthouse. The salty breeze and the smell of seaweed cleared her head for the first time that day. The car ferry from Bergen slid past on its way to the dock further up the river. Hannah remembered a family holiday in Norway. Rosie had been six. She'd been sick on the boat. Jonathan had sulked all week because the food in the farmhouse hadn't lived up to his expectations and he hadn't been able to get hold of a decent bottle of wine. Even before the arrival of Eve the temptress it hadn't been much of a marriage. 'You'll be better off without him,' her friends said. Until now it had been too much like admitting failure to agree.

The cemetery was almost empty. In the distance a workman was mowing the grass paths but the sound of the machine hardly reached her. At first she wandered aimlessly, her attention caught and held by unusual names, ornate carvings, simple messages of bereavement. Then, as the shadows lengthened she brought more order into the search. The modern graves – those dug within the last twenty years – were at the far end, the furthest inland. Those could be ignored. The remaining plots were in a more random jumble. There seemed to be no chronological order. The space was divided occasionally by a high cypress hedge or a stone arch. Rooks were gathering in the trees which separated the graveyard from the road. She walked up and down the lines of headstones to the jarring sound of the rooks, moving on quickly if the deceased were a man or too old, only stopping for a woman and if the date was right.

Most of the women had been elderly when they died. Most, it seemed, had been widows. The Elsies, the Mays and the Maggies had all joined dear departed husbands. She had almost given up hope when she came across one which fitted her dates. The grave had been planted with ivy and she pulled the plant away from the headstone to read the letters. Frances Lumley, aged thirty, daughter of Elizabeth and Miles. Hannah crouched on her heels to clean the rest of the text, convinced that her search was over. But Frances Lumley had been drowned at sea and there was no mention of a husband or child. And she had died in September, not a season for crocuses.

Michael's mother was buried in the grave next to Frances Lumley's and, despite her care, Hannah nearly missed it. In comparison to Frances's headstone the white marble was clean; the engraving looked as if it had been chiselled the day before. And there were fresh flowers in a brass pot which gleamed in the last of the sunlight. At first she thought this was a new grave, slotted in amongst the others to fill a space. It was only when she read the date that she saw the occupant had been buried the year after Frances. She had died on 19 February.

So there were relatives who lived near enough to tend the grave. She hadn't expected that. She still thought of Michael as he had been then. Quite alone. With only her and the Brices to care for him.

She read aloud. 'Maria Jane Randle née Grey. Daughter of Anthony and Hester. Beloved wife of Crispin and mother of Theo.' The facts were as bold as the carving. There was no comforting verse or religious text.

She knew her search was over. If she had opened the shoebox in Michael's bedroom on that day after school she would have found a birth certificate, and probably a passport too, in the name of Theo Randle. She couldn't guess where Michael – because that was how she would continue to think of him – had filched his first name. The family name he'd taken from his mother's parents. All the same she continued her walk past the last two lines of graves. She had to be sure and she hated a job half done. There were no other women of the right age buried in the place. She returned to Maria's grave and though she could remember them by heart she jotted down the details of her death and her birth, copying the engraving word for word. The sun had almost gone and she was starting to feel cold.

Hannah hadn't managed to eat anything after her interview with the detectives the night before, and after her walk along the sea front she was starving. In the town she queued up with the trippers to buy fish and chips and sat on a bench looking over the sea to eat them. She finished everything, even the thick pieces of batter she usually left behind, and licked her fingers. She had to pass the Prom on her way home and looked through the open door, thinking that Rosie's urgent appointment might involve a drink with her friends. But there was no sign of her or of anyone else Hannah recognized.

She had intended phoning Porteous as soon as she got home, had been gearing herself up to it all the way home. But when she got in the answerphone was blinking and there was a message from Arthur. 'Hi, I was hoping to see you today. How did you get on last night?' The taped voice had a stronger Liverpudlian accent than she remembered, was even more mellow and laid back. He'd left his home number and she dialled it quickly before she thought too much about it. He answered after a couple of rings. 'Hi,' again, as one of the kids would. Her mother, who'd been very strong on telephone etiquette, would have had a fit.

'Arthur. It's me. Hannah. Are you doing anything?'

'Nah, a couple of reports. Nothing interesting. Nothing urgent. And have you seen what's on the telly?'

'Would you come over? I could do with your advice.' She felt breathless. She thought he must be able to tell from her voice how nervous she was.

'Do you want to go for a drink?'

'Not a drink, no.' The idea of alcohol turned her stomach. Even the fish and chips seemed a mistake. 'Would you mind coming to the house?'

She gave him directions then sat and waited, thinking she'd made a fool of herself. Melodrama wasn't her style. It didn't suit her. He'd think, as Jonathan had done, that she was menopausal and hysterical. Or he'd get the wrong idea entirely and see her as one of those pathetic women, recently dumped, who'd do anything for the company of a man.

He arrived sooner than she'd expected. It hadn't given her time to work out what to say so she opened the door and stood awkward and tongue-tied in the hall.

'Are you OK?' He'd come out so quickly that he was still wearing carpet slippers – battered suede moccasins. Jonathan would never wear slippers. He said they were old men's garments, like pyjamas.

She began an explanation for calling him, but stumbled over the words. He put his arm around her.

'Hey. What is it?'

She pushed him away gently. 'Look, I'm really sorry to have dragged you out.'

'Just tell me what's going on here.'

So she sat him on the sofa where the night before Porteous and Stout had played their double act and she told him about it – about Michael Grey whose real name was Theo Randle, about the detectives who thought she was a murderer, about her discovery of Maria Randle's grave in the cemetery. He listened. He didn't move or give any of the usual verbal encouragements to prove he was listening, but she could tell she had his full attention.

'Can you be sure,' he asked, 'that Theo's the same person as Michael?'

'There's no other explanation. Maria's the only person buried in the cemetery who could be his mother. His memory of the funeral was so clear and precise that I'm sure he was telling the truth. And it can't be a coincidence that he chose Maria's maiden name as his surname.'

'Of course, you'll have to tell the police.'

'I know. But what will they think? I could have told them at the first interview that Michael's mother was buried there.'

'They'll think you were in shock, intimidated. I don't suppose they're stupid. They know how law-abiding people can react to police questioning.' He stretched his legs. He was wearing paint-stained sweat pants. He'd bought a cottage near the prison and seemed to have been decorating for months. 'Do you want to phone now, while I'm here? Then I can stay if they want to come to talk to you.'

'Yes.' Again she knew she was being pathetic but she couldn't help it. 'Are you sure that's all right?'

The phone was answered by a young woman who said that Porteous was no longer in the office. She was polite but distant. Any secretary talking about any middle manager. Was it urgent? She could find someone else to speak to Hannah. Otherwise, if Hannah wanted to leave a message she could be put through to his voicemail.

'Yes.' It was some sort of reprieve. 'I'll do that.'

She listened for the beep. 'Hello. This is Hannah Morton. I've remembered something which might be useful for you. Perhaps you could get in touch.' She replaced the receiver. Arthur pulled a face of mock disappointment.

'Bugger. So I miss out.'

'What do you mean?'

'I was hoping for the chance to play detective.'

'You can't be serious?'

He put out his hands, palms up, a gesture of being caught in the act. 'OK I admit it. I love crime fiction. I'm a sucker for all those crappy cop shows on TV.'

'This is hardly the same!'

'I know.' He paused, continued slowly, a dream confided. 'I've always thought I'd make a good psychological profiler. At least in my work I meet real criminals and I'm not sure how many academics could say the same.'

'You're welcome to be here when the police talk to me.'

'Right.' He paused. 'What about making a few enquiries on our own? While we're waiting for the police to get in touch?'

'This isn't a game, Arthur. Not for me.'

'I know.'

But she couldn't bear to disappoint him. It was like when Rosie *really* wanted something. She always gave in. She thought, Being a mother is like trying to please the world.

'What did you have in mind?'

'We might find something which would divert attention away from you . . .'

'That's an excuse.'

'What about having a shot at tracing the boy's father? I don't mean camping out on his doorstep. Just finding out where he is.'

'How would you go about that?'

'Through the records office, the archives of the local paper. There may have been a death notice when Maria died, an address. If the Brices said Michael was going to meet his father just before he died I'd say Crispin Randle makes an adequate suspect. If we hand him to Porteous on a plate it'll give him someone else to harass.'

'Why would he kill his own son?'

'Why would he desert him? We'll have to find out.' He was like an overenthusiastic boy. Michael was a stranger to him. A puzzle to be untangled. He must have sensed her reservation, her distaste. 'God,' he said. 'What an insensitive git. Look, I'll clear out and leave it to the police.'

'No,' she said. He must have known she would give in eventually. 'You play detective. If it makes you happy.'

Chapter Nineteen

Rosie spent the day looking for Mel in some of the places she could be lying low. There were days when Mel couldn't face the Prom. Then she'd turn her back on her friends and Frank's teasing and she'd go walkabout. Usually she wanted to be on her own but sometimes on the trawls around town she'd take Rosie with her. She didn't speak much. She just waited for Rosie to follow her round the arcades, the sleazy snack bars, the tiny back-street pubs where a couple of pensioners sat all evening in silence. Everywhere people seemed to know her. Rosie stuck with her because in that mood Mel frightened her.

Rosie went first to the snack bar next to the bus station. A Formica shelf ran shoulder-high around the room and there were tall stools bolted to the floor. A water heater steamed behind a counter. The windows ran with condensation. There was a smell of frying bacon, which made her want to throw up.

A pimply youth was wiping tables with a grey cloth.

'Hey, Robbie. Seen Mel?'

Robbie was one of Mel's admirers. She had them everywhere, picked them up. Robbie was from Edinburgh, had run away from a loutish stepfather and lived now in a hostel run by a children's charity. Rosie had never talked to him about any of this but Mel had told her. Robbie was passionately in love with Mel. You could tell by the way that he blushed whenever she spoke to him. Mel encouraged him. He was into Idle-wild and they'd talk about album tracks, Mel strumming an imaginary guitar, the boy banging out a rhythm on a tabletop until the manager came out from the back to shout at him.

'No.' He squirted cleaner from a spray, turned his back to her. He could be lying. If Mel had asked him to, he'd lie.

'Her parents are worried about her. They're talking about getting in the police.'

He faced her. 'Really. I haven't seen her for ages.' He seemed scared, but perhaps that was the talk of the police.

'If you see her, tell her to get in touch. With me or Joe if she's not up to going home.'

He nodded. His face was blank. Years of practice at not letting on what was going on in his head.

The amusement arcade was next to the funfair, old fashioned in the same sort of way. It was decorated in red and gilt and a cashier sat in a booth in the entrance. Mel said the booth reminded her of one of the windows in Amsterdam where a prostitute would sit. Carol, the cashier, wasn't one of Mel's admirers and the hostility was mutual. Mel went to the arcade to play the machines, not to chat. Carol was a middle-aged, once-upon-a-time blonde, a single mum. She was outraged by the money Mel lost; enough, she'd say, to feed her kids for a week. Mel didn't taken kindly to the lectures. She played the machines as if nothing else mattered, completely focused on the patterns which spun before her. The money was irrelevant. Sometimes she left her winnings in the tray and had to be reminded to go back for them.

On rainy days the arcade was packed. Today there was a middle-aged couple playing on the penny scoop and a few teenage lads bunking off school. Carol waved to Rosie. She got bored out of her mind imprisoned in her booth and she wanted the company. She'd keep you talking all day given the chance.

'Mad Mel not with you then?'

'No. I was wondering if she'd been in.'

'I've not seen her since she went away on holiday. Portugal, was it? Did she have a good time?'

'She didn't go in the end.' Rosie inched her way towards the door. She couldn't face explanations.

Carol seemed to realize she'd not get much more from the conversation and picked up a copy of *Hello!* magazine from a shelf under her desk. She began to flick over the pages. Her nails were sugar pink. She looked up once more to flutter the nails in Rosie's direction to wave goodbye.

It was early afternoon. Joe would still be sleeping. Rosie tried a couple of pubs without much hope. There was one in a back street, near the health centre, run by an ex-jockey, a little wizened old man with no teeth. Another of Mel's fans. The bar was full of men studying form in the racing pages. Rosie had never been able to understand why Mel went in the place. She had become a sort of mascot. She sat at the bar on a wooden stool and the punters asked her advice, though she admitted she knew nothing about horses or racing. Today her stool was empty.

'She needs looking after,' said the landlord

sentimentally when Rosie explained that Mel had gone missing. 'Proper loving care.'

Rosie thought secretly that Mel had been loved too much, spoilt rotten at least. But she kept that opinion to herself.

She walked down the steep hill from the health centre towards the sea front. Terraces of pastel-painted guest-houses ran away from the road. In the windows were signs saying 'Vacancies' and 'Contractors welcome'. On the corner was the hostel where Robbie lived. A young woman was hanging sheets out on the washing line. Rosie thought Mel could hide herself away in this town for months if she wanted to. The Gillespies would make sure there was money in her bank account. Eleanor obviously wanted her found, but Rosie thought Richard wouldn't pry too much as long as he knew she was safe and she didn't cause a fuss which could be picked up by the press. At the sea front Rosie crossed the road and went down to the level of the beach. The traffic became a distant hum above her.

The Rainbow's End was a café, two arches cut out of the bank of the promenade. It was run by middle-aged drop-outs selling organic food and herbal teas and it was one of Melanie's favourite haunts. She said it was like a cave. She would sit near the counter, as far away as possible from the natural light, her back turned to the sea. She'd drink decaffeinated coffee and smoke roll-up after roll-up although there was a big sign saying NO SMOKING. Maura, who ran the place, turned a blind eye. Another example of one rule for Mel and another for the rest of the world. In the Rainbow's End, Mel was drawn to the food. Sometimes she'd buy a slab of carrot cake. She'd sit and look at it, a paper napkin folded on her lap, but she'd never eat. In the end she'd push the plate across the table towards Rosie.

'I don't feel hungry. You have it.'

Rosie was always hungry but she didn't know what to do for the best so the cake would sit there, the cream-cheese topping slowly melting, until they left.

Maura was a big woman, an earth mother in an Indian-print caftan and beads woven into her hair. She looked out for Mel. If the café was quiet – which it usually was – she'd sit with her and talk earnestly about the things which would 'get her head straight'. Things like plant remedies, hypnosis, acupuncture. Mel would listen with a bored expression on her face. So far as Rosie knew she never followed up any of the suggestions.

Today two young women sat near the window. The tide was in, right up to the concrete walkway, and it felt like being in a boat. The women had children with them – a toddler apiece in pushchairs and a baby in a sling. Maura was going gooey-eyed over the baby, talking about the benefits of terry nappies and breast milk. The women agreed about the breast milk at least. They all seemed very smug.

Perhaps that was Mel's problem, Rosie thought facetiously. She probably wasn't breastfed.

She interrupted the baby talk and ordered a sandwich – mozzarella, tomatoes and basil on ciabatta.

'Has Mel been in?'

Maura shook her head. 'Not today.'

'Yesterday?' In the evenings the place had a licence. It sold veggie meals and organic wine in candlelight.

So you couldn't see what you were getting. Often there was live music.

'Yes. Last night. First time in ages. She stopped for one beer and then she left.'

The Rainbow's End only had a table licence but that had never bothered Mel.

'Was anyone with her?'

Maura shook her head again. The beads and the braids swung and clacked. 'I felt a bit mean actually.' She had a surprisingly classy voice, very deep and well modulated. 'She wanted to talk. But we were busy. We'd hired a student band and they'd brought all their friends. You know what it's like.'

Rosie didn't really. She didn't go there in the evening. She thought the people and the music a bit pretentious. She liked something you could dance to.

'How did she seem?'

'Not brilliant. A bit jumpy. Sort of desperate actually. I let her have the drink and told her to wait. Adam was on his break. I thought when he came back I'd take her out for a walk, calm her down a bit. But when I looked again she'd gone. She didn't even bother to say goodbye.'

When Rosie had finished the sandwich there didn't seem much point in staying and she couldn't think of anywhere else to look. She went home and snoozed on the sofa in front of a black and white movie. She didn't want to talk to her mother – she couldn't face the fuss of explanation – so she wrote her a note and at five o'clock she went round to Joe's. Joe's sister Grace let her in. She was a gawky thirteen-year-old with pointed elbows like the legs of a tree frog and a mouth full of metal brace. Grace yelled up the stairs. There was no answer. She shrugged.

'He's in. You'd better go up.'

Joe's room was in the attic. It had a sloping roof with a big velux window and even more crap on the floor than Rosie's. Divine Comedy was rolling away in the background.

'I was just going out,' he said, guilty because he'd been sleeping all day while Mel was missing.

'I've been everywhere I can think of.' She sat on the bed.

'Anything?'

'She went to the Rainbow's End after the Prom. Maura said she was a bit jumpy, but nothing new there . . . It was a student gig. Maybe she met some-one . . .'

There was a pause.

'The police think she might have been kidnapped.' He couldn't keep a shiver of excitement from his voice. He was still worried but kidnapping was some-thing out of the movies, glamorous even.

Rosie frowned. 'The Gillespies went to the police?'

'Eleanor did. I think she cracked. Richard didn't sound very happy. I phoned just now and I could hear him in the background. He says everyone's overre-acting.'

So do I, Rosie thought. I think she picked up a bloke at the Rainbow's End out of boredom or desperation or devilment. She's hiding out in a hall of residence or a grotty bedsit, waiting for the maximum fuss before making her appearance. Rosie wouldn't have told Joe but it wouldn't be the first time Mel had gone home with someone she'd met on one of her walkabouts.

'Why do they think she was kidnapped?'

'Apparently it's not much more than a theory. Eleanor and Richard are high-profile parents. And there was a case a couple of months ago. The kidnappers got away with a half a million. Since then there has been a spate of copycat attempts. Mostly amateurs, the police say. Mostly easy to deal with.' He paused and sat beside her on the bed. His feet were bare. She could see every bone and joint under the skin. 'Do you remember Frank saying someone was in the Prom looking for her? An older bloke.'

'Yes. Do the police think he might have been the kidnapper?'

'I told Eleanor anyway. It's up to them. She thought they might want to talk to us sometime.'

'Me too?'

'Why not? You know her as well as anyone. You're best mates.'

Suddenly she felt sick with guilt. She remembered the good times. The girlie sleepovers with bottles of wine and soppy videos, the gossip about lads, mega shopping sessions in the city. She imagined Mel being held somewhere and what they might be doing to her. And she'd been thinking it was all some attention-seeking stunt.

'Let's go and look,' she said. 'Just in case. I can't sit here doing nothing.'

They spent the evening in the city, tramping through all the pubs, even those Mel had never set foot in so far as they knew. They asked in the arcade and the pizza places and the roller-skating rink. No one had seen her. They ended up with Maura in the Rainbow's End, shouting their questions over a flamenco guitar. Had there been an older guy in the night before? Anyone taking a special interest in Mel? Maura tried to answer their questions but in the end she got fed up with them and sent them home.

Joe walked Rosie all the way to her door. On the step he held on to her in a desperate bear hug. She pushed him away in the end, feeling confused and guilty. As guilty as if she'd played some part in Mel's disappearance.

Chapter Twenty

Hannah had been expecting Arthur to be waiting for her at the prison but she went through the gate to the library without seeing him. It was halfway through the morning when he bounced in.

'Can you spare a minute?'

She turned to Marty. 'Are you OK on your own? Dave's in the office.'

Marty rolled his eyes towards the ceiling. 'Is that supposed to be reassuring?'

'Well . . .'

'Go on. I'll be fine.'

They sat in Arthur's office drinking coffee. He was a different man: the super-cool Scouser had gone; he was bubbling, the words falling over themselves. She regretted her impulse of the night before to involve him. She could tell there would be no stopping him now.

'I've been to the Central Library, tracked down the back copies of the local rag. It's great that they've still got them.'

'Aren't they all on microfilm?' She wanted to slow him down, rein back some of the enthusiasm. Stop, she wanted to say. You don't know what you're getting into.

'Mm?' The interruption only checked him for a moment. 'It's amazing what you can find in the births, marriages and deaths columns.'

'You haven't wasted any time.'

'I started with Maria's death. The notice said she died after "a brave struggle with illness". Cancer isn't mentioned but that's the implication.'

'That would fit in with Michael's memories.'

'Then I went back a few years and found the report of her marriage. A front-page spread. Obviously a big do. The wedding of the season. Crispin Randle seems to have been a member of the local gentry. He owned land not far from here. He was an MP. Tory of course. Master of the Hunt. You know the sort of bloke. He married Maria Grey in 1952. Two years later Theo's birth was announced. He was named Theo Michael, so I don't think there's any doubt we're on the right track.'

She nodded, felt irrationally pleased that she could continue to think of her ghost as Michael.

'I almost gave up the search then. I mean, I'd got enough for the police to be going on with. But I thought Randle was still a young man. What if he'd re-married . . .'

'And had he?' Just to show she was still listening.

'Yeah. Three years later. That wedding was a much quieter event. The bride was Stella Midwood, who'd been working as his secretary. A year later they had a daughter, Emily.'

The names and dates washed over her. She thought she'd have to write it all down like a family tree to make sense of it.

'Why didn't they have Michael to live with them?' she asked. 'Why board him out with the Brices?'

'Wait. There's more drama to come. In 1964 when Theo Michael was ten, there was a fire in the family home. It was big news. The place was burned to a shell and Emily, the little girl, Michael's stepsister, was killed. Crispin Randle sold the estate and some months later he resigned his seat in the Commons. Michael isn't mentioned in the account of the fire or the resignation.'

'Is that significant?'

'Dunno. Perhaps it was too painful for Crispin to have him around. Perhaps Michael reminded him of the death of his first wife and his daughter. Perhaps Crispin had some sort of breakdown and couldn't cope.'

'Michael was only ten!'

'Old enough to be shipped off to boarding school.'

'Why did he come to Cranford then? And why the change of identity?'

Arthur shrugged. 'Teenage rebellion? It's possible he didn't get on with his stepmother. Perhaps he resented the way his father dumped him.'

'Perhaps.' It's all guesswork, she thought. Really, despite Arthur's excitement we're not much further forward. 'Do we know where Stella and Crispin are living now?'

'There's no record. But the police will find out easily enough. We've done all the hard work for them.' He hesitated. 'Don't you have an early finish today?'

'Why?' She knew he wanted something from her. Living with Rosie had given her a sixth sense about people bumming favours.

'What about going to Cranford? This afternoon. We

can give all this information to Porteous in person.
That'll stop him hassling you.'

Who are you kidding? she thought. That's not what
this is about. This is about you showing off to the
police. You want the glory. You want to sit there and
gloat.

'We could stay the night. I could meet your
friends. We could be back in time for work tomorrow.'

'Go on then.' She couldn't think of an argument
against it and, as Rosie knew, she'd always been an
easy touch.

She phoned Porteous from the library. Dave had
sloped off and Marty pretended not to listen.

'Mrs Morton,' Porteous said. 'I was hoping to speak
to you. More questions I'm afraid. Something's come
up.'

'I can't talk now. I'm at work.' She couldn't face an
interview over the phone. She wanted Arthur there.

He said he was tied up all day and that he'd come
to The Old Rectory in the evening. She sensed he was
preoccupied and wondered if there'd been a development in the case. Perhaps he'd discovered Michael's
background without Arthur's help.

Later she phoned Sally and asked if she could put
the two of them up for the night as paying guests.

'A double room?' Sally asked mischievously. 'The
honeymoon suite?'

'Of course not!' Hannah thought her humour hadn't
developed since they were children. She'd always been
a tease about sex.

Arthur hadn't quite finished his class when she
arrived at his room at lunchtime. Some form of role-

play was going on. Hannah walked back down the corridor so she wouldn't be tempted to watch. She found that sort of exercise embarrassing enough without spectators, though she'd come to realize that Arthur liked play-acting and games.

He admitted as much in the car. He'd been asking about the people who'd been around at the time of Michael's death. She described Roger Spence, Sally and her disc-jockey boyfriend, Stephen and Sylvia Brice. By the time they arrived at The Old Rectory she had the feeling that he knew them as well as she did and probably understood them better.

'What's all this about, Arthur?' It was her librarian, who's-been-turning-down-the-page-corners voice. 'I really think we should leave it to the police.'

'Come on, girl. Don't spoil my fun.' She was about to say tartly that it wasn't fun for her when he added, 'I might leave it to them if I could be certain they'd get it right.' He paused. 'You must have met men inside who don't deserve to be there.'

'I've met men who *say* they don't.'

'Well, I don't want any cock-ups in this case.' He smiled but she wasn't reassured. He worked for the Home Office. He should have had more faith in the system.

It was just after two when they arrived. Hannah had expected Sally to be at work but she was there to meet them. Curiosity about Arthur, Hannah thought, and a nose for a story. Sally hustled them into the dining-room and organized a late lunch. Later, over coffee, Roger joined them too.

They talked about Michael Grey. It was Arthur's

doing, but perhaps the Spences were eager to talk about him anyway. Sally had her own agenda.

'I had the impression he'd come from the private system,' Roger said, 'but his Latin wasn't up to much. Hardly prep-school standard. Not what you'd expect.'

'Was he doing Latin A level?' Arthur gave the impression he was just being polite. Hannah knew better.

'No, but I dragooned him in to help with one of my first-year groups. In the end I let him go. He wasn't any use at all.'

'Perhaps he just wanted his free period back.'

'Perhaps. I don't think so. It's quite hard to fake genuine ignorance, isn't it?'

'How did you get to know him if you didn't teach him?'

'Through the school play. I coached him. Individual rehearsals.'

'Were you surprised when he disappeared?'

'Not very surprised. Not at first. He liked mysteries. I remember one session when I talked about him bringing his own experience into his acting. He said he was already doing that but he refused to discuss his past with me. I was more surprised when he never returned. I kept expecting him to turn up out of the blue to astound and amaze us.'

Arthur turned lazily to Sally. 'How well did you know him?'

'Only as Hannah's boyfriend. And I'm sorry, pet, but I didn't really take to him. He was a bit arty-farty for me. There was too much pretence.'

'Whereas you . . .' Roger interrupted, 'you had your own bit of rough.'

She laughed, not offended in the slightest. 'Quite right,' she said. 'And very nice it was too. You'll be able to meet him tonight, Arthur. Chris. My ex-bit-of-rough.'

She narrowed her eyes. Hannah thought Sally knew what he was up to. Perhaps journalists and psychologists had similar techniques when it came to ferreting out a story.

Sally continued, 'There's a wedding party in the annexe and Chris is doing the disco. He's still playing the same sort of gigs. I think it's a bit sad that he's never moved on.'

In the afternoon they left the car at the hotel and walked to the lake. There was a footpath through an old deciduous wood and then a strip of forestry-commission plantation. The footpath was overgrown and looked as if it must have been there in Hannah's time, but she couldn't remember having used it, and at the lakeside everything was so different that she found it hard to get her bearings. A group of teenagers in orange life-jackets stood where once Chris had bought her vodka. A woman was spelling out the rules of safety on the water, shouting to get their attention. Hannah thought that if they capsized they'd be able to walk back to the shore. The water level was even lower than she'd expected. The beach, which she'd remembered as a narrow strip of sand, had widened to an unsightly expanse of mud, rock and shingle. The trainee sailors had to push their dinghies to the water on trolleys, lifting them occasionally over the larger rocks. A new island had been formed at the north end of the lake.

She didn't know what Arthur hoped to gain by the walk. A sense of place perhaps. She'd told him about her first romantic encounter with Michael by the bonfire on the beach. But this scene, on a sunny afternoon, with the giggles and squawks of the school party coming to them over the water, had nothing in common with the night after the exams. She felt it was an anticlimax. She'd waited so long to come back and now it meant nothing. Arthur seemed dissatisfied by it too, because he sat for a moment in the sun then suggested that they return to The Old Rectory by the lane. On the walk back she started to fret about what Porteous would want from her and how she would explain her failure to pass on the information about Maria's grave. She said nothing to Arthur. How could she tell him she felt like a schoolgirl, waiting for one of Spooky Spence's beastly tests?

Outside the hotel a battered white transit was parked. One headlight seemed to be held on by gaffer tape. Chris was standing by the sliding door, shuffling a loudspeaker towards him so he could get his arms around it. Hannah didn't want to face him yet and touched Arthur's arm to stop him from approaching. Chris shifted the balance of the speaker so he was taking all the weight and walked slowly with it round the side of the building. His hair was a lot shorter and he was a bit thicker round the waist but he hadn't changed much. It could have been the same black T-shirt as the one he'd worn to the party after *Macbeth*.

'I don't suppose you recognize him,' Hannah said.

'No. Why should I?'

'He's been done for dealing. He might have ended

up in our place. If he did he never used the library. I wondered if you'd come across him.'

'No. Look, why don't we talk to him now? Once all the wedding guests turn up it'll be impossible.'

'I wouldn't know what to say.' Again she regretted starting all this. But Arthur was unstoppable.

'Just introduce us. Leave the rest to me.'

The party would take place in a room Hannah hadn't seen before, a large one-storey annexe built on to the back of the house in stone. It had a polished wood floor for dancing, a bar at one end and a scattering of small tables around the walls. It was quite different from the rest of the hotel – more up-market working men's club than country house – but she supposed that in the winter the dos held here would make up most of the Spences' income. Chris was setting up his equipment on a low stage. He was bending over so his T-shirt had ridden up his back. He heard their footsteps and turned round.

'Hannah Meek,' he said. 'Well, well, well. The police haven't locked you up yet then?'

She blushed. She'd always known Chris was hostile. He'd thought her stuck up and prudish. But she hadn't expected such an obvious display of rudeness.

'Why should they lock her up?' Arthur sounded interested, a bit amused.

'Who are you?'

'Arthur Lee. I work with Hannah.'

'Oh? Where's that then?' He pretended to stick wires into sockets but his heart wasn't in it.

'I'm a librarian. I work in Stavely Prison.' She threw that out as a kind of challenge but he didn't seem bothered.

'I never got there. Not a long enough sentence.'

'Perhaps another time.'

He laughed. 'Nah. I'm too old for that now. Didn't Sal tell you? I'm settled. Content. I've got a lady. She's expecting our kid.'

The kitchen door must have been open. Hannah could hear the clattering of pans. There were cooking smells.

'What were you like then?' Arthur asked.

'What do you mean?'

'When Michael Grey was murdered. You weren't so settled then.'

He accepted that as a compliment. 'We were all a bit wild I suppose.' He paused. 'Except Hannah. You never did wild, did you, H?'

'What about Michael? Was he wild too?'

'I never knew him that well.'

'You didn't know anything about him before he came to live here? You'd never met him before?'

'How would I? He went to some sort of posh school.'

'Did he tell you that?'

'Him or someone else. How should I know? Anyway, what's it to do with you?'

Arthur ignored that, continued with the questions, sharp and impersonal.

'What was he like? You were older than the others, more experienced. What did you make of him?'

'He wasn't the angel they all thought.' It came out grudgingly.

'One of your customers, was he?'

'No,' Hannah said. She glared at Arthur. 'He wouldn't.'

'Come on, Hannah,' Chris was fighting back. 'You

know as well as anyone that Michael Grey was hardly the perfect gentleman. Don't you?'

She didn't answer. She wanted to drag Arthur away, to drive immediately back to the coast, but knew there was no way he'd give up now. She'd have to stick it out.

'Have the police been to see you yet?' Arthur asked.

'Of course they've been to see me. Anyone farts in this town, they knock on my door.'

'What did they want?'

'They wanted me to tell them about the party at the caravan site. The last time any of us saw Michael Grey alive. The party after the play. You remember the one, Hannah.'

'Did you tell them?' she asked.

'Of course I told them. I'm a law-abiding citizen now. What else could I do?'

He smiled. His teeth were brown and uneven. Then he turned back to the large, black speaker.

Chapter Twenty-One

Macbeth had gone well. Everyone involved in the production felt the buzz, lapped up the success. Even Hannah, who was on the edge of it. It was a manic time. Exams were only days away. People were up all night revising. You'd have thought it was the worst possible day for a party, but everyone had so much nervous energy and they felt like celebrating.

Hannah never knew whose idea it was to hire a room at the caravan site. Perhaps one of the cast was related to the manager. She thought it was something like that. She spent the afternoon at home getting ready. On her own. She'd asked Sal to come round. Sal was better than she was at clothes and make-up. But Sal hadn't had much to do with the play and anyway seemed to spend all her free time with Chris. Years later Hannah would be able to remember the clothes she was wearing that night. She wanted it to be special. After the exams everyone would move away. It would probably be the last time they'd be together.

She soaked for an hour in the bath, got dressed and looked at herself in the long mirror on the landing. She was wearing a long skirt with tiny green flowers printed on to a cream background. It had a drop waist and she'd made it herself. There was nowhere in

Cranford to buy clothes. It was the first time she'd worn it. A cream top with a gathered neck. A shawl which Sylvia Brice had crocheted for her birthday. Jesus sandals. And masses of black eye make-up. The last throes of flower power, which anyway had come late to the town.

Then, just as she was about to leave, her mother threw a wobbly. Hannah should have seen it coming. It had been building for days – resentful comments every time she went out, tearful self-pity when she returned.

Now Audrey blocked the front door, stood in front of it with her arms outstretched.

'Don't go.'

Hannah was panicking. 'I must. They're expecting me. It's to do with the play.'

She didn't say it was a party because Audrey would have played the guilt card – I never go out, you see your friends every day. That sort of thing. And Hannah had to go. During rehearsals she'd hardly seen Michael. He'd seemed to be slipping away from her.

Audrey crumpled. Her knees buckled and her back slid down the door until she was sitting on the floor. She began to sob. The tears gouged drains in her face powder. Hannah could see the tops of her tights and her knickers. Words came in muffled, snotty bursts.

'I'm so sorry. You mustn't mind me. I only want you to be happy.'

Hannah couldn't leave her like that, though more than anything she wanted to ignore the tears, step over the body and force her way out of the door. She took Audrey's arm and coaxed her to her feet, settled her on the sofa and made her tea. She switched on the television. Immediately Audrey became absorbed in one of her favourite programmes.

'I'll go now, Mum, shall I?'

Audrey turned, waved briefly and returned her attention to the set.

They'd hired a minibus to take party-goers to the lake. Courtesy again of some anxious parents. A disabled lad had gone missing a couple of years before and for a while there'd been a fuss about youngsters out on their own. Hannah was too late to catch it. She began to walk, sticking out her thumb for a lift every time a car went past. She'd never hitched on her own before but now she was too desperate to think of all the adult warnings. It was still light and the road was busier than she'd expected – mostly families on their way back to the site. They didn't seem to see her. Each time a car sailed past she stared after it with loathing. Her sandals were new and a strip of leather cut into her toes.

Then, when she was thinking she'd have to walk the whole way, someone stopped. A young bloke in a rusting estate car. He was chatty and in the few minutes it took to drive the rest of the way she found out he was visiting his girlfriend. She worked on reception in the site office and had been given a free caravan for the season. He was obviously smitten.

She heard the music as soon as she got out of the car.

'Some party, that,' he said, before driving off through the maze of caravans to find his love.

The party wasn't in the bar, but in a room next to it, which sometimes held bingo for the older visitors and talent competitions for the kids. In natural light it would be gloomy, but Chris had rigged up some coloured spots and someone had decorated it with balloons and streamers. It was full. The dancers jostled for space. The first person she saw was Mr Spence, who was dancing with the fifth former who'd played Hecate. Some of the cast had dressed up in their costumes and hers was black, floaty and long. Ribbons of frayed black cloth trailed from her cuffs. Mr Spence danced with his eyes half shut, his body twisting and swaying to the music. Hannah saw at once that Michael wasn't there.

She didn't ask any of her friends if Michael had been with them on the minibus. The music was so loud that her ears were already singing and the room was full of people she didn't know well. Boyfriends and girlfriends and stray hangers-on had gatecrashed. Sally was there, though her only contribution to the play had been to hand out programmes at one of the performances. She was beside Chris, dancing on her own. She already seemed drunk. Hannah didn't want to ask her about Michael. Chris would have made some sarcastic comment. He always did.

She went outside, walked down towards the lake where the noise of the music wasn't quite so loud. She told herself that Michael might have gone for a walk on the shore, that he might be waiting for her there. The sky was a crazy mix of colours. Violet streaked in the west with gold and grey. Soon it would be completely dark but now it was light enough for birds still to be singing and she could make out the paler strip of sand and the reflection of the last light on the water.

They were lying on the spiky grass between the road and the lake. Jenny Graves, otherwise known as

Lady Macbeth, was sprawled naked on the grass with Michael Grey, otherwise known as Theo Randle. The picture had the quality of a photographic negative. The background was grey, their bodies milky. Michael's hair was startling white, her black braid lost in the shadow. It wasn't a shock. She'd looked out for Jenny in the dancing crowd too and registered that she wasn't there. Hadn't even expected her to be. Throughout the rehearsals she'd watched Michael and Jenny, his charm, her flirting. But Hannah hadn't felt able to demand an explanation, because then he'd have told her, not using the exact words of course, that he wanted her as a friend and an audience, not a lover. That is was Jenny Graves he'd write his poems for. Hannah stood for a moment staring, fascinated despite herself by the entwined limbs, the panting, the moans, thinking in a dispassionate way – So that's what happens, that's what it's all about.

Then she turned and ran. They must have heard her footsteps on the shingle but she didn't care. She hoped Michael did hear, that the encounter would be spoiled for him. It serves him right, she thought. Over and over again, spiteful and childish, a schoolyard chant. She stumbled back towards the music, not because she could face going back to the party, but because it was the only way home. A figure was standing outside the building. He leaned against the wall rolling what she realized later was probably a joint. It was Chris. There was an outside light fixed to the bar and she was caught in the glare of it. He saw her tears. He gave a mocking smile and beckoned her towards him. She turned away and hurried down the lane. She didn't try to get a lift. By then it was pitch black and she had more sense. And she didn't want anyone to see her crying.

She was home earlier than her mother had expected. Audrey was still watching television, though she'd moved from the sofa to her usual upright chair and there was a plate with some crumbs on the coffee table. The earlier panic was forgotten. She was touchingly pleased to see Hannah, who sat on the floor beside her to watch the end of the programme. She found herself making allowances for her mother's behaviour now, as she would with someone who was very old or very sick. Audrey seemed not to notice that Hannah was upset until they went upstairs together, then she asked suddenly, 'Are you all right, my dear?'

'Of course.' Audrey would be the last person she'd talk to about her troubles. What could parents know?

'You should leave this place,' Audrey said sharply. 'As soon as your exams are over. I stayed far too long.'

'Oh yes,' Hannah said. 'I will.' She spoke as if it had been her plan all along but it had never crossed her mind before that evening.

'Good.' She shut the bedroom door firmly behind her, but Hannah still heard her repeat the word to herself. 'Good.'

The next morning Michael phoned. It was Sunday and her mother was still in bed. Hannah hadn't been able to sleep. She knew it would be him before she picked up the receiver but she couldn't let it go unanswered.

'Hannah, I have to see you.'

'No.'

'You don't understand. I'm scared.' He did sound

terrified, as if he'd just woken from a nightmare. But she told herself he was a good actor. 'No one else will believe me.'

She didn't say anything.

'There are things you should know. We should talk.'

'Talk to Jenny.' She knew it was petty but she couldn't help it.

'This isn't anything to do with Jenny.'

'And it isn't anything to do with me.'

If Chris hadn't seen her running away from the beach she'd probably have agreed to meet Michael. She wanted to see him. But Chris had seen her and she could tell from the way he'd grinned that he knew about Michael and Jenny. He'd have told Sally. Hannah was proud. She couldn't bear to be seen scuttling back to Michael after she'd been so publicly betrayed. She wanted to help him but knew it was impossible.

'I'm sorry,' she said, as firmly as her mother had said the word 'good' the night before.

She was replacing the receiver when she heard him say goodbye.

That was the story she told Arthur as they sat on the terrace waiting for Porteous to arrive at The Old Rectory. It was quiet. The newly-weds and their friends hadn't yet arrived. It was the story they agreed she would have to tell the detectives.

Porteous was late and when he did arrive he was looking crumpled and breathless. She was thrown because he was on his own. She felt she should ask after Stout. It was as if a husband had turned up at a dinner party without his wife.

'Oh,' Porteous said. 'We're very busy . . .' She had the impression that he'd been rushing around all day.

'You don't mind if my friend joins us. He's responsible for most of the information.'

'No,' Porteous said. 'Of course.' Though he seemed surprised. Perhaps he thought she wasn't the sort to have friends.

They sat in the lounge where he had interviewed her on the evening of the school reunion.

'I remembered something. Michael once mentioned the cemetery on the coast . . .'

Porteous's head shot up. He'd been taking notes. It seemed an overreaction.

'Which cemetery, Mrs Morton?' The voice as bland and polite as always.

'Near the lighthouse. Do you know it?'

'I've heard of it certainly.'

'I looked at the graves, narrowed down the possibilities. I think I've found Michael's mother. She was called Maria Randle. If we're right, Michael's first name was Theo.'

Arthur took him through the dates and the family history. Eagerly. A magician pulling each new bit of information from his hat. 'Theo's father, Crispin, remarried his secretary Stella. They had a daughter. She died in a fire in the family home. Since then there's been no mention of the boy.'

Porteous wrote meticulous notes, but Arthur seemed upset by his lack of reaction. He must have been expecting gratitude, to be welcomed with open arms into the investigation.

'You don't seem surprised,' he said. 'Had you worked all that out for yourself then?'

'No, Mr Lee, you've been very helpful.' Still polite but dismissive. Porteous turned his attention back to Hannah. 'When did you say you were at the cemetery?'

'Yesterday evening.' She added in a rush, 'I did try to phone you then.'

'Did you?'

'There's something else. I've remembered the party after the school play.'

'Ah,' Porteous said. 'Michael and the young Lady Macbeth. Yes. Mr Johnson told us about that.'

'Yes. And the next morning Michael phoned me. He sounded anxious, scared even.'

'Tell me, Mrs Morton, why are you telling me this now? It's not something you'd have forgotten. Seeing your boyfriend with another girl. Not when you remembered other details so clearly.'

She was saved from the need to answer because her mobile phone rang. It was Rosie.

'Mum. Something terrible's happened.'

She was almost screaming and Arthur and Porteous couldn't help overhearing. They both stared out of the window but Hannah could tell they were listening.

'What is it?' Her first thought was Jonathan. A car accident. He drove like a maniac.

Rosie was panting, trying to steady her voice so she could speak.

'It's Mel,' Rosie said. 'She's dead. Someone found her body today on one of the footpaths by the cemetery. She was stabbed.'

Hannah's first thought was, Thank God it's not

Rosie. Then she pictured her daughter frightened and alone in the house.

'We're coming,' she said. 'Leaving straight away.'

She clicked off the phone and stood up. Porteous was already on his feet, blocking the door. 'Do you know Melanie Gillespie, Mrs Morton?'

'Not well. She was my daughter's best friend.'

'Why?' Arthur asked.

Porteous looked down at him as if he were considering whether or not to answer. 'I'm running the investigation into her murder.'

'A bit far from your patch, isn't it?'

Hannah knew what Arthur was up to. Being deliberately provocative in the hope of prising more information from the detective.

Porteous hesitated then chose his words carefully. 'We have reason to believe that the deaths of Michael Grey and Melanie Gillespie are connected. Go back to your daughter, Mrs Morton. Of course she's upset. I'll be in touch shortly when I've checked the information you've given me.' He paused. 'You've nothing more to tell me now? About your visit to the cemetery?'

'No!' She understood for the first time how Audrey had felt, when she'd crumpled in a heap on the floor.

'There will be more questions. Of course you understand that.' He turned and let himself out.

PART THREE

Chapter Twenty-Two

Peter Porteous stood in front of them looking more than ever like a teacher at a second-rate college for further education. He'd set up a flip chart and there was an overhead projector to show slides of the victims and crime scenes.

'If Carver hadn't done the Gillespie post-mortem we'd probably never have made the link,' he said. 'But the Michael Grey inquiry was still fresh in his mind. He's convinced the same knife was used in both murders. If not the same, so similar that it's still significant. Not an ordinary kitchen knife. A dagger. Short bladed but wide. Very sharp.'

He flicked through half a dozen slides – grey flesh, Carver's hands holding steel instruments, wounds which looked now very tidy and clean – then he paused. It was hot again. He'd taken off his jacket, loosened his tie just a touch.

'So, let's look at the victims.' He turned a page of the flip chart. Stuck to the next page was the old photograph of Michael Grey playing Macbeth. Porteous stretched and wrote in felt-tip at the top: Theo Randle. He had no problem accepting the new name of the boy. He had more important things to worry about. He flipped the page again and scrawled a rudimentary family tree. The felt-tip squealed on rough paper.

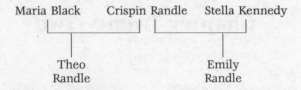

Maria Black   Crispin Randle   Stella Kennedy

Theo
Randle

Emily
Randle

'Maria died when Theo was very young. Crispin remarried and had a second child, Emily. She was killed in a house fire when she was still a baby. Two tragedies. Perhaps that explains the family breakdown and the fostering.'

A young DC at the back stuck up a hand.

'Yes?'

'How did we get a positive ID on the boy in the end, sir?'

Porteous thought the man already knew the answer and intended to rub salt into the wounds. He was a cocky little sod. And it did come hard to admit that an enthusiastic amateur had got there before him. But he kept his voice friendly.

'With the help of a member of the public. A psychologist who works for the Home Office. He had information we didn't have access to, but I'll come to that later.

'Let's turn now to what we know about Theo Randle. Quite a lot, considering how much time has elapsed. He was bright, well educated, personable. He seems to have come from a wealthy family. Just before he died he had a row with his girlfriend because she caught him making love to someone else. He was a talented actor and was starring in a production of *Macbeth* in the week before he disappeared. One of his props was a dagger. According to witnesses it was very sharp. I'd like to trace it. The school is doing its best but I don't hold out much hope . . . He was lodging with a couple called Sylvia and Stephen Brice. Everyone says they were very fond of him. There was no question of ill treatment or abuse and I think we can rule them out. They're dead now, but perhaps we can trace friends who knew Theo, knew how he came to be living there. None of this might be relevant, but I want to know.'

He turned to the next page on the chart. This was covered with a montage of photographs of Melanie Gillespie. Before she'd dyed her hair red she'd been blonde. In the centre there was a picture of her, blown up. She was half turned, caught unexpectedly. She had a wide mouth, high cheekbones and she was super-model thin.

'Despite the gap in time these two have a lot in common. Not just their age. The Gillespies are wealthy. They're both prominent business people, often in the news. Theo's dad was an MP. Melanie was bright and articulate. Her teachers say she could be moody but she was often charming. She wasn't into art and acting like Theo, but she was a skilled musician. So they had similar backgrounds. Now, let's look at the differences. Most obvious, of course, is gender . . .'

The cocky DC raised a hand, languidly, as if it were hardly worth the effort. 'Is that important?'

Porteous wanted to yell: Don't be fatuous. *Everything's* important. Two young people have been killed.

'We don't know at this stage. There was no indication of sexual assault on Melanie Gillespie, according to Carver.'

He turned his back on the audience as he regained control, wrote DIFFERENCES on the flip chart, added GENDER, then AGE with a question mark. 'Theo was a year older than Melanie, though as they were both in their A-level year, that hardly seems important.'

'Could we be looking for a teacher?' Claire Wright asked.

'Possible, isn't it? I'd be very interested to know if anyone who taught Theo at Cranford Grammar went on to work at Melanie's school. Can you take responsibility for checking that out?'

She nodded.

'Then there are the temperaments,' he went on. 'Not so easy to pin down, but we seem to have a difference here. Theo is described as organized and conscientious but he doesn't seem to have been over-stressed by exams. He still felt able to take part in the school play. One witness says he told stories, you couldn't believe what he said, but she was his girlfriend and he betrayed her. I'm not sure we can rely on her objectivity. There was no record of any emotional problems, nothing more than you'd expect in any adolescent. On the other hand Melanie was moody, given to bouts of anger and depression. For the past two years she'd been seeing a psychiatrist for an eating disorder.'

Porteous looked out at his team. Some were scribbling notes. He thought that soon they'd have no need for that. Soon they'd know these teenagers as well as they knew their own families.

'So,' he said. 'Two victims. The big question is – Are there any more? Would a killer keep a knife for nearly thirty years, resisting the temptation to use it, then murder again, out of the blue? We need to check the old files and make sure this isn't a part of a wider pattern. Pull up all the post-mortem reports for stabbings when the victim was a teenager. I don't want the search restricted to the local area – I'm sure we'd have picked that up. But the killer might have been working away.'

He stopped again, abruptly, and seemed lost in thought for a moment. A fan on one of the desks in a corner hummed. Someone coughed uncertainly. His audience didn't know him well enough to tell whether or not he'd finished the briefing. He let them sit in an awkward silence for a few minutes longer before continuing slowly.

'So that's one theory. We've got an undetected serial killer. We'll find other crimes that fit the pattern – teenage murders and that particular knife. At least it's something we can check. Carver's happy to work with us on it.' More than happy, Porteous thought. The pathologist had almost begged to be involved. He'd seen the chance for fame, mentions in influential journals and the opportunity to star as an expert witness in an important court case.

'The other theory is that the second murder came about as a result, somehow, of the discovery of Theo Randle's body, that there was a causal link between the incidents. If that's the case it won't be an obvious connection. Melanie hadn't been born at the time of Theo's death.'

'Couldn't we be talking a random nutter?' The

contribution came from Charlie Luke, who'd been sitting in the front row, his brow furrowed with concentration throughout the presentation. He had the build and squashed features of a boxer. Approaching middle-age he was still a constable and would remain one. No one was quite sure how he'd slipped through the assessment process to get into the service. Claire dismissed him as having the IQ of a gnat, but Porteous didn't care and rather liked him. He was dogged and did what he was told. He didn't let the job get under his skin. Beer and sport would always be more important.

'Nothing's ever completely random, is it, Luke? The killer must have met these young people somewhere. Their paths crossed even if he only came across them opportunistically, if he had no other motive than the thrill of killing. It should be possible to learn something about the pattern of his life from theirs.'

Luke seemed bewildered by the concept but he nodded enthusiastically.

'Of course,' Porteous went on, 'we've already discovered one connection between Theo Randle and Melanie Gillespie . . .' He turned towards Stout who was already rising to his feet. 'Eddie, perhaps you'd like to tell us that part of the story.'

'Hannah Morton,' Stout said. 'Maiden name Hannah Meek. She works as a librarian in Stavely nick. She's recently separated from Jonathan, who's deputy head of a high school on the coast, the high school where Melanie Gillespie was a student. There's one daughter, Rosalind, aged eighteen, still living at home and waiting to go to university. On the surface you couldn't find anyone more respectable than Mrs Morton. Anyone less likely to commit murder. But she did know both victims.

'We were already interested in Mrs Morton before the Gillespie murder. She was Theo's girlfriend, the love, she thought, of his life. She caught him . . .' Stout hesitated, seemed to be searching for an appropriate euphemism.

'Shagging?' Luke suggested helpfully.

'Quite.' Still Stout couldn't bring himself to say the word: ' . . . the young actress who played Lady Macbeth. *They* were together by Cranford Water after an end-of-performance party. That's the last record we have of the boy alive. Mrs Morton claims he phoned her the following day but after all this time it's impossible to check.'

Stout paused. 'She has a surprisingly clear recollection of all the details. That, in itself, raises suspicion. She didn't tell us about Theo two-timing her until she knew we'd find out anyway. She was stage manager for the school play so she'd have access to the dagger which could well have been the murder weapon. She had motive and opportunity. There's no one else in the frame.' He rocked back on his heels. 'But I don't see it. I don't see her as the sort of person who'd stab the boy she was in love with, tie an anchor round his body and hoy him in the lake. I certainly don't see her living with herself for thirty years afterwards—'

'Unless she'd repressed the memory,' Luke interrupted. He looked round as if he expected congratulation from his colleagues for the contribution. When none came he added defensively, 'Well, it happens. I saw this programme on the telly . . . And when the boy's body was dredged up from the lake perhaps it all came back.' He looked at Porteous for help.

'You'd have to ask a psychiatrist,' Porteous said. 'Not my field.' Recognizing the irony of the words as he spoke.

'Unless she repressed the memory,' Stout said impatiently. 'But then why kill Melanie Gillespie? She had a motive for killing Randle, but none at all for murdering the girl. Melanie couldn't have been a witness to the first murder. She couldn't be any threat.'

'How did Mrs Morton know Melanie?' Claire Wright asked.

'Melanie and Rosalind Morton were best friends. They went to the same school. Hannah met Melanie when Rosalind had friends to the house.'

'Quite a tenuous connection then.'

Porteous, who'd been leaning against a table at the front of the room, stood up to answer.

'Quite tenuous,' he said. 'And as Eddie's said, Hannah Morton has no motive for the Gillespie murder. She does, however, have opportunity.'

He picked up the remote control and another slide was projected. It showed a narrow footpath with a stone wall on one side and a hawthorn hedge on the other. The footpath was crossed with blue and white tape. 'Melanie's body was found wrapped in black plastic at the bottom of the hedge.'

He clicked the remote and there was a shot of a lay-by on a main road, the entrance to the footpath. 'Melanie wasn't killed where she was found. The murderer must have parked here and carried the body the fifty yards or so to where it was dumped.

We've already said she was anorexic so she wasn't heavy. But not a pleasant job. It would have taken nerve.'

Another click and the footpath was seen from a different angle, so it was possible to see over the stone wall to a row of headstones.

'Hannah Morton admits to having been in the cemetery the evening before the girl's body was discovered. She claims to have remembered suddenly that Randle had told her where his mother was buried. She found the grave and that's the information Arthur Lee, the Home Office psychologist, used to dig out the boy's identity. If she's telling the truth, then it's some coincidence.'

The screen went blank. 'All the same,' Porteous said, 'I don't think we should become too fixed on the Morton connection. Not yet. Certainly there are other avenues to explore. I haven't spoken to the Gillespies today. The doctor said they needed time. But before Melanie's body was found they gave important information to the team looking into her disappearance. The case was taken seriously from the beginning because it was thought to be a kidnap. Melanie left home some time after ten, and went to a pub, the Promenade. When none of her friends were there she went to a café on the sea front called the Rainbow's End. We need to trace everyone who was in either establishment that night. It was the last time she was seen alive, though Carver thinks it more likely she was killed the next day.'

He paused for long enough for them to catch up with their notes. 'There's someone else we need to get hold of too. A middle-aged man went into the Prom-enade looking for Melanie the week before she disappeared. Who was he?'

He let the question hang. Luke's mobile rang. Embarrassed he fished in his pocket and switched it off.

Ignoring the interruption Porteous went on, 'This afternoon I'm going to see Stella Randle, Theo's step-mother, his only surviving relative. Perhaps something will come of that. Some other connection to make more sense of both cases.'

Eddie Stout listened and he thought that his boss had no soul. A fish on a slab had more emotion. Port-eous spoke about connections and links as if he were forming a mathematical theory. Not as if a young girl had been stabbed to death. He thought of his Ruthie, excited and dressed up to go out, and said suddenly, trying to shock Porteous, 'Wouldn't there have been a lot of blood? A stabbing like that.'

'Certainly.'

'Not an easy thing to hide then. There'd have been stained clothes, marks on a floor, walls. Someone would have seen. Shouldn't we put out the usual plea through the press? Wives and girlfriends who noticed anything odd . . .'

'Of course, Eddie. It's already in hand.'

Porteous stayed behind when they all filed out, collecting his papers into an ordered file. On the way to the door he stopped and glanced behind him. Melanie Gillespie, half turned in the photo, her mouth wide in a grin of recognition, seemed to be looking at him. He had an image of her alone and in pain, heard the screaming. He turned his back on the photo, deliberately distancing himself from the smile. That way lay madness.

Chapter Twenty-Three

Crispin Randle, father of Theo, former Tory MP, had died. Porteous thought, with some satisfaction, that the fat psychologist hanging round with Hannah Morton had missed that bit of information. *He'd* dug it out from the registrar. Crispin had died five years before from liver failure. The doctors Porteous tracked down suggested that alcohol consumption had been a major contributing factor.

Stella Randle, the widow, was living in Millhaven, in a flat close to the sea front, not very far down the coast from the cemetery where Melanie Gillespie's body had been found. Porteous had made the appointment to visit by phone and she had been strangely uninterested, rather vague, so he turned up not even sure that she'd be in. The flat was in a crescent built around a communal garden. It had always been a poor Victorian imitation of Georgian grandeur but now it looked shabby and down at heel. A locked wrought-iron gate prevented him from parking right outside so he left his car on the promenade and walked. The grass in the garden was long, the borders overgrown.

Stella Randle opened the door to him herself. She had a faded charm, which matched the building. When he introduced himself she seemed not to recollect that they'd spoken earlier in the day and throughout the interview he was unsure whether her vagueness was genuine or an attempt to deceive. She was in her mid-fifties, dressed in what seemed to Porteous to be a parody of the character she was playing. She wore a pleated skirt, a little cashmere cardigan and even a string of pearls. In her youth she would have been pretty, a little foolish but aware of her limitations. Now she still tried to be girlish.

'Come in. An inspector. What fun! You will stop for tea?'

There was a wide hall, then a huge high-ceilinged room with a bay window looking out to sea. He had been expecting clutter, furniture from a big house crammed into a flat, but the room was surprisingly empty. There was one sofa – well made but modern – and a couple of coffee tables. On one lay a library book, a romantic novel, face down. The floor had been stripped and varnished and in front of the marble fire-place there was a Moroccan rug of a startling indigo blue.

She must have sensed his surprise.

'Crispin drank everything away,' she said. 'If he hadn't died when he did the flat would have gone too.' She looked round the room, saw it perhaps through his eyes. 'Why don't we go into the kitchen? We'll be more comfortable there.'

The kitchen was shabby too but less austere. There were herbs in pots on the window-sill, a bunch of flowers and a brightly coloured oilskin cloth on the table. A portable television stood on one of the counters. A plate and a cup were draining next to the sink.

'Tea then,' she said and set a kettle on the gas

ring. Still she hadn't asked Porteous what he was doing there.

'I'm afraid I may have some bad news,' he said.

'Oh?' She seemed untroubled. Perhaps years of living with an alcoholic had inured her to the possibility of bad news.

'It's your stepson Theo.'

'Theo?' It was as if she barely recognized the name. She seemed to trawl back through her memory before it made sense.

'Have you seen him recently?'

'No, no. Not for years.'

'Had your husband kept in touch with him?'

'My husband was very ill, Inspector. Long before he died.'

It was hardly an answer but he let it go.

The kettle gave a piercing whistle. She seemed grateful for the distraction. Her attention was taken up then with warming the pot and making the tea. Porteous set the photograph of Theo as Macbeth on the table. 'Is that him?'

'Oh goodness, after all this time, really I couldn't say.' She'd only glanced at the picture, was more intent on looking in the cupboard for matching cups among a jumble-sale assortment.

'Please look at the photo carefully, Mrs Randle.'

'I haven't seen him since he was a young boy.'

'All the same.'

He spoke firmly and her resistance went. She sat at the table, took a pair of reading glasses from the pocket of her skirt and studied the photograph.

'It could be him,' she said at last. 'That hair. Yes, I rather think it is.'

'Do you have any photos of him as a young boy?'

He could tell she was about to say no without thinking about it, then she caught his eye and changed her mind.

'There was one. He was pageboy at our wedding. Even Crispin didn't have the heart to get rid of those. Not that they were worth anything . . .' She jumped to her feet. He thought she was about to fetch the album, but she poured out the tea and arranged chocolate biscuits on a plate.

'If I could look at it . . .' he prompted.

'Yes.' The forced gaiety disappeared quite suddenly. 'I don't see why not.' She left the kitchen, shutting the door behind her. When she returned some time later her eyes were red. He wondered what had made her cry. He hadn't told her yet that Theo was dead. She hadn't asked.

She had certainly been happy when she married. She beamed from every shot. The photos were in a red leather album, separated by flimsy sheets of tissue paper. They had been taken in a garden. She hadn't worn a traditional wedding dress but a short white frock with a lacy white coat over the top. She must have been in her early twenties but had the enthusiastic grin of a school girl. She held a posy of garden flowers and there was a circlet of ox-eye daisies in her hair. Randle stood beside her, proud, rather paternal. His face looked a little flushed and Porteous thought he might have been drinking heavily even then.

'They were taken at Snowberry,' she said. 'That was Crispin's house. It had been in the family for years. It was foolish of course but I thought I'd grow old there. I imagined it full of grandchildren at Christmas. I was very young. Perhaps I fell in love with Snowberry as much as I did with Crispin.' She gave a sad little laugh. Her hands had stopped turning the pages of the album.

'You said there was a photo of Theo,' Porteous prompted gently.

'Theo. I did try very hard with Theo. I'd hoped he might dress up for the wedding. I can't remember now what plans I had . . .' She stopped, lost in thought. It seemed to be very important to her to remember what she had wanted the boy to wear. She looked up smiling triumphantly. 'A sailor suit,' she said. 'I think that was it. I'd seen a picture in a magazine . . . I didn't have bridesmaids. It wasn't a big affair. Crispin didn't want the fuss. He'd done all that the first time round. Anyway Theo wasn't having any of it. I don't think he resented my taking his mother's place. I don't think it was anything like that. Crispin said not at least, and we always seemed to be good pals. Perhaps it was his age. At the last minute anyway, he refused to wear the costume I'd chosen for him. Had an almighty tantrum.' She smiled and it seemed to Porteous that she remembered the boy with genuine fondness. 'Crispin was furious. I said it didn't matter. Why should it? So Theo came to the wedding in his school clothes. Short grey trousers and a cherry-red tie. Very festive and perfectly appropriate. He was very sweet actually. He came up to me later and said he was sorry for making a fuss. I said I supposed the sailor suit *was* a bit sissy and he gave me a kiss. First time ever.'

'Where was Theo at school?' Porteous asked.

'A place called Linden House. A little prep school. He went as a day boy. Crispin had been sent away as a boarder as a very young child and he didn't want that for Theo. Not then.' There was no hesitation. As she talked, the details of her life at Snowberry seemed to become sharper. She had more confidence in her memory.

'The photograph . . .' Porteous prompted her again.

She turned a page and there it was. A boy of about seven or eight standing on his own, looking into the camera, apparently enjoying the attention and the chance to show off. Instead of a traditional buttonhole he had a daisy pinned to the lapel of his blazer. There was a scab on one of his knees and his socks needed pulling up. He looked as if he'd been eating chocolate sauce.

'I did want a photo of him,' Stella said, 'but I knew he wouldn't stand being cleaned up first.'

Porteous was looking at the face, at the shock of white hair, the long straight nose. It would take an expert to check both pictures to confirm the identification but he was prepared to bet a year's salary that Theo Randle had turned into Michael Grey.

'I'm afraid,' he said, 'that Theo's dead.'

She had been staring at the photograph, apparently lost in memory, and he had to repeat the words to be sure she'd heard. Then she gave a little moan. 'Oh no,' she said. 'Not him too.'

'We believe he died a long time ago,' Porteous said. 'When he was only eighteen.'

'How?' Her eyes were bright, feverish. The question demanded an immediate and an honest answer.

'He was stabbed.'

She seemed almost relieved by the words. 'Quick then?'

'Oh yes. He wouldn't have felt any pain.'

'That's good.' She got up from the table and poured more hot water into the teapot. Then she stood at the sink with her hands over her eyes as if she wanted to pretend Porteous wasn't there.

'Mrs Randle,' he said gently.

She lowered her hands and asked fiercely, 'Did Crispin know about this?'

'I don't see how he could have done.' Unless, Porteous thought, he was responsible. 'The body was only discovered last week.'

'Crispin didn't tell me everything,' she said. 'He kept things from me. He didn't want me upset. He said it was for my own good. But I never knew what was going on. It's very confusing, Inspector, to be kept in the dark. Sometimes I thought I was going mad.'

'Would you like me to phone someone to be with you? A relative perhaps?'

She shook her head.

'I will have to ask questions,' Porteous said. 'About Theo and your husband. Would you like me to come back another time to do that? Perhaps now I should call your doctor. You've had a great shock.' He wasn't sure he should leave her on her own.

'No.' Her voice was sharp. 'No doctors.'

They sat for a moment in silence, looking at each other.

'Ask your questions, Inspector. It'll give me an excuse to talk about it. Talking helps. Isn't that what the doctors say? That's what they said after Emily died. It was a lie of course. Nothing helped. Except the pills. Crispin drank and I became a junkie. Not heroin. Nothing like that. Prescription medicine. All quite legal. Nothing for you to worry about. Professionally.'

'Are you still taking medication now?'

'No,' she said. 'I took myself off them when Crispin was very ill. I needed to feel angry. The pills stop you feeling very much at all.'

'That must have been hard.'

'The hardest thing ever. At least it stopped me blaming Crispin for his drinking. He'd been through more than me. First Maria. Then Emily. How could I expect him to give it up? When I knew what he was going through. It brought us together at the end.' She wiped her eyes with the back of her hand. 'I did love him, Inspector. People thought I was after him for the money and the house and there was some of that in it. How could you separate them? It was all a part of what he was. But I wasn't a gold-digger. I loved him. And Theo. I took them on as a package.' She looked at him across the table, gave him her young woman's smile. 'So, Inspector, why don't you ask your questions?'

'When did Theo stop living at home?'

'It was after the fire,' she said. 'After Emily died.'

'Would you mind telling me about that?'

She shook her head. 'I don't mind but it's very confused. You mustn't be cross if I get things wrong.'

'It's a long time ago.'

'No,' she said impatiently. 'It's not that. When Emily was born I was ill. Post-natal depression. I thought it would be easy. Like with Theo. I loved *him* without any bother. Why couldn't I do the same with my own child?'

'Not so easy building a relationship with a baby.' As if, Porteous thought, I'd know.

'But she was my own daughter. They wanted me

to go into hospital. I refused. I thought Snowberry was the only place I had any chance of getting well. You don't know what it's like, Inspector. Sometimes I'd wake up in the morning feeling better. For no great reason. The sun coming in through a gap in the curtains. The taste of toast for breakfast, though they brought me toast on a tray every morning. And I'd think – This is it. The start of the recovery. Sometimes the feeling would last for days. Crispin still had his seat in the House then and I'd send him off to London telling him I'd be fine and I didn't need him. Then the depression would return, as bad as ever. It was at the end of a really bad period of depression that we had the fire.'

'Was Crispin at home when it happened?'

'Yes. He came back that night. It was unusual to see him in the middle of the week. He'd been spending more and more time in London. He had a flat there of course. I think he probably had a mistress though I didn't ask. I couldn't blame him. I wasn't much of a wife.'

'Do you remember what happened on the night of the fire?'

'Not very well. As I said, it was all very confused.'

Porteous didn't push for details. There should be a fire investigator's report, a coroner's judgement. But Stella added quickly, 'I think it might have been my fault. I smoked then, heavily. We had a nanny for Emily. A nice girl. We hired her before the baby was born even. I thought we'd be friends. We were about the same age. I thought we'd be able to share Emily. In the end of course she looked after her pretty much single-handed. But that evening she asked for some time off. She bathed Emily and put her to bed and then she went out.'

'Do you remember the nanny's name?' Porteous asked.

'Lizzie. Lizzie Milburn. She came from Newcastle. Her parents were teachers and she was crazy about babies. Just as well.'

'You think your smoking might have started the fire?'

'No one said. I told you Crispin tried to protect me. But going back over the facts I think that's most likely. I went to look at Emily. Crispin came with me. There were no baby alarms in those days and I did feel responsible for her. Perhaps if I'd had the nerve to let Lizzie go, if I'd been forced to look after Emily myself things might have been different, but really I don't think so. I was very ill.' She paused. 'I'm sorry, I'm rambling. Crispin and I had dinner together. He'd come back from London in a foul mood. He'd always been ambitious and someone had said something to make him believe he didn't have a chance of promotion in the next reshuffle. He probably blamed me. I was hardly an ideal MP's wife. Certainly nothing like Maria, who was perfect apparently in every way. A saint is a hard act to follow. Crispin had a lot to drink over dinner. I had a couple of glasses with him. Not sensible considering the strength of the medication I was on. When we went up to the nursery we were both a bit unsteady. Crispin didn't stay long. He wanted to get back to the brandy. But I loved to watch her sleeping. That was the one time I could really believe I loved her . . .'

'You think you might have been careless with a cigarette?'

'I think it's possible. I'm sure Crispin blamed me. I wonder sometimes if he thought I did it on purpose. An act of madness. He thought I was crazy. Certainly he believed I was responsible for the fire one way or another. That's why he took Theo away. He said he couldn't trust me to look after him any more.'

Chapter Twenty-Four

'She says the boy never lived at home again after that,'
Porteous said. 'I've seen the fire investigator and the
coroner's reports. There was no real structural damage
to the house. The fire started in the nursery and was
contained there, but the girl was trapped in her cot
and when the bedding and nightclothes caught, there
was no hope for her.' There had been a photograph in
the fire investigator's report of a small charred body
pushed to one end of the cot as if she had been trying
to escape the smoke and the heat, the arms raised in
the pugilistic stance common in burn victims.

'I suppose it *was* an accident.' It was evening. Eddie
Stout had come out to Porteous's home. It had never
happened before. Porteous had reciprocated the Stouts'
hospitality with a meal in a restaurant. He'd told them
it was because he couldn't cook, but that wasn't true.
He liked home and work kept apart.

He'd been home for an hour and had almost
finished writing up the notes of his interview with
Stella Randle, when his doorbell rang. He'd seen Stout's
car from his window and had gone down, planning to
keep him outside, thinking they could talk in the
garden, even walk to the pub at the end of the lane if
it was going to take a while. But Eddie had been so

diffident and apologetic that a response like that was impossible. It called for something more friendly.

'Of course, you must come in. No, really, it's a pleasure. I was just going to have a beer. I'm sure you'll join me.'

And Porteous had found it helpful to describe again his conversation with Randle's widow. They were still standing, each with a glass, looking at the view down the valley. Stout continued without waiting for an answer to the original question.

'It couldn't have been an insurance scam turned tragic? Nothing like that?'

'No. The fire officer said it was consistent with a cigarette or match having been carelessly dropped, not an attempt at large-scale damage. It started in or near the nursery. If it had been deliberate they'd not have done that. I know the technology wasn't so precise then, but the officer was experienced and he was confident of his decision. When the fire really took hold the parents were at the other end of the house and hardly conscious – Crispin was drunk and Stella doped up to the eyeballs. Luckily the nanny came home earlier than expected or they might all have been killed.'

'Where did Randle take the boy?'

'Stella was very vague about that.' After her description of the fire and her daughter's death she'd hardly seemed to hear his questions. 'Perhaps to stay with relatives until Crispin could arrange a boarding place for him.'

'We've finally found out where he was at school then?'

'No. Crispin would never tell her where Theo was.

Not precisely. It was as if she'd relinquished all her rights over the boy. A way of punishing her for the death of his daughter. Theo came home occasionally for holidays, she said, but she was never allowed to be alone with him. As he got older he seems to have found better things to do. It can't have been much fun at Snowberry. Randle had resigned his seat in the Commons and was drinking. I presume Theo invited himself to friends' homes for the vacations. By all accounts he was a charmer. I don't suppose it was difficult. Or there may have been other relatives.'

'Where do the Brices fit in?'

'I don't know. Stella didn't recognize the name.'

'Not much further forward then.' Eddie didn't sound too disappointed by the lack of progress.

'Oh, I think so. We should be able to trace Theo's school with the information we've got now. Two schools probably if he was only ten when he went away. There must be someone who remembers him ... I've been thinking that the reason for his leaving boarding school could have been financial. Crispin could have run through the family money very quickly. Perhaps he just couldn't afford the school fees.'

'Is this background relevant to the murder do you think?'

Is it? Porteous thought, and realized that he'd hardly considered the real business of the murder investigation all afternoon. He'd been wrapped up in the domestic tragedy. They'd all suffered – Crispin, Stella, Theo and Emily. When the wedding pictures were taken they must have seemed an ideal family. Porteous could imagine them posing for a similar photo to go with the constituency Christmas card. But the happiness had been shattered even before the fire.

'I can't imagine Stella Randle tracking down Theo and sticking a dagger through his ribs if that's what you mean. She wouldn't know where to start. And why would she?'

'Could she have blamed the boy for the little girl's death?'

'She might have been psychotic when she was very ill, and dreamed up something like that, but she didn't strike me as delusional today.'

'Perhaps it wasn't a delusion.'

'What do you mean?'

Eddie shrugged. 'Perhaps he did kill his sister. An unsupervised boy playing with matches could have the same result as a cigarette fire.'

'There was no mention of that at the time.'

'It would give another slant on Crispin keeping Theo away from his stepmother. Perhaps she was threatening to harm him even then. Much easier to blame the boy than take responsibility for her own negligence.'

'It's a possibility . . .'

'But you don't think it's likely.' Eddie finished his beer and grinned. 'It's OK. You don't have to humour me. I'm not a kid. I'm . . .' he paused. 'What's that technique they always use on the team-building courses? Brainstorming.'

'I'm not dismissing any ideas. It's just that Stella *did* take responsibility for Emily's death as soon as I asked her about it. And she'd almost forgotten about Theo. I don't think she'd have been able to do that if she'd killed him.'

'Did you ask her about the Gillespie girl?'

'Yes.'

On the way out. He'd stood on the doorstep looking across the garden to the wide sweep of the bay, with the lighthouse at one end and the mouth of the Tyne at the other, then turned back to her as if the question had just come to him: 'Does the name Melanie Gillespie mean anything to you?'

She'd stood with her arms clasped across her chest as if she were cold. A breeze was coming off the sea and her cardigan was thin, but Porteous still felt warm. Then she'd giggled. 'What's this, Inspector? A sort of quiz?' Then she'd gone into the flat shutting the door behind her without answering the question.

The sun was so low now that it shone up at them through the long window of the barn and they were dazzled. They turned away and sat down. Porteous offered Eddie another beer but he shook his head and for the first time Porteous saw how excited he was. It had been a struggle to contain himself in the conversation about Stella Randle.

'What is it, Eddie? What have you got for me?'

'I went to see Jack Westcott. You remember, he was the history teacher in the high school. Just retired.'

Porteous nodded.

'I turned up before opening time this morning. Caught him when he was completely sober. We went for a walk in the park. His wife's the house-proud sort. You could tell she was glad to have him out from under her feet. He was glad of the company, I think. He'll miss those kids.'

Porteous nodded again, thought Eddie would get to the point in his own time.

'I just wanted to get him talking. Claire Wright hasn't found any teacher who moved from Cranford to the school on the coast, but I thought there might be some informal connections – specialist music teachers, drama festival, sport. That sort of thing.'

'Anything?'

'Not that Theo was involved in. So I asked about the other kids in the school. It occurred to me that Melanie's mother and father would be about the same age as Theo if he'd lived. But Westcott couldn't remember a Richard Gillespie or an Eleanor of any description, so I could kiss goodbye to that theory.'

'Worth checking though. And it's possible that Richard Gillespie was at Theo's boarding school.'

'Aye. From what I've seen of him on TV he's got the air of a public-school boy about him . . . I'd pretty much given up hope of anything useful when Jack said he'd been digging around at home and he'd found some more photos of the *Macbeth* production. Would I like to see them? Most likely an excuse so he wouldn't have to face that dragon of a wife on his own, but I thought he might have a sharper photo of the boy we could give to the press, so I went along with him.'

Porteous was finding it difficult to give the story his full attention. He didn't mind Eddie Stout being here as much as he'd expected, but the evening sun was making him drowsy.

Eddie continued. 'You'd have thought he was a schoolboy himself, the way he spoke to his wife. He took me upstairs to a sort of den where he hides away from her. There were cardboard boxes full of snaps. There must have been pictures in there of every school play in the past thirty years, but he'd sorted out the ones he thought were relevant.'

'Anything of Theo we could use for the media?'

'No. Jack must have had the shakes even then. None of them were brilliant. But amongst them I found this.' Carefully, holding the picture by the edges with his fingertips, Eddie handed it over. It was a black and white photo of the audience, taken probably from the side of the stage just before the show was about to start. Parents clutched hand-printed programmes on their knees and chatted to their neighbours. There was no indication that they'd been aware of the photographer. Eddie pointed to a couple in the front row.

'Those are the Brices.'

They looked ordinary, elderly. They could have been anyone's grandparents. Stephen wore a hand-knitted sweater over corduroy trousers. Sylvia had made more of an effort about dressing up and had a high-necked blouse over a long black skirt. There was a brooch at the neck. They were holding hands.

'Interesting,' Porteous said. He always found it helpful to put a face to names. But he couldn't quite understand Eddie's excitement. It was hardly worth a trek into the country at tea time.

Eddie took a deep breath. 'That,' he said, pointing to a pale, insignificant man sitting next to Sylvia, 'that is Alec Reeves.'

Then Porteous did understand the excitement. This was Alec Reeves who'd worked as assistant manager in the hardware store in Cranford high street. Alec Reeves, uncle to Carl Jackson, the lad with the learning disability who'd disappeared not long before Theo.

Alec Reeves, who, according to Eddie, liked young boys and had gone off to get a job in a children's home.

'I thought Sarah Jackson said he'd left Cranford by then.'

'She did. He must have come back.'

Porteous looked again at the photo. Although Sylvia was holding Stephen's hand she was talking to Reeves. Her head was turned to him and she was smiling. It was the relaxed conversation of friends. 'You said they knew him.'

'Aye,' Stout said bitterly. 'You'd have thought they'd have had better taste.'

'This changes things,' Porteous said. Slowly. Not wanting to wind Eddie up any further. But Eddie was buzzing already.

'Of course it does. Alec was there that night. It must have been the last performance, because Hannah Morton says that's when the Brices were in the audience. No reason why he couldn't have got hold of the knife. I bet when we check the records we'll find other lads in his care who've mysteriously disappeared.'

'Theo wasn't in his care,' Porteous said. 'Not as far as we know.' And Melanie Gillespie wasn't a lad, he thought.

'He could have been. Perhaps the Brices asked Alec to have a word with the boy. Perhaps Theo was depressed because of the mess he'd made of his love life and they asked Alec to help. He was always a sympathetic listener. I'll give him that. Maybe he offered to take Theo out for the day, offered a shoulder to cry on. He was nearer the boy's age than the Brices. More like a father.'

'How would he explain Theo's disappearance?'

'I've been thinking about that.' Eddie's words tumbled over each other. 'Someone told the Brices that Theo had decided to go back to his dad. It must have been Alec Reeves.'

'It's certainly a plausible theory,' Porteous said. Then gently, 'Where does Melanie Gillespie fit in?'

'Maybe she's the last of a string of teenagers who've disappeared. We don't take missing teenagers very seriously, do we? Not the restless, unsettled ones. We put them down as runaways and hope the Sally Army will do the business for us.'

'Melanie didn't disappear though, did she? Her body was found. No attempt was made to hide it.'

'Perhaps Reeves was disturbed. Or all the publicity about the body in the lake made him want to come out into the open. Could be he's been enjoying the glory.'

Porteous said nothing. He wished he knew more about the subject. Perhaps after all he would have to talk to Hannah's fat psychologist, ask his advice. He drank his beer absent-mindedly. He hadn't eaten and felt it go to his head, mixed with the medication he'd taken earlier in the day. Like Stella Randle, he thought, I should take more care.

'Sir?' Eddie was on his feet. He was obviously desperate to move the case forward.

'Peter. Call me Peter here, please.' He set the glass on the table, stood up too, tried to sound decisive when all he had were questions. 'I want to know where Reeves is. Don't go to Sarah Jackson. I don't want him frightened off. Put a watch on her bungalow. But be discreet. When you find Reeves, don't pull him in. Tail him but leave him where he is. We'll need more evidence, any evidence, before we question him. At present he doesn't know there's anything to connect him to Theo Randle and that's how I want it. Show this photograph to the barman in the Promenade who said someone was looking for Melanie. Reeves will have changed since then, but it's better than nothing. Tomorrow we'll talk to her parents. See if the name means anything to them.' He paused. 'Go easy on this, Eddie. Bet will be expecting you back for a meal. Most of this you can do from home.'

But as Eddie bounded down the stairs Porteous knew he was wasting his breath. Eddie was a man with a mission and was losing the power of rational thought.

Chapter Twenty-Five

When Porteous arrived at the police station the next morning – early for him though he'd still walked, still kept to the same routine – Stout was already there. He looked as if he'd spent all night at his desk. He'd shaved but he was wearing the same clothes and he spoke too quickly, feverish through lack of sleep.

No use to man nor beast in that state, Porteous thought. Then recognized that as the pious sentiment of the newly converted and he listened to the steps Stout had already taken to track down Alec Reeves.

'There's an empty bungalow over the road from Sarah Jackson's. The council were going to do it up before the next tenant anyway. I talked to a chap in building services who goes to our church. He pushed the work to the top of the list. They're going to start this morning.' He looked at his watch. 'Should be there already. I've sent Charlie Luke along as part of the team.'

'Won't the council workers talk?'

'No, they think he's a management trainee. They have to do work experience in every department.'

Porteous smiled at the thought that Luke could pass as management material, but Stout was continuing. 'He'll have a key and can let our people in at night. If the neighbours get used to workmen being in the place it shouldn't cause so much gossip.'

'Good.' Porteous thought the plan unnecessarily elaborate. They had no evidence that Reeves would try to contact his sister. But he knew Stout wasn't in the mood to take criticism. Counselling had taught him the futility of knocking his head against a brick wall.

'I got an address for Reeves from the DVLA. He lives in a small town in the Yorkshire Dales.'

'Back to Yorkshire,' Porteous said. 'Hannah Morton thought Theo had been at school there but we didn't get anywhere when we checked earlier. Could Alec have introduced Theo to the Brices, I wonder? I suppose it's more likely to be coincidence. Theo would have been in a boarding school and Alec a care assistant in a Social Services assessment centre so it's hard to see where they'd have met. Not that I've traced either establishment yet. But it shouldn't be difficult now.'

'I've found out where Reeves worked.' Stout was jubilant. Porteous tried to be gracious in his moment of glory. 'It was a place called Redwood. It wasn't run by Social Services. Not officially. They bought in places there for difficult kids they couldn't persuade anyone else to take. It was operated by a charitable trust. It closed about a year ago when the person in charge retired. A woman by the name of Alice Cornish. Apparently she's famous.'

'Oh yes,' Porteous said. 'She's very famous.'

He was surprised Stout had never heard of her. Alice Cornish had been committed to providing quality care for children before the improvement of residential services became a fashionable cause. She'd worked in local-authority children's homes in the late sixties and resigned, very publicly, exposing a series of scandals. The press hadn't known what to make of her and in some quarters she'd been portrayed as an idealistic but rather hysterical trouble maker. She'd gone on to qualify as a doctor and then to set up an establishment of her own – Redwood – in a farmhouse in the country. Her peers found it hard to understand why she was bothering with grubby and disruptive children when she could be earning a comfortable living within the health service, but her qualifications made them take her seriously. She welcomed research teams into Redwood and they had to admit that her methods worked. She had gone on to be hugely respected in the field of social welfare. She had been made a Dame and chaired committees of inquiry into widespread abuse. Yet still she maintained her personal contact with Redwood and the children who'd lived there spoke of her with great affection. It seemed inconceivable that she would have employed anyone suspected of abuse. Porteous said as much, tactfully, to Stout.

'She wouldn't have known, would she? He was never convicted. Never even charged.'

'I just don't see how he would have got away with it at a place like that. Dr Cornish's whole philosophy was about listening to children. The kids wouldn't have been frightened to talk if Reeves had tried anything on.'

'He's clever,' Stout said stubbornly. 'Cunning. You don't know.'

Again Porteous saw no point in arguing. 'Is Reeves at home now?'

'I got in touch with the local nick. They sent a

community policeman round there yesterday evening. If Alec had answered he'd have got a pep talk about the neighbourhood watch, but nobody was in. According to the neighbours he's a model citizen, keeps his lawn cut, does his stint driving meals on wheels round the village and – get this – he helps organize the Duke of Edinburgh award scheme at the local high school.'

'Perhaps that's how he met Theo Randle,' Porteous said, almost to himself.

'Perhaps that's still how he gets to meet young lads.'

'Had the local bobbies heard that anything like that's going on?'

'They didn't say.' Stout sounded disappointed. 'But he's known as a loner. Well thought of in the village, but no real friends, no wife, no ladyfriend.'

You could say the same about me, Porteous thought.

'Did the neighbours have any idea where Reeves had gone?' he asked.

'Away for a week to visit an old colleague. They think he'll be back today or tomorrow.'

'I don't suppose they mentioned where the old colleague lives?'

'No. The old lady who lives next door asked but he wouldn't say. It wasn't like him. Usually he was happy to have a cup of tea with her and a chat.'

'Suspicious . . .' Porteous said, but only to please Stout. He didn't want Reeves to be uncovered as a child-abuser and serial killer. His employment at Redwood would be seized upon by the press. Alice Cornish would lose her credibility. And it would mean that Stout had been right all along. He hated to admit it but an element of competition had crept into the inquiry. Stout had found an address for Reeves, but still Porteous hadn't discovered where Crispin Randle had taken Theo to be educated after the fire. He didn't want Stout to be proved right about this.

'I've made an appointment to visit Mr and Mrs Gillespie,' he said. It would be the first formal interview with Melanie's parents. According to Richard Gillespie the doctor had said Eleanor wasn't up to it before. Gillespie still wasn't keen but Porteous had persisted and he'd reluctantly given way. He must have realized it would have to happen eventually. 'One o'clock. Is that all right with you?'

'You want me to come?'

'I don't want to miss anything. And while we're at the coast I thought we'd see Melanie's friends. Rosalind Morton and the boyfriend. You're good at teenagers.' He'd thought Stout would be pleased to be asked. 'Don't worry. They'll let us know if there's any news on Reeves.'

When Stout left the office Porteous made his decaffeinated coffee and spent most of the next hour on the phone. His first call was to an official in the Department for Education. He needed to find out where a child had been at school thirty years ago. It was urgent. A murder inquiry. Was there any way of finding out? There was a moment of silence and Porteous sensed the usual shock and excitement.

'State sector or private?'

'Private.'

Another silence. Then: 'Did he take any public examinations?'

'O levels. He must have taken O levels because he went on to the sixth form.'

'You could try the exam boards then.' The official hesitated then offered tentatively: 'If you don't mind giving me the details I can phone round for you. Call you back later.'

Porteous didn't mind. He gave both Theo Randle's names and his date of birth. 'We think he was in school somewhere in Yorkshire.'

He replaced the receiver and felt he was easing back into contention in the race with Eddie Stout. Then he remembered two kids had died and wondered how he could have been so petty.

The next phone call was to Hannah Morton's house. It was answered sulkily by a girl who sounded as if she'd just woken up. If anything when he identified himself she was even ruder. 'Don't come to the house,' she said. 'I'll be working. The Promenade. A big white pub on the front. You'll need to talk to Frank anyway and I'll make sure Joe's there. Make it mid-afternoon when we're not so busy.' She replaced the receiver before he had a chance to object.

He was wondering whether to break his routine and have another cup of coffee when the DFEE officer phoned him back.

'I think I've traced your lad.'

'Go on.'

'He took O levels in the name of Michael Grey. Passed seven well. A grades in Art and English. Failed Latin.'

That's all it took, Porteous thought. One phone call. Why didn't I think about the exam boards before?

'Have you got the name of the school?'

'Marwood Grange. It doesn't exist any more. I checked.'

'Where was it, when it did exist?'

'Out in the sticks. Yorkshire.' He paused. He was good at dramatic pauses. 'I tracked down one of the teachers. He works in the state system now. You can phone him if you like. Name of Hillier. This is his number.' Porteous was just about to replace the receiver, when he added, 'By the way. There's no record of A levels.'

'No,' Porteous said. 'There wouldn't be.'

Hillier must have been waiting for his call because he answered immediately. 'Marwood Grange,' he said. 'What a nightmare. It put me off private education for life.'

'Do you remember Michael Grey?'

'No. I was only there for a couple of terms before the place closed down and that was a bit of a blur. Like I said. A nightmare.'

'Why did it close?'

'Well, the fire was the final straw, but I don't think it would have survived long anyway. A couple of parents had complained and several more had taken their kids away.'

'Tell me about the fire.'

'It started late one night. I was junior house-master. It started in a classroom they think, but it spread to the dormitories. We got all the boys out but only because a kid got up for a pee. There were no fire doors. No extinguishers. There should have been a court case. It was gross negligence. I'd have been a witness . . . The guy in charge must have had friends in high places because it never came to that. He cut his losses, claimed the insurance and agreed not to run a school again.'

'You're sure you don't remember a boy called Michael Grey?'

'Certainly. I really only remember the boys in my house.'

Porteous saw Stout hovering outside his office door, ready for his trip to the coast, and waved him in. Another fire, he thought. Can that be a coincidence?

Chapter Twenty-Six

The Gillespie house had the dense quiet of an old church. It struck Porteous so strongly because he could tell that usually it wouldn't have been like that. As they approached the front door he saw through the living-room window an electric guitar and a practice amp, a battered upright piano with music on the stand and scribbled manuscript in a pile on the floor. In the hall the telephone had been unplugged.

Richard Gillespie let them in and took them to a room on the first floor which he called his office. It had a desk and a computer but it was big enough for a leather sofa and a couple of armchairs. He left them there while he went to fetch coffee. The room was at the back of the house and looked over the garden to public tennis courts. Two women were playing a scrappy if energetic game and occasionally shouts of triumph and cries of 'well done' floated through the open window, emphasizing the quiet inside.

When Gillespie returned with a tray he was still alone.

'Mrs Gillespie will be joining us?' Porteous asked.

'If you insist that it's necessary. She's resting.'

'It is, I'm afraid.' Porteous was glad Eddie Stout was with him, solid and unimpressed. He found Gillespie intimidating without being able to work out exactly why. Perhaps it was an impression of anger, only held in check with great self-control. Without Eddie as minder he wasn't sure he'd be able to stand his ground.

'While we're on our own I want to know what's going on,' Gillespie said. 'No one's told us anything. I've a right to know.'

'Of course. We're linking your daughter's murder to that of a boy called Theo Randle, nearly thirty years ago. Does the name mean anything to you?'

'Any relation to Crispin Randle?'

'His son.'

'Crispin never told me his son had been killed.'

'He didn't know. We retrieved the body from Cranford Water a couple of weeks ago.'

'*That* body?'

Porteous nodded. 'Did you know Crispin well?'

'Through business really. We had a couple of boozy nights together, but everyone who worked with Crispin ended up drinking with him.'

'Was Mr Randle involved in the computer business?' It was hard to picture.

'Hardly. No. And I was never a computer scientist or engineer. Still don't really understand the technology. I trained as a lawyer and worked my way up through the company's legal department before becoming MD. When I first qualified I worked briefly for a firm of solicitors in town. We sold some property for Crispin.'

'Snowberry?'

'No, he'd already sold that. This was a house in Gosforth. We got a good price for it considering it was nearly falling down round his ears.'

'Tell me about your daughter,' Porteous said.

Gillespie shifted in his seat. For the first time the suppressed anger gave way to uneasiness.

'It must seem like prying but we'll need all the information you can give us.'

Eddie sat with his pencil poised over his notebook, waiting.

'She wasn't my daughter.'

'I'm sorry?'

'I mean, not biologically. Legally of course. I adopted her when I married Eleanor.'

Porteous wondered if that explained the anger. His position was compromised, ambiguous. Eleanor's grief would be more straightforward. Had she made him feel he couldn't possibly understand what she was going through?

'Does Melanie's natural father know that she's dead?'

'I shouldn't think so. We've no way of tracing him. He's a musician. That, at least, is what he calls himself. I think there was a card at Christmas. From North Africa, Marrakesh, somewhere like that. He travels a lot. I don't know how he supports himself. Not now.'

'What do you mean? "Not now"?'

There was a pause. Eventually Gillespie said, 'I gave him money. Enough to last for a while.'

'Why did you do that, Mr Gillespie?' Eddie Stout spoke for the first time, shocking them both. Both, too, sensed the disapproval in his voice. Not now, Eddie, Porteous thought. Now's not the time for a moral crusade.

But though the question seemed to make Gillespie defensive, he wanted to explain. 'It was when Eleanor and I married. I didn't want Ray around, dropping in every afternoon with his unsuitable friends, confusing Mel. I wanted to be her dad.'

'So you paid him to go away?'

'And to agree to the adoption, yes.'

'How old was Melanie then?'

'Five. Six by the time we went through the whole process.'

'And he just disappeared from her life?'

'Yes. Look, I thought it was the best thing at the time, all right? Ray Scully was mixed up in all sorts. He'd been convicted of fraud. He'd even been to prison. What could someone like him give Melanie?'

'Did Mrs Gillespie know about the financial arrangement?'

'Look, it was no big deal. A one-off payment. I wasn't stopping him keeping in touch for ever. Like I said, he wrote to her, sent her cards.'

'So Mrs Gillespie knew?'

'No. She just thought it was Ray being irresponsible again. He'd been disappearing on and off since Mel was born.' He stood up and stared blankly out of the window. The tennis game was over. 'I shouldn't have told you.'

'No,' Porteous said. 'I'm very pleased that you did.'

'You won't tell Eleanor?'

'I really don't think that's any of my business. Though we'll want to trace the father. Is there any possibility that he's been in touch with Melanie recently?'

'She didn't say anything. But I don't suppose she would have done. Communication had pretty well broken down here.'

'You know a middle-aged man went into the Promenade looking for her. It didn't occur to you that it
might have been her father?'

'No. He knows where we live. He could have come
to the house.'

'That wasn't part of the deal, was it? You'd paid
him to stay away.'

Gillespie shrugged. The fight seemed to have gone
out of him. 'Eleanor thought that was the start of all
Mel's problems. Ray going away.'

'What problems?'

'She was never an easy child. Bright of course, but
attention seeking, hyperactive. Then in the last few
years there's been the anorexia.'

'Was she being treated for that?'

'Oh, she's been treated for everything.' He must
have realized that sounded callous. 'We wanted her to
be happy. I don't think she ever has been, really. When
we moved here and she started making friends I
thought things were looking up. But in the couple of
weeks before she died she was more disturbed than I
remember.'

'Who was her psychiatrist?'

'Dr Collier at the General. He seemed a decent
enough bloke, but I don't know how effective he was.'

Oh, he's effective, Porteous thought. Trust me. I
know.

'He wanted to treat Mel as an inpatient. She hated
the idea. He was talking about sectioning her. Not
on the food issue. She was eating enough, just, to keep
her alive. But because she seemed to be depressed.'

'How did that manifest itself?' Porteous thought he
sounded a bit like a doctor himself.

'Listlessness, insomnia, withdrawal.' He paused. 'Sometimes I thought she'd lost all touch with reality.'

'In what way?'

'She seemed to hate her mother and me. She couldn't believe we were trying to help her. There was some fantasy about us trying to control her.'

Just because you're paranoid, it doesn't mean they're not out to get you, Porteous thought and stopped the facetious words slipping out just in time. It was true. In hospital he'd met a man who was convinced he was about to be blown up by the IRA. The staff thought he was psychotic. A week after leaving the place he'd been killed by a car bomb. He dragged his attention back to the present, was aware of Eddie staring at him. He nodded at Eddie to take over the questions.

'Had Melanie complained of any unwanted attention? Unusual phone calls, perhaps, strangers trying to engage her in conversation.'

'I told you. In the last few days before she was killed she didn't go out.'

'She hadn't had a problem with her boyfriend?'

'What do you mean?'

'They hadn't had a row, for example?'

Clever Eddie, Porteous thought. On the look out for another connection. But Gillespie shook his head.

'I don't know how Joe put up with her but he was always remarkably patient. Eleanor and I like him a lot. He's respectable, despite the hair and the clothes. Comes from a good family. He was devoted to Mel. It was a relief when they started going out together. It was someone else to keep an eye on her. You know?'

Porteous nodded. 'Would it be possible to speak to

Mrs Gillespie now? We could talk in her room if that would be easier.'

'No. She won't want that. But you'll have to wait while she gets ready.'

'Perhaps in the meantime we could look in Melanie's room. Is it as she left it?'

'Yes. The police said not to touch anything. I'll show you.'

The room was on the next floor, long and narrow, with two bay windows, each with a padded seat. The furniture was expensive, much of it custom built to fit the space, but the posters and cards on the walls, the candles and joss-sticks, the piles of clothes and papers turned it into any other student pit. On the desk there was a CD player and a rack of tapes. A door in the opposite wall led to a small bathroom.

'You'll have to excuse the mess,' Gillespie said. 'She wouldn't let our cleaning lady in. Something else to fight over.'

'You can leave it to us, sir. We'll come down when we've finished.'

Gillespie turned. They waited in silence until they heard his footsteps retreating down the polished wood stairs.

'Well?' Porteous asked. 'What do you think of him?'

'He's told us some of it.' Eddie had already started on the dressing table. He pulled the top drawer right out and began feeling carefully through an octopus of tights. 'Thrown us a few crumbs – like the fact that he'd paid the dad to go away. But he's not told us everything. Not by a long chalk. Perhaps it's not relevant. If he's having an affair with his secretary, for instance. I don't suppose that would have anything to do with the murder. But he's keeping secrets and I don't like it.'

'I'm not sure.' It was unlike Eddie to get so heated. Lack of sleep, Porteous thought. He felt more sympathy for Gillespie. 'Perhaps he just feels guilty because he sent the father away and screwed up the kid.'

'No,' Eddie snorted. 'His sort don't do guilt.'

They sorted through the mess but they didn't find a hiding place. No cache of love letters. No diary, which Porteous had been hoping for. He'd thought an introspective young woman like that would have kept a written record of her thoughts and feelings. No photo of her father, which he'd been looking for too. He'd have liked something to show the manager of the pub.

In the bathroom there was still a dirty towel on the floor. There was a small wall cupboard empty except for a bottle of anti-depressants on a shelf inside. It was dated a month before but it was still full. Had she stopped taking her medication because she thought she could manage without? Or was she saving the pills for a grand suicidal gesture?

Eddie was replacing the final drawer. 'Nothing. Still, if Gillespie knew there was anything incriminating he'd have had plenty of time to get rid of it. There's this . . . for what it's worth . . .'

It was the National Record of Achievement from her school. The academic reports were glowing. There was a number of unaccounted absences, but allowance had obviously been made. The teachers had written sympathetic comments about Mel's courage in the face of her medical difficulties. Eddie snorted again.

'You don't think she had serious health problems?' Porteous asked.

'Well, it's not like cancer, is it? Self-induced and self-indulgent. If you ask me she could have done with a bit of healthy neglect.' He opened the door of one of the wardrobes. Porteous had already been through the clothes checking the pockets. 'Look at all that stuff. She didn't get that in C&A or New Look. My Ruthie would give her eye-teeth for one of those frocks.'

'Not a justification for murder though, is it?' Porteous said quietly. 'Being spoiled by your parents.'

Stout stopped, horrified, his arm still flung out in a gesture of righteous indignation.

'You're right. That was crass. I don't know what came over me. It was that man. I let him get to me. One of the first rules, isn't it? Don't blame the victim.'

'Have we finished?' Porteous asked, a bit embarrassed to have had such a dramatic effect.

'Just a minute.'

Stout straightened the cover on the crumpled bed. It was dark blue with gold stars and moons, too young for the sophisticated young woman they'd come to know, perhaps a relic from childhood. He felt under the pillow and came out with a photograph in a small silver frame.

'The boyfriend?' Porteous asked. Then more interested. 'Or the father?'

'Neither.'

It was of a small girl, perhaps eighteen months old, with blond curls tied with a ribbon. She had a plump face and dimples.

'There's no younger sister, is there?'

Porteous shook his head. He slipped the photograph from the frame. On the back of the print was written 'Em'. 'Another coincidence,' he said. 'The Randle child who was killed in the fire was called Emily.'

'The photo's much more recent than that,' Stout said. 'Unless they had Teletubbies thirty years ago. Look at that top she's wearing.'

'Perhaps the Gillespies will know.'

'Aye,' Stout said. 'And perhaps they'll tell. Which is another thing altogether.'

Eleanor Gillespie had joined her husband in his office. Porteous thought perhaps they didn't want their personal space contaminated by the police. Eleanor wore jeans and a big sweater. She seemed very small inside it. She hardly looked up when they came in. Porteous apologized for the intrusion but couldn't tell if she was listening.

'It won't take long.'

She shrugged. 'We've got all the time in the world.'

'We need to trace your husband, Mrs Gillespie. Do you have any idea where he is?'

She shook her head.

'Is there anyone who might know?'

'His mother, if she's still alive.' She gave an address.

Porteous handed the photograph of the baby to her. 'Could you tell us who this is, please?'

Eleanor looked down listlessly, then seemed to jerk awake. She shot a look at her husband.

'It's Emma,' she said. 'Emma Leese. Just a little girl Mel used to babysit for. Before she got tied up with exams. I didn't realize she'd kept a photo.' She gave a sob. 'It's so unfair. If Mel had gone away on holiday when she'd planned she wouldn't have been here. She'd have been on some beach in Portugal soaking up the sun.'

'What made her change her mind?'

'I don't know. Perhaps Joe wasn't keen. He never seemed very happy about the idea. Perhaps Mel was so low that she just couldn't face it.'

She turned again to her husband. 'We should all have gone. As a family.' An accusation. He turned away and didn't respond.

Porteous stood to go.

'Does the name Alec Reeves mean anything to either of you?'

She seemed about to answer but Gillespie stood too and spoke for both of them. 'No,' he said firmly. 'I've never heard of him. Have you, Ellie?'

She said nothing and stared dumbly after the men as her husband led them down the stairs.

Chapter Twenty-Seven

Eddie said he was starving so they queued at a baker's for a sandwich and sat on a bench on the sea front like trippers to eat.

'I wouldn't give that marriage long.' Eddie cupped his hand to catch the oozing tuna mayonnaise before it splashed on to his lap.

'No?' It wasn't the first time Porteous had been surprised by Eddie's cynicism. 'I thought they were well matched. He seemed supportive. Protective even.'

'Nah. She blames him already for the lassie's death. I'd give it six months. She doesn't trust him. We should get her on her own.'

'What have you got against him? Besides his money?'

'That'll do for the time being. And the fact that he was lying.'

After the glare of the afternoon sun the pub was inviting. Rosie had been right. At this time of day the place was quiet. She was on her own behind the bar, chatting to a thin lad with a pony tail. She realized who they were as soon as they came through the door, and went to the back to call a plump, balding man, before greeting them.

'Do you want a drink?' It was an offhand snarl.

Porteous thought if she was as ungracious as that to all the customers she was lucky still to have a job.

'Orange juice.' He raised his eyebrows to Stout, who nodded. 'Two.'

She poured the drinks then turned to her boss. 'Can I have my break now, Frank?'

'Aye. Take as long as you like. We're hardly rushed off our feet.'

She helped herself to a Coke and led them to a table in the corner. The skinny boy followed after.

'This is Joe,' she said. 'Mel's boyfriend.'

'It was good of you to come.'

'What do you want?'

'To talk about Mel, that's all. To try to get a clearer idea what she was like. Her parents are upset.'

'We're upset too.'

Porteous wished Eddie would help him out. He hadn't expected the girl's hostility. Didn't Eddie know about teenagers? But Eddie drank his orange juice and seemed content to let his boss struggle on.

'It's not just that. She'll have told things to you that she'd never let on to her parents. Wouldn't she?'

'Yeah. I suppose.'

'So just talk to us. Describe her. Joe?'

'She wasn't like anyone else I'd ever met.'

That hardly helps, Porteous thought.

'She was delicate, fragile. It wasn't just the anorexia. I mean, I could never get to the bottom of what that was about. It didn't seem to be about food. Not image even. I mean, it didn't seem to be about the super-model thing. She didn't want starvation chic. She had more about her than that. It was as if she didn't feel she deserved to eat. Which was crazy when you knew her, because *everyone* thought she was brilliant. Not just the teachers but her mates. People liked being around her. I couldn't believe it when we started going out. I was on a high for months.'

Hadn't that been how Hannah Meek had described her relationship with Michael Grey? Porteous thought. But perhaps it could be a description of any teenage infatuation.

'Did she talk to you about her dad?'

'You know about that?' Joe seemed surprised. 'My God, you'd have thought *he* was a murderer the way Richard Gillespie made her keep it secret. I think that made her dream about him even more. She had this romantic notion that Ray Scully, the great musician, was going to turn up and take her away from all that respectability.'

'Richard wasn't Mel's real dad?' Porteous could tell Rosie was hurt.

'No.'

'You never said. Even when she went missing.'

'I couldn't,' Joe said. 'She'd made me promise . . .' Like a six-year-old in the playground.

'Had she heard from her dad recently?' Porteous asked.

'No, I'm sure she would have said.'

'How were things between you before she died?'

'I hadn't seen her for a few days. Her parents said she was too ill.'

'You'd spoken on the phone though?'

'They'd said she wasn't up to it. I don't know. Maybe she didn't want to talk to me.'

'Why wouldn't she? Had you had a row?'

'No!'

'But?'

'But something had happened to freak her out. I don't know what it was. Maybe it was something I'd done or she'd thought I'd done, but she wouldn't say.' He paused, drank his beer. Porteous thought that despite his grief part of him was enjoying this – the attention, the drama. At university it would make an unusual chat-up story. The murder of the love of his life would demand sympathy. Women would go for it in droves. 'We were going on holiday. It was her parents' idea. They thought she should get away. The stress of waiting for exam results was getting to her. They knew someone with a villa on the Algarve.'

'Eleanor said you weren't very keen on the idea.'

Joe seemed shocked by the interruption. Porteous thought he'd already conjured a fantasy in which there'd been no disagreements in their relationship.

'I just wasn't sure I wanted the responsibility.'

'She could be disturbed?'

'Not mad!' Joe said. 'Troubled, depressed maybe. I'm not saying she was insane.'

'So you were all set for a holiday to the Algarve. What happened?'

'We were in here. All packed. Our suitcases with us. It was an evening flight and we'd arranged for the taxi to pick us up outside at six. We were having a few drinks, saying goodbye to our friends. Not Rosie. She'd gone away with her mum.'

Porteous turned slowly to Rosie. 'That was the day of the school reunion?'

She nodded.

'Was the television on in here?'

'Yes.' Joe had finished the beer. He put the empty glass on the table. 'Why?'

'An idea. Humour me.'

'Mel started watching it. Suddenly she shouted for everyone to keep quiet. She was ratty. I mean really ratty. The moment before, she'd been laughing, then suddenly she was screaming at people because she couldn't hear.'

'What was on the television?'

'I'm not sure. Local news, I think.'

That was the day they'd issued the press release naming the boy in the lake as Michael Grey and shown the photograph. Porteous felt a hit of adrenalin, breathed slowly to keep his voice calm.

'Did she say what had interested her?'

'Not really. Nothing that made sense. She got up and switched off the telly. Not angry any more, but serious. I asked her what was so important. "Nothing," she said. "I think I've just seen a ghost. That's all." Then she said the holiday was off. "You go," she said. "Take someone else. Take Rosie if you like." But she didn't mean it. And anyway I couldn't just fly off and leave her like that. The taxi turned up then and we got it to take us home. The driver was moaning because he'd been expecting the full fare out to the airport and he'd turned down other work. I said we'd pay him anyway. I sat in the back next to her and she was shaking. She wasn't causing a scene. She was really upset. She wouldn't let me go into the house with her. "You've paid all that money. You might as well get him to drop you at your doorstep." That was the last time I saw her.'

'Rosie, did you ever see her after that, after you came back from Cranford?'

She shook her head.

'Does the name Alec Reeves mean anything to either of you?'

'Is he the suspect?' Joe asked, almost with relish. Again Porteous thought the boy would survive this experience without too many scars. He wasn't so sure about Rosie.

'Just someone we're trying to trace.'

'Never heard of him.'

'Rosie?'

Again she shook her head.

'What about Emma Leese?'

'Wasn't she the little girl Mel used to babysit?'

'Do you know her?'

'No. It was before Mel moved round here. But she used to talk about her. About how cute she was.'

'When did Mel move to the coast?'

'A couple of years ago. At the beginning of the sixth form.' Rosie gave Joe a brave grin. 'That's why all the lads fancied her. Because she was new, exciting. Him and me started infant school together. No secrets at all.'

Another connection with Theo, Porteous thought, almost automatically. But his mind was moving on in wider speculation. Wasn't the relationship between Mel and the baby girl more intense than that between a young babysitter and her charge? Could Mel be the child's mother, the photograph her only souvenir of a baby handed over for fostering or adoption? It would explain Richard Gillespie's hostility and his reluctance to answer questions. Even after her death he wouldn't want details of a teenage pregnancy made public. It might explain too why the family had moved just before she started her A-level course, why Mel was so mixed up.

'Did Mel ever talk about having children?' he asked.

Rosie picked up on what he was on about at once. 'You *must* be joking.'

'Where did she go to school before she started with you?'

'Don't know. Some private place inland, I think. Did she ever tell you, Joe?'

Or a special unit, Porteous thought, for pregnant schoolgirls. With very wealthy parents. Then immediately – I wonder if Redwood would take a kid like that. But wouldn't Carver have picked up the fact that she'd had a child at the post-mortem? Perhaps it was in the final report which still hadn't arrived.

'Don't you want to know,' Joe demanded, 'about the guy that came in here looking for her?'

'Of course.'

'I'll get back behind the bar,' Rosie said. 'Then Frank can come and talk to you.' She walked away from them. Joe watched her wistfully, unsure whether or not he should follow.

Porteus could tell immediately that Frank wouldn't be any help. There'd been a brief discussion with Rosie behind the bar. He'd been reluctant to let her take over. Now he did approach them his face was greasy with sweat.

'Look.' He held out his hands, palms outward, a gesture to distance himself from the policemen and their questions. 'I can't remember anything. Honest. I wish I could. It was really busy. A guy came in asking about Mel. I didn't tell him anything and he left. That's all.'

'Middle-aged, you said. Respectable.'

'Aye.'

'Not elderly then? Not an old man?'

'Compared to these kids they all look old, don't they?'

Stout had got hold of a recent photograph of Alec Reeves. He'd been in the paper in his home town handing over Duke of Edinburgh awards to a bunch of school children. He looked younger than his years. It must have been all that walking in the hills. He stood, fit and tanned, in the centre of the frame smiling shyly. It was hard to think of him as a monster.

'Could that be him?'

'Do you know how many faces I see in here?'

Porteus could feel Eddie beside him, winding himself up for a row.

'Please concentrate,' he said quietly.

'All right. Aye. It could have been him. But I wouldn't swear to it. Certainly not in court.'

Chapter Twenty-Eight

At the police station in Cranford, Claire Wright was waiting for them. 'I've traced Elizabeth Milburn, the woman who was Emily Randle's nanny. She's head teacher now of a nursery school in the city but she lives out this way. She'll be in this evening after eight if you want to get in touch.'

'Any news on Reeves?' Eddie demanded.

'Nothing. He's not visited his sister and he's not gone home.' She was sitting at her desk and didn't look up from her computer screen. Eddie walked away. He knocked an empty Coke can off the desk and didn't bother picking it up. 'What's wrong with him?'

'Reeves,' Porteus said. 'Eddie's convinced he killed a disabled lad before Theo Randle, and he likes him for these two. If there are only two.'

'Looks that way at the moment. We've pulled up all the serious-crime reports that might be relevant. I can't see anything which fits into a pattern with Randle and Gillespie. Not yet.'

'Anything else?'

'Members of the public have been ringing in all day, claiming they saw Melanie on the evening she died. It's taken time to sort through. We're following up anything that looks promising this evening. OK?'

'Sure.'

He went to his office to start tracking down Ray Scully. Scully's mother still lived at the address given to him by Eleanor Gillespie and she answered the phone on the first ring, shouting a little so he realized she was hard of hearing.

'Yes? Who is it?'

He explained, repeating the questions louder when she didn't seem to understand.

'Ray isn't here.'

'I know that Mrs Scully. Where is he? We want to talk to him.'

'What about?'

It was obvious that she didn't read the newspapers and the Gillespies hadn't bothered telling her. He didn't want to break the news of her granddaughter's death over the phone.

'He's not in any trouble, Mrs Scully.'

'Are you sure?' The deafness made her sound truculent.

'Absolutely.' Crossing his fingers, wondering if this was true.

There was a long pause.

'Mrs Scully?'

She made up her mind suddenly. 'He's in Cromer. Norfolk. Summer season in the theatre at the end of the pier. Playing in the band for the musical turns.'

'Has he got a telephone there?'

Suspicion returned. 'No. He phones me. Once a week. Regular as clockwork.'

'Can you ask him to contact me? Tell him it's about Mel.'

He repeated the question to check that she'd

understood, but she'd already gone. He left a similar message with the theatre manager.

It was six o'clock. Too early to visit Lizzie Milburn, so he could make a start on finding out everything there was to know about Frank Garrity, the manager of the Prom. A treat to himself after a dispiriting day. There was nothing he liked better than a dig through the files and records. He found what he was after quickly, made himself a celebratory mug of coffee and went to look for Eddie. He was at his desk, engaged in an earnest discussion with Charlie Luke, who was holed up in the bungalow opposite Sarah Jackson's.

'Nobody's been there all day except a bloke selling dodgy dusters.'

'I know why Frank was so reluctant to talk to us,' Porteous said.

'Why?'

'He was charged with rape twenty years ago. It never came to court. The girl changed her story. But he was held on remand for a few days. It must have made an impression.'

'Could he have killed Melanie? No one else saw the bloke who asked for her. He could have made it up to muddy the waters.'

'He could. But he'd have still been in primary school when Theo Randle was killed.'

'Could Carver be wrong about the links between the deaths?'

Could he? Porteous thought about it. It wouldn't be the first time a team had wasted weeks following up connections which didn't really exist.

'I don't think so. I don't like the man, but he's a good pathologist. And he's put his reputation on the line.' Another thought occurred to him. 'Has his completed report been sent over yet?'

'I've not seen it.' As if he didn't really care. As if all he cared about was nailing Reeves.

'I want you to talk to the Spences and Chris Johnson tomorrow,' Peter said.

'Why?' As truculent as Mrs Scully.

'Back to basics, I suppose. They were at the party where Theo was last seen alive. Ask them about Reeves. Did they know him at the time? Show them a photo. Both photos. Did anyone see Reeves and Theo together? Has he been knocking around recently?'

'Yes,' Eddie said slowly. 'I could do that.'

Then he was on the phone again, asking for an update from Charlie Luke.

Lizzie Milburn was in her fifties, but rather glamorous in an efficient, power-dressed sort of way. Certainly more glamorous than he'd expected someone who spent her days with three- and four-year-olds to be. But it seemed she ran the Early Years Centre on a big council estate on the edge of the city and spent little time these days with paint and sand. Porteous arrived at her home before her. She had a flat in what had once been a large country house. When there was no reply he was about to walk back to his car to wait, but she drove up, very quickly, and pulled to a stop beside him, scattering gravel. She was in a convertible Golf and the roof was down. She slid one slim leg out and stood up to greet him. She smelled expensive. Her skirt was short. Her shoes were dusty.

'You wouldn't believe the mess on the estate,' she said. 'It's like a dust bowl. They're knocking down most of the flats and putting up houses. A good thing. No one wanted to live in those high rises. But they seem to be taking for ever. And it's worse in the winter. You need wellingtons to get from your car.' She didn't expect any response and went on, 'Sorry I'm late. Parents evening. In a place like ours it's hard to get the parents there and we don't feel we can chase them away.'

At the door she slipped off her shoes. 'I'm sorry, Inspector, but I really must have a very large G and T. I don't suppose you . . . ?'

'Just a tonic,' he said.

She'd been married, it seemed, but it hadn't worked out. He had the impression that she'd got rid of a husband who hadn't lived up to her expectations, re-assumed her maiden name, and carried on as if he'd never existed. There had never been any children but she'd done well financially out of the divorce. All this he gathered in the first few minutes. They sat, without ceremony at the kitchen table and he was reminded of his conversation with Stella Randle. Another kitchen. Two women of a certain age, but remarkably different.

'What's all this about, Inspector?' Her hair was rinsed auburn and cut short. Her make-up was still intact. Despite the difference in their ages, despite the fact that she wasn't at all the sort of woman he usually went for, he found himself attracted to her.

'Theo Randle.'

'Oh? Usually when the police come to see me it's because one of the fathers has been suspected of abuse. Or the mums have been shifting stolen property on our premises. Or some little vandal has set fire to the place again.'

'It is about a fire I want to talk to you.'

'Is it true that the body you found in Cranford Water was Theo?'

'Yes. He'd changed his name before he died but it was Theo.'

'Poor boy.' She went to the freezer to fetch ice for their drinks. 'You'd have thought he started out with every advantage. Compared with the children I work with now. But he didn't. He didn't stand a chance of a normal life.'

'Why?'

'Before I arrived at Snowberry he'd been left almost to his own devices. Crispin went to pieces after Maria died. Kept up a show for the constituents but he was hitting the bottle even then. Theo was minded by a series of women whose main job was to keep the house clean. He got whatever he wanted so long as he left them in peace. And it was much the same when Crispin was there. I suppose things were better when he started school but it was a snotty little prep place and I think it must have been pretty bleak. Theo must have been well screwed up even before Crispin married Stella.'

'Did he resent his stepmother?'

'No. Quite the opposite. He worshipped her. She took time to listen to him, read him stories, played with him. She wasn't much more than a girl herself – a bit giggly and silly – but she made a real effort to get on with him. I met her first when she was pregnant. We were about the same age but she made me feel about a hundred and one. She treated the whole thing as a game. As if having a baby was all about parties and presents. She'd been totally sheltered. Mummy and Daddy were friends of Crispin's. She'd done boarding school, a year's finishing in Switzerland. The job as Crispin's secretary was to give her something to do with her time before marriage and of course she didn't have to look very far for a husband. It was hardly surprising that she went to pieces when Emily was born. Her depression was a nightmare for everyone at Snowberry but especially Theo. He thought he'd found someone who cared about him. Then suddenly she didn't care about anyone. She couldn't. The doctors Crispin got in didn't help. They just pumped her full of drugs. I tried to spend as much time as I could with Theo, but I couldn't replace her and I was pretty busy with Emily.'

'Did you keep in touch with him when he went away to school?'

'I didn't keep in touch with any of them. Crispin made it quite clear my role in the family was over when Emily died. The day after the fire he gave me a month's wages in lieu of notice and he sent me away.'

'Tell me about the fire.'

She swirled the remaining gin in her glass. 'I'd been out. It didn't happen often. Snowberry was miles from anywhere. The only entertainment was the pub and those days a woman didn't go out drinking on her own. One of the lads on the estate asked me to go to the pictures in town. He had a car. That was the only reason I went and I made sure I wasn't late back. The nursery was at the back of the house and I couldn't see the fire from the front. The first thing I did was check on Emily but I couldn't get near her room. You wouldn't believe the heat and the smoke. Sometimes I wake up at night and I can still taste it. Theo was asleep but I managed to get him out. Crispin and Stella were still up. They'd both been drinking and they hadn't noticed a thing.'

'Was anyone else there?'

'Not in the house itself. There was a couple who looked after the place, but they lived in a cottage at the end of the drive. They didn't know anything until the fire engines woke them up.'

'Are you sure it was an accident?'

'You think the fire's related to Theo's murder?'

He shrugged. 'I hope I've got an open mind.'

'Stella wouldn't hurt a fly, even in her maddest moments. Crispin had a fearsome temper. I can imagine him lashing out at Stella, but he loved the baby. And even if the fire was his fault, why kill Theo after all that time?'

And what, Porteus thought, could any of this have to do with Melanie Gillespie?

Chapter Twenty-Nine

Porteous had made an appointment to see Melanie's psychiatrist. Walking from the car park to the day hospital, all glass and concrete like the superstore next door, he tried to walk in her footsteps, see it through her eyes. On the step by the entrance, a young couple stared blankly into space, smoking cheap smuggled cigarettes. In the waiting-room a middle-aged man with wild hair paced backwards and forwards talking to himself about God. Sitting on one of the orange plastic chairs in the corridor a plump woman in a neat, grey raincoat sobbed discreetly into a handkerchief. What would Melanie have made of them? Would she have considered herself different and sat apart? Would she have visited the place alone, her parents too busy to be there? He found it hard to imagine Melanie here at all. He thought Richard Gillespie would have arranged somewhere private, an exclusive clinic where discretion would be guaranteed, the sort of health farm where customers were force fed instead of starved.

The receptionist on the main desk gave him a brief smile of recognition, but when he showed her his warrant card she shook her head. A sort of apology for mistaking him for one of the patients. The waiting-room was unusually busy. The hospital tried to see patients on time. If they were kept hanging around some lost their nerve and walked out. Others turned nasty. Porteous had a sudden qualm of conscience about taking up the doctor's time.

'Mr Porteous, the doctor will see you now.'

They watched him, aware he was jumping the queue, but too apathetic or too cowed to comment. The nurse started walking with him.

'It's all right,' he said. 'I know the way.'

He followed the corridor with its jolly posters promoting healthy eating and adverts for self-help groups, until he came to the door. He stopped outside, feeling for a moment the old anxiety, the breaker of rules outside the head teacher's study, then he knocked lightly and went in.

Collier was a red-headed Scot with freckles and blue eyes. He ran marathons and looked horribly fit.

'Peter. You're looking very well.'

Despite himself he felt pleased. Collier had always been honest. If he looked lousy he'd have said so. This meant he must be doing OK.

'I'm not here for me. Didn't they say?'

'Yeah. There's a note somewhere.' He scrabbled through a pile of scrap paper. Porteous would have loved the opportunity to go through the desk, to reduce it to a series of neat piles. 'And I had a phone call,' the psychiatrist continued. 'From Mr Gillespie.' He lay back in his chair. 'What you might call a warning shot across my bows.'

'Oh?'

'Oh aye. I'm to respect Melanie's confidentiality although she's dead. The cheek of the man. You'd think he was paying me.'

'Isn't that odd? I mean Melanie being treated on the NHS. He must have private health insurance.'

'I'm the best,' Collier said, quite seriously. 'If he'd asked around he'd have been told that. And I don't do private.'

'I do know. That you're the best.'

Collier grinned. 'And they might have gone private before they came here. They said not, but I wouldn't have been surprised if they'd tried something else. Herbal remedies. Acupuncture. Hypnosis. Any damn thing to avoid having to face what was going on. You'd be surprised by the number of patients who've been fooled by some quack but who're too embarrassed to admit it.'

'So,' Porteous said cautiously. 'There's nothing you're prepared to tell me. You've been warned off.'

'I can't tell you about the lassie's illness.'

'When did you last see her?'

Collier opened a desk diary. The pages were covered in scribbled notes and crossing out. The lack of order made Porteous wince.

'A week ago. It was a house call.' He paused, frowned. 'Oh bugger Gillespie! But just be discreet. He says he'll sue. He couldn't, of course, but he could make things awkward. Eleanor, the mother, phoned up in a state. She said Melanie was delusional, in the middle of some sort of crisis. She needed to be in hospital. I offered to send in a community nurse but that wouldn't do. By the time I could get there Gillespie had turned up. He said the same as his wife but more forcefully. I had to treat the girl as an inpatient.'

'But you didn't admit her?'

'No. I wasn't going to be bullied. I'd have liked to

talk to Melanie alone but the parents weren't having any of it and I didn't think I could insist. It was an awkward situation. I was on my own. Sod's law. I'd been trailing a female student around with me the rest of the week.'

'How was Melanie?'

'Angry. She'd had some sort of tantrum, throwing furniture around, smashing plates. It was over by the time I got there but I presume that was why Eleanor phoned.'

'The anger was directed at her parents?'

'That was the impression I had.'

'Was it about the anorexia?'

'Melanie used food as a weapon in every situation. But as to what triggered the scene . . .' He shrugged.

'Could it have had anything to do with her natural father?'

Collier looked up at him sharply then shrugged again.

'I don't know. By the time I arrived Melanie was very controlled and she wasn't giving anything away. She insisted she didn't want to be in hospital and I don't have the beds to admit every young person who causes their parents grief. She was perfectly rational and I didn't think she was suicidal. No grounds for sectioning. I made her an outpatient appointment.'

'When for?'

'I would have liked to have seen her immediately. Get her here, away from home territory. I felt there'd been some sort of breakthrough, that, you know, she trusted me for standing up to her father. But I couldn't make it for a couple of days. I was speaking at a conference in Edinburgh. I gave her a chance to see a colleague but she wasn't happy about that.'

'When was the appointment?'

'The morning her body was found in the cemetery.'

There was a pause. Porteous was aware of the patients in the waiting-room, their nerves twisting to breaking point as the minutes ticked on. He knew Collier was thinking of them too.

'Had she ever been in Redwood?'

'The assessment centre? Alice Cornish's place? Not so far as I know. Why?'

'One of our suspects was a social worker there. It would be a link. And that's privileged information too, even if I can't sue.'

'They never said. I mean, I took a history. Schools. You know the sort of thing. But I didn't check. Why should I?' He paused, tilted back in his chair. 'Redwood was an amazing place. I did a residential placement there. One of my options. There's no reason why the Gillespies wouldn't have admitted to her having gone there. It was harder to get into than Eton. Something for them to brag about.' His eyes flicked to the clock on the wall and Porteous realized his time was up.

Outside the sun splashed off the big glass windows of the hospital and the superstore. His car, trapped between the buildings, was sweltering. He opened all the windows but didn't start driving. He couldn't face Cranford and Eddie's obsession, the rest of the team expecting answers and leadership.

When he did start it was to go up the coast towards Stavely Prison, knowing he was running away. In the low fields on the coastal plain the combine harvesters moved relentlessly over the crop, followed by swarms of herring-gulls, as if the machines were trawlers. By the time he'd arrived he'd persuaded himself that the trip was vital. Hannah was still the best link they had between the killings.

Because he hadn't told the prison in advance that he intended to visit, he had to wait at the gatehouse while they found someone to take him to the library. There was a tiny room which he shared with a nervous young solicitor, who farted loudly then blushed. The walls were posted with mission statements about racism and bullying. They weren't as colourful as those in the hospital but they had the same improving tone.

He'd led the officer on the gate to believe that Hannah was expecting him. 'No. Don't disturb her. Just get an escort to take me over.'

The escort was a stocky young woman who seemed new to the job. They walked past a group of inmates who were weeding a huge circular bed, planted with geraniums in the shape of an anchor. The inmates whistled and shouted and the officer turned scarlet. Porteous didn't think she'd stick it long.

The library was closed and the officer had to unlock it. Inside, an orderly sat at a desk, covering books with transparent plastic.

'Mrs Morton about?'

'In the office. Hannah, there's someone to see you.'

She came out carrying a pile of new books. She seemed so shocked to see him that he thought he might drop them, but she recovered her composure well. She ignored him and spoke to the officer. 'That's all right, Karen. You can leave us to it. I'll see Mr Porteous back to the gate.'

The officer went reluctantly, obviously curious about what he was doing there.

'Do you want to go out for a smoke, Marty? Just give us a few minutes.'

When they were on their own she turned on him with a ferocity which surprised him.

'What the hell do you think you're doing here?'

'I had another appointment on the coast and I thought I'd call in, see if you could spare a few minutes.' I'm playing hookey. Hiding from my team.

'You don't get it, do you? In a prison a visit from the police means arrest, guilt, trouble. It'll be around the place in minutes that you've been to see me. There'll be rumours, stories. It's hard enough to work here as it is.'

'I'm sorry.'

'What do you want?'

'Really just a few questions. Would you like Mr Lee with you?' He would quite have liked to talk to the psychologist, get some informal advice about what might be going on with the Gillespies.

'Arthur can't be here. He's taking a class. If you'd phoned in advance we could have arranged it.'

'Really, it's no big deal.'

'Yes, Inspector. It is a big deal. Two murders nearly thirty years apart are linked by the same weapon. I knew both victims. I'm not stupid. I know how it looks.'

'I talked to your daughter yesterday.'

'She told me.'

'They're nice kids. Her and Joseph.'

'What is this about, Inspector? Marty and I have work to do. The library opens in twenty minutes.'

'Did Theo mention anyone called Alec Reeves?'

There was moment before she reacted. He saw that she still wasn't used to the boy's new name. Then she shook her head. He was disappointed. If she had met him, he thought, she'd have remembered. She remembered everything else. But he persisted.

'He was a friend of the Brices. You might have met him at their home.'

'I didn't meet anyone else there. They were content with their own company.'

'He was sitting with the Brices for the final production of *Macbeth*. In the front row. You told me you chatted to the Brices in the interval. You would have seen him then.'

She sat with her eyes shut and he knew she was trying to re-create the scene. He had heard of photographic memory but he'd never before met anyone with such vivid recall.

'A little man,' she said. 'Nondescript. Grey.'

'Yes.' He tried to keep the voice measured but she picked up his excitement.

'Did he kill Michael?'

'We want to talk to him.'

'So you're looking at someone else? Not just me.'

He smiled. 'No,' he said. 'Not just you.'

'You're right. He was staying with the Brices. He *had* been a member of the church but he'd been working away. There was a special service on the Sunday – a confirmation, I think. He'd come back for that and they'd persuaded him to stay the whole weekend.'

'What did Theo think of him?'

'He said he was boring. Boring but worthy.'

'He wasn't frightened of him? You said Theo phoned you on the Sunday to say he was scared and he needed to talk to you. Could he have been frightened of Alec Reeves?'

'I don't know. If he was, he didn't say.'

'Mr Reeves worked at a place called Redwood. Did Theo ever mention that to you?'

'Wasn't that the name of his school in Yorkshire?'

'No,' Porteous said gently. He didn't want to do anything to stifle her memory. 'I don't think it was.'

'Yes. I'm almost certain. Isn't it strange? I'd been trying so hard to remember if he ever told me the name and couldn't come up with a thing. Then you mentioned Redwood and the conversation's come back to me almost word for word.'

'Could you tell me? It is important.'

'It was the George Eliot essay.' She looked at him. She'd told him so many details of her time with Michael that she thought he knew it all. 'He was a George Eliot fan. As was I. There was a teacher who inspired him. When I reran the conversation in my head first he talked about "someone in the old place". But that wasn't what he said. Not at first. He corrected himself straight away but what he first said was "someone in Redwood".'

She beamed at him, delighted to have got it right. He could see why the fat psychologist fancied her.

So, Porteous thought, after the fire and Emily's death, Theo was sent to Redwood. He'd attended Marwood Grange as a day boy. That's why Hillier the housemaster hadn't remembered him. He must have lived at Redwood for years, until he moved to live with the Brices. Why? Because it was a place of safety and Randle had thought he was in danger from his stepmother? Or because he was so traumatized by the death of his sister, that he needed long-term help? If they could establish that Melanie had been there too, they'd have their link between both teenagers and Alec Reeves.

Hannah walked with him back to the gate. Marty was sitting outside on the grass. As they walked past him the orderly gave her a look which was almost protective.

Chapter Thirty

When he returned to the station Stout wasn't there. Claire Wright had sent him home to get a bite to eat.

'He was bushed,' she said. 'He was here most of the night again and then he went over to the old folks' bungalow to talk to Charlie Luke. And spent the rest of the morning mooching around town.'

'Looking out for Reeves?'

'What do you think?'

Porteous thought Stout was driven, losing it, but he didn't answer.

'Ray Scully's been on the phone.'

'And?'

'He's here. At the coast. He came up last night to stay at his mum's.'

'Can you go to see him? Check out his alibi of course, but let him talk. Anything Melanie might have told him. Did she write? Has he kept the letters? Find out if there's any possible connection between him and the Randles. Any gossip on the Gillespies would be useful too.'

'Sure.'

From his office Porteous phoned Carver. The pathologist was out and nobody else seemed willing to tell him if the report on Melanie Gillespie had been sent.

He sat at his desk for a moment then felt the old restlessness creeping up on him and went out.

He found Eddie Stout asleep in his garden. Bet opened the door to him. She'd been washing up and had on big yellow gloves like motorcycle gauntlets.

'Look at him.' She pointed through the open kitchen window to a neat patio, sheltered with a trellis covered by clematis and honeysuckle. Eddie sat in the shade in a green garden chair. His head was tilted back and his mouth was slightly open. He was snoring. 'I came in to make him a sandwich and when I went out he was off. He's still not eaten.'

'Leave him.' Porteous could smell the honeysuckle. 'He's been doing too much. It's not urgent.'

'No. He'd never forgive me if he knew you'd been and I'd not told him.'

Eddie woke with a start like a small boy startled from a dream. Bet left them. In the kitchen they heard her singing along to Classic FM, the sound of water running into a kettle. Eddie moved stiffly, easing the stiffness from his body.

'It looks as if you're right,' Porteous said. 'About Alec Reeves.' But even as he spoke he was trying to make sense of it. What had the Brices been playing at? They must have heard the rumours about Reeves but they'd invited him into a house where a young kid was staying. Then he thought – No, it was the other way round. Theo knew Reeves before he came to live with the Brices. Reeves must have introduced them.

'It looks as if Theo Randle was at Redwood,' Peter went on. 'Hannah Morton remembered his mentioning it. I haven't checked but I bet Melanie was there too, just before it closed.'

Stout shut his eyes, a silent prayer of thanks.

'Have they found him yet?'

Porteous shook his head.

'You'll be going public then? Tell the press we want to talk to him?'

'Tomorrow. I promise. I'm still worried about lack of evidence. Coincidence. It could be no more than that. If we come to trial I want nobody saying there can't be a fair hearing because of the ranting of the press. You can be sure all the old rumours will come out. Publicity works both ways. I've arranged to see Alice Cornish and she might have more information on Reeves. In the meantime you could ask again around the town. Discreetly. If he's come back here someone will know about it.'

'When are you seeing her?'

'I'm going straight from here. She still lives in Yorkshire.'

Eddie nodded with approval. 'I'm seeing the Spences as you suggested. And Chris Johnson.'

'Any problems?'

'Not with the Spences. She's a reporter, isn't she? All over me like a rash. Johnson wasn't so happy but he knew better than to object.'

'Look,' Porteus said. 'Take a couple of hours off. The rest of the day if you need it. Those interviews can wait until tomorrow.'

Stout didn't even bother to answer that. 'I think Reeves has done a runner. He's not gone home. He's not visited his sister. He's guessed that we're on to him.'

You're obsessed, Porteous thought, recognizing the signs. You're thinking of nothing else. Reeves is haunting your dreams. 'Alice Cornish might know where he's hiding out,' he said mildly.

'Please do me a favour.' Eddie leaned forward, put his hand on the arm of Porteous's chair, almost touching him. Fervent as he'd be preaching in the chapel on Sunday. 'Give me a ring when you get in. Let me know what she's said. Even if there's no news.'

'It could be late. You'll need some sleep.'

'I'll not be asleep. You phone me.'

Alice Cornish's house was less grand than Porteous had expected. She was a celebrity of a kind, a Dame, the author of a handful of books and dozens of reports. When he'd spoken to her that morning she hadn't exactly welcomed his visit. 'I don't understand, Inspector, why this conversation couldn't be conducted by telephone. I value my privacy.'

But he'd wanted to meet her. Not only because he thought he'd get more out of her face to face. He'd admired her work. And still he was itching with the need to run away. When he'd persisted in his request for a meeting she'd given in gracefully and instructed him precisely on his route from the motorway. It was an area he didn't know, too close to industrial centres to be of interest to second homers and holiday makers. As he left the main road there were views of the Pennines to the east and Emley Moor to the west. He drove down a steep hill into a valley bottom, turned at a disused mill and then he was there. A small stone cottage with a meadow beyond it and a garden in front so tangled with perennials that when he walked up the brick path he scattered pollen with his legs. A ginger cat was sleeping on a window-sill.

'Inspector.' She had the door open before he knocked, while he was still stroking the cat, and he was caught off guard and felt slightly frivolous to be petting the animal. But she must have liked cats because her mood was softer than it had been on the phone. 'Shall we talk in the garden?'

There was a small patch of lawn at the side of the house, the edges ragged with long grass where it hadn't been properly trimmed. They sat side by side on a wrought-iron bench.

'What is all this about? You said on the phone it was about Redwood. But I've retired. The centre is closed.'

'You employed a man called Reeves?'

'Alec, yes. One of our longest-serving employees. By the end he was part of the architecture of the place. He wasn't a demonstrative man. He never drew attention to himself. But it was impossible to imagine Redwood without him. His retirement and my decision to give up control coincided. I felt that was appropriate.'

'You liked him?'

'He didn't let anyone else get close enough to him for that. Not adults at least. He was very different with the children. But I respected him.'

'Were you aware when you appointed him that there were rumours he'd been involved in child abuse?'

'No!' She turned her face sharply so she was facing him. She wore her grey hair in a severe bob which must have been fashionable when she was a small child in the thirties. 'I don't believe it.'

'You had no suspicion when he was working for

you that he had an undesirable relationship with any of the children in his care?'

'None.'

'You didn't think it was odd that he'd never married?'

'Are you married, Inspector? Because I'm not.'

He could sense her hostility and sat for a moment in silence searching for words which might appease her, but she came at him again.

'Do you suspect Alec of child abuse, Inspector? A recent case?'

'Not exactly.'

'I'm sorry!' The sarcasm could have come from a ferocious headmistress. 'I'm not sure that I understand you. What do you mean "not exactly"?'

'We want to question Alec Reeves about two murders. We've been trying to trace him for a number of days. We hoped you might help us find him.'

She sat quite still with her hands folded in her lap, staring ahead of her.

'You've come from the north-east, Inspector?'

He nodded confirmation.

'Then one of the murders you're investigating is that of Michael Grey?'

'His real name was Theo Randle, but yes, I'm the senior investigating officer in that case.'

'I recognized the name when it appeared in the papers. When you phoned I thought you had questions about Michael . . . It never occurred to me that Alec was implicated.'

'We've no proof against Alec Reeves. But he was staying in Michael's home the weekend he was murdered. He had an unsavoury reputation in the town and was linked to the disappearance of another boy, a child with a learning disability of about the same age. You can understand why we want to talk to him. His disappearance is a cause for concern.'

'Yes,' she said slowly, 'I can see that it would be.' She turned towards him again. 'But I don't believe it, Inspector. I'll cooperate with you because I think that's what Alec would wish. But you're wrong about him. It's not unusual for him to disappear for a week or two in the summer. He's a hillwalker and he likes wild places and he avoids other people. He'll appear suddenly from the Highlands or the Peak District and make himself known to you.'

I hope he does, Porteous thought. But I'll not hold my breath.

'Can you tell me about the boy you knew as Michael Grey?' he said. 'You never knew his other name?'

'Not so far as I remember.'

'Perhaps you could check with your files?'

'There are no files. Not that we kept. It was part of the Redwood philosophy. The files remained the property of the children. They had open access to them while they stayed at the centre and they took all the records with them when they left.'

'Didn't that cause problems if you needed to liaise with other agencies?'

'No. It meant that we all had to involve the young people about their futures from the beginning.'

'There must be some records. A list, at least, of the children you cared for.'

'I have an autograph book. The children all signed their names when they left, added any comments they wanted. Towards the end of my time at Redwood there were names that I hardly recognized. I was so busy – lectures, reports, committees. Much of the day-to-day administration was left to my staff. That was when I knew it was time to leave.' She paused. 'At the beginning it was very different. We had so little money and we had to do everything ourselves. If it hadn't been for a generous benefactor the place would have closed only months after we started. It was a round of fundraising, the school run, keeping the house from falling down and most of all finding time for some very disturbed children.'

'Was Michael Grey very disturbed?'

'Not as disturbed as some.'

'How was he referred? Social Services?'

'It was a long time ago, Inspector.'

'But you do remember?' He was sure that she did. Since hearing the news of Michael's murder, she would have gone over the details of his stay at Redwood. It was natural, what anyone would do.

'Michael was a private referral. It did happen occasionally. We were registered through Social Services and most of the children came through them, but sometimes we were approached by desperate parents who'd seen stories about us in the papers. Of course, they kept legal custody. Michael was unusual because he stayed with us for such a long time.'

'His father brought him to you?'

'I believe he did.'

'Don't you remember?'

'I wasn't here. I was in Geneva. Receiving some award.' She waved her hand as if it were of no importance. 'I wasn't keen but the staff thought I should go to raise the profile of the house. We'd not long opened. We were a democratic organization. I went. When I returned there was a new little boy. Michael. White hair, beautiful manners. Very distant. Very withdrawn. He didn't speak for months. I was told his mother had severe depression and his father a drink problem. A sister had been killed in a fire. The family didn't want Social Services involved but they thought we could help. I thought we could too. We were a good team . . .'

'Why the change of name?'

'I don't know. To me he was always Michael. Perhaps the family were in the public eye and afraid of publicity.'

'Perhaps.' Porteous thought it an extreme move. Once interest had died down after the fire, would anyone care what happened to a small boy?

'Did the family visit?'

'The father. Occasionally. Usually he was drunk when he turned up. When Michael was ready to leave we tried to arrange meetings with family members to discuss his future. But the appointments were never kept.'

'Michael attended a private school as a day boy?'

'It was what his father wanted. He made the arrangements. If Michael had been allowed to choose I think he'd have gone to the local grammar.'

'There was a fire at the school.'

'Yes.'

'Was Michael implicated?'

'Not in any way. The police came here first of course. We housed "problem" children. But he had an alibi. A member of staff was with him all evening.'

'Alec Reeves?'

'No. Not Alec Reeves.'

'How did he end up with the Brices?'

'Was that the name of the couple who took him in?'
He nodded.

'When Michael was sixteen we had a problem.
Frankly he was taking a bed which could be better
used by another child. He'd turned into a bright and
well-adjusted young man. He'd enjoyed being at
Redwood and he hadn't wanted to move, and we didn't
want to throw him out. Of course we waited until
he'd completed his O levels before thinking about it
seriously at all. There was no interest from the family
– we'd even had to subsidize his school fees because
they'd stopped paying. So what to do with him? The
fire in the middle of his lower-sixth year brought
matters to a head.'

'Alec Reeves came up with a solution?'

'Yes. He'd not long started working with us. There
was a retired clergyman and his wife, he said, in his
home town. Childless, but full of love. We all met.
Michael liked them. It seemed a wonderful solution.'

'Until he died less than two years later . . .'

'I never knew about that. Not until the press reports
of his death.'

'Tell me about Melanie Gillespie.' If he hoped to
shock her into some admission or indiscretion he was
unsuccessful. She seemed lost in thought. The ginger
cat had moved on to the grass beside her feet and she
stopped absent-mindedly to tickle its ear.

'I'm sorry, Inspector. I don't recognize the name.'

'Melanie Gillespie was one of the children in your
care. Much more recently. Within the last three or four

315

years.' At least, he thought, I hope she was. Otherwise I've nothing to work on at all.

'I don't think so.'

'She had an eating disorder. Probably another private referral.'

'I've explained that in recent years my contact with the centre has been minimal.' She seemed tired now, rather than hostile. 'But we can check. Come inside and I'll show you my book. My record of achievement you might call it. More precious to me at least, than all the awards put together.'

She took him into a dusty and cluttered study. The book was gigantic, leather bound. It wouldn't have looked out of place in a cathedral. In it successive children had signed their names, written scraps of verse, drawn pictures.

'When do you think she left us?'

'Two years ago. Three perhaps.'

She turned the pages slowly.

'You see, Inspector. No Melanie Gillespie.'

'May I look?' Theo Randle had changed his name. Perhaps Melanie had too.

He found it immediately. *Mel Scully* written in spiky italics. Beside it a cartoon. A stick figure with cropped hair holding an electric guitar, with a balloon coming out of her mouth. Inside the balloon the words: *What now?*

'Scully was her father's name,' he said.

'I do remember her! Very bright. Very articulate. Self-destructive with her eating. A lot of aggression directed at her parents. Not nearly as confident as she wanted everyone to think her.'

'Had there been a child, do you know?'

'You think she'd been pregnant? Certainly not while she was here. Before?' She shrugged. 'She was someone we never quite got through to. She never felt able to trust us.' Porteous remembered Collier saying something similar. She closed the book suddenly. The air displaced by the heavy covers stirred the dust. 'What's happened to her?'

'She's dead too.'

Chapter Thirty-One

Despite his sleep in the garden Eddie Stout was tired. As he drove to The Old Rectory he found his concentration slipping, the car bouncing suddenly on the Cat's-eyes in the middle of the road. The Spences had agreed to see him at four. That was their quiet time, they said, between lunch and dinner. Sally would leave the paper early especially.

And they were waiting for him. A young woman in a black dress met him at the front door and led him to the lounge where the Spences sat, expectant and curious. Between them a small table was set for tea. There was a silver pot and china cups, tiny sandwiches, a double-tiered plate with scones and cakes.

'Just in time, Sergeant. I was about to pour.' Roger Spence wore a white shirt and a red bow-tie. He handed a cup and a plate to Stout, who juggled with them awkwardly, in the end balancing the plate on the arm of his chair. He noticed that Spence's fingers were very long, the nails beautifully manicured. Spence set down the teapot and rubbed his hands together. 'Now, how can we help?'

They both turned towards Eddie and smiled in a predatory way. Sally was dressed in a grey silk tunic over trousers. She filled the armchair, a huge grey walrus. He wondered how she would manage to prise herself to her feet. Jack Sprat and his wife, he thought. Throughout the conversation images and words came into his head unbidden as in a dream. Perhaps he should have followed Porteous's advice and waited until he was less tired. He felt he was no match for these two, especially now.

'I've been hearing rumours,' Sally said when he didn't answer immediately. Her tone was confidential, slightly flirtatious. She leaned forward and he could see the top of her bra. 'People are saying that you've linked Michael's murder – I still think of him as Michael – with that girl on the coast.'

'We're ruling out nothing at present.' The standard line. If she were any sort of a journalist she'd know anyway. And he thought she probably was very good at her job. She had the necessary ruthless streak

'We didn't know her,' Sally went on. 'The girl on the coast. We'd never met her.' She seemed very keen to make that point.

Eddie struggled to stamp his authority on the interview. 'It's the first murder I'd like to talk about.'

'Oh?' She smiled again, took a chocolate éclair from the plate and bit it in half.

Eddie turned to include them both in his question. 'You were at the final performance of *Macbeth*? The Friday before Michael disappeared.'

'That's right, Sergeant. I was selling programmes and Roger was helping to direct.'

Eddie watched the second half of the éclair disappear into her mouth. He unclipped his briefcase and took out the photograph given to him by Jack Westcott.

'Do you recognize the gentleman sitting next to Mr and Mrs Brice?'

Roger flicked his eyes towards the picture and immediately away again.

'I don't think I do,' he said casually. 'Why?'

'We're trying to trace as many people as possible who were there that evening. If you could try to remember, Mr Spence.'

'I know who it is!' Eddie almost expected her to clap her hands like a little girl who's just come top in a spelling test. 'It's Mr Reeves, isn't it? You must remember Roger. Alec Reeves, the scout master. There was talk . . .'

'Was there?' Roger licked his fingers with a long, darting tongue and patted his chin with a napkin.

'Probably all rumour,' she added quickly. 'You know what this place is like.'

'What exactly did the rumours say?' Stout asked, as if the information was new to him.

'Oh, you know. That he liked the company of young boys too much. I'd never met him. Not really. He ran the hardware store next to where my father worked, and I went into the shop sometimes on errands. My dad thought he was all right but then my dad said that about everyone. I didn't think there was anything particularly creepy about him, but then I was only a kid. But I'm sure Mr Reeves had already left the town when Michael disappeared. There was a new bloke in the shop when I was in the sixth form. Younger. Good looking in a dark, moody sort of way . . .'

'But Reeves came back for the performance of *Macbeth*,' Eddie said.

'He must have done, I suppose, if the photo was

taken that night. But I don't remember him. I was backstage, helping with the costume changes. Roger was a real dictator. He wouldn't let us out during the interval.'

She grinned at her husband but he didn't respond.

'Do you remember seeing that man, Mr Spence?'

Spence took the photograph, holding it with exaggerated care by the edge of the print.

'No, I'm afraid not. Quite impossible after all these years.'

'Of course, he looks a lot older now,' Sally said.

They both stared at her.

'You've seen him recently?'

'About ten days ago. Don't you remember, Roger? He came in here with Paul Lord and his wife. I knew there was something familiar about him. I'm surprised that they stayed friends. Poor Paul, he was tainted by his association with Reeves when he was young. I mean, he was never going to be the most popular boy in the school. Not with that acne. Though I remember one night Hannah coming pretty close to snogging him . . . And he was a boy scout, wasn't he? His picture was in the paper when he won some award and he never lived it down. That awful uniform. But then it came out that he was big buddies with Alec Reeves, and when all those rumours started he was teased dreadfully.'

She continued talking but Eddie had stopped listening. Paul Lord was the lad who'd given Alec Reeves an alibi after Carl Jackson had disappeared. Eddie had interviewed the boy himself. He remembered a stuffy sitting-room, a mother, flustered and embarrassed, and Paul, hidden as Sally had said behind a layer of acne, stubbornly refusing to change his story. At last Eddie had given up and soon after Reeves had left the town.

'Is Mr Lord a regular customer?'

Roger answered. 'Yes. Mostly at lunchtimes. He's a businessman. He brings his clients here.'

'What is his business?'

'He's some sort of computer consultant. He and his wife are partners. They work from home. They turned the outhouses of the farmhouse where they live into an office.'

'The address please?'

But he knew it already. Porteous had phoned there when they were trying to identify the body in the lake. Balk Farm. Home to Balk Farm Computing. Once home to Carl Jackson, the lad with learning disability, and his parents.

In the car Eddie tried to phone Porteous, but his boss's mobile was turned off. Eddie saw that as an opportunity and didn't leave a message. He thought he'd be late for his interview with Chris Johnson, but that didn't seem important. Now he had to speak to Paul Lord, who'd been with Alec Reeves ten days ago, who must know where he was hiding out.

He drove too fast, still in the daze he'd been in since his sleep in the garden, his thoughts woolly, his eyes prickling with exhaustion. He came over the brow of the hill and had a flashback of himself, young and fit, standing in a line with other men and women, searching for Carl, prodding into the heather and bracken with a long pole. They'd improved the entrance to the farm, widened it and he sailed past, seeing out of the corner of his eye a big sign advertising the computer consultancy. It was only as he pulled into a lay-by to turn back that he thought what a fool he was being. Alec Reeves might be hiding out at Balk Farm but what could Eddie do about it, single-handed and without a warrant? Only warn him and drive him away. He drove slowly back to the town, his heart racing with panic at the damage he'd almost done.

He arrived at Chris Johnson's house without remembering how he'd got there. He was late and the conversation started badly. Johnson had recently moved into a small terraced house on a modern private estate. A woman, very young and very pregnant, opened the door. She wore a sleeveless dress which clung around her stomach and heavy breasts. Her frame looked as if it would snap under the weight.

'You're late,' she said. 'He's gone.'

'But his van's still here.' Stout nodded towards a transit pulled on to the pavement.

'He's not got time to talk to you. The soundcheck's in half an hour.'

Stout was too tired to argue. 'Just let me in. It'll not take long.' He pushed past her, not roughly, hardly touching her, but usually he would have been polite, and he was surprised at the change in himself. He walked straight into the living-room. Chris Johnson was watching television. In the corner was a flat-pack cot, still in its box, and a white fur rabbit. Eddie picked up the remote from the floor and zapped off the television. The woman followed him in and levered herself carefully into an armchair. There was nowhere else to sit so he leaned against the door.

'I want to know where you were one evening last

week.' He gave the date Melanie had been taken, but all the time his thoughts were racing about Alec Reeves. His hands were shaking at the thought of how close he had come to wrecking the whole investigation, and then he imagined Reeves driving down the track to the road by the reservoir before he'd had a chance to have it watched. He should have sorted out surveillance before coming here. He was losing it. 'Now!' he snapped. 'I've not got time to mess about.'

'I was working.'

'Where?'

'An eighteenth birthday party. Some village hall out in the sticks. Why?'

'Can you prove it?'

'You can check. Some of the kids got a bit wild. The police were called. It was that sort of place. No fun after nine thirty or the neighbours have a seizure. The cops came in and told me to turn down the sound.'

'What time did you get home?'

'About midnight.'

'Can you confirm that?' To the woman. Going through the motions. Though no way would Johnson have been able to pick up Melanie from the Rainbow's End and be back here at midnight.

'Of course.' There was a mischievous look in her eye which said – But how can you trust me? I would say that, wouldn't I? Eddie ignored it. Duty done.

'Does the name Alec Reeves mean anything to you?' The question was directed at Johnson. The woman wouldn't have been born when Alec was running the hardware shop in the high street.

Johnson shook his head. Stout got out the photographs. Reeves as he'd been at the performance of

Macbeth. Reeves more recently handing out Duke of Edinburgh award certificates. 'You don't recognize him?'

Johnson stood up quickly. 'I've told you no. I've got to get to work.' He pulled a leather jacket from the back of his chair, felt in the pocket for car keys.

Running away, Stout thought. What scared him?

'You weren't one of Alec's little boys were you, Chris?'

'Jesus, are you crazy?'

The blasphemy hit Stout, as it always did, like a slap.

'Nothing to be ashamed of if you were. Not your fault.'

'I told you. I didn't know the man.'

Chris went up to the woman, bent to kiss her on the forehead, stroked her belly, then he stood in front of Stout, challenging him not to let him out. Eddie opened the door for him. He watched for a moment as Johnson slid open the door of the transit, climbed in and drove off. The woman didn't move or speak. She looked at him from her chair, waiting for him to go.

Chapter Thirty-Two

They decided to go into Balk Farm early the next morning. Not mob handed. Porteous and Stout would knock on the door, very polite, very civilized. There'd be a car at the end of the track and someone on the hill behind the house with binoculars in case Alec tried to get out on foot. Because, as Eddie said, Reeves knew every inch of that hill.

The team had all crowded into Porteous's office to make the final arrangements, and Eddie stayed, even after the rest of them went. So wired up that Porteous knew he wouldn't sleep. Porteous wanted to get home and felt the nerviness was contagious. He tried to wind up the discussion.

'Then a team to search the house,' he said. 'Like we decided. Good people. Tidy and careful. It's all sorted, Eddie. Nothing left to do.' Still Stout didn't take the hint, so he added, 'Let's go home. We'll have an early start.'

But Stout wouldn't move until he'd gone through it all again.

Peter woke before the alarm went off. It was just light, a grey mist in the valley, the first blackbird screaming.

No walk to work today. A break from routine. He'd arranged to pick up Eddie from home and knew he'd be awake too, probably already dressed, pacing the floor. Porteous understood his sergeant. He'd been there. Like a reformed smoker he wanted to preach. He wanted to yell: It does you no good. All that stress and adrenalin. It'll make you crack up. Except it probably wouldn't make Eddie Stout crack up. *He* was tough, with a wife who was there when he came in at night, to help him relax and to stroke away the tension.

Peter showered, made tea, toasted a piece of wholemeal bread, forced himself to eat it. He was scared. Not of Alec Reeves, who was probably pathetic, not half the monster Eddie had described. But of cocking this up. If he made a mess of it he didn't think he'd be able to work with Eddie Stout again.

He was early but Eddie must have been looking out because he was halfway down the drive before Porteous had switched off the engine. He was carrying a foil-wrapped packet, which he threw on to the back seat.

'Bet insisted on making sandwiches. I told her it would all be over before dinner.'

They met up at the police station and drove in convoy round the reservoir, held up at one point by an ancient tractor. The only other traffic was a post van. They pulled into the lay-by where Stout had turned his car the day before while the team got into place. Stout didn't mention that. He didn't mention how close he'd been to going it alone.

At seven thirty exactly they drove up the track. That was the time they'd decided on. Not too early to cause offence if it did all turn out to be a mistake and Reeves wasn't there at all. Stout dismissed the possibility, but went along with the theory. These were business people, keen surely. They'd be checking their emails, planning their day. But it was still early enough to catch them on the hop, to emphasize that they were here on serious business.

'This has changed a bit. I don't think I'd have recognized it.' Stout was driving. He pulled into a marked parking bay in what had once been the farmyard. A brass sign by the door of a converted barn said 'Reception' but they ignored that and went towards the house. Everything was smart, spruce, clean. The garden was landscaped. A conservatory had been added. Porteous took a breath and rang the doorbell.

The door was opened by a child, a boy of about twelve, half dressed for school, his shirt hanging out, his buttons undone. Porteous hadn't expected that. There'd been no mention of children.

'Could I talk to your father please?'

The boy grunted. He still seemed half asleep. He led them through the house to a large kitchen, all new oak and terracotta tiles. There was a smell of coffee and faintly of cinnamon. At a table by a big window sat a couple, the woman in a silk kimono, the man, his hair wet from the shower in a short towelling dressing gown. The table was laid for three but it seemed the third place was for the boy because there was no sign of Reeves. Either the couple hadn't heard the doorbell or they thought the boy had dealt with it because they didn't look up. They were discussing work, planning a meeting for later in the day. If Reeves was there, Porteous thought they weren't aware of what he'd done. They had no sense of danger.

The boy stood dreamily. His bare feet had made no sound on the floor. Eventually he seemed to remember what he was doing.

'Dad.' Then they did look round and he nodded over his shoulder in the direction of the visitors before wandering off.

Paul Lord must have taken them for potential clients. If he was surprised or annoyed that they'd turned up at such an inconvenient time, he didn't show it. Perhaps it wasn't unusual. He stood up, held out his hands, a gesture of welcome, but also of apology for the dressing gown, the half-eaten breakfast. He was confident, rather good looking. There was no sign of the spotty schoolboy. His makeover had been as dramatic as that of the farm.

'Can I help you?' Then he turned to Stout. 'Don't I know you? I remember, you were a policeman. That dreadful case when I was a boy. Do you know, you've hardly changed.'

'Still am a policeman, sir. Here to ask you a few questions.'

And still Lord remained courteous and composed. Too courteous? Porteous wondered. Wouldn't most people be irritated, hostile, if they were interrupted in the middle of breakfast. But perhaps it had become a habit to be pleasant. Perhaps that was why he was so successful. He treated them now with a puzzled good humour.

He asked to be allowed to dress first and they let both of them go, because even if Reeves was hiding out somewhere in this big house and tried to do a runner the team outside would get him. That might be better even. Save them having to search and it would look better in court if he had been trying to escape.

'Does Phillippa have to be involved in this, Inspector?'

Phillippa, the wife, had remained silent throughout.

'We do have questions for both of you.'

And he accepted even that without a fuss.

While they were waiting in the kitchen the boy came in for breakfast. He shovelled in cereal, then, well trained, stacked the bowl in the dishwasher and returned the milk to the fridge. He showed no curiosity about who they were.

'Do you need a lift to school, lad?' Stout asked.

'No thank you.' Very polite, very well brought up. 'I get the bus from the end of the track.'

Like Carl Jackson, thirty years before. Doesn't that haunt Paul Lord? Porteous thought. He was involved in the case even if it was only as a witness. How can he send his son up that lane every morning without a worry?

They carried out the interview in the conservatory, drinking the best coffee Porteous had tasted for years from chunky, hand-thrown mugs. Stout took the lead. That was what they had decided.

'A bit of a coincidence you living here,' he said. 'After you were involved in the Carl Jackson case.'

'Not really involved,' Lord protested mildly. 'I gave Alec an alibi. That was all. And not really a coincidence. I'd kept in touch with Alec. When Sarah's husband died he knew she was wanting to sell. I was looking for bigger premises and he knew that too . . .

He put us together. She saved on agents' fees. We got the place for a good price.' He shrugged.

'It's Mr Reeves we're here about.'

'Why?'

'We'd like to talk to him. He seems to have disappeared.'

'I mean, why do you want to talk to him?'

Stout paused. 'It's in connection with a murder inquiry.'

'The body in the lake? Michael Grey? You've got things all wrong. Again. Alec had left town before Michael disappeared. Before he arrived even.' He kept his voice amused. Still he wasn't rattled.

'He came back,' Porteous said quietly. 'To watch a production of *Macbeth*. It was special because Michael was the star and Alec knew him very well. We'll call him Michael shall we, though that wasn't his real name. Michael had been staying at Redwood, where Mr Reeves was working as a care worker. Were you aware of the connection at the time?'

'No.'

'Don't you find that strange? You were the same age as Michael. Wouldn't Mr Reeves have introduced you? So you could help the boy settle into his new school.'

'He might have done I suppose, but he didn't. It wasn't necessary. Michael was confident, immediately popular. Alec would have recognized that he didn't need any help from me. Besides, after the business with Carl, all the gossip at the time, my parents didn't want me to have anything more to do with Alec. I expect he was trying to save me embarrassment.'

There was a pause, then Stout turned to Phillippa,

changing his tone. 'Are you a local woman, Mrs Lord? Had you heard about all this?'

'Only what Paul's told me. We met at university.' When she'd gone off to dress she'd put on make-up. Her lips were glossy, her complexion flawless. She was dressed in a neat little skirt and a sleeveless top. A jacket was hung carefully on the back of a chair.

'When did you first meet Mr Reeves?' Stout asked.

She gave a frown, not because the question worried her but because she wanted them to see how irrelevant all this was. It was eating into the important business of her day. 'He came to our wedding.'

'Did he?' Stout raised his eyebrows, a pantomime of surprise.

'Paul doesn't have many relatives. His side of the church would have been rather thin.'

'And Alec is an old friend,' Lord broke in. 'He was very good to me.'

'You've kept in touch ever since?'

'Yes. Phone calls. Christmas cards. If he visits his sister he calls.'

'Did he talk to you about his work?'

'A little. Not in detail. He wouldn't consider that ethical. Confidentiality must be very important in social work.'

'Quite.' Stout deliberately set down his mug. 'You can tell us now, Mr Lord. After all these years. You were under pressure at the time, we all know that. A boy. But now there's a chance to put things right . . . Where was Mr Reeves on the afternoon Carl Jackson disappeared?'

'With me. Just as I said.'

Phillippa looked again at her watch. 'Look, I've got a meeting. I really should go.'

'A few more minutes, Mrs Lord.' Stout didn't even look at her. He continued to hold Lord's stare. 'When did you last see Mr Reeves?' he asked suddenly.

'I can't remember the date. He phoned the day after the school reunion. He said he was going to be in the area, he'd like to take us out for a meal. We arranged to meet at The Old Rectory the following evening.'

'What did he want?'

'Want? Nothing. Our company perhaps. He's a kind, elderly man. Occasionally he must get lonely.'

'Did he talk about Michael Grey?'

'I think we must have discussed the identity of the body in the lake. It was a matter of interest. Everyone in Cranford was talking about it.'

'Did you introduce the subject, or did he?'

'I did. I remember Michael going away in the middle of exams. We all thought he'd gone back to his father.'

'At the meal at The Old Rectory, did Alec tell you that he knew Michael, that he'd worked with him at Redwood?'

'No.'

'Odd that, isn't it? You were gossiping about the body in the lake. Enjoying the drama even. Nothing wrong with that. But Alec didn't tell you it was through him that the boy had come to town?'

'I've told you. Alec was scrupulous about confidentiality.'

'So you did. Did he stay here the night after the meal?'

'No. We offered to put him up, but he'd made other arrangements.'

'What were those?'

'I don't know. I presumed he'd be staying with his sister.'

'How did he seem that night?'

For the first time Lord hesitated before answering. 'He seemed suddenly very old. We wondered if he might be ill. He said not, but it occurred to me that he'd arranged to meet us . . . almost as a way of saying goodbye.' He looked up, gave a little smile. 'Probably just my imagination. All that talk of death.'

There was a pause. Porteous could sense Phillippa's impatience but still Stout held the stage and she didn't dare move. When Stout spoke at last he was cheerful, a jolly surrogate uncle who should have been invited to the wedding too.

'You said you got a good price for Balk Farm. You've made a lovely place here, a real family home. Why was the price so low? A payment was it, for backing up Alec's story all that time ago?'

Lord stood up. At first Porteous thought Stout had succeeded in provoking him into losing control, but he held it together. All the taunting and bullying as a child had held him in good stead.

'I think you'd better take your sergeant away, Inspector, before he says something else you'll both regret. You're welcome to search the house if you don't believe me about Alec. Phillippa and I will be working in the office. We've wasted enough time already.'

The team searched the house but Porteous left them to it. He could tell it would be futile. He had to get Stout back to the police station, find some way to deal with his disappointment. In the car the sergeant sat mute, shaking his head. He didn't speak until they were in Porteous's office.

'I played it all wrong. But I don't know what else I could have done.'

'Perhaps he was telling the truth.'

Before Stout could answer the phone rang. Porteous listened, said little, replaced the receiver.

'You'll need those sandwiches of Bet's after all,' he said. 'Reeves's neighbour contacted the Yorkshire lads. She thinks he came home last night.'

Chapter Thirty-Three

Reeves lived in a tidy bungalow at the end of a cul-de-sac of similar houses. Porteous parked at the end of the street and they walked down, but still he was aware that they were being watched. Not from Reeves's place. The curtains there were still closed. But in the other bungalows neighbours were twitching behind the Venetian blinds and the bleached fancy nets.

'The old lady next door said it was very late when he got in. One thirty at least. Though according to the local lad who spoke to her she's as deaf as a post and he didn't think a car would wake her.'

The car, a red Metro, was parked on the drive, pulled right up to the garage door.

'She says it must have been late when he got here or he'd have put the car away. He always kept it in the garage. Security conscious. Head of the neighbourhood watch.'

'A model citizen,' Stout said sneering.

They knew there was no way out from the back of the bungalow. A thick leylandii hedge separated the garden from a railway embankment. Occasionally high-speed trains roared past, making conversation impossible. Porteous rang the doorbell. They stood back and waited. Nothing happened. He rang the bell again, then tried the door. It opened.

They stepped into a wide hall with a door on either side, and a corridor ahead which led, Porteous presumed, to bedrooms and bathroom. There was a pale grey carpet on the floor, a small table with a telephone.

'Mr Reeves?'

There was no answer. He opened the right-hand door into a kitchen. A yellow roller blind covered the window, but let in enough light to show empty workbenches, a spotless tiled floor. There were no plates or cups draining by the sink and the dishcloth folded over the mixer tap was dry and hard. Porteous looked in the fridge. It had recently been defrosted and was empty.

'He must have gone straight to bed,' Stout said. He couldn't stand still. He was fidgeting like a kid. 'Let's wake the bastard up.'

But Porteous shook his head. He went back into the hall and opened the opposite door into the living-room. The bay windows were covered by thick velvet curtains and it took his eyes a moment to adjust to the gloom. Stout came up behind him impatiently and switched on the light. The room was lit by two lamps on the walls. They had bulbs like imitation candles and heavy fringed shades. The central light was operated by another switch and didn't come on, but it was a chandelier with similar fittings. It must have been more substantial than it looked, because it supported the weight of Alec Reeves, who hung by a noose of blue nylon rope, twisted around the chain which fixed the chandelier to the ceiling. A kitchen stool, overturned, lay on the floor beneath him.

Stout was about to go into the room but Porteous pulled him back.

'There's nothing we can do. It might be a crime scene.' He wondered why he wasn't more surprised. Had he been expecting this as soon as he realized the door was open?

'What are you talking about? He knew we were on to him and he topped himself.' Stout was almost weeping with frustration. This wasn't the way it should have ended. He still had things he wanted to say to Mr Alec Reeves.

'Perhaps.'

'What do you mean, "perhaps"? He came in last night and killed himself.'

'Why didn't he lock the door?'

'What!' It came out as a scream.

'Suicide. It's a private thing. You wouldn't want to be disturbed.' Peter thought he was an expert. At the depth of his depression, he'd contemplated suicide in all its forms. Walking into the sea. Taking pills. Hanging. Jumping off a bridge like his dad. One of the things that had stopped him in the end was the possibility of an audience. The terrible embarrassment of being caught in the act.

Eddie was looking at him as if he were mad. 'Maybe he just forgot.'

'He wasn't that sort of man. He was careful. He had a routine. And the key was in the lock on the inside of the door. He used it to get into the house, took it out and put it in on the inside. A deliberate act. Why didn't he turn it then?'

'Maybe he didn't care.'

'Oh, I think he cared.'

'What are you saying?'

'That I think he was murdered.' He spoke quietly, apologetically. For thirty years Eddie had thought of this man as a monster, the human form of the devil he talked about in pulpits on Sundays. It was like expecting him to accept he'd got all the other Sunday stuff wrong too.

'Why?'

'I don't think he killed Theo and Melanie. I don't know about Carl. Perhaps not even him. I think we got it wrong.'

'Not "we"!' Eddie bellowed. A child having a tantrum. Wanting to be important, even if it meant taking the blame. 'If anyone got it wrong it was me.'

'We need the scene-of-crime team.'

'Why was he murdered if he wasn't involved?'

'To make us think he was. If the house had a Yale lock we'd have been taken in by it. The murderer would have been able to pull the door to behind him and we'd never have known any different. The pathologist should throw some light.' He paused, turned to Stout. 'Look, I might be wrong. I'm just saying how I see it.'

'No,' Stout said. 'I don't think you're wrong.' Then, muttering, just loud enough for Peter to hear. 'I don't think you're ever wrong.'

Porteous left him waiting for the local team and went to see the old lady who'd reported Reeves's return. She took a while to answer the door. She used a Zimmer frame and she was a big woman. Walking was an effort. But she'd moved as quickly as she could, frightened that he'd go without giving her the low down.

'Anything up?' she said, moving awkwardly aside to let him in.

'I'm afraid Mr Reeves is dead.' She'd see the trolley soon enough.

'I knew something were wrong!'

'Why?'

'Like I told that lad on the phone, he hadn't put his car away. I know it were late when he got in, but he always did.' She had a heavy Yorkshire accent. He saw the hearing aid, remembered what they'd said about her being deaf.

'Did you hear his car?'

'Saw the lights. I was awake and got up to get a cup of tea. You don't sleep so well when you get older. I was in the kitchen waiting for the kettle to boil.'

'Did you see him get out of the car.'

'No. I took my tea back to bed. The bedroom's at the back.'

'What time was it?' Just checking.

'Quarter to two.'

'It *was* just the one car?'

'What do you mean?'

'He didn't have a visitor? Someone who parked at the top of the road perhaps?'

'Not that I saw. Anyway he wasn't one for visitors at any time. Certainly not in the middle of the night.'

He was halfway down the path when she shouted after him. 'What was it that killed him then?'

He pretended he was deaf too and didn't turn round.

Eddie was waiting in the kitchen of Reeves's house, subdued. 'I had another look,' he said. 'Just from the door. You're right. It's the way that stool's lying. If he'd kicked it away it would be further from him.'

'The old lady didn't see anything.'

'The local lads are on their way,' Eddie said. 'We've made their day. It's two years since they had a murder.'

'Do you mind waiting for them?'

'Nah. Where are you off to?'

'I want to talk to Alice Cornish. I don't think we got it all wrong. Redwood's still the place that links the killings together.'

'You think she knows something?'

'I want to talk to her.' He thought, I don't want to be waiting here when they cut down Alec Reeves. I don't want to see Eddie realize it's partly his fault. He hounded Alec out of Cranford because he was lonely man who only felt comfortable in the company of kids. I want this over, with no more drama.

It was the last thought that stuck with him on the drive to Alice Cornish's cottage. It made him take the bends too quickly and hit his horn at a slow, elderly driver hogging the middle of the road. He felt the pressure and when he saw a café by the side of the road just before the turn-off into Alice's lane, he forced himself to stop. It was an ordinary living-room with two tables covered with gingham cloths; a jolly middle-aged woman brought him Earl Grey and a home-made scone with jam which she said she'd bought at the WI market. He ate it and told her how good it was, but he couldn't face waiting for her to bring him change, so he stuck a five-pound note under the plate when she was out of the room and he left.

He hadn't phoned Alice Cornish in advance. Partly superstition. If he phoned she wouldn't be there.

Partly because he needed to get out of Reeves's immaculate bungalow even if it were on a wild-goose chase.

She *was* there. The cottage door was open. Her briefcase and an overnight bag stood just inside. When she came to greet him she was dressed for a meeting – a smart trouser suit with a loose silk jacket. Her grey fringe was ruler straight. She was wearing lipstick.

'Inspector, I haven't time to talk to you now. I'm expecting a taxi to the station.'

'Alec Reeves is dead.'

'What happened?' The colour had drained from her face but her voice was even.

'I think he was murdered. It could have been suicide.'

'No. Alec wouldn't have killed himself. He'd have seen it as an act of cowardice.'

'Is there anything you have to tell me?'

She looked directly at him. 'Nothing.'

'I need to look at your book again. The book with the children's names inside.'

She hesitated. Down the track came a red Mondeo. It sounded as though the exhaust had a hole in it. He was aware that he'd been listening to it approaching for some time.

'My taxi. I'm appearing before a select committee. Not something I can put off.'

'Please.'

She paused again. 'All right. But you'll have to see to yourself. Just shut the door behind you when you leave. It's a Yale lock.'

She picked up her bags and went out to meet the

taxi. He stood, watching her. She turned back before getting into the car.

'Inspector?'

'Yes.'

'There's some coffee in the kitchen. It should still be hot.'

He smiled and waved his thanks.

He poured himself a mug of lukewarm coffee and took it to the study. He opened the big book with its scribbled signatures, its jokes and its drawings, turning the pages slowly, looking for anything he'd missed the first time round. Anyone else would have given up, but this was the only thing he was good at, this persistence, this love of the detail. When he found nothing the first time, he worked through it all again. And this time he saw it, wondered how he could have been so blind not to have picked it up earlier.

He shut the cottage door carefully and sat in his car to call Eddie and then the office. It was late afternoon. The car window was open and he could hear woodpigeons calling beyond the meadow. The ginger cat was back in its favourite spot on the window-sill. In the office he spoke to Charlie Luke.

'The pathologist's report has finally come through,' Luke said. 'Melanie Gillespie's never been pregnant. And we traced that kiddie you were interested in. Emma Leese. It all seems like the Gillespies said. Melanie used to babysit for her. But the baby died. Cot death. No wonder she was upset.'

That was it then, Porteous thought. The final piece of information. The tag line to the joke. The final connection.

PART FOUR

Chapter Thirty-Four

The afternoon the police came to talk to Rosie and Joe in the Prom, it was hotter than ever. Rosie thought that was why the conversation seemed so unreal. The heat seemed to shimmer, even inside the building, stopping her from thinking clearly.

When they walked in she was behind the bar. It had been one of those quiet afternoons she spent daydreaming. She'd look at the big clock in its heavy wooden frame and see that an hour had gone by and she knew she must have served half a dozen customers but she couldn't remember any of them. Then Joe had bounced in, excited somehow despite his grief, shaking her out of her reverie, and soon after that, the policemen. She'd never met them but she guessed at once who they were. Hannah had described them as a double act and Rosie knew what she meant. It was hard to imagine them working apart. But she couldn't work out why her mother had been so scared of them. They looked like two ordinary, middle-aged men. Out of place in here. They were dressed for the office, not the seaside in a heatwave. Doughy faces covered with a sheen of sweat.

They stood for a moment just inside the door and then the younger man came to the bar. He introduced himself and ordered orange juice. He was pleasant enough, but she couldn't forget he'd upset her mother and found it hard to be polite. Joe took a beer off him then they sat round one of the tables in the corner, staring at each other, not sure how to start.

'This isn't official,' the inspector said. 'Nothing formal. We just want to talk about Mel.'

Somehow that started them off, so he didn't have to ask any questions. It was like a real conversation, friends chatting. Frank wasn't there – he was minding the bar – but the rest of them did what Porteous wanted. They just talked about Mel.

But right from the beginning Rosie couldn't recognize who they were going on about. Slow down, she wanted to say. I mean, what *is* going on here? It was as if the person who'd been her best friend throughout the sixth form had disappeared to be replaced in their collective memories by a total stranger. Joe was worse than any of them. Really she wished he wasn't there. She felt constrained. While he was going on about how delicate Mel had been, how fragile, she wanted to yell at him: No, she was more than that, stronger than that. You know what she was like. She could be a manipulative cow. Ruthless. She had to get her own way. She wasn't the victim you're all making out.

But she couldn't do it to him. Not yet. Someone would have to put him straight, but it couldn't be her. She had too much to lose. What if he never forgave her? So she sat quiet while they warbled on, pussy-footing around the subject.

'What about you, Rosie?' Porteous said at last, leaning across the table, giving her a seriously deep and meaningful look, as if he expected *her* to give them the truth. 'What have you got to tell us about Mel?'

'Nothing new. Nothing that's not already been said.'

She could tell he was disappointed. They went on to talk about Mel's music, how talented she was and how she'd already got a confirmed university place at Edinburgh, the same old gushing stuff.

'They were so impressed,' Joe said, 'that they'd have taken her even if she'd failed all her A levels.'

Then Porteous tried again. He wanted to know if Mel had ever been pregnant. Not now, but at some time in the past. The question was so delicately put together that not even Joe was offended.

'No,' Joe said. 'Of course not. She'd have told me.'

'Would she?'

Joe didn't answer that because there were lots of things Mel hadn't liked to talk about.

Rosie though was certain. 'It's not possible. Mel would never get pregnant. She was paranoid about it, wasn't she, Joe?'

Joe nodded sadly in agreement and Rosie continued.

'She had to be in control of her body. Completely. That was what the food thing was all about. And if there was some accident, some mistake, she'd get rid of it immediately.'

'Was there ever any accident?'

'No,' Joe said. 'Not while she was with me.'

'Are you sure?' When there was no reply, he added. 'No matter. The pathologist will be able to tell us.'

Rosie was daydreaming again. She and Mel had talked about children on one of their girlie nights together. She'd slept on the sofa bed in Mel's room and they'd got through a bottle of wine each when they'd got back from the pub. Mel had got a bit soppy about the kid she used to babysit, but she'd made it clear a family wasn't part of her future. 'Your life's not your own if you're a mother,' she'd said, shuddering. Though what could she know?

'Eleanor seems to manage OK.'

'That's different. I'm old enough to look after myself. I don't bother her any more. She wasn't so keen when I was little.' She'd paused. 'I want to be someone. You can't concentrate on what you want to do if you're surrounded by screaming kids.'

And then, lying on top of her bed, propped up on one elbow, Mel had squinted across at Rosie. 'What about you? I can see you as an earth mother. Married. A cottage in the country. Four or five kids, a goat and some hens scratching about in the garden.' Rosie had laughed then, but something about the image still appealed.

She was brought back to the pub by a sudden blast from the jukebox, a couple of bikers laughing. Porteous gave her another pleading look but she ignored it. She told him she had nothing else to say and offered to look after the bar so they could talk to Frank.

Frank must have realized that Porteous would want to talk to him about the bloke who'd been in the Prom asking after Mel, but he didn't seem very pleased about it.

'Look, I don't think I can be much help . . .'

'Don't be daft, Frank. No one else can remember him.'

And she gave him a playful little push, sending him out into the room. He looked shaky, panicky, walking towards the policeman as if he were already about to go into the witness box. From the bar she couldn't hear exactly what the group in the corner were saying, but Frank was facing her and she saw him staring blankly, occasionally shaking his head. His eyes were unfocused, wandering. It was as if he wasn't really thinking about the questions and the answers. He was just trying to survive the interview, waiting for it to be over.

The next day she tackled him about it. She'd been thinking about it all night. Frank had liked Mel, in the way that he seemed to like all the young people who came into the Prom. He'd joked with her, acted sometimes as father-confessor, standing at the bar for ages listening to all her troubles. So why had he been so reluctant to discuss her with the police?

She waited until about five o'clock when they had their meal break together and she could get him on his own. They sat in the little staff-room which led off the kitchen. They propped the outside door wide open and sat beside it on old bar stools, their plates on their knees, looking out at the pavement. Families were already trailing back from the beach, the children fractious and covered in sand, the parents loaded with towels and toys. There was the hot smell of drying seaweed and frying onions from the burger stall at the fair.

'What was going on yesterday, Frank?'

'What do you mean?' He was defensive. He had the same unfocused look in his eyes as when he'd been talking to Porteous. She thought: But he can't be scared of me. Frank had always been the boss. He knew everything there was to know about running a bar. She'd been the dippy teenager who couldn't pour a decent pint, who couldn't get up in the mornings, who turned into work with seconds to spare. He teased her and poked fun in a slightly flirty way which kept her wary. Something new was going on here which she didn't quite understand. The power in the relationship had shifted.

'Well, it didn't look as if you were being particularly cooperative,' she said, carefully keeping her voice neutral.

He wiped his forehead with the back of his hand.

'Don't you want to catch the bloke who killed Mel?'

'I don't think the chap that came in that night did kill her.'

'How did you know that, Frank?'

He shook his head, a refusal to answer.

'If you knew anything you should have told the police.'

An open-top bus rattled past. A party of kids on the top deck all held helium-filled balloons. Rosie imagined the bus rising slowly in the air, carried slowly out to sea. Frank took a mouthful of sandwich, muttered something which she couldn't make out.

'What was that?' Sharply. Sounding like her mother trying to teach him table manners.

'I said I've had dealings with the police. I know what they're like. They'd set *me* up given half a chance. Best policy's not to say anything.'

'Nobody's saying you'd ever harm Mel. Why would you?'

He turned to her. Grateful, sad puppy eyes were focused properly on hers for the first time. 'I've got a record. That'd be enough for them.'

She hadn't known about the record. Again she looked at him in a new light. She wondered what he'd been done for and if he'd ever been inside. She imagined him in Stavely asking her mother to find him books, then thought she couldn't see him as the reading type.

'But they'll know you couldn't have done it. You were working the night she disappeared.'

'Only until closing time. I could have done any- thing after that. I live upstairs on my own, don't I? Lisa won't let the kids come to stay any more.'

Lisa was his ex. It was an old complaint. Rosie was irritated by the self-pity but she tried not to show it.

'Did you go out?' Rosie asked. She wanted to shake him. It was like speaking to a surly child.

He shook his head. 'But if they make out I'm tied up in this case I'll lose any chance I ever had of access.'

'That's ridiculous. The kids have nothing to do with this.'

Then she wondered if she'd been too hard on him. Frank doted on his children. Before Lisa started being awkward they'd come to stay at weekends. Rosie tried to understand what it must be like for him, how lonely he must feel. Perhaps that was why he was good at his job. He made an effort with the staff and the customers because without them he'd have no one to speak to. He ever talked about friends or other family.

'Why did you say that about the bloke that came in here looking for Mel? I mean, how did you know he didn't do it?'

'He wasn't the type.'

'Come on, Frank. What is the type? You must listen to the news. Anyone can commit murder. Teachers, doctors, anyone. And if they find him, you'll get the police off your back, won't you? There won't be anything to get in the way of the access application then.'

He put his empty plate on the floor. 'You're a good lass, Rosie. I'll miss you when you go to college.'

Oh God, she thought. A revelation. He wants to get inside my knickers.

'I've got a lot to lose,' he said.

'What are you talking about?'

'This place. It's all I've got.'

'So?'

'So people could make things awkward. With the brewery or the authorities.'

'Has someone been threatening you?'

He looked at her with those eyes again.

'For Christ's sake, Frank. Go to the police. Get it sorted.'

'Leave it,' he said. 'They always catch murderers, don't they? No need for us to get involved.'

'Yes, Frank, there is.'

But he hardly seemed to be listening. By now she knew exactly what was going on. Joe might not go for her heavy-bosomed, hippy look, but it appealed to middle-aged men. She fended off the flattery and the clumsy approaches every day at work. She'd always suspected that Frank fancied her. Now she was certain. She pulled her chair closer to his.

'Tell me,' she said. 'You don't have to see the police again. I can talk to them. I'll say one of the customers remembered seeing the guy that night. Give me a description, a name even. I'll pass it on. That way we can find Mel's killer and keep you out of it.'

He didn't answer immediately, but she knew she

had him hooked. It crossed her mind that it wouldn't be much fun working with him after this. Then she thought, Sod it. She'd just leave. She could do with a holiday anyway before she went to university. Her dad could pay up some guilt money.

She reached out and touched his arm and lowered her voice. She knew what a tart she was being, but found she was enjoying the role. The power thing again.

'Please, Frank. I'd be really grateful.'

Chapter Thirty-Five

Rosie's shift ended at seven. She tried to phone Hannah then. She was standing on the pavement outside the Prom, her hand cupped round her mobile, blocking out the sound of the traffic. She'd wanted to talk to her mother ever since Frank had spilled out his story. In the end he hadn't treated her as any sort of object of desire. There'd been no groping, none of the usual crap about how lovely she was. She'd felt like his mother, for God's sake, as he stumbled through his confession. She'd put her arm around him and told him she'd make everything all right. And she believed that she could.

Rosie hadn't liked to phone her mother while she was still at work. She didn't want everyone listening in and she didn't want Frank to know how important she considered his information. Not that he'd been around much after their talk. She supposed he was embarrassed. At one point he'd gone to the flat upstairs as if the exchange between them had exhausted him and he needed to rest. He looked as if he hadn't slept properly for weeks.

She let the phone ring until the answerphone was triggered, then she remembered Hannah had said she'd be working late at the prison. She tried the work number but no one answered in the library. A gate officer came on.

'Sorry, pet. You've just missed her.'

She switched off the phone. Before starting the walk home she glanced back at the pub. Both double doors were wide open and she had a clear view. Frank was staring out at her. She'd left without saying goodbye to him and she thought about going back in. It would have been pleasant to sit on one of the high stools on the right side of the bar, drinking a long glass of white wine and soda, plenty of ice. But perhaps she shouldn't lead him on. Anyway, he turned to serve a middle-aged couple, a big woman and a thin man, who had their backs to her. Something about them was familiar. She hoped they were regulars, customers who were as near as Frank got to friends. As she crossed the road to walk past the infant school, she had the sense that everyone in the pub was staring at her. Of course when she glanced back over her shoulder they weren't even looking.

He must have been watching for her outside the Prom but there was always a line of parked vehicles along the road and she wasn't aware of him until she reached the middle of the street where Joe lived. It was still warm. The tar oozed black where a patch in the road had been mended. Somewhere in the neighbourhood there was a barbecue. The street was quiet. She could hear children playing in one of the back gardens, the splash of water from a paddling pool, the occasional snatch of television through an open window, but no one was about. And until she got to Joe's house she took no notice of her surroundings. She was running scenes in her head. Rosie as heroine, giving the police vital information which would lead to the capture of Melanie's killer. Rosie talking to reporters outside court. Perhaps with Joe at her side.

That was when she arrived at Joe's house. The attic window was open and she could hear the thump of his music. She thought his parents must be out or they would have made him turn it down, then she remembered his saying he was looking after Grace that evening. At first Rosie didn't think of going in. She couldn't face listening to more delusions about Melanie and she wanted to talk to Hannah. But she liked Grace. She'd always wished she'd had a kid brother or sister. Even now she was almost grown up Grace was passionate about animals. Rosie enjoyed being shown the latest additions to the menagerie she kept in the garden – the motherless kittens, the baby hedgehog, the house sparrow with one wing. She stopped walking and looked towards the house, tempted.

A small grey van came up the street behind her. It was moving very slowly as if the driver were looking at the house numbers. It had a wing mirror held on with black electrician's tape and a loose bumper which rattled as the van went over the speed bumps in the road. When it pulled up at the kerb Rosie turned to face it, expecting the driver to ask for directions. But instead of winding down the window – it was a very old van and certainly wouldn't have had electric windows – the driver got out. He was a young man, about the same age as Rosie. She didn't recognize him and he didn't look as if he belonged in this street of wealthy professionals, even as someone's black sheep. He was thin with cropped hair and a tattoo running all the way down one arm. Still she paused, curious to see if it was someone who'd come to visit Joe. Joe had copied Mel's habit of gathering up strangers and oddballs and it wouldn't have surprised her.

But he went to the back of the van and opened the door. She decided he was making a delivery and lost interest. She turned and carried on walking down the street.

'Hey!' He didn't shout but his voice was urgent. She stopped. 'Are you Rosie?'

'Rosie Morton. Yes.'

He stood looking for a moment, squinting against the low, evening sun.

'Morton . . .' he repeated. 'Your mam must be librarian at Stavely nick.' As if this was a surprise, a new piece of information which needed consideration.

She didn't like being rude but she didn't want to encourage him. She continued walking. He covered the distance between them quickly. She didn't hear him running, but suddenly she could smell him, a strangely clean, chemical smell. He was behind her, so close that they almost touched, his bony chest against her shoulder blades. From a distance it would look as if he had his arms around her. She turned back to Joe's house but the sunlight was reflected on the windows and she couldn't tell if anyone was watching. Still she thought he might be some weird friend of Joe's, and any moment Joe would come out and rescue her, save her from having to make a scene.

'Get in.'

'What?'

'In the van. Now.'

Then he did have his arm around her. One hand

stroked her neck, in the other, clenched as a fist, was a Stanley knife, only the blade showing.

'Not a sound.' The voice was almost caressing.

His head moved, turning quickly, his eyes darting up and down the street. In the distance an elderly woman in bowling whites stepped out into the road at the zebra crossing. He waited until she walked away in the opposite direction. Joe's music changed tempo, became more melodic. As if they were dancing, the boy moved Rosie to the back of the van.

'Get in,' he said again. Inside there was an old quilt with a faded paisley design. It was shedding feathers. She climbed in. He shut the door. The back of the van was a sealed unit, separate from the front seats. Everything was black, except for a thin crack of brilliant light where the door didn't quite fit. He started the engine and the rattle of the broken bumper vibrated through her legs and her back. She opened her mouth to yell, but it was like a nightmare, when you scream and scream and no sound comes out.

Later she spoke to Hannah. She sat on the floor of a flat which was empty except for a sleeping bag and a portable television. As far as she could tell. She'd only seen one room and the toilet. Her hands were tied behind her back, but the young man held her mobile so she could speak. The flat was on the second floor of a block on an estate she didn't recognize. It hadn't taken them long to get here. Twenty minutes perhaps. He'd parked at the bottom of the tower block by a couple of skips, pulling her out of the van as if he didn't care if anyone saw. She'd had a few minutes to look around. There was a low building, some sort of school or community centre perhaps, and next to it a children's playground, which seemed surprisingly new and in good repair, though no children were playing there. There were giant hardboard pandas and chickens on huge black springs, with black seats and handles, swings made from tyres, a wooden fort.

In contrast most of the flat windows were boarded up and beyond the tower blocks there was a building site, where a crane and a couple of diggers were marooned on the hard-packed earth. A woman came out of the school. She had a bunch of keys like the ones Rosie's mum used at the prison, and she locked up the building, pulling at the doors to check they were secure. She looked smart and efficient and walked briskly round the corner out of sight. Her car must have been parked there because they heard the engine. She hadn't seen them standing in the shadows. Even if she had, she'd have taken them for a couple of lovers, mucking about. They hadn't passed anyone else on their way up the stairs to the flat.

'Hi, Mum.'

'Yes?'

'I'm not coming home tonight. Don't worry about me.'

'Where are you staying?'

She almost said Mel's because it came automatically. Perhaps she should have done. Perhaps her mother would have picked up the mistake and somehow understood. But the boy wasn't stupid.

'Laura's,' she said. 'She's having a party.'

'When will you be home?'

'I'll go straight to work tomorrow.'

He switched off the phone. 'Good,' he said. 'Very good.' But he seemed unsettled. He paced up and down the floor. She watched him, not terrified any more, her emotions somehow slipped out of gear, but her brain working like fury. Very sharp, very clear, as if this was the most important exam of her life.

'Can I ask you something?'

'What?' He stopped pacing, crouched beside her, so she could smell him again.

'Did you kill Melanie Gillespie?'

Chapter Thirty-Six

Hannah replaced the phone with satisfaction. She was proud of herself. At one time she'd have demanded details. Who was Laura? She'd never heard the name before. Where did she live? Was there a contact number? Today she just accepted Rosie's explanation and let it go. Treating Rosie as an adult. Besides, she had other things to think about.

For example, Porteous's visit to the prison earlier in the day. She could have died when he just turned up, unannounced, though he'd actually behaved with more discretion than she'd have expected. She wasn't sure Marty had been taken in by the detective's casual reference to needing witness statements, but Marty wouldn't talk. It wouldn't be all around the prison that she was a suspect in a murder inquiry. She could tell, though, that the orderly had been unsettled by Porteous. For the rest of the shift he'd been moody, demanding that the radio be turned down, snapping at prisoners who jostled to have their books stamped. Occasionally she caught him looking at her and she wondered if he'd say something when the place was quiet. But they were never alone. He asked to leave early, saying he had something important to see to. It wasn't like him. He always preferred to be in the library than on the wing, would have worked twelve-hour shifts given half the chance.

The other preoccupation was that Arthur was coming to supper the following evening. She'd invited him on impulse and immediately regretted it. She hadn't seen him all day, then met him in the car park on her way home. He must have been working late too. He'd seen her leaving the gate and was standing by his car waiting for her. His appearance had almost made her laugh out loud. He was wearing shorts which almost reached his knees and a shirt with horizontal stripes which made him look like an upended deck-chair. Dear God, she'd thought, with a jolt of affection which surprised her. Whatever is he like. No wonder the officers want rid of him.

'Are you OK?' He must have heard on the grapevine that Porteous had been there. And he'd be curious, of course, about what had happened. Since tracing Michael Grey's identity he thought he had a stake in the case.

'Of course.'

'I don't suppose you fancy a drink?'

She hadn't. At least not in public. What she'd fancied had been a long, hot soak to take away the smell of prisoners, a good book, a glass of very cold, very dry wine. But he'd looked so tentative, so sure of rejection, that she hadn't wanted to hurt him.

'I'm sorry. Not tonight.'

He'd given her a sad smile. 'Better things to do?'

'Just shattered. Why don't you come round for a meal tomorrow evening? Rosie will probably be working, but I'll get rid of her if she's not.'

'Haven't you got enough on your plate?'

'I'll enjoy it.'

But now she wasn't sure that she would. She hadn't entertained anyone in the house since Jonathan had left, and when he'd been around dinner parties had been daunting affairs, taking days of planning, sleepless nights of anxiety. She'd always admired friends who could throw together a bowl of pasta for half a dozen people, drink out of jumble-sale glasses, eat from ill-matched crockery. She'd never had that sort of confidence.

Now she worried about what she should cook for Arthur and whether she really wanted him in her house. He'd insist on going over the inquiry, picking at the threads of it. Would he be a rampant carnivore like Jonathan, who bragged that he never ate anything that hadn't breathed? She supposed there would have to be a pudding. And would he read more into the invitation than she'd intended? What would be expected of her?

She was about to set off to the all-night supermarket where Rosie's friend worked, in search of inspiration, when the phone rang again. It was Sally Spence, eager for a gossip. She had information to give, but throughout the conversation Hannah thought she was fishing too. She had a reason for calling which was never made clear.

'We had one of those detectives here again this afternoon. The ugly little one.'

'Oh?' Perhaps Stout had told Sally that Porteous had been to the prison. Perhaps she was phoning to see if Hannah had been arrested.

There was a pause, lengthened by Sally for dramatic tension.

'You'll never guess who's mixed up in this business.'

No, Hannah thought. Probably not. It was hard to remember that once Sally had been her very best friend, that she'd confided everything to her.

'Who?' she asked.

'Paul Lord. You remember him?'

'The spotty boy scout.' Hannah smiled despite herself. She remembered sitting next to him by the bonfire at Cranford Water the evening she'd first kissed Michael.

'Not spotty any more,' Sally said. 'Quite a hunk these days. You met him at the reunion, the night they identified Michael . . '

'Of course.' Hannah replayed it all in her head – the curse of a memory which would let nothing go. She heard the conversation with Paul, his description of his computer business and the conversion of the farmhouse, the music in the background, Chris Johnson's muttered introduction to the next record. 'Why do the police think he's involved?'

'He's a friend of a man called Alec Reeves. Apparently this guy's disappeared from the face of the earth. They want to trace him because he knew both dead kids.' She paused again before adding grandly, 'At least that's what my sources tell me.'

'So Paul's not really implicated. Only by association.'

'Don't be silly, H. You can't see Paul Lord *killing* anyone, can you? He was always such a nerd.' As if she might admire him more if he did turn out to be a murderer.

Hannah thought the conversation was finished

then. She even began to say goodbye. But Sally seemed eager to prolong it.

'How's that lovely daughter of yours?'

'Fine. Out partying. As usual.'

'Oh.' Sally sounded shocked. 'I thought Melanie Gillespie was one of her best friends.'

'She was.' Hannah could have kicked herself. She didn't want to make out that Rosie was an insensitive little cow. Especially to a reporter. What right did Sally, who was obviously enjoying every minute of the investigation, have to disapprove? 'She's been really upset. I thought she needed some time out with her friends.'

'Right,' Sally said. 'Of course. Right.'

Hannah wondered if Sally had been hoping to talk to Rosie, to turn her memories of Mel into an article. Just as well she wasn't at home. There was a muffled conversation at the other end of the line.

'Roger sends his love.'

But I don't want it, Hannah thought. Really, I don't. I don't care if I never see either of you again.

She decided on a casserole for Arthur, something she could cook that night and heat up the next day. Chicken with tarragon, she thought. Then she could use some of the wine she had chilling in the fridge and she wouldn't end up drinking the whole bottle. The supermarket was quiet. There were a couple of single men in suits carrying wire baskets of ready-cooked meals and designer lager, sad disorganized women like her who had nothing better to do at nine o'clock at night than shop. She looked out for Joe. She would never do it because Rosie would be mortified, but she wanted to say, 'Look at my daughter. I mean really look at her. She's a beauty and she fancies you like crazy. What are you doing, letting her go?' She expected to bump into him at the checkout or filling shelves but he wasn't there. She hoped it was his night off and he was at Laura's party too.

The next day, Marty wasn't waiting outside the library for her to unlock the door and he still hadn't showed when the papers arrived. She tried to rouse Dave, the prison officer, but he was stretched out in the chair in the office and the rhythm of his snoring didn't alter a beat even when she shook him. She phoned the wing.

'Haven't they told you?'

If they had, I'd not be ringing, she thought. She didn't say it because she knew the wing officer and liked him. She didn't have so many friends in the place that she could afford to offend him. But she came closer than she ever would have done when she was living with Jonathan. Perhaps living on her own with Rosie was making her assertive.

'Where is he?' She thought Marty might have been shipped out to an open prison before release. Sometimes it happened without warning.

'He's in hospital.' The officer was from North Wales and spoke with a sibilant hiss which was mimicked by the inmates and other staff.

'The sick bay?' She was still thinking of it only as an administrative inconvenience. She ran through the library rota in her head, wondering if she could draft in another orderly, trying to think of a suitable candidate.'

'No. The General.'

That brought her up short. 'Serious then?'

'Yeah.'

'What's wrong with him? He seemed fine yesterday.'

'There was a fight. Nastier than most. We didn't get to it in time.' He paused. 'Marty started it. They all say that. Some new lad was winding him up. He can kiss goodbye to his parole, if he lives that long.'

'It's that serious?' What's happening to the people I know? She thought. He can't die. Not him too.

'I've not heard how he is this morning. The Governor will know, I suppose, but you know what he's like. He tells us nothing. It looked bad last night.'

'It's crazy,' she cried. 'Marty had so much to lose. I always guessed he had a temper, but he told me he'd learned to control it.'

'Did anything happen yesterday to upset him?'

She thought immediately of Porteous, but what did that have to do with Marty? 'I don't think so.'

'You two didn't have a row?'

'No. Why?'

'He seemed wound up anyway. I had a bit of a run-in with him earlier in the evening. I mean, sometimes you could tell that he was getting tense, but he'd take a deep breath and walk away from it. But yesterday, before lights-out, he had a go at me.' There was a silence at the end of the phone and she thought he'd finished, but he continued in a rush. 'I'm afraid it was about you. He wanted me to give him your home phone number. He said it was urgent, vital that he talked to you. I told him if it was that urgent to give me a message and I'd pass it on. And anyway he'd see you today. He calmed down in the end, but like you said, usually he managed to hold it together, and last night he was way over the top. I couldn't do it, Hannah. I couldn't give an inmate your home number. Not even Marty.'

'No,' she said, meaning it. 'Of course you couldn't.'

During the day Hannah tried to find out more about Marty. He hadn't had any close friends in the prison. He'd always worked on his own. But she thought someone might know what was behind the fight.

'Who was the lad he went for?'

'Don't know, miss. He was new. Just out of reception.'

'What did he do to wind Marty up?'

'I didn't see. Honest, miss. It all happened so fast.'

Apparently no one had seen. Or they weren't telling. She thought they were scared, but perhaps she was deluding herself. Perhaps she didn't want to believe Marty could have been such a fool.

At lunchtime she phoned the General Hospital, but the sister on ICU wasn't giving much away either. She said Marty was 'serious but stable'. And no, he wasn't fit to receive visitors. She sounded disapproving. Perhaps the prison officer who would be sitting on the end of Marty's bed was making a nuisance of himself. It wasn't always the most house-trained member of staff they chose for escort duty.

Hannah wished she had the name and number of Marty's girlfriend. Perhaps it would be possible to trace it through the bail hostel where she'd worked as a volunteer. But Hannah didn't feel she had any emotional claim on Marty and she didn't want to look as if she were interfering. In the end she shut the library early and went home. When Dave roused himself to complain she said it was a gesture of respect.

Chapter Thirty-Seven

The incident with Marty had stopped her worrying about dinner. She was glad now that she'd invited Arthur. He might know what had happened. Despite his outsider status he always seemed to understand what was going on in the prison. She took pleasure now in the preparations, set the table carefully, polished glasses, opened wine. She was coming out of the shower when the phone rang. Usually she'd have let the answerphone take it, but she thought it might be about Marty. She'd asked his wing officer to let her know if there was any news.

'Mrs Morton?'

'Yes?'

'Can I speak to Rosie?'

Because she was thinking about the prison it took her a moment to place the voice: Rosie's friend Joe.

'She's not here,' Hannah said. 'She's at work. Sorry.'

There was an awkward pause.

'No,' Joe said. 'I've just been to the Prom. Frank said she'd called in sick.'

Hannah's first response was irritation. It wasn't the first time Rosie had phoned in sick if she felt like a day's shopping or an expedition up the coast with her mates. Then she thought that Rosie would have told her what she was up to. Not just to cover in case Frank got in touch, but because she knew Hannah would be worried after what had happened to Mel.

'Did you see her last night?' she demanded.

'No. I met her the day before with the policemen, but not yesterday. My parents were out. I had to look after my sister.'

'You weren't at Laura's party then?'

'Sorry?'

'She was at a party last night and she stayed over. She phoned to tell me. Laura's party.'

'I'm sorry,' he said again. 'I don't know anyone called Laura.'

'She's not one of your friends from school?'

'No.'

Then she lost control of her body. She still had the towel wrapped round her but she started to shiver.

As if from a distance she heard Joe on the other end of the phone. 'Don't worry,' he said. 'I don't know everyone she does. She phoned you last night and Frank at lunchtime. She must be OK. I'll call round and ring you back.'

She replaced the receiver and dressed quickly. The shivering didn't stop. Feeling foolish for not having thought of it sooner, she dialled the number of Rosie's mobile. She heard her daughter's voice, delightfully normal, saying she couldn't come to the phone right now, but she'd return the call as soon as she could. The doorbell rang.

It was Arthur. He was clutching a huge bunch of flowers in one hand and a bottle of red in the other. Of course, she thought, he would be a red-wine drinker. She burst into tears. He didn't say anything then. He took her in, sat her on the sofa, poured her a glass of wine from the fridge and dumped the flowers in the sink.

'What is it?' he said. She saw he'd opened the red, poured a big glass for himself. 'News from the hospital?'

'Nothing like that.'

'Rosie?'

She explained about Joe.

'He's right,' he said. 'Rosie must be OK if she phoned you and the pub. Perhaps she's feeling the pressure and wants to go off on her own for a bit.'

'No. She wouldn't. Not without telling me.'

He sat beside her, put his arm around her shoulder. 'Could she be at her father's? She might feel awkward about letting you know she was there.'

'He's away. The Dordogne.' With Eve, the temptress. 'He gets back tomorrow. Rosie doesn't have a key to their house. It's something she complains about.'

'Do you think you should phone the police . . .'

She sensed he was thinking of Mel and that he was going to add 'in the circumstances'. She didn't want to hear it and cut him off.

'We'll wait ten minutes. See what Joe has to say.'

As if on cue the telephone rang. She answered it in the living-room so Arthur could hear what she was saying.

'Mrs Morton.' The same two words but it wasn't Joe. 'Mrs Morton, I've got a message from your daughter.'

'Where is she?'

'Not far away.'

'But she's safe?'

'She is at the minute. You could say I'm looking after her. You should be grateful.'

'Can I speak to her?'

He seemed to think about that. 'I don't think so. Not just yet.'

'When is she coming home?'

There was another pause. 'That depends on you.'

'What do you mean? She knows she can come home. Anytime.'

'I need something from you, Mrs Morton, before I can let her come back.'

'Money?' It was almost a relief. Something she could catch hold of. 'A ransom. How much?'

'I'm not greedy. Twenty thousand. You can manage that.'

'Not immediately,' she said. Her mind was racing. 'There are savings, bonds. Some things need my husband's signature.'

He lost his temper suddenly, shocking her. 'Listen lady, she should be dead already. Tomorrow. Eleven. I'll phone back then. And if you go to the police I'll know. And I'll kill her.'

She heard herself screaming as if it was somebody else. 'Of course I won't go to the police. I won't tell anyone. I want her safe.'

The line had gone dead and she wasn't sure he'd heard her.

Arthur took the receiver from her and dialled 1471 then held it to her ear so she could hear the number repeated.

'Rosie's mobile,' she said. 'He must have her.' She jabbed her finger on 3 and waited for the number to connect, only to hear Rosie's answering service say she couldn't come to the phone right now. 'He's switched it off.'

They sat together on the sofa, each clasping an undrunk glass of wine, double handed, like bridesmaids each holding a posy of flowers, one white, one red.

'I know who it is,' Hannah said. 'That boy.'

She hadn't recognized the voice until he lost his temper, then the memory which was a curse, but which also served its purpose, replayed the scene in the prison library which had initially sent her back to Cranford.

'You know him too. Thin, cropped hair, young. He's got a tattoo of a snake running from his shoulder to his wrist. He can't have been out for long. You took his pre-release course.' She screwed up her eyes, saw the list of names on Arthur's desk. 'He's called Hunter.'

'Yes,' Arthur said. 'I remember. Are you sure it's him?' He kept his voice flat, but she could tell it wasn't good news.

'Certain.' She set her glass on the table. 'What was he in for?'

Arthur hesitated. 'Assault, I think.' He added quickly, 'Not rape. Nothing like that. He was a small-time dealer. Someone tried to muscle in on his patch.' He paused again. 'You know you must tell the police. They'll have an address.'

'What happened to the man he assaulted?'

'I don't know.'

'Don't lie to me, Arthur.' The anger was wonderfully liberating. 'You know all about these kids. That's what you do. You tackle their offending behaviour.' She was sneering as she used the jargon, just as the officers did when they talked about his courses.

'Hunter stabbed him, then slashed his face. He's got a scar.'

'But the victim lived?'

'Hunter isn't a murderer, Hannah,' Arthur said gently. 'He didn't kill Melanie.'

'He was out of prison in time.'

'What motive would he have? And he wasn't even born when the lad in the lake died.' He turned to her. 'You must tell Porteous about this.'

Again she ignored the point he was making. 'Why is he doing it? Why me? Personal revenge, perhaps. I upset him that day in the prison. Or is it Rosie? Has she done something to disturb him?'

'I don't know,' he said. 'You must tell the police. This is their area of expertise. They'll be able to trace him.'

'No!' The anger returned. 'What do the police know about why people do things? They haven't got very far in finding Melanie's murderer. And I can't risk it. What if he was telling the truth? What if he knows someone who works with Porteous?'

'He's a kid, a smack-head. He's not in league with the police. That's paranoia.'

She seemed about to give in, to agree to his phoning Porteous. Certainly she presented as the old Hannah, diffident and unassuming. She straightened her skirt over her knees and clasped her hands on her lap.

'You always wanted to play at detectives.'

'What are you talking about?'

'Well, now's your chance.'

'Hannah, what do you want me to do?'

'Bring Rosie back.' As if it were the most simple thing in the world. 'You must still have access to Hunter's file at Stavely. They won't have cleared it yet. You can find an address for him. You worked with him. You know what he's like. You're a psychologist, for Christ's sake. You'll know what to say to him. He won't be expecting anything to happen until eleven tomorrow. We can catch him off guard.'

'I don't know.'

She looked at her watch and was surprised that it still wasn't eight o'clock. 'If you go now to look at the file you won't even cause a stir on the gate. They're used to your working late.'

Still he paused.

'I'm sorry,' she said. 'I shouldn't have asked you. It could be dangerous. Just get the address and I'll go myself.'

'No.' It came out as a wounded bellow. 'It's not that.' He turned to her. 'Sod it,' he said. 'Sod the Prison Service and the Home Office. I'll do it. I bloody want to do it.'

Chapter Thirty-Eight

In the flat the boy was becoming more jumpy. Rosie thought of him only as 'the boy'. She hadn't asked his name. She didn't care. The television was on. He'd switched it on as soon as it got light, but he kept the sound low and the flashing images couldn't hold his attention. In the distance there was the scream of a police siren. He jumped to his feet and stared out of the window. Rosie saw his knuckles clenched white around the handle of his knife. He only started to relax when the noise disappeared into the distance. She couldn't see her watch because her hands were tied behind her back, but it was starting to get dark, the second night. He wouldn't put on a light. He didn't want anyone to know he was using the flat.

She'd stopped being scared. Now she was only hungry and uncomfortable. The water to the flat was still connected. The toilet flushed and when she'd complained of being thirsty he'd brought her a drink in a blue plastic mug with a moulded handle. They'd had an identical set to take on picnics when she was a kid. He'd given her a biscuit too because she'd said she was starving. It was soft and stale.

'Is this all there is?' she'd demanded.

At that, he'd been flustered and said she'd soon be

out of there. It wouldn't hurt her to go without for a couple of days.

Yeah, she'd thought. She could live off her bum for a week. If she came out of this thinner perhaps the adventure would be worth it. That had led to a picture of a skeletal Mel. She had pushed the image from her head. Remembering Mel, dead in the cemetery, had made her panic. She needed to think straight.

It was clear to her that there'd been no forward planning in the boy's decision to bring her to the flat. If he'd thought about it in advance, he'd have got food in. Even if he didn't mind starving her, he'd have wanted to eat and as far as she could tell he didn't have a stash hidden away. With the arrogance of someone who usually thrived on the challenge of exams, who found learning easy, she'd put him down as a bit dim. She'd worked out the sort of lad he was; there'd been someone like him in every class since she'd been an infant. The name for them in her school was 'charvie', meaning scally, loser, someone you wouldn't be seen dead with socially. Charvies were the kids who started school without being able to tie their laces. They wet their pants and came last in spelling tests. Teachers hated them. In primary school they started fights in the playground and failed their SATs, and in high school they got involved in petty crime, dealing in single cigarettes, then blow or smack. When they were at school, which wasn't often.

When Hannah heard Rosie talking like that, out would come the lecture. 'How on earth can you be so judgmental? You don't know anything about those kids. You don't know where they come from or what their families are like. Of course people can change if you give them a chance.' She thought she could change her prisoners by giving them books. What planet was she on? Rosie knew this boy was a charvie, always had been, and so he was no match for her.

She sat now with her hands behind her wriggling her fingers so she wouldn't lose the feeling in them, and she tried to work out the best thing to do. She couldn't rely on Hannah to go to the police. Hannah would do just as the boy said. She wouldn't take any risks. But Rosie wasn't going to see the boy walk away with all that money – money which could see her through university, buy her a holiday somewhere seriously hot, a little car and driving lessons. Then she wondered if Mel had died because her parents had refused to pay up.

When they'd come into the flat the boy had opened the door with a key, but he hadn't locked it behind him. It was a Yale lock with a snick, so if she got to it she'd be able to get out. Although he was thin and wiry she didn't think he was as fit as she was. He'd been smoking since they'd got there, tiny roll-ups. He crouched over a shiny tin to make them, so no stray strands of tobacco were lost and he used both hands. So while he was making his cigarettes he couldn't hold his knife. She wondered what he'd do when the tobacco ran out.

He hadn't made any sexual advance towards her. Even when he'd had his arms around her pulling her to the car, when his finger was stroking her neck, she hadn't thought he was interested. He had other obsessions. Her body wasn't something she could bargain with. She could tell.

It was possible that he didn't think she'd try to

escape. He'd probably grown up with the same sorts of prejudice about her as she'd had about him. He'd see her as a lardy wimp who couldn't look after herself. He even left her while he went to the toilet. It was off the hall right next to the entrance to the flat, and he left the bathroom door open, but if he'd thought she'd make a run for it, he'd have tied her legs. He just didn't think.

All the time she kept her eyes on the blade. She knew he could move quickly over short distances. He'd done that in the street outside Joe's. But she thought that once she got out of the flat she'd be able to outpace him down the stairs and into the road. Usually the knife was in his hand. Otherwise it was on the floor just beside him. He was as connected to it as some of her mates were to their mobiles. You couldn't imagine him without it. He'd said, as he let her out of the car when they'd first got here, 'I've used it before, you know.' Boasting. As if he were just waiting for an excuse to use it again.

As it grew dark, she let her head drop forward so her chin was on her chest, pretending to drowse. She'd slept a couple of hours the night before. Hannah always said it was a gift being able to sleep anywhere. But she wasn't sure the boy had. He must be exhausted. Despite his nervousness and his restless energy, he wouldn't be able to stay awake for ever.

There were no curtains at the window. She couldn't see from where she was sitting but on the way in she'd glimpsed the river, cranes, and the skeleton of an oil platform, half constructed. Light came in from the glow of the city on the horizon. It reflected on the blade on the floor beside the boy. He still had his palm flat on the handle, but his breathing was regular now. Rosie was leaning back against the wall, her knees bent. She stretched one leg, tensing and relaxing the calf muscles. The boy didn't stir. She repeated the movement with the other leg. Still his breathing didn't change.

It crossed her mind that it might be a trick. Perhaps he wanted her to try to run. Then he'd have an excuse to chase her and hold her down and threaten her. Perhaps that was what excited him. But she didn't think so. Charvies could be devious, but he hadn't tried on anything like that before. He saw her as a means of making money. That was all.

She bent her knees again and bent down, so her back slid slowly up the wall until she was standing. She shook the stiffness out of her legs. Still the boy slept. She walked quickly into the narrow hall towards the front door.

She had already realized there was no way she could free her hands. She'd spent hours the night before trying. She'd seen films where magically ropes had loosened sufficiently to allow one hand to slide out. That wasn't going to happen here. When she moved, the nylon twine cut into her wrists. They were still firmly fixed behind her back. She stood at the front door and turned her back to it, leaning forward so she could raise her straightened arms high enough to reach the Yale snick. The joints in her shoulders seemed to tear with the strain. Even when her fingers touched the catch, it was more difficult than she'd expected to open it blind. At last the knob turned. She gave a gentle tug and the door opened. The boy, caught in the orange glow from the window, muttered in his sleep. She froze but he didn't wake and she moved out on to the landing.

She'd reached the first floor when she heard him come after her, bellowing and stumbling as if he'd wakened suddenly and was still half asleep. She thought then that all the flats must be empty, because there was no response to the noise. She'd have to get out. There was just enough light to see where she was going, some dim, emergency lamp high on the wall. She carried on down, pumping her legs, one step after another, keeping the movements small and tight, saving her energy for when she reached the bottom. Her shadow danced ahead of her.

At the bottom the steel-plated double door was open. She supposed it had been left like that the day before when they'd come in. Outside it was warm and dusty and she thought she could smell the dry mud of the river. She paused for a moment. She didn't think the boy was gaining on her but in the distance there was muffled, amplified rock music – some sort of festival or outdoor show – and she wasn't sure she would have heard his footsteps anyway. She needed a main road, lots of people. The music was too far away. There was a general hum of traffic and she got her bearings. She saw the lights of speeding cars in the distance beyond the building site. She started to run towards them, moving awkwardly because her tied hands threw her off balance. In the distance there was a bang and the splatter of fireworks from the festival. No sign of the boy.

The scene was lit suddenly by car headlights. They shone on the animals in the children's playground behind its wire-mesh fence, a nightmare zoo.

He's fetched his van to head me off, she thought. Then: I underestimated him. Not such a charvie after all.

She heard the engine revving and sensed it coming towards her, but blinded by the lights after the gloom of the flats she was paralysed. She couldn't decide which way to run. At the last minute she twisted and started to move, but knew it was too late.

Then there was a shout. She felt the soft thud of another body, pain as she was thrown to the ground, winded and battered. Then came the movement of the vehicle past them, air on her face, and an enormous crash as it swung, out of control, into a wall.

Chapter Thirty-Nine

Hannah sat by the living-room window, counting the cars go past, telling herself, When I've counted ten more, Arthur will arrive with Rosie. But Arthur didn't arrive, so she counted twenty, then thirty, then fifty. She'd wanted to go with him to the estate by the river, Hunter's last known address, but he'd said she'd be better there, next to the phone, and he'd suddenly seemed to inspire confidence so she'd done what she was told. When the car did stop she thought it was a mirage, her imagination playing tricks. But the first person she saw, the only one that mattered then, was Rosie, who got out of the back seat. And she looked dishevelled and shocked, her white work shirt stained. Too solid to be a dream.

Hannah ran to the door and held her. She felt herself crying and wiped her eyes on her sleeve, because Rosie always said she was soppy, that she cried at the drop of a hat. When she looked up she saw Porteous and Stout coming up the path. No one else was with them.

'Where's Arthur?'

'They'll explain,' Rosie said. 'Is there anything to eat?'

'He's in hospital,' Porteous said.

'Shouldn't Rosie be too? For a check-up at least.'

'Nah.' Rosie shook her head and went to the kitchen to forage for food.

'Is Arthur badly hurt?'

'Serious but stable, they say.'

Like Marty, she thought.

Rosie wandered back in. She was drinking from the glass of wine Arthur had poured for himself earlier. In the other hand she held a slice of the cheesecake Hannah had finally decided on for pudding. Crumbs from the biscuit base were dribbling on to the floor. 'Any phone calls?' It was what she always asked. It was as if she'd only come back from a four-hour shift at the Prom.

She doesn't want a fuss, Hannah thought. 'Joe,' she said. 'Several times. He's been frantic.'

'I'd better phone him.' She drifted away upstairs.

Hannah watched her then turned to Porteous. She wondered what he was still doing there, hovering just inside the door like a Jehovah's Witness or a Kleeneze salesman. Shouldn't he be taking statements?

'Arthur is all right?' she asked. 'If it's serious, perhaps I should go to the hospital.'

Then Porteous and Stout walked in, flanking her on each side, so she thought for a crazy minute that they intended to arrest her after all. They sat beside her on the sofa.

'I don't think you should do that,' Porteous said. Hannah saw that both men looked exhausted, much worse than Rosie. He rubbed his eyes. 'Arthur Lee's under arrest. He's been charged with the murders of Theo Randle, Melanie Gillespie and Alec Reeves. And the attempted murder of Rosie.'

'No.' Again Hannah thought she was going mad. 'Rosie was abducted by a youth called Hunter. He phoned here for money. Arthur went to rescue her. I asked him to.'

'Mr Lee's just driven his car straight at her at fifty miles an hour,' Stout said crossly, grumpy as an over-tired boy. 'If the boss hadn't thrown your daughter out of the way she'd be dead.'

There was a silence. Porteous stood up. 'I think this should wait. You'll want to spend some time with your daughter.'

Hannah stood at the door and watched the policemen walk to their car. Through the ceiling she could hear Rosie's voice chatting, almost naturally, to Joe. There was a burst of laughter, tension relieved. Suddenly Hannah felt angry. How could her daughter be so arrogant, so foolish, not to be scared, not to recognize how close she'd been to danger? But later, when Hannah was in bed, pretending to sleep, Rosie crept in beside her and they spent the rest of the night cuddled together and occasionally Rosie cried out.

Porteous invited her to Cranford to explain Arthur's guilt. He was apologetic. He was so busy, he said, tying up loose ends. He didn't think he could make it to Millhaven. Would she mind coming to him?

It was the evening of the following day and still the sun was shining. They met at the picnic site at Cranford Water. The press was still at the police station, Porteous said. And anyway she wouldn't want to go there. They sat at one of the bench tables. A respectable, middle-aged couple taking the air. Porteous had brought an old-fashioned wicker shopping basket covered with a tea towel and fished out a bottle of wine and some smoked-salmon sandwiches. There were real glasses, linen napkins. Hannah wondered if this were another apology. I'm sorry I thought you were a murderer.

'How's Arthur?' she asked, wanting to start them off. Really rather hoping he was dead.

'Well enough to talk. Just. Did you know he'd worked as a psychologist at a centre for disturbed children called Redwood?'

She shook her head. 'He didn't talk much about the past. I knew he'd done research into families. The causes of delinquent behaviour. I don't think he ever said where he was based.'

'He was there for years. Almost since the place started. He went on to run training courses for other professionals, but he kept his links with the centre. He was a leader in his field. That's why the Home Office headhunted him for Stavely when Redwood closed down.' Porteous stretched back and closed his eyes against the sun. 'It started with Theo Randle, the boy you knew as Michael Grey. His mum died of cancer and his dad remarried. There was a little girl. Emily. You know all that. Arthur told you, didn't he? Once he knew we'd find out anyway. Theo's stepmother suffered from severe post-natal depression. His father started drinking heavily. The family was falling apart. A suitable case for Mr Lee's research. Theo hated Emily. She was only months old but he hated her. If she'd never been born he thought they might be happy.

It would have been like before his mother died. So he decided to do something about it. He started a fire in the nursery when the nanny had a night off. Emily was killed.

'Afterwards he was probably sorry. He went to his father and told him what he'd done. But his father didn't go to the police. He was a public figure. His wife was already suffering from depression. Imagine what the press would make of it. A boy that age charged with murder. Yet he couldn't face living with Theo either.

'Redwood hadn't long opened and was desperately short of money. There was a possibility that the place would shut before Alice Cornish had a chance to prove her ideas. Crispin Randle made a generous donation and Arthur accepted care of the boy. He probably saw it as a professional challenge. He promised he wouldn't tell the authorities that Theo had killed his sister and agreed to the change of name.'

'Was that wrong?' Hannah asked. 'Would Michael have been better off in a secure unit? A prison?'

'He would have been safe there,' Porteous said. 'And he wouldn't be a danger to other people.' He paused. 'There was another incident of arson. This time at Theo's school. He started the fire there too. Apparently he hated the place. Arson was his answer to difficult situations. His way of hitting out. Arthur provided an alibi for him. He didn't want people making awkward connections. Again Alice Cornish never knew. Soon after, the time came when Theo had to move on. He couldn't be protected in Redwood for ever and Arthur couldn't let on that he might still be a risk. Alec Reeves, a care worker at Redwood, knew the Brices. They agreed that he could live with them.'

Hannah didn't answer. She was thinking of Michael, sitting on the shore here at Cranford Water, so bewitched by a bonfire that he couldn't take his eyes off it.

'Then Arthur had a tricky moment,' Porteous said. 'Theo wanted to confess. Perhaps it was the Brices. Being surrounded by all that religion. Perhaps he kept getting flashbacks of Emily in her cot. He'd never been allowed to admit the truth of the memories. He phoned Arthur, telling him what he intended to do. Very self-righteous. Very dramatic.'

Oh yes, he'd have been that, Hannah thought.

'At first Alec was sent to sort him out. I don't think he was ever told the complete story but he knew the reputation of Redwood was at stake and he'd have done pretty well anything to protect that.'

'Did he have a blue car?'

'Why?'

'I saw him. He came looking for Michael here one night.'

'Poor Alec,' Porteous said. 'All those rumours about his nephew and he was just a lonely, middle-aged man who got on better with children than adults. He persuaded the boy to keep quiet, but in the end Theo couldn't let it go and Alec was sent back.'

'The weekend of *Macbeth*?'

'Yes. He realized immediately it wouldn't work and Arthur came up himself. He and Theo met on the Sunday evening after the performance of *Macbeth*, the day after the party, here on the shore. It was late at night. Theo must have had the dagger with him.

The prop from *Macbeth*. We'll never know if he intended any harm with it or if he'd kept it as a souvenir. He was a disturbed young man and he'd already tried to kill twice. There was an argument. Arthur says Theo got wild and angry and started to wave the dagger about. They had a scrap and Theo was killed. Hard to believe it was self-defence when the boy was stabbed in the back. And considering how cool and efficient Arthur was in dealing with the death. He weighed down Theo's body and threw it in the lake. Then he phoned the Brices and said that Theo was in the middle of some sort of crisis and had decided to go back to his father. Of course they believed him. Why wouldn't they? Theo had been their gift from God, only theirs on loan. Presumably Alec was given a similar story.

'And that's how it would have stayed if it hadn't been for global warming and a drought and a canoeist called Helen Blake, who found the body.'

'I don't understand where Melanie comes in.'

'Melanie was at Redwood too, briefly.'

'For her anorexia?'

'No,' Porteous said. 'It was history repeating itself. She killed a baby. A little girl called Emma. She was babysitting. The baby wouldn't stop crying, she got frustrated. She smothered it with a pillow. It was put down as a cot death. She confessed too. To Richard Gillespie. I couldn't accept the coincidence. Two babies dying. Richard was a public figure like Crispin Randle, but I don't think he was considering himself when he shipped Mel off to Redwood. He couldn't put her through a trial. There'd been all the publicity about the killers of the little boy in Liverpool. Even after her death he didn't want it to come out that she was a murderer. When he was young he'd worked as a solicitor for Randle. Apparently Randle got drunk one day and let slip about Theo and Redwood . . .'

' . . . so Melanie got shipped out there too.'

'Yes,' Porteous said. 'For a price. No wonder the girl was so screwed up.'

'Why did Arthur kill her?'

'Melanie was bright,' Porteous said. 'She knew what was happening to her. She was nearly fifteen when she killed Emma Leese, not a child like Theo. She was confused and mixed up and she wanted someone to blame. She knew Arthur was working locally. Rosie had talked about her mother's new friend at Stavely. She tracked him down, phoned him a couple of times at the prison. You can imagine the sort of thing. "You really screwed me up. How could you do that to me?" Wanting sympathy, someone to take her seriously. Arthur got jumpy and went to the Prom to try to talk to her. He knew Rosie worked there, thought it would be somewhere Mel would hang out.

'Mel might have let it go but she saw the photo of Theo on the local news in the pub on her way to the airport. She recognized him. Redwood was plastered with pictures of the kids who'd stayed there. The coincidence freaked her out. And she couldn't understand why Arthur didn't go to the police about the Redwood connection. Later that week the press reports were still talking about the mysterious boy with no past. She phoned him again and said that if he didn't tell the police Michael had been at Redwood, she would. He must have been frantic but he still thought he could reason with her. He couldn't get to her at home. She was so disturbed by then that her parents almost had her under house arrest. So he became more devious. He even followed Rosie and Joe home from the Prom one night, hoping they might lead him to Mel. At last he found her in the Rainbow's End. He persuaded her there was a reasonable explanation for keeping quiet about Theo. If she went back with him he'd tell her all about it. But whatever story he'd dreamed up she wouldn't accept it. She was hysterical . . .'

'And he killed her.'

'In his cottage.' Porteous hesitated, seemed to make up his mind to continue. 'The next night he took her body to the cemetery at Millhaven. He knew you'd been there. You were already a suspect and he wanted to implicate you.'

She sat in silence for a moment wondering how she could have been so foolish, so easily taken in. 'What about Rosie?' she asked. 'She can't have known anything about all that.'

'Rosie suspected him.'

'How could she?'

'Arthur got to know a nasty little boy inside, thought he might be useful.'

'Hunter.' Marty knew, she thought. Or guessed. It was impossible to keep secrets in prison. He'd wanted her to know too.

'Hunter went to see Frank at the pub and persuaded him it wouldn't be a good idea to remember the man who'd been looking for Mel. We thought Frank was uncooperative because he didn't like the police, but it was more than that. Rosie got an accurate description out of him.'

'Arthur.'

Porteous nodded. 'Later Frank had second thoughts and told Hunter what he'd done.'

'And Arthur told Hunter to kill her?'

Porteous didn't answer directly. 'Hunter recognized the name. Got greedy.'

'How did you work it all out?' *In time to save my daughter.*

'Dr Cornish had saved a book from Redwood. It was a record of all the kids she'd worked with, but Arthur's name was in the staff register at the back. I missed it first time. And his car was seen close to Alec Reeves's house on the night he was murdered. By then Arthur was panicking, desperate to throw suspicion elsewhere. Like Mel, Alec was starting to ask questions . . .'

There was a silence. 'Rosie's tough,' Porteous said. 'Brave. She'll be OK.'

Perhaps, Hannah thought. But will I? She looked out over the flat water to the hills on the opposite bank. In a few weeks her reckless daughter would be away to university. She'd live on her own and Hannah wouldn't know where she was or what she was doing. Hannah would retreat to the safety of the prison with its rules and its walls, but Rosie would dance and shimmy through the strange town in the south and there'd be nothing Hannah could do to protect her.

As Peter Porteous filled her glass his hand touched hers. 'Really,' he said. 'She'll be OK.'

Yes, Hannah thought. Of course we will. Both of us.

extracts reading groups events
competitions books new
books discounts extracts
competitions extracts discounts
books new extracts events
events books reading groups
new extracts new titles reading groups
interviews events new
events extracts extracts books
discounts new books
new books events interviews new books extracts
events new events
discounts extracts discounts books
www.panmacmillan.com
extracts events reading groups
competitions books extracts new

PUFFIN BOOKS

GIRL WONDER'S
WINTER ADVENTURES

Malorie Blackman is an ex-computer-programmer who now writes full time. She has had a number of jobs – database manager, systems programmer, receptionist and shop assistant. As a database manager she travelled extensively to places such as Toronto, Geneva, New York and Dallas.

Not So Stupid! her first collection of short stories (Livewire Books for Teenagers, The Women's Press), was a Selected Twenty title for Feminist Book Fortnight, 1991. Since then she has published over fifteen books, including *Hacker* (Doubleday Books/Corgi Books – which was a Federation of Children's Book Groups Pick Of The Year 1993 title, and *The Betsey Biggalow* series (Piccadilly Press/Puffin Books). She has contributed to numerous anthologies for both adults and children. She lives in London with her partner and several pets – including a frog, some bears, an owl, a haggis, a whale and a penguin – all stuffed toys!

By the same author

GIRL WONDER AND THE TERRIFIC TWINS